BLOODBOND

Nick Bastin

Nick Bastin

DISCLAIMER

This is a work of fiction and all characters, with the exception of well-known historical figures, businesses and events are products of the author's imagination or used in a fictitious manner. Where real-life historical figures appear, the situations, incidents, and dialogues concerning those persons are entirely fictional and are not intended to depict actual events or to change the entirely fictional nature of the work. Otherwise, any resemblance to actual persons, living or dead, or actual events is purely coincidental.

BLOODBOND

Nick Bastin

ACKNOWLEDGEMENTS

I would like to acknowledge the patience of my wife (the real author in the family) and my children in my pursuit of writing this. I would also like to thank Emma Darwin and Duncan Campbell for their advice.

THE FREE REPUBLIC OF
THE GAELS

Nick Bastin

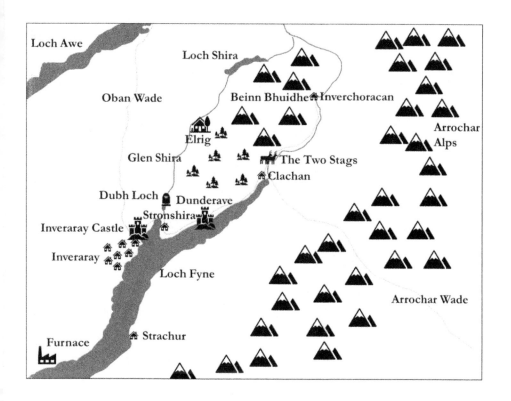

DUNDERAVE AND
SURROUNDING AREA

PROLOGUE

11.30 am, 16 April 1746, Culloden Moor, Scotland

The bloody evidence of disaster was growing all around him. The shouts and war cries had turned to screams and moans, the crump of cannon and whip-crack of musketry to the clang and ring of steel. Though the smoke and rain hid much of what was happening at the enemy line, he could see enough to know that Lochiel and the right wing were in trouble: momentum was ebbing. On the left, the MacDonalds had started their charge but had been slow off the mark; with farther to run, they were not going to reach the enemy in time to make a difference. The featureless moor that stretched before him, soaked by the rain and ploughed by cannonballs, was now being churned into a foot sucking mire.

The rain stung; its cold drops joining the hot tears of shame and rage that trickled down his face. Why had he agreed to fight the battle here? This godforsaken moor! It was too flat, too exposed and his poor men were too exhausted: it was asking too much. Cumberland must have double his numbers, not to mention those damned cannons. All his bickering advisers with their tactics, stratagems and maps and plans: look where they'd left him. After all they had been through, all they had fought for: was it really going to end here?

O'Shea galloped over, his horse wild-eyed and streaming with sweat and blood. "Your Highness, you must leave." He shouted. "The day is lost; you must save yourself. There is nothing more to be done here." His face was urgent; eyes shining white through a mask of black powder and mud.

His own horse shied at the distress of O'Shea's mount, and he pulled the reins tight to hold it still. "Where the hell is Murray?"

"Damn Murray! There's no time!" O'Shea pleaded. "You must escape now, or all will be lost."

"It's lost anyway you fool; can't you see that?"

He'd had enough of running. He had run all the way from Derby, chased relentlessly by that bastard Cumberland. The long-promised welcome from the supposedly loyal English Jacobites had never come. The very same cowards that for decades had been toasting his father and grandfather as the rightful Kings Over The Water had turned away. They had abandoned him.

But his poor loyal Gaels had tramped the length of the Kingdom, far from their homes, fighting and winning. They had trusted him, fought and died for him. After all they had achieved in his name, in the name of his father, in the name of the true religion and of freedom, they were now being butchered. They deserved better.

Had he not chanced it all on the turn of a card when he had landed at Glenshiel those few short months ago? They'd said he was mad, a fool; but hadn't he proved them wrong time and again? Was he now going to save himself and leave his men to die?

"Get me MacDonnell and Elcho. Bring all our horse to me, now!" He waved off O'Shea's entreaties, primed his pistols, and pulled a telescope from his saddle bag. He swept the enemy line, choosing his target with care.

As soon as the tattered collection of cavalry arrived, and without waiting for further discussion, he dug his spurs deep into his mount's side, driving it towards the distant red line. As he left the relative safety of the rear, the air grew thick with smoke and the whine of musket balls. Fortunately, the smoke was thickest where they were crossing, and they'd already covered most of the open ground before the enemy realised they were in earnest.

His Life Guards were on either side, few though they were, faces grim and set: brave lads. O'Shea to his right was leading the FitzJames, and Elcho to his left brandished his sabre as if it alone could ward off the ball and grape that sang around them. The damned moor seemed to go on for ever, but at last the smoke parted and they burst upon the red wall. He hacked to left and right: cleaving, hewing, slashing, through and through he pressed onward. Nothing existed beyond the point of his sword over his horse's ears. He laughed at the freedom of it, the red-soaked joy of it: revenge for the failure, the indignity and shame.

Suddenly, he could see Cumberland, sitting like a fat toad, surrounded by lace-fretted lords and lackeys. The crowd around him was thick - too thick, surely - could they cut their way through, after what they had just endured? But this was the moment; he could not stop now. Sheathing his sword, he pulled a pistol from his saddle and brandished it at his remaining cavalry, who cocked their weapons in response. Together they rode hard at the press of troops around Cumberland, loosing a desultory volley before urging their exhausted mounts into the enemy.

It was as if the hand of God directed that ball, shepherding it through the heaving horseflesh and waving arms, guiding it to its destination between the eyes and ears of Cumberland's mount, leaving a perfect puckered hole at the top of its white blaze. The horse dropped like a dead weight, taking its rider down with it. As Cumberland disappeared from view, his entourage, which had seemed so impenetrable, scattered like chaff in the wind.

A roar went up behind him. As the redcoats turned to see their leader fall, their courage wavered; their resolve so firm until now teetered in the balance. By contrast, the spirit of the highland army was redoubled; scenting their opponents' doubt and fear, the remainder of his force charged across the moor.

Seeing Cumberland pinned beneath his fallen horse, struggling to wriggle free, he dismounted. As one Prince to another, he reached out to help pull his enemy from under the horse, resisting the urge to shoot him then and there. But Cumberland fumbled with his saddlebow and produced a pistol. Its round black hole filled his vision.

How could it end like this? After everything? Surely this wasn't God's plan?

A flash of light shone out. He closed his eyes, waiting for the impact and the darkness to swallow him.

A scream pierced the air: not his. Opening his eyes, he saw Cumberland staring at the bloody stump where his treacherous right hand had been, his mouth twisted in pain, his jowls and chins rolling and shaking. A bloodied and battered highlander stood over him, sword drawn and dripping with blood.

The joy of salvation filled him from boots to brow, but with it came a wild anger. Grabbing his sword, he fell on Cumberland, swatting aside his entreaties. Moments later he held his enemy's fat and lifeless head above his own for all to see, the streaks of gore running hot and thick down his face, mingling with the rain and sweat.

The roar from his men swept the field, consuming all opposition and dissolving the resistance of the redcoats into the mud and sleet.

Nick Bastin

Following his unexpected victory at the Battle of Culloden, Prince Charles Edward Stuart became King of the Gaels and split the highlands and islands of Scotland from the rest of Britain. Upon his death, Am Poblachd Shaor nan Gàidheal – the Free Republic of the Gaels - was declared. Since then, the Gaelic Republic has maintained its culture and language, ploughing its own idiosyncratic furrow to the present day, a constant irritant to its larger and more powerful neighbour......

1 - THE STRAIT

The pain was sharp and pointed as if someone was trying to excavate their way out of his forehead from the inside with an ice pick. The blows chipped away frenetically, gradually slowing until they aligned with his pulse. It was pitch black; he was soaking wet, lying on his back in freezing water. He tried lifting his head: nothing, just darkness.

"Fuuuuuuuuuckkhhh, argh, what's going on? Where am I? What are you doing? Arrghhh faaahk, my head." Gillespie groaned, squeezing his temples hoping to release some of the pain that was gouging behind his eyes.

He breathed in a lungful of salty air: they were at sea! He tried to push himself up; an unseen hand gently but firmly pushed him back down. A hard-edged whisper reached him through the darkness: "We are in the Strait. Don't move or make any sound."

He was lying in the bottom of some sort of boat, surrounded by feet and calves. There was a good inch of seawater down there with him and it lapped around his head as the boat climbed and slid down each wave of the moderate swell. The only sounds were the slap of water on the hull and the very faint thrum of their engine: they were barely moving.

Gillespie swallowed, closing his eyes again against the pain in his head which promptly erupted in starbursts.

A flurry of whispers flew around the gunwales. A woman – Brighid? - leant down and with her lips practically pressed to his ear muttered apologetically: "I am sorry. We knew you would be reluctant, but it was important you came with us. Once we have had the choosing you will be free to go. I'll even bring you back myself. But you must be quiet until we are in safer waters. If we are spotted, well…. you know what will happen."

She spoke in the old tongue, hardly surprising if his cousin Duncan had sent them from the Republic. Thanks to the many painful lessons of his youth, he could understand her, but it was an effort, as the cogs of his brain ground slow through the throbbing of his pulse.

He lifted his head out of the bilge water. As his eyes adjusted, he saw the very faint glow of the boat's binnacle, its feeble illumination giving a green radiance to Ninian's face at the helm. He could just make out the shadowy figures of his motley companions hunched on the rubber tubes of the gunwales, each with a hand on a grab rope and the other holding a weapon; their dull clunks an unsettling reminder that they were heavily armed.

He struggled to remember the names of the others. There were the two redheads; one short but stocky: powerfully built with a barrel chest and bulging arms; the other with a fierce face and peat spade of a beard. Then there was the one called Iain the Rat, with his memorably pointed face, as pale as milk. He looked like he had been pulled teeth first down a funnel, the tarry yellow incisors leading, his nose and cheekbones scurrying behind. There was Ninian – Nin - who was now on the helm, Gillespie could still feel the firm grip of his handshake and the power of his cornflower blue eyes, and Kirstie, their leader.

His brain churned. Was he going to die out here? Drowned or gunned down for the crime of being abducted by this bunch of caterans? Given all those Gaelic smugglers sunk or impounded that he read about in the Antrim Gazette, it seemed a certainty. Gillespie had never even been to the Gaelic Republic and the very thought of visiting it gave any right-minded person pause. He began to shake – whether from cold or fear he wasn't entirely sure. He tried to focus, to calm himself, to think. A slow-moving boat this small and low-lying surely wouldn't show up on radar. If they'd made it over the Strait in one piece, then surely they must be able to return.

The boat was moving incredibly slowly, barely outpacing the slip and slide of the waves. Over their heads the quiet crinkle of a low foil awning helped to explain why it was so dark. Through a peep hole at the front he could just see patches of moonlight rolling on the swell and a dark line on the horizon.

He thought back to the news they had brought, that his distant cousin Duncan was dying and his two sons, Callum and Oisean, were already dead. Duncan must be an old man, but Callum and Oisean? They were his age: far too young to be dead and buried.

"What time is it?" His lips were parched and cracked from the sea water. His head throbbed from whatever it was they had drugged him with, the sweet, chemical wave that had burst upon his senses, drowning them in utter blackness.

"Three thirty," Brighid replied. "We have been out here since shortly after one. We are nearly at the border. Once across, we can get some speed on."

His mind did a few quick calculations, two and a half hours at a couple of knots meant that they were probably not far off the maritime boundary. While the boundary was not much respected, the closer they were to the Republic's shore the safer they would be, at least from the Kingdom although not necessarily from the locals.

As this thought dissipated into the thudding of his temples he could hear a new sound: the far-off thrum of another engine.

"Shite, can you hear that?" Ninian said from the stern. "The bastards are sailing up the line. They're going to spot us for sure."

"Hold your nerve. We'll be able to outrun them even if they do," Another voice – Jamie? - growled. "With luck they won't see us."

Gillespie's spirits soared: if only he could attract the attention of this approaching boat then they could save him. Should he shout? Could he grab one of the guns? He tried to be calm, to wait for the right moment.

The tension in the boat rose as the other engine came closer, the voices of her crew carrying over the water: they were almost upon them.

"Has someone got the fifty cal ready?" Kirstie whispered. "I can't see shit in here."

"Aye, I've her locked and loaded," came a steadfast voice from the bow.

The other engine note changed, as if it was heading towards them.

It was now or never. Gillespie pushed himself upwards, scrabbling and tearing at the foil above his head and shouting at the top of his voice. Almost as soon as he had risen from the deck, arms were wrestling him back down from all sides, pinning him to the bottom of the boat. A rough hand was clamped over his mouth and he felt the flat of a sharp-edged blade press into his cheek.

"If you do that again, I will cut your throat," came a hard whisper in his ear. "If you even fucking move an inch."

He lay still, waiting to see if he had been successful; had the boat heard him? Everyone's ears and eyes strained, muscles, sinews and nerves tensed, ready to explode into action.

Malcolm, who was lying across the bow with a large object in his hands, turned back to look at Ninian in the stern. "Think we are about to get fucked. I vote we light them up first, and then fire up the afterburners to get us the hell out of here. We should be faster, and the confusion will give us an edge."

Ninian nodded through the gloom. "Okay, on the count of three, and for fuck's sake hold on; we are not stopping to pick up any swimmers."

"One, two, thr...."

Malcolm tore back the foil awning. They could see the boat now: an inshore patrol boat. It was so close that it was a miracle that they had not been spotted before. At that instant Malcolm let rip with the fifty-calibre machine gun; its barrel spitting a jet of flame into the night; a hail of empty cartridge cases pouring over Gillespie and the other occupants of the boat. Malcolm's burst stitched the side of the hull before erupting into the wheelhouse, splashing red up the shattering windows. Screams and shouts pierced the night.

Nin gunned the engine: the boat springing to life in his hands, skimming across the swell, throwing a cloud of salt spray each time it kissed off the top of one wave before thumping down onto the next. Malcolm's aim became more erratic as their speed increased, but he continued to pour fire into the patrol boat until it was out of range astern

A flare arced into the sky and began a slow descent, illuminating the sea with its burning phosphorous: the patrol boat's crew were getting their act together. Now tracer from their bow gun began to puncture the dark around them, throwing up great spouts of water as the bolts of light flashed ever closer. Gillespie was mesmerised and terrified. Just as their march onto the boat seemed inexorable, Nin threw over the helm turning sharply to port. Picking up even more speed he started to weave, making for the distant shore.

Looking up, Gillespie saw that Jamie had a rifle in his hand that he was leaning on the Rat's shoulder, aiming back at the patrol boat. The Rat grimaced as the barrel bit into him every time the boat crested a wave but said nothing. Jamie was focused, staring down the sight, held around the waist by Kirstie to stop him being flung out of the boat. As the boat cleared a big wave, he pulled the trigger, emitting a grunt of satisfaction as the patrol boat's gun fell silent.

The sea spray soaked them as the knots accelerated; they were pulling away. Nin did not pause or slow down, keeping the boat flat out for the Republic's shore. From the bottom of the boat Gillespie was beginning to think that they had escaped, that they had shown a clean pair of heels, when the bow erupted in a sheet of flame and Malcolm exploded in a cloud of blood and brains.

"Raptor!" Kirstie shouted, her index finger tracking the drone that passed metres above them.

"Fuckfuckfuckfuckfucksake." Nin worked the helm trying to wrongfoot the pursuer.

The raptor started to turn, returning for another pass.

Brighid lunged between Gillespie's legs, clawing desperately with one hand to free the clasp on a small box that was bolted between his feet, while holding on to the grab rope for dear life with the other. Each wave was trying to buck her out of the boat, wrenching her grip on the hawser. But she couldn't grip the clasp to work it free.

Without thinking, but driven by the desperate look on her face, Gillespie stretched his left arm as far as he could reach and was just able to grip the small metal bolt and pull it open. Brighid scrabbled for the small tennis ball shaped object inside. Bringing it to her lips she gripped the ring that hung from its side with her teeth and pulled it out. Rolling backwards over Gillespie, she tracked the pursuing drone, timing her throw perfectly as it swooped overhead.

The ball rose into the air and then shattered with a pulse of invisible energy. The shockwave pummelled the boat and shook the occupants violently. Gillespie gasped as the air was jolted from his lungs and his ears rang like a bell. The drone stopped dead in the sky, as if it had run into a wall, before dropping like a stone into the black waves below.

"Let's just hope they don't have another one of those." Nin muttered as he slalomed the boat towards the rapidly approaching shore.

2 - THE SHORE

The pursuit seemed to have been called off. The patrol boat was moving slowly away back towards the Antrim coast and the trailing smoke suggested that Malcolm had done more damage than was immediately evident. No more drones were launched, and Gillespie thanked his lucky stars that Brighid had been so quick and accurate with her throw.

With no more need for stealth, Gillespie grabbed a rope and hauled himself up to look around. The first blow caught him by surprise: "What the fuck did you think you were doing?" shouted Jamie as he rained down punches. "You stupid cunt! Standing up like that. You fucking showed them where we were! If you had kept your mouth shut Malcom would still be alive." Gillespie's ears rang.

It was the click of the safety catch that stopped the blows. Kirstie pointed the gun right in Jamie's face. "Sit the fuck down and shut the fuck up!" She shouted; her authority cowing him instantly. "If I hear another fucking word, I promise I will put a bullet in you. Do you understand me? This is your last warning!"

Jamie nodded sullenly. Kirstie slowly lowered and then holstered her pistol, but the tension between them remained.

It was Nin that spoke, trying to answer the question on everyone's lips: "I don't think that boat heard Gillespie, even if what he did was fucking stupid. In any case, they were going to find us. If we hadn't got them first, then we would be the ones at the bottom now."

The crew nodded in agreement; all except Jamie who turned away. Gillespie felt sick. He looked to Brighid, who seemed like she was about to say something, but instead she gazed glassily at Malcolm's carcass hanging over the bow, a bloody pulp where his head had once been. His right hand still clutching the handle of the machine gun and his left hand wrapped around the grab rope. Brain and blood were spattered liberally over the bow and there was now a deep red pool sloshing back and forth in the bilge.

"Jesus," said the Rat trying to pick his feet up and away from the bloody tide at the bottom of the boat. "Malcolm is making a bit of a mess here. We are going to have to clean this up before the crossing if we are to have a chance of getting over. There is no way we can take his body back with us."

"Just you leave him where he is," growled Jamie, "or you'll join him."

Brighid turned to look at Malcolm's remains: her face pale, her cheeks running with tears. She reached out and ran her thin fingers over the back of Malcolm's thick and powerful hand. Choking back the waver in her voice she turned to Kirstie, "Much though I regret it, I think the Rat has a point. We'll never get over the crossing with a dead body in the boat. It'll be hard enough as it is. Fiona and Mara will understand, you know they will."

Kirstie said nothing, instead fixing her fierce gaze on the shore watching the distant surf pound on the rocks, throwing spumes of water high into the air. Finally, she turned back, "Brighid's right. We can't pass the crossing with the body in the boat. I don't see that we have a choice – unless someone else has a bright idea?"

She scanned the boat, daring the crew to respond. No answer came, but Jamie shook his head disconsolately.

"Fine – Rat, since it was your bright idea you can prepare the body, and for God's sake make sure that it can't float or be found."

The Rat nodded and produced a wicked looking knife from his armpit. He worked swiftly in the bottom of the boat cutting the webbing off Malcolm's body before wrestling the jacket off and handing it to Gillespie.

"You better take that – at least till we're past the crossing. Six went out, fewer questions if six come back."

Gillespie took the sodden black jacket, the strips of familiar tartan down the inner arms now seemed a richer red. The smell of blood mixed with salt water caught in his nostrils. A wave of nausea swept over him - was that seawater or blood running from the hem? He rubbed it in his fingers. Was it really his fault that a man was dead? Had the patrol boat heard him? As if he could've escaped, here in the middle of the Irish Sea with a bunch of heavily armed Gaels. What an idiot. He held the jacket close, tears running down his face.

In the bow, the Rat turned to the body and cut off the right-hand sleeve of the shirt. Then, gritting his teeth, he used his knife to cut the deep blue tattoo of a castle tower out of the flesh of Malcolm's upper arm. The sharp blade working away under the skin until it finally came free. Without a pause, the Rat threw the tattered patch of flesh into the water. He then manhandled the body on to the gunwale and drew his knife firmly and deeply across Malcolm's belly. Turning his head away from the foul smell, the Rat then pulled out the still steaming guts like strings of sausages and threw them into the wake. He paused, uttering a few words under his breath, before taking a box of ammunition which he inserted into the cavity. Then, having bound the body with rope, and without a further word, he heaved it over the side. They watched it sink into the depths.

The whole process had taken less than ten minutes, but Gillespie felt he'd been watching for hours. He was numb, and not just because of the cold. How could these people be so callous, so cold hearted? He knew that life was cheap in the Republic, he'd heard the stories, but the dispassionate gralloching of Malcolm shook him to the core. He wrapped the jacket tight around him, rubbing his arms against his sides to try and inject some warmth. Meanwhile, Jamie and the Rat were splashing sea water over the charnel house of the bow.

With the immediate threat from the patrol boat over, Nin came off the throttle. They were now just a mile or so off the Republic's shore, tracking the coast north. It took Gillespie a few minutes to realise that the shore was on their starboard and not their port bow.

"Where are we going?" he said. "Surely, we should be going around the Mull and up Loch Fyne?"

"Well, if you were going for a wee pleasure cruise, maybe that is the way you would go. But it's too exposed to Kingdom vessels coming up from Gourock and Glasgow. Having dodged one, I am not keen to tangle with another."

"But this will bring us miles away from where we need to be – surely it's even more dangerous going up through the islands and across the hills?" Spluttered Gillespie.

"Aye, right enough. If that was what we were going to do, we would need to be braver or better armed than we are. No, we are going to take the crossing place at Tarbert. That will hopefully save us from both the Kingdom's navy and from the hospitality of the Lamontation. Although, to be fair, we'll still need a little luck and a following wind to dodge that pleasure."

The maw of the unknown gnawed at Gillespie's gut as the Republic came ever closer. He stared out at the coast; it was low-lying here, with long stretches of pale sand rising through green fields to a moorland backbone that ran as far as the eye could see. This was the more accessible flank of the Republic. The long finger of Kintyre that dipped far to the south of the country, suspended like a probe into the Irish Sea. With its relatively rich farmland and flat topography it was known for being more accessible and open. But this accessibility fell away the further north you went and as the landscape changed. The Republic was famously mountainous and jagged, rucked in great folds east to west. Its tattered hem flared out into the Atlantic, calving islands into the grey ocean, its weft torn open by deep sea lochs running far into its mountainous interior. These were old rocks, some of the oldest on the planet. They had been ground down and eroded, hammered into a hard and unyielding landscape.

His father had always told him that the Gaels had been shaped by the landscape: that they thought differently. Their culture of kinship, of hospitality, their unbreakable connection to the land and a love of nature ran through them like a watermark. As did the need to safeguard and defend their meagre resources. Over centuries this had bred and fostered the dichotomies of self-reliance and mutual dependence, hospitality and suspicion, generosity and parsimoniousness, affability and bellicosity, the open hand and the closed fist. Some saw this as volatile and threatening, but his father had always refuted that, seeing it instead as vital and life affirming.

He had often looked across the narrow stretch of water between Antrim and the Gaelic Republic, and wondered what life was really like there. Could it be so bad? But any wish to visit had been tempered with a well-honed desire to stay alive. Hadn't his grandfather escaped all of that by leaving? Why would he go back?

His father had rarely talked about Clan matters, but he had told him tales of his cousin Duncan. He had been Chief of the Clan for many decades. A distant, near legendary figure, he had seemed a fiction, a convenient vehicle for cautionary tales or showboating glamour. But the family had chosen to leave all that behind, trusting to the few short miles of sea to insulate them from the Republic and its dangerous ways.

How much of what he had heard on his father's knee was true and how much was misty-eyed bullshit? He was about to find out.

3 - LIFT AND CARRY

Even at the slower pace, it wasn't long before the Isle of Gigha came into view off the port bow, it was flat and smaller than he had imagined. A cluster of wind turbines crowded its only hill. Unsurprisingly, there were no lights showing the length of the coast here. Anyone foolish enough to show lights would doubtless be on the receiving end of unwelcome visitors. But the land looked rich and well-kept: he hadn't expected that.

After another half an hour of hard pounding, a rocky promontory jutted out from the coast shielding the mouth of a long sea loch. Brighid said it was Ardpatrick Point, the entrance to West Loch Tarbert, the gateway to the crossing place. As Nin turned the boat into the long and narrow loch, all eyes scoured the shoreline for unwelcome watchers. It was still early, not much past six, and the lightening thread of dawn was rising behind the low ridge of Kintyre to the east. To the north, the sharper hills of Knapdale marched up the loch to their left, disappearing into a soggy mist that clung to their pine clad slopes.

Nin slowed the boat, steering it in the middle of the channel as if charting an imaginary tightrope leading from the sea to the loch head. They passed a shuttered and dark building on their left, with a few boats moored outside. The loch had narrowed at this point and the shore was only 150 yards away, no more. A door suddenly swung open and a dark figure stepped onto the jetty and stared at them.

Gillespie froze: was that a gun?

Kirstie stood up quickly and waved an arm, calling in a low but carrying voice, "Greetings from Dunderave."

The figure said nothing but waved them on before returning inside and pulling the door closed. Kirstie turned to Gillespie, as if guessing his thoughts, "We and the MacAlistairs go way back. When you are a small Clan sandwiched between such neighbours as we have, you do well to have firm friendships."

Gillespie shivered and looked ahead as the brightening sky revealed their destination. As they approached the head of the loch, there were more buildings and obvious signs of habitation: fields with horses and small black cattle surrounding doughty whitewashed houses most of which had solar panels clamped to their roofs and wind turbines standing sentry nearby.

Kirstie gave her orders: "Okay, you all know the routine. When we get to the jetty, leave the talking to me. I don't want any trouble kicking off – and that means you Jamie and you Rat. Gillespie, keep your mouth shut, I don't want to have to be answering any unnecessary questions."

There was a harbour at the end of the loch, with a series of pontoons jutting out into the dark water. There were a few bigger boats, some of which looked like they could happily cruise from ocean to ocean, and plenty of small ones, many ramshackle and down at heel. Nin steered into a space and gently rubbed up against the mooring.

After so long sat in the boat, much of it in freezing seawater, Gillespie was glad to be able to get out and stretch his legs. They were stiff and recalcitrant, and he swayed slightly as he helped the crew unload their gear onto the dock.

From the shipping container that served as the harbour master's office came four men, one armed with a tablet, the rest with an assortment of weaponry. Gillespie toyed briefly with the idea of asking them to help him, to rescue him. But now that he was in the Republic his clansmen were the only friends he had.

The man with the tablet turned to Kirstie and said: "That didn't take you very long now did it. Will you be wanting the lift and carry service again?"

"Er, yeah, thanks Duncan. Just a short trip." Kirstie mumbled, "and yes, a lift and carry would be great thanks."

"OK, that will be 50 Cùinn for the boat and five each for you, so a total of 80 Cùinn please..." said Duncan, punching the numbers into his tablet. His forehead was smooth, and his brown eyes peered out at them under curiously fine brows.

"Now," he said, leaning close to Kirstie and speaking in a conspiratorial whisper that Gillespie could only just hear, "I don't imagine you know anything about a little incident out in the Strait last night? We've heard that some troublemakers shot up a Kingdom patrol boat: very unwise. I gather that Lord Lamont is keeping an eye out for them. And, if it was me, I would want to avoid that eye if at all possible."

Raising one of his delicate eyebrows he gave Kirstie a knowing look, before pursing his lips and returning his gaze to the screen of his tablet.

"We don't know anything about that," Kirstie lied. "We've come down from the North of Jura."

Duncan lent in closer yet, pulling her so close the flecks of his spit shone on her cheek. "Aye, well, you would be wise to make yourselves scarce. While Lamont has no friends here, we have to sit and look at him day in and day out. And I can assure you, I don't want him sticking a red-hot poker up my arse any more than you do."

Duncan jerked his head back, releasing her arm. Kirstie nodded, rummaging around in her inner pocket and took out her phone. She held it close to Duncan's tablet and swiped the transfer over to him.

".....and keep the change," she muttered, before turning on her heel and heading back to the others.

The boat was unceremoniously picked up and put on a trailer attached to the back of the big 4x4 at the end of the jetty. Waving Duncan off, they all clambered into the back and were soon bouncing very slowly down the rutted and torn track that led to the ancient harbour of Tarbert. As they drove, Gillespie realised that the isthmus between the two coasts was very narrow, barely a mile wide. It was only this sliver of rock and earth that stopped the long peninsula of Kintyre from being an island.

As they approached Tarbert, Gillespie saw the church first, crowned with its distinctive steeple. The houses of Tarbert were clustered round a tight sheltered anchorage. Some of the buildings had been painted in bright colours bringing some cheer to the otherwise gloomy stone and harl that stood round the harbourside. The brightest was the unlikely primrose yellow of the Boar's Head Inn. A tall building, its upper storey windows were dark sockets punched through the façade, below them a deep bow window spilled out into the road and looked out over the water.

Gillespie's stomach was growling. He hadn't eaten anything since lunch the previous day. He felt weak and feeble, the adrenalin of the journey was fading. Turning to Kirstie he pointed at the rough looking door of the Inn and raised a questioning eyebrow. "Can we get something to eat? I'm starving." Kirstie first looked at her watch before scanning the still and silent town. She nodded.

"Jamie, we need fuel. Can you take the boat round and fill her up? Rat, I want you to keep an eye across the water in case of any unwelcome visitors. Nin, Brighid, I want you to come with me and Gillespie to get some food and coffee before we head up the loch. RV back here in 15."

They all helped to shoulder the boat from the trailer into the water. Jamie immediately jumped in and started up the engine, puttering across the harbour to the fuel store that was dimly illuminated on the other side. The Rat trudged away up the quay with a keen eye out of the harbour mouth and across the loch.

Kirstie mounted the steps to the battered door of the Inn. Turning the thick ring of the handle she pushed it open, revealing a passage beyond. They followed her a few feet before pushing past a felted wool curtain, exchanging the cold dark of the hall for a warm and inviting saloon.

The room was quiet, unsurprising given the hour. A huge fireplace at one end held a hearth filled with ashes from the previous night's fire: a clod of peat still burned, a dull red at its heart. The fireback had the head of a boar embossed across it: its tusks long and sharp.

Nin gestured for them to take a seat while he went to the bar where a man was watching. Gillespie pulled up the stool nearest the fire and sat, hoping to quell the swoop and swirl of the sea. Brighid and Kirstie sat opposite and rubbed their hands, not ready yet to shed any of their layers of clothing.

The man at the bar unfolded his arms and turned to Nin with a bleary smile. It seemed they knew each other, and Nin reciprocated with a dodge of his shoulders, a pointing finger and a wide grin.

Within a few minutes, Nin returned with a tray of steaming coffee and some bread rolls stuffed with cheese and ham. Gillespie could hardly restrain himself and he wolfed down a roll while scorching his tongue with the bitter black liquid. His stomach turned cartwheels at these riches, and he briefly wondered if he was going to be able to keep them down.

Stuffing a few rolls in her pockets for Iain the Rat and Jamie, Kirstie wrestled with the lids of the coffee cups, swearing hard at the scalding splashes that inevitably spattered her hands. Successful at last, she led the way out of the saloon, pushing past the curtain and out into the morning light.

Jamie had already finished filling the boat's tank and was waiting alongside the quay. The Rat came back down the harbour wall grabbing a roll and coffee from Kirstie on the way. They clambered aboard and swiftly stowed the gear while the Rat swept the quiet harbour looking for signs of life. There were none: Tarbert slept.

Nin helmed the boat through the moorings out of the sheltered bay and into Loch Fyne. The loch was wide at this point. To the south. it funnelled outwards into Kilbrannan Sound and the Clyde, away from the Republic and into Kingdom waters. To the north, its long silvery finger pointed deep into Argyll towards their destination at the head of the loch.

Immediately opposite were the low, thickly wooded hills. Pulling on Gillespie's elbow, Brighid pointed; "Over there is Cowal. And you see there? Just to the right of that hill?" Gillespie stared out across the water at a castle, half hidden by trees, a short walk from the shore. "That's what we are trying to avoid; Castle Ascog, the seat of Clan Lamont and the home of their Chief, John Lamont of the Sorrows. People here know him as The Lamontation. Although don't ever call him that to his face, not unless you wanted yours peeled from you. He is a cruel and powerful man."

Gillespie shuddered: the knot in his stomach tightening.

4 - THE LAMONTATION

John Lamont wrinkled his nose in thought. He turned from the window and focused on the imposing partner's desk that stretched out before him, its acres of green leather disappearing beneath multifarious papers and the double screen of his computer. The cursor winked impatiently, keen to be off. Sighing, he rubbed his eyes and turned his attention to the demanding pixels.

In his position as Warden of the Clyde, he had already fired off messages to Westminster and Edinburgh, his ill temper rising with each sentence that he'd had to write explaining the attack on the patrol boat. Since being roused from his bed with the news, he had written to the families of the three dead crewmen and had ordered flowers to be sent to the other two in hospital. The media was going to have a field day.

The phone on his desk rang, sharp and demanding. Grabbing the receiver, he heard the voice of Allan Stewart on the line.

"Your Lordship, I thought you'd want to know that we've located a suspect for the patrol boat incident."

"Really? That was quick. Who and where are they?"

"If your Lordship looks out of the west window of his study, he may see the dubious looking crew making their way up the loch. Our man in Tarbert told me that they came in this morning from the west. In a boat like that they could've easily made it from the incident in the time. I believe that the helm is Ninian MacNachtan, a notorious layabout."

"Hhmm, I wonder what a small band of MacNachtans could be doing so far from home? And why would they attack one of his Majesty's patrol boats? Very unwise I would have thought, and at this time most of all with Duncan about to croak his last. Poor old Duncan: he used to be ever so useful. The stone in MacCailean Mòr's shoe I called him. Still, we can't tolerate such blatant acts, can we? Hhmm? Where would it end…?"

"Shall I arrest them?" asked Stewart.

"No, I think not. At least not yet. This fits perfectly with my plans. Let them go for now. We'll deal with them soon enough."

With that he hung up the phone to consider his next move, the tip of his tongue moistening his lips, the thin crease pulled taut with concentration.

5 - THE RETURN

Ninian turned the boat out of the harbour, piling on the speed as they rounded the seawall. Gillespie was sitting in the bow holding on to the grab rope for all his worth as the boat skitted and thumped over the shallow waves. The hills that lined either side of the water had names that were so familiar from songs and dances, stories and films, that he felt he really did know them. It was as if his connection to these places, despite being severed by generations, still itched through some vicarious phantasmagoria.

The landscape was already becoming more imposing, with the Cowal shore rolling away towards the Republic's southern border. To the west, the hills of Knapdale were dotted with forestry; dark and pointed conifer plantation, still naked deciduous woods, stands of aspen and rowan, and bushes of goat willow and blackthorn. Despite the passage of winter, the landscape was still green here, the relative shelter and the regular rainfall cloaking it in emerald and tourmaline, chrysoprase and peridot.

They passed stubby Loch Gilp before turning the corner at Otter, leaving the wider expanse of the lower loch behind and moving into the narrower confines of its upper reaches.

Nin swung the boat to hug the western shore, skirting a small island. Gillespie saw that Kirstie was on her phone speaking earnestly while looking towards a massive emplacement shrouded in camouflage netting that covered much of the island. It was dotted with loitering groups of men and there was a tall pole on its summit that flew a flag showing a castle with three towers. He searched his memory for that crest, dredging up MacLachlan of MacLachlan from a deep, seldom touched recess. From the snatched words through the wind roar it seemed that Kirstie was making a payment to ensure safe passage. As they passed, Iain and Jamie waved across at the small group of men who waved slowly back.

He leant round to Brighid and was opening his mouth to speak when she cut across him: "That is the Tiger's Mouth – sometimes known as MacLachlan's Folly. We have to pay a toll to pass, not much, but it keeps him in the style to which he has become accustomed." Brighid laughed sarcastically, turning her face towards him. "Old MacLachlan thinks he's a big noise, but he sits there sandwiched between MacCailean Mòr and the Lamontation. Do you think they pay him for passage? No, but it suits them to have him do their dirty work, guarding the loch and risking a blood feud for every gallowglass he sends to the bottom. MacLachlan may think he's the big man - Tiger's Mouth my arse - but he could be snuffed out like that if it suited them." She said, snapping her fingers. "It is only poor wee clans like us that have to pay. Still, better to toss a coin in the beggar's bowl than risk the alternative."

Ordinarily, Gillespie would probably still be sat at home reading the paper while finishing his breakfast. Instead he was cold, wet, tired, and his head still ached. He had been thinking about trying to escape again, but he knew it was hopeless. He wouldn't last five minutes, either in the water or on the shore. The first person he met would probably sling him into a dark hole and wait for a ransom that would never come. He was not a timid man, he had travelled far and wide, and could handle himself in most situations. But this was different, he was isolated and alone.

The further they sped up the loch the more dramatic the landscape became with high hills in all directions. Farms and dwellings were scattered along both sides of the shore. It was better tended than he had expected and gave an impression of calm prosperity. It still surprised him that it wasn't a smoking ruin.

As they rounded a bend in the loch there was a white township on the port bow. It could only be Inveraray, the capital of Clan Campbell with its fine white buildings and hulking great black castle. They passed swiftly by; the small groups of men gathered on the quayside seemingly uninterested.

They were coming towards the end of their journey; Gillespie knew that much. The head of the loch was their destination and as they approached he could feel his sense of foreboding rise, tightening its grip on his chest.

As they raced along the final stretch, he watched jagged Beinn Bhuidhe rise ahead of them; this was the mountain that famously dominated MacNachtan stories and songs. The thickly wooded hillside spilled down onto a nubbly promontory that jutted into the dark water. In the middle of this stood Dunderave, the ancient stone tower that had been home of the MacNachtan Chiefs for more than 500 years. Surrounded by the loch on three sides, it stuck out like a pimple into the water and commanded the upper reaches of the loch.

A beach of rough shingle rose to meet them, and Nin grounded the boat to allow his companions to jump ashore and start unloading: they had arrived.

6 - THE WELCOME

For the first few minutes ashore Gillespie staggered drunkenly. His legs were stiff and sore from being crumpled beneath him and his arms ached from holding the grab rope for so long. His whole body was zinging from the vibrations of the engine, something he only noticed now that it had stopped. He thought he might be sick.

A hand clapped him on the shoulder. "Cheer up," said Kirstie brightly, "and a warm welcome home."

He wanted to punch her, to vent the suppressed anger that was pooling in his gut, but instead he leant backwards, arms akimbo, filling his lungs with air and trying to hold on to his breakfast. It was no good, and seconds later he threw up on the shingle.

"A fine omen," sneered Jamie.

Even the Rat sniggered at that.

Gillespie spat the last lumps from his mouth, brushed his hair back behind his ear and turned to them. "Fuck all of you," he said, "I never wanted to come, remember? You kidnapped me, remember? I have been drugged and shot at and am now stuck here in the arse end of nowhere surrounded by heavily armed psychopaths. And you expect me to feel welcome! You are all mad!"

"Now just be careful with the choice of your next words," said Kirstie. "There are plenty here who might take offense and we wouldn't want anything to happen to you while you are our guest."

Nin, chuckling, said: "You've got to understand that we may not have much, but one thing we do have in abundance is pride and short tempers:

that can be a dangerous combination. Our ways may seem a little strange but try and be patient with us."

Kirstie trudged up the beach towards a small group that were coming towards them across the shingle. They were all dressed alike in a mix of dark green and faded black: each having the same tartan panel stitched on the inside of their forearms. The men were all wearing kilts, some tattered and torn and others crisply pleated. Like his companions they were all heavily armed and not just with the obvious weapons: the unlikely bulges in unexpected places showed that all too clearly. An assortment of swords swung from hips or were strapped on backs.

Gillespie had never seen such a sight before; few had unless they had visited the Republic. It was an incongruous sight in the 21st century, one that was both exotic and slightly terrifying. It wasn't just the weapons, although those were anathema to citizens of civilised society, but also the confidence and ease that these people wore their unconventional clothing.

He looked down at his dishevelled condition. He was still dressed in Malcolm's bloodied jacket, his soaking wet trainers covered in mud and worse, and his jeans were ripped open at the knee. He felt like a fish out of water; he was cold, wet, battered, dejected and degraded: it wasn't much of a home coming.

"Fàilte, fàilte," said a balding middle-aged man with a beaming smile who stepped forward from the gaggle on the beach. "We welcome you back to the land of your fathers. I am Aodhan, Duncan's Seanchaidh, and I've come to see that you are made to feel at home."

The surrounding group all jostled him, shaking his hand and introducing themselves with genuine warmth and polite enquires as to the journey. His head span trying to take it all in.

Introductions completed, Kirstie and Nin related the details of the crossing. There was much sucking of teeth and furrowed brows when they described the encounter with the patrol boat and when they came to

Malcolm's death a sombre and subdued mood descended. Aodhan spoke for the group when he said, "This is sad news indeed. Malcolm was a kind and generous companion and friend. Fiona is going to be devastated. Angus, Uisdean, go and find her quickly and bring her to the hall. We must tell her before she hears the news from others." Two of the group peeled off and walked swiftly away into the woods, while the remainder of the group continued to the tower.

7 - THE TOWER

During their brief walk Gillespie had a chance to study his surroundings. As they approached the dour looking tower they passed a large wind turbine and series of stone outbuildings. Through the windows he could see rows of desks covered in banks of computer screens and an earnest looking group of men and women holding a vigorous discussion.

Iain the Rat followed his gaze and before he could ask said: "Online gaming. And to be more precise Fan Tan. You know, the Chinese game? We also have a very strong offering in poker and piquet."

"What really? You are running online casinos from here?" sputtered Gillespie, incredulous. "How?"

"Well, you didn't think we still made our money from cattle rustling, did you? Gambling software is our niche. We have been doing it for decades, ever since old Diarmid MacNutt wrote the Highland Raider fruit machine code back in the 1980s. Check out our earth station," Iain pointed towards a six-metre satellite dish mounted behind the building, "That is the latest tech."

"Don't tell me you have your own satellites." Gillespie gaped.

"Don't be so fucking ridiculous, of course we don't have our own satellites, we rent capacity from whoever has space. You'd be amazed who has a few spare transponders for the right price – Chinese, Israelis, Russians, Indians – there's so much capacity floating around up there," Iain gestured upwards with a sharp yellowing finger, "that we can always find someone to take the signal."

"But what about the Brits? Surely the Kingdom doesn't tolerate this on its doorstep."

"Well, what they don't know, won't hurt them. We're deep on the dark net and our audience are high rollers and professional gamblers, mostly in Asia. You seem surprised, but what else do we have round here? If we want to earn money we need to bring it here from outside. We have been doing that for many centuries, this is just the latest in a long line of schemes and dreams. Fortunately, this is working out quite well for the moment, the internet and digital communications have been a godsend, but it won't last — they never do."

The Rat led him through a robust looking steel door in the ten-foot-high wall that ran around a large enclosure at the base of the tower. Gillespie looked up; the tower was peppered with small deep-set windows that didn't seem to reflect any obvious floor plan behind, and from each corner bartizan turrets swelled out of the corbie-stepped gables. The mighty round tower faced down the loch. While modern weapons had rendered it largely redundant, it was still an impressive construction.

The door in the gate was already open and they walked through into the outer ward that was filled with picnic tables and benches. There was a low-lying wing to the far corner that was connected to the main tower by a loggia on the first floor and an archway on the ground floor level. Walking under this arch, wary of its ominous assortment of murder holes and gun loops, he came to a surprisingly peaceful courtyard with a dark pool at its centre.

The pool surrounded a fountain of black basalt in the shape of a high round tower, the same as in the MacNachtan crest. Its steep sides rose to a flared crown surmounted by crenulations, the parapet of which had been eroded by the water that dribbled and seeped from an unseen source at the top, running down its flanks and splashing into the water below. The constant babble was very calming and quite a contrast to the martial surroundings.

Skirting the pool, they approached a small door tucked into a corner, it was framed by an eroded moulding and five heavily weathered carved heads that were sunk into the stone around it. The features of long dead Pictish kings and warriors stared out from the stone; frozen in time but eaten away by the wind and weather. He knew that one of them was supposed to be Nechtan Mòr, the great king who had been the founder of the Clan in the 8th century, brought here from an earlier building, but which it was, none knew.

More impressive was the ancient script carved above the door. Like any self-respecting MacNachtan he knew the words by heart already:

"Behold the end, be not wiser than the highest. I hope in God"

He clenched his fists in his pockets to bolster his resolve, he was determined not to embarrass himself. The thick steel blast door suddenly swung inwards, leaving a pitch-black portal. Following the Rat's disappearing back, Gillespie stepped into the darkness.

8 - PASSING ON DOWN THE LINE

Andrew Balfour, First Minister for Scotland, carefully replaced the receiver in its cradle, the British Prime Minister's furious threats still ringing in his ears. He raised his eyes to the room. A cluster of advisers and flunkeys twitched on the other side of the desk. He said nothing for a few moments, passing his penetrating stare from one to another. God, they were all so young, what the fuck use would they be in the knife fight that was about to ensue.

Sighing, he poured himself another cup of coffee and picked up the receiver again. "Claire? Yes, hello. Could you please get me John Lamont on the phone? Tell him it's urgent."

Moments later the sound of a phone ringing came down the wire, after a few rings it was answered.

"Andrew, or should I say First Minister, how very nice to hear you. What an unexpected pleasure, as always." John Lamont's measured voice dripped passive aggression down the line.

Balfour's head twitched as if unconsciously shrugging off the barbs: "Lamont, listen. I don't have time for your pleasantries. I've just got off the phone with the Prime Minister and she has told me that she is going to cut off your balls if you don't get this situation gripped. You are the Warden of the Clyde and securing our sea border with the Republic is your responsibility. What the hell is going on out there?"

A profound silence came down the line. The longer it lasted the greater the pressure grew on Balfour to blink first and fill the void. Just as it got to the point that he could bear it no longer, Lamont hissed:

"I am quite aware of my responsibilities, but am ever grateful to be reminded of them, of course. Now turning to your question. I'm on the trail of the perpetrators and expect to have them in custody soon. I will be able to make a more complete report in the coming days. As you know, it's never easy to get information in this lawless place, but you can assure the Prime Minister I am doing my utmost. I've also filed a formal complaint and request for information to the Seanadh in Oban. But I think we all know how effective that will be." He audibly yawned down the phone.

Balfour paused, scanning the assembled faces before him; they carried expressions ranging from gormless to pained concentration. He felt his ire rise, constricting his throat with fury as the bile churned and roiled in his gut. They were all so fucking useless, how was he supposed to manage the vicious cretins across the border with such a bunch of spineless imbeciles. The Gaels were a problem that should have been answered long ago; they were an inconvenience in the modern age, with their funny clothes, exclusive language and pompous feudal chieftains. They had only ever brought him problems. Turning his attention back to Lamont, he poured vitriol down the line:

"Listen carefully you self-important Gaelic cunt. I am the elected First Minister for Scotland and you are our errand boy to that shit hole you style as the Gaelic Republic and don't you forget it. Just think of all that money we pay you. Maybe we can spend it somewhere more useful like Inveraray or Dunvegan? What would happen I wonder if you had to pay all those retainers out of your own pocket? How long would it be before someone decided to string you up by your own guts? Not very long I imagine."

"You have two days to report back. I hope I've made it clear that I don't want to hear anything other than success. I am holding you personally accountable and any failure will result in your funding being terminated forthwith. Is that clear!" He thundered, surprising even himself with his intemperate tone.

"Oh aye, you are very clear," replied John of the Sorrows, so softly it was almost a whisper.

And then the line went dead.

9 - SCHEMING

As soon as Colin Campbell, MacCailean Mòr, Duke of Argyll, Colonel of the Black Watch, Warden of the West and Chief of the Clan Campbell, stepped into his office the phone started ringing. He crossed the room to pick up the receiver, waving away Morag, his PA, as he did so.

"Yes, MacCailean Mòr here." He always answered the phone with his Gaelic title as that was what Clan members seemed to expect. In any case, he had grown so used to being addressed by it since his father died that he was now only called Colin by his oldest and closest friends.

"Ah, it's you John. I must admit that I've been expecting your call. A nasty business last night I see."

Amongst those he recognised as his equals, few and far between though they were, John Lamont could be charming. With MacCailean Mòr he was always at his most engaging, especially when seething under the surface about some perceived slight or other. Today was no exception.

"Yes, frightful isn't it. Edinburgh is really quite upset and even London have been on the phone to complain. It's fair to say, they are looking to us Wardens to deliver something to quench public outrage. I was hoping that a man of your reach and influence might have some useful information to share?"

Lamont's obsequious tone grated on MacCailean Mòr's ear, but he brushed the irritation aside.

"I am afraid I've heard nothing yet, have you?"

"Well a little bird did whisper something in my ear," Lamont continued, relishing the moment. "From what I've heard, it sounds very likely that this outrage was perpetrated by a boatful of marauding MacNachtans. My sources saw them coming back from the Irish Sea and crossing into Loch Fyne at Tarbert."

"Fortuitously, this dovetails with another matter I wanted to discuss with you for some time and that is the small matter of Clan MacNachtan. With old Duncan breathing his last, isn't this the moment to draw a line under that old song? This is the 21st century after all. They are a distraction and a nuisance, particularly with all that illegal gaming they do. They sit there thumbing their noses at you, practically at your front door. Surely, we need to consolidate small clans like the MacNachtans into bigger operations – like yours. You know it makes sense. The current situation presents us with a rather wonderful opportunity to, how should I say, kill two birds with one stone....."

Lamont did not do pleading, and this was as close as MacCailean Mòr had ever heard him. He stared out of the window and across the boggy lawn and gardens towards the loch. After a few moments, he replied:

"Mmmmm, and what exactly do you have in mind?"

10 - DUNCAN TAPAIDH

As he stepped under the lintel and into the dark, Gillespie found himself in a narrow hallway almost entirely filled with a staircase. Following the Rat's disappearing legs, Gillespie mounted the stairs two at a time coming out of the gloom onto a surprisingly bright and open landing. Two bulky clansmen barred their way. The Rat spoke to them rapidly and the two hulks shuffled aside to let them pass.

The walls were hung with a few very faded blue tapestries and what appeared to be an Andy Warhol portrait of the Chief in his younger days – dark glasses to the fore, a flourish of eagle feathers in his bonnet and the drape of a great kilt over his naked torso in what could only have been Studio 54, the famous New York nightclub.

Following his glance, the Rat responded: "Aye, he was a wild one back in the day. Andy gave him that after Duncan taught him how to throw a knife. Different times then."

They arrived at a pair of stout oak doors each of which had a finely cast brass tower set in the middle. As the Rat reached to open them, they swung inwards to reveal the room beyond. Gillespie knew that this must be the famous Red Banner Hall, the centre of Clan life for 500 years. It was not as big as he had imagined, and it had windows on two sides that brought in shafts of light, but due to the high ceiling the corners of the room shrank away into shadow. His gaze was drawn to the huge fireplace surmounted by a heavy carving of the by now familiar tower. Underneath it read: I Hope in God.

In front of a fire, on which you could've roasted an ox, was a chair in which sat an elderly and plainly very unwell man.

BLOODBOND

Duncan Tapaidh MacNachtan, 35th Chief of the Clan MacNachtan and Keeper of the Black Tower, was swaddled in many layers of clothing and even though the fire was roaring behind him he shivered and shook. His long face was gaunt, like yellowed ivory, his cheek bones pushed higher by the deep recesses below. His eyes were now rheumy, their blue power diffused by cataracts and time. His aquiline nose, once so admired by Warhol and Mapplethorpe, was gnarled and mapped by the contours of burst capillaries. Gillespie had heard many tales of Duncan: some inspiring, some cautionary. But all of them had been extravagant tableaus soaked in the technicolour of projected dreams and half-truths; the clannish pride of his father inflating and burnishing the legend. It seemed impossible that this shrunken body could be the same person.

Aodhan stepped out of the shadows and leant down to his ear: "My Chief, this is your cousin Gillespie come home from across the water. Iain the Rat has brought him as you requested."

Duncan turned his bleary eyes in Gillespie's direction. Gillespie felt sure that he couldn't see but he was wrong. Duncan started to laugh; a low chuckle at the beginning, building to a raspy wheeze, finished by a hacking cough. With a grimace he spat a yellow sputum in the fire and watched it sizzle before turning his face back to Gillespie.

"Ach well, so you are just like your father and his father. I would recognise that hair and those eyebrows anywhere. Fine men they were too. We could've done with more men like them staying closer to home. But ach, that was all so long ago." He paused, as if having lost his train of thought, before continuing:

"Gillespie, do you know why they brought you here?"

Aodhan and Iain exchanged glances while Gillespie contemplated the question.

"I understand that you are dying and that there will need to be a choosing of the next Chief. For some reason, you thought it important to have me kidnapped and brought here." Gillespie could feel his cheeks flushing, as his anger rose. "But I know nothing about you or the Clan, or even the Republic. My grandfather left all this behind for a reason; to seek a new and better life. A life without all the pointless violence and the stupid blood feuds you Gaels seem to love. I am a farmer, not a warrior! I've no martial skills to offer. Why on earth would anyone even want me as Chief?"

Duncan laughed again, more vigorously, until his body shook, wracked by spasms. Another sputum went on the fire: this time thicker and redder. Recovering his composure, Duncan gestured at Gillespie to pull up a chair next to him and once he had sat down, said:

"I know, I know and I'm sorry. It was selfish of me to want you to be here and I'm sad that a good man had to die to achieve it. But there is a logic and a reason why it matters. We're surrounded and hounded by our neighbours on all sides. MacCailean Mòr is just one of the threats we face; that bastard Lamont is also greedy for what little is left us. No, our enemies are a long list and they all want to take us over: our land, this house, but most of all they want our gaming operation."

"Ever since the brilliant Diarmid MacNutt put us on the map for the first time in a hundred years those buzzards have been circling ever lower. I can feel them here," he clawed at his hollowed-out face, "just waiting for me to croak my last. But I'll be damned before we give it up so easy."

"The Clan is small now and we are sick of the sight of each other. I wanted to bring in some fresh blood to the choosing. They may not want you; they probably won't want you, but at least they will have had a choice. Then they can lie in a bed of their own making."

"Once they have chosen, you can go home. I've asked the Clan treasurer to compensate you for your inconvenience. If my memory of your house is anything like the reality you may be grateful for a little financial assistance and I've told him to have an open hand. So, have patience Gillespie. I won't detain you too much longer."

Then, exhausted by this speech, he slumped in his chair, chin on his chest, the mucus-filled wheezing the only noise.

Aodhan nodded at them both, gesturing that they should leave. Gillespie followed Iain the Rat to the door, wondering if he would ever meet his cousin again. As he was almost through the doorway, Duncan called out. A clawed hand beckoned Gillespie to come closer and as he approached Duncan's chair it gripped his hand tightly, pulling him down.

"Is that what your father told you? About why your grandfather left?" The wheezy whisper trailed away, but Duncan's milky eyes were resolute.

Gillespie nodded.

The hacking cough that followed was awful; blood foamed at either corner of Duncan's lips: his lungs were losing their battle. Gillespie wanted to pull away; to leave this dying man to pass in peace. But the hand would not release him. It pulled him closer still: his whisper faint.

"Don't believe everything your father told you."

Exhausted by this effort, Duncan closed his eyes and slumped deeper on his chair; the clawed hand relinquished its grip on Gillespie's giving a final squeeze as it was withdrawn.

11 - THE CANUN

Gillespie felt relief when he walked outside into the cooler air. The Hall had not only been stifling but was permeated with the expectation of death's imminent arrival. The stillness and shadows, combined with the oppressive heat, had been quite overwhelming. While Gillespie was no doctor, Duncan was clearly on the last lap and he knew it. The parchment-like skin pulled taught across those once fine cheekbones; the liver spots insidiously spreading across his hands; and that cough, well, they told their own story.

He turned Duncan's last words to him over and over in his mind. What did he mean? What shouldn't he believe? It had all seemed so straightforward before: his grandfather sensibly leaving his benighted homeland for a better life. But now doubt crowded his mind. There was something strange about his grandfather. He would never talk of the Clan or his background and if anyone asked he would change the subject. Gillespie had never seen him wearing a kilt or any tartan either. It was as if he had left that all behind when he had crossed the water. But meeting Duncan hadn't given him any answers after all, only questions.

Leaving the Rat to have a smoke in the outer ward, Gillespie walked out through the scrub oak and Scots pine woods that came down to the shore of the loch. The tall pine trees soared high above him; their trunks scabby with grey scaly bark and naked of branches until high in the air, as if shrinking from the touch of the humans far below. Beneath them, the oak trees were still leafless, waiting for winter's passing before pulling on their new spring coat: their stubby upstretched boughs resilient. In this sunshine Gillespie could sense their expectation too: soon, but not yet.

There was a light but regular flow of people along a well-worn path that led up through the woods and as he walked under the trees he saw that the path turned into a more substantial track beyond. This followed the loch shore and was rutted and potholed and covered in loose chippings between pools of muddy water. Ahead, he could see a small group gathered by the side of the track and as he got closer he realised that they were in fact an angry bundle of gesticulating arms and voices.

Pressing his way through the crowd he saw two figures in the centre of the makeshift circle fingers jabbing and voices raised. One carried the familiar red, green and blue tartan, while the other had a dark green and blue, almost black tartan.

"Ya Campbell cunt! I know it was you who thieved my Kat. It took me three days and 50 Cùinn to fetch it back from the other side of Rannoch. I should open you up here and be done with it! To hell with your MacCailean Mòr: he should keep you rabble in your place."

The MacNachtan shook with rage, eyes wide and wild and dark red beard bristling. At that moment Gillespie twigged it was Jamie; the rage had so transformed him that he was barely recognisable. His fellow clansmen had pinioned his arms but were struggling to hold him back from his adversary who stood calmly waiting for Jamie's rant to conclude.

He was a blond-haired man of average build, his hair was scraped back tightly across his head and tied in a ponytail, and his blue eyes sparkled cheerfully as if enjoying the moment.

Gillespie looked around the group and saw the usual arsenal of weaponry hanging from every shoulder and hip. Why was the blond so relaxed? He was outnumbered 20 to one! Why hadn't someone put a bullet in this arsehole?

The Campbell inspected his cuff and, as if seeing some dust on the pristine black drill cotton, he brushed at it with the back of his hand sardonically turning to fix Jamie with his unperturbed gaze.

Jamie's rage was duly raised another notch.

"Enough!" came a commanding voice – Kirstie! "Jamie Ruadh are you accusing Niall Campbell of stealing your Kat?"

"Aye, I am. And the bastard should pay me for the time and money it cost me to get it back." Jamie replied, shaking off the restraining arms. "And if the cowardly Campbell cunt doesn't want to pay, well let's settle it according to the Canun."

The accompanying sneer would have curdled milk, but the Campbell still remained calm and raised his hand to speak.

"There is no need for such language. It is perfectly clear that I did not steal your clapped-out Kat. Why would I? I can't imagine it could even get me from here to Inveraray. How it made its way past Rannoch I've no idea; the Griogaraich must have carried it there. But if you are invoking the Canun then you leave me little choice."

Kirstie nervously turned to face Jamie: "Are you sure you want to invoke Canun. It's not too late to retract."

Jamie nodded slowly, eyes narrowed and fixed on the blond: "Aye, I am sure. It's about time this piece of shit paid his bill."

Kirstie nodded and the bystanders stepped backwards to clear a wider circle for the two protagonists.

"OK, as the senior representative of Clan MacNachtan present I declare that Canun has been invoked by James MacNachtan of Kilblaan against Niall Campbell of Ardbreknish. According to Canun this matter must be settled with blood. The first to draw will prevail."

With that she withdrew, and the two men carefully prepared themselves. Both had been carrying claymores in back mounted scabbards and having removed all other unnecessary accoutrements they retrieved their respective blades and stood facing each other in the centre of the circle.

While Jamie was thick set and short; Niall Campbell was lithe. Both had similar swords although Niall's looked the finer blade. It had a fine red leather lining to the elaborate basket, whereas Jamie's had a more agricultural look, but the glitter and flash were identical as they slashed at the air to warm through their muscles.

The men completed their warmup and faced each other. Kirstie stepped forward a final time and said, "Canun has been invoked, only by blood can it be settled. You must fight until the blood flows; may the first drop not be your last."

"May the first drop not be your last" echoed the crowd, who now started to cheer on Jamie, calling his name and clapping in a slow menacing rhythm.

Jamie's face was set hard. While Niall was superficially calmer, even he had now shed his smirk. Both men circled each other; Jamie aggressively adopting a hanging guard while circling to his right, his left hand on his hip; while Niall calmly adopted a half-circle guard, with his sword blade and basket facing to the inside of his posture, his arm well bent and below the level of his wrist.

Gillespie thought this looked like a weak position from which to defend against a concerted attack from hanging guard. To anchor him to his heritage, his father had forced him to spend many hours of his childhood going to fencing classes and learn the eight guards and the seven cuts, the traverse step and how to compass a blade. He had never enjoyed it much and was relieved when in his mid-teens he was at last able to leave the bruises and batterings of the sword yard behind.

Jamie lunged with a lightening quick cut to Niall's head. Niall ducked and slipped his lead leg backwards, withdrawing from the reach of Jamie's blade. Jamie returned to the hanging guard; the point of his sword leading down across his body.

It was now Niall's turn to probe. Circling to his right, he cut to Jamie's left cheek; was parried with a cross guard that pushed his sword away above his head. The blades were held in tension for a moment; then Jamie released, recovering to an inside guard momentarily, before rapidly lunging and laying a cut to Niall's right side.

Niall moved smoothly and elegantly, parrying and pushing Jamie's sword to his right before stepping in and punching Jamie hard in the face with his free hand. Smarting, Jamie stumbled backwards, eyes watering, blinking away the unwanted tears.

Niall moved so easily; he flowed. Stepping in to lunge and back in slip, his sword seemed to barely move – a twist here, a turn there, the basket hilt moving from inside to outside posture, the tip seeming to remain the fixed point around which he moved.

As if he could sense that he had to win quickly if he was to win at all, Jamie feinted a cut at Niall's shoulder, while compassing his blade around his opponent's to strike at his leading right leg. Niall parried easily and pulling on Jamie's overstretched arm with his left hand sent him tumbling to the floor. With a flash of steel, it was over; a deep cut drawn across Jamie's prone posterior, which immediately started to seep blood in a determined manner.

The crowd scattered, breaking the circle. Several, including Kirstie, rushed to Jamie's aid, staunching the blood and starting to apply field dressings. Jamie groaned but did not rise, accepting the indignity that went with their succour.

Niall bowed obsequiously in Jamie's direction and slowly gathered his gear, wiping his sword point on his sleeve. Without further ado, and unhindered by the attendant crowd, he set off down the road towards Inveraray with a spring in his step and a tune on his lips.

12 - CLIÙ

Gillespie was shocked at how quickly the events had unfolded and the unexpected consequences that had been left behind. Having watched the skilful application of a spray-on field dressing that stopped the bleeding and bound the cut together, he helped to lift Jamie to his feet. Then, supported on both sides by his fellow clansmen, Jamie slowly and painfully walked away back towards the Tower.

Gillespie stared after him as he disappeared down the track.

"If you don't shut that mouth, you might catch a fly," said Kirstie from behind him.

"What the hell just happened? I mean, what the fuck! Is this normal? Do you always try and butcher each other like this? And why did you lot just stand around? You all had guns; any one of you could've put a bullet between his eyes at 100 yards!"

Kirstie considered him, her face impassive, letting him finish before responding.

"There is a lot you'll find strange and different here, even though you've grown up in the tradition. This is not some textbook. You need to be patient and try to understand why things are the way they are. I'll try and answer your questions, but please calm down."

"As you might have guessed, our Jamie has had a long dispute with Niall Campbell running back over many years. The latest expression of this was Jamie's belief that Niall had stolen his Kat and sold it to a bunch of MacGregors over Rannoch way. To be honest, I don't know if I believe that; partly because, as Niall said, I don't think it could've driven that far. It is forever breaking down. In any case, it doesn't really matter, as once Jamie had invoked Canun there was nothing any of us could do to stop what happened next."

"From that moment it can only be settled by blood, cliù - honour - demands it. Neither Jamie or Niall could walk away, and neither would the Clan let them. After all, honour does not belong to them alone."

"But he was outnumbered 20 to 1, you could've easily stopped it!"

"Look Gillespie, you have to understand, we are a small Clan. Yes, we outnumbered Niall here today, but he's a Campbell and an important duine uasal for MacCailean Mòr. The duine uasal make up the professional fighting corps of the Clan and MacCailean Mòr can put 5,000 men in the field. How many have we got? 100, maybe 150 if we scrape the barrel. We're small fry and know our place. Why do you think we've survived this long?"

"And as to guns, it's forbidden under Canun to shoot a fellow Gael in the Republic. It is one of the core tenets of our constitution. Do you think there would be any Gaels left if we ran around shooting each other? No! Any Gael that breaks Canun like that brings a blood feud down on his head and that of his family. Even his Clan is obliged to offer him up. This is why we still carry claymores and the like: under Canun blades don't count. This was the balance that the founding fathers created to satisfy the need for honour while preserving the ability for Gaels to protect themselves and ensuring that the Republic didn't wipe itself out. Canun stops small trifles becoming big problems."

Gillespie paused, thinking. "So, it's OK to kill each other with swords but not ok to shoot each other."

"Kind of," replied Kirstie. "Canun dictates that you fight to first blood. That could be anything from a scratch to a fatal blow. Very occasionally someone will be killed outright, but the winning participant then risks a blood feud with the family of the one they have killed. Generally, if it's perceived as an unfortunate accident, it will go no further. But if it's considered deliberate, then all hell can break loose. Blood feuds apply to you and all your immediate family any one of whom can be killed to repay the debt. That is why people are so keen to avoid them and also why we are still here over 250 years after King Charlie freed us."

His head swam. All those crazy stories his father had told him about the Republic and its ways; he had never really believed half of it. It was so preposterous. Nonetheless, it was here taking place in front of his eyes.

He idly started to shuffle stone chippings over the blood stains that Jamie had left on the ground. He had almost forgotten Kirstie was there when her voice suddenly cut into his reverie.

"Hello, is there anybody in there." She waved a hand in front of his eyes.

He snapped back into focus. "Sorry, I was miles away."

"Hhmm, I could see that. Well I, for one, am starving. Let's go and find some lunch. Come on, I need to show you the village and where you will be staying." Pulling him by the hand she led him like a lost child down the track.

13 - THE DUBH LOCH

As Gillespie and Kirstie walked along talking, he suddenly realised that she was much shorter than him, even though he had always felt her to be much larger. The force of her personality more than made up for any lack of stature. She was stout but not fat, solid, with wide hips and strong thighs that rucked and creased her trousers as she walked. Her upper half was slighter, almost as if the wrong top had been joined to the wrong bottom in some flip book game. Her roundish face was topped with spiky black hair that she picked at and preened as they walked.

She was busy explaining the topography to him as they walked, pointing out where further along the loch MacNachtan territory abruptly ended and Clan Campbell lands started. Most MacNachtan territory that remained was north and west of the loch, lying between it and Loch Awe some ten miles away. As they rounded Strone Point they got a good view down the loch to the South and across to Inveraray, the white walled township of the Campbells. Following her finger, Gillespie could see the black turreted hulk of the castle lying just outside the town and dominating its approach.

Swinging round the point they continued to follow the shore, passing a few modest houses at Stronshira where Kirstie pointed out Brighid's home, before leaving the loch behind and heading inland up Glen Shira. They walked beside the river Shira as it spilled its load into Loch Fyne. It was hardly the mighty torrent of his imagination, but it was still too wide to cross easily except by the rather battered looking bridge. Ignoring that, they proceeded to the Dubh Loch, the hereditary heartland of the Clan.

The Dubh Loch was not large, not much more than a millpond really. Kirstie pointed out the islet on which the MacNachtans had built their first stronghold, until plague had carried them off and it had to be abandoned. Nothing remained of it now, but the islet endured and was where the Chiefs were buried, albeit it now suffered the indignity of being joined to the shore by a causeway.

They followed the river backwards up Glen Shira towards its source, through bulrushes and clumps of bog myrtle that released waves of astringent scent as he and Kirstie pushed through their straggly branches. The sun burst through the clouds at that moment, and, combined with the heady smell, Gillespie felt almost relaxed.

At each house along the way, Kirstie methodically named the tenants and their children, their parents and grandparents and great grandparents, until Gillespie's head span with names and the associated epithets that seemed inalienable one from the other – the tall, the short, the fair, the dark, the wily, the slow, the fisherman, the steam, the IT, the Katman, and so it went on. The houses had a similar descriptive nomenclature based on what you see is what you get – View Mount, River Side, Big Field and for Gillespie it revealed a society at one with its environment and comfortable with reality, rather than pretending to something other.

The glen was long but fairly straight and having crested a rise they could look far away to the north. The slopes of either side were thickly wooded with a mix of pine and scrub oak. The pine tending to the higher slopes, while the oak preferred to be lower and more protected. Beinn Bhuidhe rose high and imperious above them, its three ridges dusted with snow. But the sun was at their backs and warmed them as they walked.

Immediately in front of them there was a fine oak tree, its limbs flung wide enjoying the relative shelter of the glen. Its leafless branches with spread fingers poked and rustled in the light wind. The glen continued into the distance, the hiatus between the hills filled with the ebb and flow of fields and woods and the river meandering its way from side to side.

"A fine view." Gillespie said to himself as much as to Kirstie.

"Aye, it is that," Kirstie replied. "Which is why we have held it through thick and thin. It's pretty much all we have left now, squeezed as we are by Campbells all round, MacArthurs to the north, MacNabs to the east, and Griogaraich anywhere they choose. Duncan Tapaidh's passing is going to throw all of that in the air again. Still, we have been here before and will just have to wait and see how that all unfolds."

Ahead of them was a fine stone house, its rough blocks almost certainly liberated from the vanished fortress on the Dubh Loch. It sat up above the river and commanded the glen, its five bays tied together under a narrow pediment. The garden in front was littered with bits of dead machinery, an incongruous contrast to the rather fine structure behind. Old tractors, hoes, muck spreaders, balers and troughs were casually strewn, seemingly with little thought to place or visual amenity.

A mud-spattered vehicle stood with its bonnet raised and an array of tools and parts laid on the grass beside it. It was unlike any vehicle that Gillespie had seen before; it was shorter than a normal car and had six tightly bunched wheels, three on either side, and its body was moulded from what looked to be toughened composite plastic. At the front there was a covered cab which could take two passengers, or three at a push, and this was bound in a stout steel rollcage, to protect the passengers in case of an unexpected tumble. Behind, it was open to the sky, with some hard-moulded seats on either side and a load-bay in the middle. As they approached, they could hear humming interspersed with the occasional expletive coming from under the dull green bonnet.

"Hullo Nin. No rest for the wicked I see, and Lord knows you are wicked." Kirstie said mischievously.

A sharp thump was followed by a torrent of swear words as Nin withdrew his grease smeared face from the engine bay collecting a whack from the bonnet's leading edge as he did so. "Bastard! You fucking piece of shit useless bastard!" He swore, lashing out with his foot at the Kat which sat impassive, soaking up the abuse. Rubbing the back of his head and thereby transferring more grease to it, Nin turned and smiled, his teeth blinding in comparison with the surrounding grime.

"Well look who it is, if it isn't Captain Kirstie and our long-lost cousin having a tour by the look of it."

Kirstie smiled, kicking at one of the Kat's many studded wheels: "And I see this is still keeping you busy. Should have known better than to buy it off Euan Cameron of all people. Still, there is no helping some folk."

"Aye, well maybe you were right, but I am nearly done and then this beauty will purr. Here Gillespie come and have a look at the cream of Republic engineering."

Nin stood back, grease covered arms spread wide, ushering Gillespie in to have a closer look at the rugged vehicle.

"Look in there," he pointed under the bonnet, his smile gleaming with pleasure. "That is a 450-horsepower Gael-Tech V4 engine; it produces over 550 lb-ft of torque at only 2,000 revs! This will take you anywhere you want to go, it's a beast! Comfort may not be high on its list of attributes, but it's tough as fuck. All I need to do is get the bastard to work." At which he lashed out another kick at the plastic moulded bodywork.

Gillespie stood admiring the surprisingly neat engine bay. Kirstie mused: "Hhmm, I will believe it when I see it. When it is, you can whisk me away to the hydro for a romantic weekend."

"In your dreams …..and my nightmares," he laughed. "Come on in and have a brew."

Wiping his hands with a shiny black rag that served only to spread the dirt rather than remove it, he led them across the mechanical graveyard and through the blue front door of the house.

14 - ELRIG

Gillespie found himself in a small vestibule strung with coats and hats and scarves and littered with sticks and boots and frisbees, shrimping nets, fishing rods, reels and bags. An all-pervading odour of dry mud and wet dog lingered in the air. Long dead deer stared down from the wall, some mournfully, others enquiringly, their shiny glass eyes at odds with their moth ravaged fur.

"This way, this way," Nin cheerfully led them on. Once their coats and boots had been added to the pile, they tumbled through a glazed door and out into an unexpectedly modern white hallway. "Welcome to Elrig." Nin said, arms spread almost as wide as his smile. "Make yourself at home and I will see if Charlie is about. Hopefully I can rustle up some of his home baking – his drop scones are the best by the way."

Nin then stage whispered to Gillespie behind a conspiratorial hand: "Now would you rather tea or coffee or something stronger?"

Kirstie opted for tea and Gillespie followed her lead, more out of politeness than because he wanted it. Nin bustled out to the kitchen, waving them through to the sitting room on the way.

Like the hallway, the sitting room was a modern room. Gillespie wasn't sure why he was surprised, but somehow given the exterior he had expected it to be all dingy dark colours with plenty of tartan. The white walls held some striking modern prints, very much in the style of late-Matisse, and over the fireplace was a Soviet Realist painting of two young men in military uniform standing side by side in front of a billowing Soviet Flag, they both clutched machine guns with large drum magazines. While one looked down demurely, the other's gaze was fixed purposefully on the horizon.

BLOODBOND

A large L-shaped oatmeal sofa was drawn up in front of the fire with a red and green geometric carpet laid under a low-lying coffee table. This groaned under weighty tomes dedicated to subjects like 'The life and loves of Wassily Kandinsky' and 'Shields of the Pacific'.

Kirstie flopped on the sofa, immediately kicking off her shoes and ranging her legs across its arm. Meanwhile, Gillespie continued to look around the room, admiring a pair of Eames chairs grouped by the window as if to enjoy the view. The inevitable flat screen TV took up much of one corner, at odds with the variety of ancient weaponry that were artfully arranged on the wall behind it. The stripped floorboards were a mellow yellowish grey, giving the room a warm feel. He noted, admiringly, that they ran the full width of the room and were tightly fitted, a skilled job worthy of a Shoreditch studio.

At that moment, Nin came through the door carrying a laden tray, his spiky black hair just fitting under the lintel. Following right behind him was another man of average height and short cropped hair. He had unusually smooth and fine skin that positively glowed with health. This was contrasted with a roughhewn nose that had clearly sustained a break or three and slightly protruding ears that were only accentuated by his shorn hair. His greeny brown eyes were soft and friendly and he strode across the room to shake Gillespie by the hand.

"Hello, hello, look at what Nin has dragged in," he exclaimed, pumping Gillespie's hand warmly. "He has told me a lot about you, but not how good looking you were, cheeky wanker that he is." He cast an amused glance over his shoulder at a protesting Nin. "My name is Charles, Charles Farquharson, but please call me Charlie – like the King!" He said, barely suppressing a giggle.

Time seemed to accelerate over tea and scones as they spraffed and laughed; Kirstie, Nin and Charlie all trying to out gossip each other, giving Gillespie the download they felt he needed about the reality of the Clan and the Republic. It was so warm and convivial that it wasn't long before

Gillespie felt his eyelids drooping, the long stressful journey and lack of sleep weighing them down.

As he battled to follow the conversation and keep his eyes open, Kirstie suddenly turned to the now dark window and clapped her hand to her forehead.

"Shit, I was supposed to be walking Gillespie to the Two Stags to book him in for his stay. We're never going to get there now."

Charlie glanced at Nin and then at Kirstie. "We would be very happy to put him up here, we've plenty of space." Turning to Gillespie, he continued. "Well how about it? Much more fun to stay with us than at that boring inn: Two Stags my arse, more like two donkeys! Our food is better, and our beds are warmer, not to mention we have cotton sheets, none of the nylon and polyester shite yon hovel will give you."

Gillespie was in no shape to argue and with a wave of tiredness sweeping over him, he simply relinquished his grip on wakefulness and slipped under its cosseting tide.

15 - COMHAIRLE

John Lamont knew he had to tread carefully. Even for one as powerful and feared as he there are moments when caution and cunning come to the fore. But despite the risk, or maybe because of it, he loved these moments. Like the alpinist reaching for new thrills - ever higher, no ropes, no oxygen - he performed his best when under the greatest pressure.

Following his call with MacCailean Mòr, he immediately summoned Allan Stewart and swiftly briefed him on the unfolding plan. Next, he messaged the heliport, alerting Fraser Murray to prepare his aircraft to fly to Oban. Finally, thrusting the necessary papers, change of clothes and toiletries into his bag, he left his office and carefully locked the door behind him.

Stepping smartly through the castle, he had arrived at the heliport just as Fraser had finished securing clearance from Air Traffic Control at Spean Bridge. Without further ado, the helicopter was towed out of its hanger and prepared for immediate departure. The short flight to Oban was mostly spent peering at the terrain below, particularly when they passed over the head of Loch Fyne. In fact, he made Fraser circle Beinn Bhuidhe twice before he was sufficiently satisfied to continue his onward journey.

As they approached Oban they flew over the Riaghaltas on the hill above the city, its Bonawe granite arcades encompassing the two great chambers from which the Republic was ruled. The Seanadh, or Senate, was the elected chamber, populated with perfectly normal elected representatives, who were focused on day to day administration and getting things done. The other chamber was the Comhairle, the unelected, unrepresentative, unruly and arcane face of the Gaelic Republic - the Council of Chiefs. This was where he was heading.

Ever since he had first attended the Comhairle as a boy he had hated it. As far as he was concerned, it was full of old coffin dodgers, puffed up with their sense of entitlement, languishing on laurels that were frequently several hundred years old, and with little interest in, or understanding of, the 21st Century. The protocol of centuries weighed heavy on the house and despite the fact that the ancient house of Lamont was as established as any, he somehow was always made to feel like the new boy, the arriviste.

Lamont walked briskly though the corridors of the Riaghaltas, passing endless portraits of former members dead and buried. Many were dressed in tartan, ranging from demure to outrageous. He shuddered as he passed their gilt frames, feeling the weight of their disapproving sneers. The sooner this lot could be put on a bonfire the better as far as he was concerned. The cockades and bonnets and jabots and doublets belonged to another time, another place. The Republic's infantile adulation of the past, its ancestor worship and obsession with history and tradition was, in his view, totally inappropriate in 21st century Europe. Lamont had long promised himself that he was going to abolish this anachronism forever.

But that was only the beginning, he also needed to change the mentality of this benighted people, yoked to the traditions of the past. It was time for the dregs of its feudal past - the violence, the Canun, the clothes and the language - to be consigned to the dustbin of history. They were a barrier to communication with the world, to trade and modernism. To forge a new nation, they needed to throw off the mental shackles of the past. English was the world's lingua Franca and he would make it the Republic's too.

But to do that he had to play on the mutual enmity and rivalry of the other magnates, to keep them occupied and their eyes off the main game.

Stopping at the first available mirror he smoothed down his ruffled hair and adjusted his great kilt. Traditional garb was required when addressing the Comhairle, another black mark against it as far as he was concerned. His forefathers had never had to get out of a helicopter in such ridiculous apparel. Plus, the heating was always on too high in the chamber for such a warm garment, designed as it was to keep you alive on the hill with not much besides. Sure enough, as he entered through the high double doors into the chamber he could see a good few Chiefs were already snoozing, chins on their chests, spittle pooling on their collars: God how he hated them.

Bowing to the chamber and receiving a few nodded acknowledgements from those still awake, he shoogled along the front bench to his seat on the right of the Labhraiche, or Speaker of the House, who was sat in his grand but rather uncomfortable-looking eagle backed throne. Lamont had always rather admired the bird, depicted rousant, with its wings poised to take flight, its talons gouging into the chair's back. It had been a gift from the last King of Montenegro and was finely carved in pale Mediterranean olive wood, an exotic touch in the otherwise dark and dull, oak furnished chamber. He had often thought that Ross Urquhart, the Speaker, looked like a babe about to be carried off, dwarfed as he was by the eagle's spreading wings.

Briefly turning his attention to the debate, he clocked that some islander - was it MacPhee? - was droning on about fish net sizes and the need for alignment with European Union directives or some such dull subject, and so he used the time to look around the chamber to see who was in that day.

Across the aisle he saw MacLean of Duart was following the debate closely; immediately to her right was Murdoch Clanranald, a cut throat of renown not otherwise known for his interest in the fisheries; behind them were a few empty spaces, but Mackinnon of Strath and MacNeil of Barra could just be spotted sharing a joke on Mackinnon's phone – highly irregular, he made a mental note to submit a complaint to the Master at Arms. Still further back, he could see MacIan of Ardnamurchan and MacDonald of Knoydart. No sign of MacDonald of MacDonald, the Warden of the Isles, or the ghastly Keppoch – thank goodness for that at least. A reasonable turnout though from the West.

Looking down the chamber, he caught the eye of Seaforth, the Warden of the North and his coterie, all sat hugger mugger. Seaforth nodded acknowledgment and Lamont tipped his head in response.

Moving to his own side of the aisle, there was Gordon, the Warden of the East, his corpulent frame swagged and swathed in tartan, with Grant and Graham – the G-unit as he liked to call them – sat on either side. To complete the north eastern alliterative set, Forbes, Farquharson and Ferguson were sat on the bench behind, but no Fraser.

Finally, behind him he had Athol, Drummond and Menzies. He was alone on the front bench, MacCailean Mòr's space lying unfilled. So, at least no Cameron or Macleod, that was good, and he turned his mind to the job in hand.

Signalling to Urquhart that he wanted to speak next, he patiently bided his time until MacPhee, for it was she, ran out of things to say about codling sizes and sat down. The Speaker called his name and he rose to address the chamber.

"My Lords, Ladies," he started, determined to put them in a good mood with a little politeness. "I have come with shocking news of an incident in the Irish Sea last night in which a Republic ship attacked and all but destroyed a Kingdom patrol boat in an unprovoked attack. Three Kingdom servicemen tragically lost their lives in this cowardly incident." He paused for effect and let the words sink in.

"I've been called by the First Minister of Scotland who has conveyed in the strongest possible terms the displeasure of His Majesty's Government. The Republic has been threatened with sanctions, both against individuals, many of whom are in this room, and against the nation, if we do not find and punish those responsible."

"First Minister Balfour conveyed in no uncertain terms the British Prime Minister's anger and frustration that these attacks could be perpetrated from such a close neighbour and one with whom, whatever our past differences, she is keen to build a fresh relationship. For too long, we have enjoyed tweaking the tail of our neighbour. But this time the lion is stirring."

"Rubbish." Said a voice.

Lamont froze: blood pounding in his ears, bile rising in his throat.

Urquhart scrambled to his feet to calm the Chamber as it erupted in shouts and arm waving. Glowering, he turned to Catriona MacLean of Duart, for it had been her utterance, and purple faced he demanded: "My Lady can you please retract or rephrase your interjection."

MacLean turned towards Lamont, tucking her mane of red hair behind her right ear and fixing him with those cool grey eyes. She repeated: "Rubbish, John. You have spent too long with your nose so far up the First Minister's posterior you can't see the wood for the trees. We have never and will never punish our citizens just to please the Kingdom. This house is not accountable to the First Minister, but to our people. Whatever happened last night, we are not at the beck and call of Balfour, or the Prime Minster of the Kingdom of Great Britain for that matter."

Urquhart, whose apoplectic visage looked fit to burst, stood up and although unable to speak due to rage gesticulated at MacLean ordering her from the chamber. As she took her leave, she bowed obsequiously to the Speaker and flicked her hair dismissively at Lamont before sweeping out.

Lamont did not fluster easy but the fury that boiled inside him threatened to make him do something foolish. Very slowly and calmly, he focused on containing it and pushing it out of his mind. He returned to his feet to continue his address.

"Apologies my Lords and Ladies for that interruption. However, we need to take action. We need to show the Kingdom that we can be relied upon to maintain the peace. And, above all, we do not want to allow the Kingdom to try and settle its own scores, as who knows where that will end. Therefore, I am asking the Chamber to appoint MacCailean Mòr, the Warden of the West and Colonel of the Black Watch, to a commission to find the perpetrators and to bring them before this house for justice to be dispensed."

With a final flourish he bowed low and sat down to await the response. His face was impassive apart from a slight flush of colour and the twitching of the vein on his forehead, the one that meandered its way from right hand hair line to eye socket. For those that knew him well, that was not a sight to be welcomed as it generally presaged a bloody and unrelenting retribution.

Sometime later, after the votes had been counted and written into the great book of State, he left the chamber accepting congratulations from some of the usual brown nosers on the way out. He was relieved; he had MacCailean Mòr's commission in his hand and could now put the first part of his plan in to action. He would deal with that bitch MacLean soon enough and that was something he was looking forward to.

16 - THE BREAKFAST OF CHAMPIONS

Gillespie woke with a start. The room was completely black. He rummaged and fumbled for the light switch before realising that it wasn't where he expected it to be. He wasn't in bed at home! It hadn't been a dream. In a panic, he reached for the wall and, having found it, edged very carefully along trying not to bump into anything. Feeling a door jamb, he felt up and down for a switch without success. Trying the other side, he finally located the elusive square of plastic. He flicked the switch banishing the darkness.

Aside from the bed, there was a colourful rag rug on the floor, its many colours cheering up what was otherwise rather an austere room. Bare floorboards and white walls made it cool not cosy and the prints that decorated it were all grey green monotypes. He looked at his watch: 7.30 am, shit, he had slept for at least 14 hours. The very thought made him feel hungry. Wrapping himself in a towel, he opened the door to find a bathroom.

A long corridor stretched away from him under the slope of the eaves. It was pierced with an occasional window and had a deep red ottoman carpet leading him onwards over its lozenges and paisleys. Having tried a few doors and found more bedrooms his hand was just reaching for the next brass doorknob when the door swung inwards, revealing Charlie wrapped in a towel leaving the bathroom in a cloud of steam.

Looking him over, Gillespie observed that he had the hard, carved physique earned through heavy work rather than hours at a gym. The alabaster white of his skin was traced with pale blue veins and on the tricep of his right shoulder was the tattoo of a lion rampant emerging from a wreath and holding a sword in its right paw. It was in the same spot that Gillespie had seen the Rat cut the black tower from Malcolm.

"Good morning." Charlie tootled, "Slept well, I hope? Breakfast downstairs in five, if you are hungry."

Charlie suddenly stopped and with a confused look pointed his finger at Gillespie's right-hand shoulder: "How come you don't carry the mark of the black tower?" His finger circled the top of Gillespie's arm that was as pale and white as the rest of him.

"Dunno, it's just not something that we do in Ireland. We don't have the same need to brand ourselves like so much cattle as you real Gaels over this side of the water." Gillespie's attempt at humour slightly backfired; the words coming out more harshly than he meant.

"Wow, that is surprising. Well maybe tomorrow, we can put that right and take you down to Tavish's Tattoo parlour and get you a permanent memento of your visit." And with that he disappeared down the carpet with a hum on his lips leaving a damp trail of footprints behind him.

Gillespie spent a long time in the shower, as if he could wash away all the aches and sprains from the previous day. It felt like even his bruises had bruises, but the hot water helped. Wrapped again in his towel he padded back to his room to get dressed. On his bed he found a pile of clothes, including a faded and slightly moth eaten MacNachtan kilt and the necessary accoutrements. A note from Charlie on top read: "I dug this out of the back of Nin's wardrobe, you are thinner than he is nowadays, so it should fit, more or less. It's important for you to blend in if we go into town." He had signed off the bottom with a smiley face and a multitude of exclamation marks.

Leaving the room, Gillespie dutifully flicked the switch and pulled the door to. The sound of the radio and the smell of frying bacon drew him like an invisible thread through the house towards the kitchen.

Nin and Charlie were both already there. Nin was nursing a coffee at the table looking at something on his tablet, while Charlie was hard at work over the stove. Gesturing to Gillespie to pull up a chair, he mounded a plate with sausages, crispy bacon, slightly runny scrambled eggs and sloppy baked beans.

Nin looked up from the screen, nodded in his direction and pushed a cup across. Wordlessly, he pointed at the tea pot and cafetiere that sat on a cast iron trivet in the middle of the table.

Gillespie wasn't sure when he had felt so hungry. Apart from those few drop scones the previous afternoon, he had only really eaten a ham and cheese roll since being dragged from his house. He demolished the plate in front of him, not pausing for breath until the last fork of egg swirled with tomato sauce had been despatched. Feeling much improved, he concentrated on his coffee.

Charlie sat at the far end of the table, observing Gillespie's ravenous despatch of the plate with amusement. No one had yet said a word.

"What happens now?" Gillespie asked, looking from one to the other. "I mean, don't get me wrong, I am truly appreciative of your hospitality and that was," he nodded at Charlie, "an exceptional breakfast. But I really should be getting back home. Apart from anything else, I've a farm to run."

Nin lifted those absorbing blue eyes from the screen and peered thoughtfully at Gillespie. "I know. I know. It's hard. But much though I would like to give you an answer, I don't have one. You saw Duncan yesterday. He could pass today. Maybe he even died last night. Whatever. It can't be long now. The choosing will happen straight after, at which point you'll be free to go."

"What if I get selected." Gillespie asked. "What then? Can I still leave?"

"It won't happen," Charlie said. "No disrespect to you and your many doubtless wonderful qualities but no one knows who you are. You have made no contribution to the Clan; you have not served in the independent company and you haven't even worked in the gaming operation. The risk would be too great. The Clan are pretty smart about these things."

Gillespie turned on his phone. He wondered if he even had roaming rights in the Republic. The first network that flashed up was An Tùraidh Dubh, the Black Tower, clearly the Clan's provider. He had four bars, so he excused himself while he sent some emails to Eamon and Kate at the farm, making his excuses for the next few days. Luckily, given the time of year, there wasn't much to do, and they were more than capable of holding the fort. In any case, what other choice did he have?

17 - INVERARAY

A distant clock chimed, shortly joined by the radio which interrupted the relentless hip hop that had boiled and mobbed the kitchen with nine plucked notes on a clarsach to announce the hour.

Charlie asked Nin if there had been any word from the Castle yet on the state of Duncan. Shaking his head, Nin returned his attention to the latest shinty results. Charlie pondered a moment and then brightened. "I know what we should do today. We should take Gillespie into Inveraray. We could stroll into town, do a little light shopping and sink a few pints over lunch at the Galley. What do you think?" He looked from one to the other for encouragement.

"Certainly not the worst idea you've ever had," said Nin, and without waiting for Gillespie to offer an opinion, got to his feet, pushing back his chair with a scrape. "Meet outside in five." And without further ado, he ushered Gillespie out of the kitchen.

Charlie was the last to leave the house, pulling the bright blue door closed and turning the various keys that secured Elrig against unwanted intruders. In his hands he carried a bundle of items that he passed to Gillespie one at time. The first was a black jacket with the MacNachtan tartan panel on its forearm which he gestured to Gillespie to put on. Gillespie was glad of the extra layer; the temperature having dropped overnight. The jacket was slightly too big for his weedy frame, but it didn't matter as it was going over all the other clothes he was wearing.

Charlie then handed him a sword.

Gillespie paused as he reached out to take it. It had been at least ten years since he had done any formal fencing. He could more or less remember the seven cuts and about half of the guards but putting any of the elements together and actually fighting anyone, let alone a Gael, well that was something else altogether.

As if reading his mind, Charlie said "This is just to help you blend in. For God's sake don't draw it, whatever you do. If you don't carry one, people will know for sure you are an outsider and that will set tongues wagging." He handed him a back mounted scabbard of black webbing, identical to the ones that he and Nin were wearing.

The final touch was a dark blue bonnet that Charlie put on his head and pulled rakishly to one side. Standing back and admiring his handiwork he beamed "That'll do." Nin gave Gillespie the once over and grunted his agreement, only pausing briefly to roll his eyes at the trainers that still stuck out incongruously below the borrowed kilt.

Nin reversed the Kat, dodging through the piles of junk in the front yard. Gillespie climbed in the back sitting in the hard-plastic seat behind the driver's cab. Charlie climbed up next to him and, as Nin fired up the engine with a roar and crunched the beast into gear, shouted down to Gillespie, "You would do better to stand, even though we are not really going off road. If you sit down there your kidneys are going to take a battering." Grinning, Gillespie stood up and held on to the robust roll cage that covered the cab. Fortunately, he had just got his grip as the Kat leapt forward and started down the hill almost throwing him off the back in the process.

They followed the river to the end of the glen, past the Dubh Loch, and coming to the collection of houses at Stronshira. Nin pulled in and went to rap on the door of Number 6. After a short pause, Brighid came out still in her pyjamas and with her blond hair frizzed and tousled. After a brief exchange with Nin, she shut the door and Nin returned to the Kat. "She'll follow us down and meet us either at Khan's or at the Galley for lunch."

Leaving Stronshira behind, they almost immediately came to the battered bridge over the river. "We are now leaving MacNachtan land and it's as well to be aware of the fact. This is now Clan Campbell territory and while we get on OK at the moment with MacCailean Mòr," Charlie shouted above the roar of the engine while pointing at the great turreted castle to their right, "they are not Clan and you should remember that."

Although the Kat was by no means comfortable, once they were on the track it ate up the bumps and ruts with ease and they were soon pulling up the fine stone bridge over the Aray River. Nin cheekily stopped the Kat at the apex so that Gillespie could get the best view of the Castle, before he crunched the gears and roared down the final stretch into town.

It was a pretty town and lay along the loch. Successive waves of development had expanded the it from its 18th century core and there were now rows of well-tended modern houses that surrounded the old burgh and stretched out to the south. The harbour was teeming with boats like the one Gillespie had crossed from Ireland; small, fast and manoeuvrable.

Nin nosed down a side road, more of a passageway, and came to a small yard where he pulled in and parked. Gillespie jumped down; he could still feel his teeth chattering from the vibration of the engine and the thumps of the suspension. Following his two guides, he found himself back on the main street.

The Galley, a much-loved looking inn, stood across the road, a highland galley with sail furled and set oars adorning its sign with the yellow and black Campbell gyronny behind. However, it was too early for lunch, so Nin and Charlie set off in the other direction, as they had promised to help him buy some more appropriate footwear. Having rounded the corner, they came to an impressive shop overlooking the harbour, its windows laden with bolts of tartan and tweed, gumboots and gaiters. Over the door in fine gothic script it simply said: "Khan's Highland Supplies of Inveraray" and underneath enclosed in a ribbon:

"Superior Highland Wear for the Discerning – If Khan Can't, No One Can."

As they climbed the steps to enter, Gillespie saw an ornate shield stuck to one side of the steps which proclaimed:

Official Warrant Holder for the Riaghaltas 2007, 2009 and 2013.

Sometime later, after a heated debate with Ali Khan, the owner, a high-tech pair of Smiths of Elgol brogues had been picked out as the best brand for comfort, longevity and drainage. They cost a little more than the Nike or Adidas trainers that Gillespie was used to, but they bore the slogan "No bog too tough", so he felt sure that they would be worth the extra. After much rummaging under counters and in cupboards, the right size was located: Gillespie was really starting to look the part.

18 - THE GALLEY

As they left Khan's the sun came out and they paused to look up the loch towards Dunderave, soaking up all the heat they could from its weak rays before heading to the Galley for some well-earned lunch. The bar was nearly empty, and they secured a table in the window overlooking the street. Brighid hadn't arrived yet, and Gillespie idly wondered what she would think of him in his new clothes.

Waving away Gillespie's weak protests, Charlie ordered each of them a pint of Boar's Head heavy, the local brew, while they started to look at the menu. Gillespie suddenly realised that sitting at a table on the far side of the room was the blond-haired Campbell that he had seen fighting with Jamie the previous day. Pointing him out to Nin and Charlie, they both looked round and, having caught his eye, returned his nodded acknowledgement with a glower.

At that moment, Brighid entered and, after a flurry of hugs and kisses, sat down to join them. Sometime later, as they were finishing their meal, a languid voice floated towards them as Niall Campbell crossed the bar. "Well look at what we have here two MacNachtans that have flown from their nest, the Farquharson and a mystery man. Who might you be stranger? Another hooded crow blown in to feast on the carcass of poor old Duncan Tapaidh before his blood is even cold. How very touching."

Charlie put his hand on Nin's shoulder to calm him and with a voice dripping with sarcasm said: "Ah, Niall Campbell. What a pleasant surprise. And how unexpected to find you in here so early in the day. At a bit of a loose end, are we? Not got any widows or orphans to make? Well we would hate to disturb you. We're just enjoying the last of our lunch and will be on our way soon enough."

Niall almost seemed to enjoy Charlie's venom, leaning in with a smirk to say: "And do tell me, how is your red headed friend? You know, the one with the beard like a bog brush? I do hope he will be able to sit down in time for the feast after they have planted your Chief in his much deserved grave. I don't believe I cut him too deeply. Although it can be hard to tell sometimes, particularly when your opponent has his back to you."

It was Brighid's turn to interject turning her gaze from Charlie to Niall: "I would very much appreciate it if you lot could take your bawbags out of my face while I am finishing my meal. This is neither the time nor the place for your petty arguments. If you want to show off, you can do it outside."

Niall pouted, murmuring something under his breath, before nodding at Brighid and moving away towards the door and out into the street beyond.

"What was that all about?" asked Gillespie, grateful that the situation had not deteriorated further.

"Ach, he's OK. Just a bit of a wanker," Brighid said.

The words had barely flown her lips when Nin and Charlie simultaneously parroted "A bit of a wanker!" and fell about laughing. Through his tears, Nin explained to Gillespie, "That is Niall Campbell, from over Loch Awe way. He's a wanker as Brighid says but a dangerous and vicious one you would be well advised to give a wide berth. He has always had the hots for Brighid: don't we all? Ever since primary school, when she used to sell him kisses behind the bike shed."

Ducking from Brighid's well aimed blows that rained down on him from across the table, Nin and Charlie collapsed in a heap of helpless giggles.

"Bastards, the pair of you!" Brighid said exasperated. "The one piece of information where Nin is correct is that yon is a dangerous man. He may not look like much...."

"Streak of warm piss really…" said Charlie.

"But," she continued, silencing Charlie with an icy stare, "he's one of MacCailean Mòr's leading duine uasal and commands the Kilmartin Company. Their track record in Yemen and Libya probably doesn't need any introduction."

"Yeah, I saw him dual with Jamie yesterday. He was pretty handy, I must say. Jamie was outclassed."

"Aye, there are not many that could win out over Niall blade to blade." Ruminated Nin. "And Jamie was taking a big risk thinking that he was the one to wipe the smile from that bastard's face. But I comfort myself with the thought that he's still a wanker and nothing will change that."

19 - THE DEPARTURE

Aodhan held the cold hand in both of his, the feeble pulse was still fluttering, but its signal was fading. Duncan Tapaidh's race was almost run. Gently placing the hand back on the counterpane, Aodhan called to one of the clansmen that was stood by the door. "Fetch the Beaton, quick man."

Archie Beaton arrived moments later from the next room where he had been trying to catch up on some sleep after many disturbed nights. He took Duncan Tapaidh's left hand and gently clipped a peg on the index finger to measure the oxygenation of his blood, pulse and blood pressure. Aodhan did not need to look at the screen to know what was happening, it was unfolding before his eyes. Duncan's organs were shutting down, giving up the battle of many months, releasing him from his ordeal.

He looked at Duncan's face, remarking that at death's approach the cares of the world always seem to fall from his victim. Duncan's brow and cheeks were now smooth and unlined, as if the energy required to power their emotions had gone for good.

Looking across to Archie, who had done so much to care for Duncan in the past months, the tears were flowing down his cheeks, his eyes red and swollen. "I can do no more," said Archie. "He can do no more. It is time for him to go." Aodhan nodded, head bowed to the inevitable.

Archie pulled the medication trolley over to the bed and rummaged through the phials and bottles in the middle drawer. Finding what he was looking for, he held it to the light and gave it a shake to check that it still contained the medicine he required – Fentanyl.

Aodhan didn't imagine that it was going to take much – Duncan was like a man teetering on a ledge, all it was going to take was the slightest nudge for gravity and nature to take their course.

Spiking a syringe through the rubber cap, Archie drew off all the contents of the bottle. He then held the syringe to the light, out of habit flicking the needle and pushing the plunger a fraction to expel any air – as if that mattered now anyway. Without further ado, he found the vein in Duncan's elbow. After committing a prayer to his lips, he tenderly inserted the needle, pushing through the skin's layers of resistance and into the vein. His thumb slowly but steadily depressed the plunger, expelling the liquid into Duncan's vein and the life from his body. Within seconds the heart monitor alarm sounded the continuous beep that is the last thing so many hear.

It was done.

Aodhan stood up and thanked the doctor. Time was now of the essence; Duncan had been ill for so long their enemies had had plenty of warning to put their plans in place. Aodhan called for Kirstie, Alexander MacNachtan of Albany and Gillespie to be brought to the Red Banner Hall forthwith.

While he waited, he thought back on Duncan's life, it was indeed hard to imagine that the husk next door was the same man who duetted with Ziggy in his glam rock pomp. His charm, good looks and strong right arm had been the legendary combination that had helped the Clan survive and transform. But now he was gone.

20 - GIFTS

The news of Duncan's death had ruined what was promising to be a fine afternoon. Gillespie had been dragged back to the castle at high speed and whisked up to the Red Banner Hall without his feet barely touching the ground. When he entered the Hall, he saw Kirstie was already there, as well as a powerful looking black man in his mid-50s who introduced himself as Alexander MacNachtan of Albany.

Alexander still had an impressive physique which amplified his dignified bearing. His strong rounded shoulders pulled and puckered his shirt and many thick veins wrapped his forearms like cords. He wore his hair twisted and wound into thick, impenetrable dreadlocks that he had attempted to corral with a robust band. Streaks of grey could be seen climbing upwards from his beard; soon he would be as white as the snow on Beinn Bhuidhe. Nin and Charlie had told him a bit about Alexander already. He commanded the Clan's independent company which was currently on a tour of duty in the Caribbean. They had both spoken of him admiringly, and Gillespie could see why.

Aodhan gestured for the doors to be closed before he began, tented his fingers and peered at them in turn: "As Clan Seanchaidh and Duncan's executor, it falls to me to oversee his burial and the selection of the new Chief. I've called you here as the Clan's most senior representatives, personally selected by Duncan in accordance with Canun law, so that the Clan may choose a new leader."

"I am sure that whichever of you succeeds to the honour you have the potential to be a great success. But, before we can do that, we must first bury Duncan in the Dubh Loch cemetery. Most of the plans have already been made, but we'll need to be careful. At moments such as these we are weak and there are those who may wish to take advantage."

"Alexander, I want you to organise the security for the next few days until the new Chief is appointed. Call out all the duine uasal."

"Kirstie, I want you to review our cyber security, make sure that we have full continuity protection – you know what is needed."

"Lastly, Gillespie, in a few days there will be the choosing and one of the three of you will become the 36th Chief of the Clan. Kirstie and Alexander are well known to all of us here and therefore have a natural advantage, some might say. With respect, I don't think any of us expect you to be successful and you should soon be free to leave. Please use this time to meet with your fellow clansmen and women and enjoy the hospitality of Dunderave, as under Canun law after the choosing the two losers will be immediately banished for a year under pain of death. That may seem harsh, but it's intended to remove any competition to a new Chief and ensure a smooth transition. So, make the most of the next few days and soak up your heritage. We are delighted you are here and are only sorry it's in such sad circumstances."

Aodhan indicated that the meeting was at an end and they all stood to leave. As they approached the door, he pulled on Gillespie's sleeve, so that while he ushered Kirstie and Alexander from the room, Gillespie remained.

Gillespie wished he was leaving too. It was like having to stay behind with the headmaster; he was bound to be asked something he didn't know or be made to feel stupid. Although Aodhan had always tried to be friendly, he was an intimidating figure.

He was also angry at Duncan for his enigmatic comment at the close of their meeting. What had he meant when he told him not to believe everything his father had said? What kind of man says that without offering a scrap of explanation? And now he was dead he could never ask him.

Having closed the door, Aodhan crossed the room to a fine-looking box sat on the sideboard between the windows. Over it hung a painting of a long dead Chief, sword and targe in hand, posing for the artist with a fierce eye and fine moustache but now as entombed in yellow and crackled varnish as any fly in amber. Ignoring the painting, Aodhan ran his forefinger along the top of the box which was inlaid with fine bone arabesques and ornate foliage. Opening the top drawer, he peered into the back and rummaged for a few moments before pulling out two leather bundles and a metal badge.

Moving back to the table he carefully laid them down and motioned to Gillespie to sit across from him. Looking carefully at Gillespie, inspecting his face in detail from his pointed chin to his hair line, he said: "As you know, Duncan has no surviving children. Therefore, at his death all that he owns remains with the Clan; out of the Clan it came and back to the Clan it must return. However, he asked me to give you these in recognition of the unlooked-for journey you were forced to make and the dangers you have faced. He wanted you to have them so that in years to come, when you tell your children and grandchildren the story of your journey here, you might remember him kindly and forgive him the injustice he did you."

He first picked up the badge which Gillespie could now see was actually a kilt pin. It was fashioned in the shape of the MacNachtan crest: a tapered black tower, its jagged crenulations flaring out above a small window, with an enigmatic open doorway carved below, the whole surrounded by a buckled garter which had the legend I Hope In God engraved upon it. It looked like it had been cast in solid silver.

"That was a gift from King Charles Edward Stewart to your ancestor after he saved his life at the battle of Culloden, it was made by Paul de Lamerie. You doubtless know the story of how Charlie went to the stricken Cumberland and offered to help him. But Cumberland would have shot him between the eyes had your ancestor not cut off his treacherous hand before it could pull the trigger. And so, out of the jaws of defeat was victory snatched. As you might imagine, this is an important heirloom for the Clan and one of Duncan's most treasured possessions. It is a gift not lightly given."

The badge was silver but heavily tarnished: it had not been cleaned in years, the black oxidisation robbing it of all lustre. Nonetheless, the fine chasing and detailing of the tower were plain to see. Aodhan handed it to Gillespie, adding "I see that Ninian has kitted you out with some more fitting attire, and now you have a kilt pin to complete the look, and one that is a damn sight finer than that cheap one you are wearing. I hope it will remind you of us when you have to leave."

Next, he turned to the two leather bundles on the table. Picking one up, he drew a wicked looking blade from its leather sheath. The handle was deeply carved bog oak, as hard as iron, and was wreathed in a seething mass of intricate knotwork and decorated with small gold pins. The blade was clearly Japanese; its carbon steel had been laid and overlaid, pounded and smelted, until a wood-like grain had been folded along its length. Held to the light this looked like a mountain range, with trees, clouds, peaks and valleys, soaring and plunging along its length, as if the Arrochar Alps had been captured in steel.

Aodhan pushed over the other sheath, saying: "They are a pair. They were Duncan's own sgian dubh and sgian aslaich. A leading Yakuza commissioned them especially for him from a famous Japanese swordsmith. They were a token of thanks after Duncan had rescued his kidnapped daughter. I am told that the pattern on the blade is unique. They were very special to Duncan. They are wicked sharp too, so be careful."

Gillespie looked down in time to see a trickle of blood run down his thumb and drip on to the table.

"Aye, well, you'd best be a bit more careful with them in the future. As I said, they're wicked sharp." Aodhan then leant over and showed him how to strap the sgian aslaich inside his upper left arm so that the hilt nestled in his armpit and the blade ran down his side. The fineness of the blade and the shallow handle meant that it was almost imperceptible once in place but could be quickly and easily drawn. With that blade safely stowed, Aodhan stuck the sgian dubh into the top of the thick stocking on his right leg, flat to his shin and easy to draw.

The presentation over, Aodhan stood up and shook Gillespie warmly by the hand. "Whatever happens at the choosing, don't forget us when you leave. The Republic needs all the friends it can get in the modern world and the Clan likewise."

21 - FIONA

It was late afternoon when Gillespie left the castle, passing through the courtyard of the fountain and into the outer ward. He looked to see if there were any familiar faces among the groups that were huddled together whispering earnestly; it seemed that news of Duncan's death had already flown the confines of the tower. Seeing no one he knew, he went to look for Kirstie at the gaming complex, but there was no one there and the door was firmly shut.

Feeling a little lost, he wandered down to the loch shore and contemplated the horizon. With Duncan dead, surely he would soon be able to leave and get back to his real life? After the drama of his kidnap and journey he had to admit that he was almost beginning to enjoy himself. Nin and Charlie made him feel curiously alive. And Brighid: so beautiful. The Loch and the tower had been just like those tales of his father. What a place. But he felt ready to go: this was not his home.

At that moment he felt a small hand reach out to his and looking down he saw a young girl with tight dark ringlets in her hair and large slightly sad eyes looking up at him. She can't have been older than nine or ten.

"Hey sweetheart, what's your name?"

"My name is Mara," she said a little earnestly. "You are the Irish MacNachtan, yes? You are Gillespie?" A little frown furrowed her brow. "My Mama wants you to come to our house. Come, follow me." And without waiting for an answer she trotted off up the path to the track. Following her, Gillespie saw her turn right to follow the loch north. Intrigued, he picked up his pace stretching out his strides so he could catch up with her without having to break into a run.

After 30 minutes they came to the very head of the loch where the River Fyne flowed into its waters. There was a settlement of small white harled houses gathered together as if sheltering from the cold wind and rain that was funnelled by the surrounding hills. At the entrance to the village a small sign proudly announced that it was Clachan.

Mara wove through the houses until she came to a small low building with a tussocky garden overrun with rushes and populated with a few indistinguishable bits of rusting farm equipment. The harling would once have been white but was now cracked and chipped, stained with rust streaks from old iron nails and screws. The guttering was torn from one eave and waved back and forth in the wind, banging against the slates with every gust.

Mara knocked on the front door which had a window of frosted security glass set in it and through which he could see a dark shape approaching. The woman that opened the door was the definition of careworn. Her haggard face was drawn and blotchy as if she had recently been crying. Half of her long hair still carried the faded blond memory of her last visit to the hairdresser, the other half was grey: lifeless.

"Oh, it's you," she said. "I suppose you should come in." She stood back from the door to make space for him to pass into the house. Mara ran on and beckoned him to follow, leading him into a small dimly lit lounge. It was clean and neat but simple, just a sofa, the ubiquitous flat screen TV, and a small cupboard holding animal ornaments and a few treasured glasses. The walls were filled with photographs of a happy couple and their young daughter; here as a babe in arms; here on a bicycle; here in her school uniform; all of them together smiling and laughing by a big Christmas tree in front of Dunderave. As he peered at the photos his stomach fell away, dropping through his boots - it was Malcolm in these pictures. This must be Fiona his wife, no, his widow. Swallowing hard, he turned around to look at her. "Fiona? Am I right that you are Fiona, Malcom's wife?"

"Aye, well I was, until he was sent on some fool's errand to please a dying man. And now what am I, can you tell me that? Who is going to look after Mara and me, now that he has been taken away from us? Is Duncan Tapaidh," at which she spat on the carpet, "is he going to feed us, clothe us, keep us warm in the winter? Is he going to hold me in his arms and fuck me all through the night? Like my Malcolm? No! His kind only know how to order us poor Clan around, sending us hither and yon, doing their bidding. If we fight and die who cares, there are plenty more sheep on the hill to take our place."

"And you, I heard about you and your stupid antics. But I don't really blame you. If it hadn't been for Duncan, Malcolm wouldn't have even been there."

"I'm so, so sorry." He didn't know what else to say. His earlier good mood evaporated utterly to be replaced with the wasteland of her sorrow. How could he have been so callous, so thoughtless. And poor Mara, that sweet child. Now fatherless. This was the outcome of high-minded decisions taken by others: a widow and a fatherless child.

She turned her face away from Gillespie; he could see that she was crying, her sobs caught in a clenched fist. He put his arm around her and steered her to the sofa. She wept; he sat stony faced. He looked at Mara over her mother's head. After what felt like hours, but was probably only minutes, she pulled her face from his shoulder putting her hand to her mouth in embarrassment. "Och look. I've got you all wet. I am so sorry. How stupid of me."

"Don't worry, it's quite OK." Gillespie was relieved that the well of tears had at least run dry.

Having regained her composure, she asked: "Would you like a cup of tea?"

"Sure, that would be very nice." What else could he say?

Fiona went to the kitchen and when she returned she had a tray with three mugs; two of tea and one with hot chocolate for Mara, who still watched unblinking from the window. The tea was strong but sweet; Gillespie couldn't stop himself from gulping it down, even though it was too hot.

Fiona breathed out. "I am sorry to bring you here, but I had to see what my man died for with my own eyes. I had to know that he died for something worthwhile and not just to satisfy some whim."

Silence fell between them until she lifted her gaze to look him in the eyes.

"Are you married? Have you ever been in love? Have you ever felt your heart jump like it was going to burst through your chest when your lover looks at you across the room? Have you counted the hours, the minutes, the seconds waiting for his call, his text, his voice, his touch? Have you? Have you? Aye, well I have. And now what am I left with? Just my precious Mara." At which she held out her arms and enveloped Mara in a tight embrace.

Composed again, she released Mara and stood up, walking over to a cupboard in the corner and opening the door. Reaching in she pulled out a long, heavy bundle which she roughly dropped to the floor.

"Here, take it. I want you to have it. I want you to keep it and to remember that your actions will have consequences. I want you to feel its weight on your back every day and for that to remind you of the responsibility you carry. It is a heavy load, no doubt, and don't you forget it…. ever!" She flung the word at him with a shout, knuckling her eye sockets as if to stop the tears from flowing.

She kicked the bundle over to him and sat on a chair looking out at the loch. He unwrapped the package. A two-handed sword, a Claidheamh dà làimh, fell out of the blanket in which it had been wrapped. He recognised it immediately as Malcolm's. Scooping it up, he hefted the leather-bound hilt in both hands. It was beautiful: simple but deadly. The clean lines of the forward facing quillons terminated in heavy trefoils, designed to catch and turn an opponent's weapon. The blade was at least two inches wide at the hilt and a little under five feet long from point to pommel. It was surprisingly flat and thin, wobbling slightly as he stood it on its point, but sharp, so so sharp. The whole was lighter than he had imagined possible for such a large weapon and very well balanced. The pommel, a hammered doughnut of steel, secured the tang of the blade and was a perfect counterweight to its length. The leather of the hilt was well used but not worn, the bands rising in a carefully laid spiral along its length. He noted the running wolf carved into the blade. Even he could tell that this was a high-quality weapon.

"I can't possibly accept it. I don't even know how to fence, let alone with one of these. You should keep it for Mara or her children." He held it out to her, laying it flat on both of his hands.

Fixing him with a piercing stare Fiona said: "You can't not accept it, it's my gift to you. And by heaven it will be a curse that'll hound you to the grave if you leave it with me. And I want you to know that I will be voting for you at the choosing. What this Clan needs is change; we have had enough of all this blood and sorrow. I feel that you have been sent to bring us this change. I am torn that my Malcolm had to die, to be sacrificed, to make it possible. But so be it. We cannot change the past; we can only make the future – so make sure you do."

He wanted to explain that there was no chance he was going to win. That hers would be a wasted vote and that the faith she placed in him was utterly unfounded. He had no plan, no vision for the future of the Clan. He did not even want to be there. He had been kidnapped against his will and dragged over the sea to this lawless and strange place. He felt bereft, as if he was responsible not only for the death of Malcolm and the snuffing out of the love that had burned between them, but that he was now going to fail her all over again at the choosing. Her hopes and aspirations had been laid on the donkey in a thoroughbred race.

Even the gift of this sword was ludicrous, he did not know how to hold it, to swing it, to hack and batter, to bludgeon and dismember, and he had no intention of doing so. It was a wasted gesture – grand but pointless. But she had laid it upon him, and he could not throw her words and her gift back in her face. No, that would be truly heartless and shaming. Instead, he gathered the sword and its sheath and hugged Fiona in his arms, kissing her on both cheeks, his lips stinging from the salty tears that flowed down her face. Turning to leave, he walked purposefully down the corridor and out of the house concentrating hard on putting each foot in front of the other and resisting the urge to crumple and pound the ground in anger, fear and frustration.

22 - THE GRAVE

Gillespie walked slowly and thoughtfully back along the track, past the Castle, past Strone point, and turning right up Glen Shira, he passed the graveyard that was soon to be Duncan's final resting place. It was getting dark by the time that he found himself picking his way through the junk outside Elrig. He could see that there were lights on inside and he found himself unexpectedly pleased to be back. The intensity of his afternoon had left him feeling drained and now all he wanted to do was sit and process everything that had happened.

As he entered the hallway, he hung his coat on one of the pegs by the door. A radio played somewhere, its warm and friendly sound bringing the real world into this otherwise alien and strange place. He could hear Charlie singing along, rather flat he thought, and he found it comforting. Entering the kitchen, he saw Nin sat at the table on his laptop while Charlie was putting away the detritus left over from breakfast. Nin peered over the top of his screen; those soft blue eyes boring into him. "Ah Gillespie, ma' man. How you doin? Grab a seat and park yourself. I expect you've had quite the afternoon." Gillespie pulled out one of the green chairs and sat down, laying Fiona's bundle on the table in front of him.

"What's that?" Asked Charlie, turning around from the sink, a mug in each hand.

"I'm not sure. It is either a generous gift, a portentous omen, a death warrant, or a dumb lump of metal. I can't decide. You tell me."

Intrigued, Nin pushed away his computer and leant forward. Carefully unwrapping the bundle, he flicked the final corner of blanket off to reveal the muted, brushed steel that lay in its folds. Transferring his gaze from the sword to Gillespie, he asked: "Did she give it to you?"

"Aye, she did. Although why she did so and what she expects me to do with it, I do not know."

Charlie pulled up a chair and sat down across the table, carefully drying his fingers before running them over the wolf carved deep in the steel. Both he and Nin were clearly transfixed, exploring the various features of the weapon and swapping memories of Malcolm's exploits with it; the occasional notch on the blade's edge being hotly debated, with each recalling feats or foes that might have been responsible.

This was the last thing that Gillespie needed to hear, and holding up his hands for them to stop, he took a deep breath and said: "Look, she was very upset and emotional. She pressed this on me, why I don't know. She thinks I am somehow going to win the choosing and ride to the rescue swinging her dead husband's mighty sword. But that just isn't going to happen. I hate this pressure. All these expectations; of how I should feel and what I should do. I hate this place…. this situation. I never chose to be in this position, and I can't bear the thought that people like poor old bloody Fiona think that I am somehow going to be able to help them."

"Well, I think you should just pull yourself together and show a little gratitude," Nin said brusquely. "Yes, yes, we know all about you being dragged here against your will, and yes, it's true. But it's time to let go of that and focus on the here and now. This would be a generous gift to anyone, even the new Chief, whoever they will be. The fact that she, who has so little, should choose to give it to you, who she doesn't even know, shows how important it was to her to do it."

"Don't you worry about the choosing, that'll take care of itself. You'll soon be on your way back to Antrim with a fine dust catcher for your wall and a few tall stories to tell. As for Fiona, she will be OK. The Clan hardship fund will kick in and help her out. What do you think we do with all the money we make from the gaming?"

Putting out his arm and squeezing Gillespie's shoulder, Nin's voice softened back to his usual west coast burr: "So, don't worry, her and Mara will be fine. Honest."

Gillespie shrugged. "I guess. But it was still an emotional roller coaster of an afternoon."

"Yes, indeed," said Charlie. "Very sad but inevitable. It is really a relief after everything Duncan had been through. The burial is tomorrow; they are really keen to get a move on so that the new Chief can be chosen as soon as possible."

"And, just so you know," Nin interrupted. "You are obviously required at the ceremony. You will not only be attending as a potential successor, but also as Duncan's last surviving blood relative. Consequently, there are a few things you probably need to know."

They sat for the next few hours discussing what was going to happen and how Gillespie should conduct himself, only breaking to wolf down a meal of venison burgers, sloppy with homemade tomato and chilli relish.

The next morning Gillespie woke to the sound of his phone tweeting birdsong at 8am. He groaned and swiped it silent but did not dare to snooze. Instead, he showered and dressed, pinning the kilt with his new pin and wearing his new sgian aslaich and sgian dubh. Finally ready, Gillespie picked up his sword and went down the stairs. Nin was waiting in the hallway and chucked a banana at him for his breakfast before leading them out of the house.

There was already a stream of figures coming down the glen dressed in their finest: brilliant vermillion tartan kilts and crosscut doublets, plaids, bonnets and stockings, the jangle of swords and other gear marked the tempo of their pace as they headed down towards the Dubh Loch.

Gillespie, Nin and Charlie joined their growing ranks and as they neared their destination they could see that the gathering was already well advanced, despite the early hour. The shores of the loch were ringed by clansmen and their families who were all proudly showing their colours: the men wearing kilts in red MacNachtan tartan, the women with tartan shawls pinned around their shoulders. A smattering of other clans were there too, their tartans a clear indicator as to who they were: Campbells in their dark green and blue; MacFarlanes in red and blue; the dark green with yellow stipe of the MacArthurs, and those were just the ones that Gillespie could readily identify.

They had to push their way through the ever-growing ring of spectators to get to the causeway. Here some heavily armed men had cleared a walkway through the crowd. As a Farquharson, and clearly identified as such by the dark green tartan with red and yellow check that he was wearing, Charlie was not permitted to go further, and Nin and Gillespie left him chatting with some neighbours while they approached the graveside. Around the lip were some familiar faces; Brighid was there and Jamie, who was leaning on a stick and clearly in considerable pain; Iain skulked a few rows behind, but there was no sign of Kirstie or Alexander MacNachtan of Albany. It was fortunate that they arrived when they did, as the crowd was still growing and with all the jostling tempers were beginning to rise.

It then started to rain.

After they had been there for a few minutes, Gillespie heard the sound of bagpipes in the distance. Every few seconds the wind and rain snatched the sound away, but they were definitely getting closer. The crowd started to murmur, separating so that the funeral procession could pass down the causeway to the grave. At the head of the group was Aodhan dressed in a fine great kilt that was pinned at his left shoulder by a large silver brooch. He was flanked by Kirstie and Alexander.

The pall bearers brought the coffin to the edge of the grave. It was a simple affair of woven willow branches and the six burly clansmen were clearly untroubled by its weight. They all bowed their heads as a sole piper struck up Grey John MacNachtan of Dunderave's Lament, a well-known Clan tune. The notes came slow and sombre at first, the tune evolving and unfolding as the piper picked up momentum. The assembled crowd were hushed as the tumble of grace notes poured from his fluttering fingers, the music reaching a crescendo of intensity. It drew the crowd together, unifying their emotions and cementing their shared identity, Duncan's death the catalyst for this alchemy.

The music stopped.

All eyes now turned to Aodhan. Raising his head and scanning the crowd he said: "We are here today to bury Duncan MacNachtan, Duncan the quick witted, Duncan of the strong arm, Duncan of the computer chip, Duncan of the quaich, and Duncan of the open door. Our Chief, our leader and our friend. Duncan who led this great and ancient family for the past 50 years, through thick and thin."

"We are here to lay him to rest with his father and grandfather and great grandfather and so on back through the generations. Their bodies, bones and blood lie here, steeped in this soil; our soil; our land. They are intermingled with it and indivisible from it, as are we all. We now return him to this sweet soil that he may rest forever. Between the mountains that sheltered him and the water that swept him away to the far side of the world; to adventures we can only dream of. Farewell, my friend."

He nodded to the pall bearers who lowered the coffin while the piper played. The crowd listened to the notes as they rose up into the trees and were swept away by the rain and wind.

Two clansmen then brought up a large block of wood, like a chopping block, followed by a woman bearing a heavy looking sledgehammer, its pale ash handle contrasting with its dark forbidding head.

As the rain poured down, Alexander MacNachtan of Albany stepped forward. He took the sledgehammer in his right hand and held it high in the air. The crowd was silent: expectant. Aodhan drew a fine basket hilted sword, turning it slowly so that the crowd could see. He then placed it on the block. No sooner had he done so, then Alexander brought the hammer down with both hands and with a clanging ring mashed and mangled the sword. Alexander then raised it up above his head before dropping it into the grave, shouting: "Herewith your sword; to guard and protect you on your journey."

Kirstie now stepped forward with a thin, expensive looking laptop computer. She too placed it on the block before bringing down the hammer, splintering and smashing the machine into pieces. She picked up the tattered remains and cast them into the grave: "Herewith your window on the world and its wealth. The wealth that you funnelled back to us over so many years. May it serve you on your journey and bring you all you need."

It was Gillespie's turn. He tried to remember everything Nin and Charlie had told him as he stepped forward to the block. Aodhan reached into his robes and produced a silver quaich. Gillespie held it up to the crowd, the weight of their concentrated gaze fixed upon him and the silver cup. "May this quaich be ever brim-full. May it bring you as much joy in death as it did in life."

He put it down on the block and seized the haft of the hammer. It was slick with rain. As he raised it over his head, he prayed that his aim would not fail, or his hands slip. With a shout he brought it down; the soft silver crumpled under the crushing blow, releasing the spirit of the quaich to serve Duncan in the afterlife, or so the tradition went. He looked down at his cousin's modest coffin, scattered with computer keys and wiring like so much confetti; he tossed down the quaich.

At that moment, a murmur rippled through the crowd. A roar of engines could be heard approaching; a cacophony of grinding metal and tyres slip slapping over the muddy terrain. Gillespie could not see what was going on, but there was clearly great unease sweeping through the mourners. The engines stopped, and the crowd parted to allow a green and blue/black robed figure to stalk along the causeway and up to the grave side. The man wore the three eagle feathers of a Chief and was surrounded by a tail of thirty heavily armed duine uasal. Among them, Gillespie spotted the blond Campbell that they had met in Inveraray the day before.

Nin muttered under his breath: "MacCailean Mòr. What the hell is he doing here? It's outrageous!"

MacCailean Mòr nodded respectfully to Aodhan, who was staring back at him wide-eyed and slack jawed. This was clearly unexpected.

MacCailean Mòr turned to contemplate the crowd for a moment and then looked into the grave. Reaching down, he picked up a stone, a jagged lump of flint, which he held in the air between finger and thumb. Addressing the crowd, he said: "Duncan Tapaidh, some called you the stone in my shoe. A title you enjoyed; I believe. Well here I am to return the favour. May this rock be ever under your foot, causing you pain and discomfort at every step, until the end of time." And then he tossed it casually into the grave. He paused, as if to drink in the crowd's shock and anger. Then, very slowly and deliberately he walked back to the line of vehicles, surrounded by his tail of men who were jostled and pushed by the crowd; anger now ripping through them at the insult done to their dead Chief.

Whether it was the rain, the presence of so many heavily armed and dangerous Campbells, or the sheer effrontery of MacCailean Mòr, there was anger but no violence at the grave side. The rest of the ceremony was hurriedly completed, the grave filled in and the crowds dispersed back to their homes.

As they were leaving, Nin's phone bleeped with an urgent message. Fishing it out of his sporran he stared intently at the screen as his face was illuminated by its blue light. Charlie and Gillespie waited expectantly as he read the message on the screen: "It's a message from An Tùraidh Dubh, with details of tomorrow's vote. They have got a lovely picture of you too." He flashed the phone at Gillespie, who saw an old photo that looked like it had been lifted from a social media post. Charlie grabbed the phone and immediately started taking the piss out of his terrible clothes and hair.

"God just look at the spiel they have given you. Who writes this shite, I ask you…?!"

Nin grabbed the phone back and held it up to his face so that its camera could scan his retina to register him for the vote. He grunted with satisfaction as the screen chirruped that he had been successful.

"Do you get a vote?" Gillespie asked Charlie as they started up the hill.

"Unfortunately not, or else I would definitely add a notch to your tally. As a Farquharson I've no say, despite the fact that me and yon lump have been living together for five years and I pay all my Clan dues. It's just the way it is. Of course, I could change my tartan, change my name and take the black tower, but I don't think my own folk would be too pleased about that. Just one of the many drawbacks of living in a feudal anachronism really." He sighed, but with a twinkle in his eye.

They were soon back at Elrig and stayed up late into the night talking about the next day, when Gillespie would be able to leave, and when Nin and Charlie were going to visit him in Antrim.

23 - THE BEST LAID PLANS

John Lamont washed his hands meticulously, rubbing the soap to and fro, front and back over his long bony fingers, occasionally dropping the slippery bar into the white basin where it slithered and skated away from his pursuing grip. Having finally grasped it in one hand, he tried to slosh water around the basin's bowl with his other to try and dislodge some of the streaks of blood that marbled the sink's sides. Blood he could handle, but he always found that the stench of viscera was much harder to shift, especially from under one's nails. After a long session working on a prisoner it always took him hours before he felt comfortable that he had expunged their odour sufficiently.

Looking in the mirror, he wiped a suspicious looking clot from the side of his face while shaping his brows with a damp finger. Satisfied that he was at last respectable, he dropped the pink hued towel to the floor, kicking it into the corner for the staff to collect. He really wasn't paid enough to do this anymore, the thrill had gone out of it some years ago, now it was just routine. Still, it got results, and that was all that mattered.

He returned to his study and picked up the phone to summon Allan Stewart, who scurried into the room and stood across the large partner's desk waiting for his orders.

"So that MacNachtan bitch you picked up proved quite helpful," Lamont said. "Apparently the choosing is tomorrow at midday. The moment is finally upon us. I think I may even enjoy it. According to her, and I don't think she was capable of lying by the end, there will be three candidates. Alexander MacNachtan of Albany has seemingly come over from Jamaica and is representing the independent company, as well as their other overseas interests. He's a dangerous one – smart and dangerous, much too qualified to be their next Chief I fear. Next, there's that Kirstie MacNachtan who runs the gaming operation, she is clever and tough too, but more than that she is the key to their online empire. You must be careful with her; we'll need her alive if we're to take control of the business. Finally, there is some ingenue who has apparently been brought over from Ireland. His only qualification is that he is seemingly Duncan's last blood relative. I thought we had sorted that problem when you squeezed the last gasp of life out of young Oisean. But no matter, what is one more greenhorn? This one does not sound like he will be too challenging. Besides no one knows who he is, and I don't expect he will be much missed."

"So, am I to bring her back here unharmed?" Allan's dark eyes were like pools of oil, expressionless and consuming of all light.

"Yes, either that or make sure you get the administrator access codes from her so that we can take over their servers. Their security is tough, but once we have the codes we will be able to take it over in minutes and cut them off at the knees."

"Now we need to give MacCailean Mòr a call to make sure he's up to speed on the plan, well the bits he needs to know anyway. I gather that he caused a bit of a stir at the funeral, a perfect scene setter really. I can't wait to see the look on that pompous prick's face when he finally realises what is going on."

Lamont allowed a prim little smile to flash across his lips as he picked up the phone.

24 - THE CHOOSING

Gillespie woke with a sorer head than he had intended; Nin's heavy hand on the whisky bottle had seen to that. He staggered downstairs to try and balance his system with coffee and breakfast. After munching his way through two bowls of cereal and most of a pot of coffee he felt somewhat better as long as he didn't turn his head too quickly. Nin was down next, looking paler than normal and he sipped his coffee avoiding all conversation.

With no sign of Charlie by 10.00 o'clock, Gillespie went back upstairs to have a shower and get dressed, slipping back into the clothes he had worn the previous day. His shirt was not the freshest, but he didn't imagine anyone was going to mind.

Even though he had been dragged here against his will, now that the moment had arrived he felt the need to front up and do his best. As he had seen from Fiona, and from his many conversations with Nin and Charlie, this was a moment of critical importance to the Clan. While he was going to disappear back to his life in Ireland in approximately 24 hours, they'd be stuck with the consequences of their choice for years.

He tried to decide who he would've voted for out of Kirstie and Alexander, if he had been allowed a vote. Alexander seemed like a fine fellow, the very image of a highlander, smart, strong, somewhat reserved but confident. He had clearly seen a lot and there was nothing that was going to faze him. He was somewhat aloof and unapproachable, but that could just be because Gillespie was a stranger and he was a little shy.

Kirstie on the other hand he liked a lot; she was plenty tough enough and commanded respect whenever she opened her mouth. She had also done a fantastic job on the gaming business and this was now the financial foundation of the Clan, far surpassing the security business that had been the Clan's mainstay for several centuries. She was also very local and known by all. A hard choice.

He picked up his sword and closed the door to his room behind him. Nin and Charlie were both outside dressed in their finery. They climbed aboard the Kat and were soon bumping round the corner at the bottom of Glen Shira and tearing towards Dunderave. The track was thick with people and vehicles streaming in the same destination.

Having spent ten minutes trying to find a parking space by the tower, Nin gave up and returned to the track, where he stuck the Kat on a steep verge. Wandering back down with the crowds, they entered the outer ward and bumped right into Brighid. She was sat at one of the tables having a coffee and enjoying the feeble sunlight that was trying to break through the clouds. She gave Gillespie a big hug, squeezing him slightly harder and for longer than was strictly necessary; not that Gillespie minded. They chatted about the previous day and the rudeness of MacCailean Mòr. All agreed that it had been beneath his dignity to act so pettily.

As midday approached, the ward filled up with people until there was hardly room to breathe and latecomers had to jostle outside its walls. A large screen had been erected at one end and a number of video cameras had been mounted on the parapet of the wall.

As the appointed hour arrived, a thunderflash was thrown from a window high up in the castle to hush the crowd and attract their attention. Aodhan appeared at one of the large windows and spread his arms in welcome, raising his voice so that it could be heard: "Welcome to an important day for all of us. A critical day for us and our children; our hopes and dreams; our future together; our Clan and its place in this ever-changing world."

"As you know, our beloved Chief, Duncan, has passed. Now we must choose a worthy successor to help lead us and defend our birth right from any that would take it from us. For the first time, this vote is being webcast to Clan members all around the world, so that they can participate in the choosing." He nodded in the direction of the cameras. "And so, I would like to start today by welcoming them and you to Dunderave, our ancient home. The Black Tower from which comes hospitality, hope, and opportunity for our friends; and wrath, vengeance and destruction for our enemies."

"Before you stands a choice, and for once I can say that it is a real choice. A choice of different paths. Each of the candidates brings special skills and strengths and the future course that they will set will be very different. Only you can decide which path the Clan should tread."

"As is tradition, I will read out the attributes of each candidate in turn. Once all have been announced those who are registered to vote must make their choice. You can do this through the app on the Clan intranet. I will now give those that have not registered a few minutes to do so before I move to announcing the candidates."

While they were waiting, the Clan pipe band played a medley of stirring tunes. Gillespie recognised Clan favourites like Strong Stands The Black Tower, The Hall of the Red Banner, and Gilchrist MacNachtan's Salute. All guaranteed to fire up the most patriotic feelings within any self-respecting clansmen.

As the last drone fell silent, Aodhan again raised his hands to quiet the crowd. Many of the assembled throng had been frantically logging in to the Clan intranet to register; holding up their phones and peering fixedly at them to match their retina print with that on the security system. Finally, all the phones disappeared, and everyone's attention was refocused on Aodhan at the window.

"I will now introduce each of our candidates to you in turn. The first is Alexander of Albany, who has travelled all the way from Jamaica where he commands our wonderful Independent Company. As many of you know, the Independent Company has had a tremendous period of success under his leadership. They have won security mandates with many respected and high-profile organisations and they recently won a ten-year contract to provide security on all Sunlover Cruise ships, protecting holiday makers from pirates and terrorism. Those of you who know Alexander know that he's hardworking, fair but resolute. He has a strong right arm and his prowess with a blade is well known and respected."

During this speech, the large screen showed a loop of Alexander looking stern but approachable before cracking into a warm smile. A hearty round of applause went up from the crowd with a few whoops and shouts. Alexander's picture then disappeared to be replaced by Gillespie's mugshot. He shuddered. Charlie nudged him with a smile, while Brighid blew a kiss in his direction and gave a little fist pump.

"Our next candidate will not be known to many of you unless you have had the pleasure of meeting him during his stay at Dunderave in recent days. Gillespie hails from our cousins across the water in Antrim. He is Duncan's last blood relative and it was for this reason that Duncan brought him back to us. He felt it was important to offer the Clan an outsider's perspective; someone who knows about the world beyond the Republic and our parochial ways; someone that can bring a new vision to the Clan, to preserve and promote us in the 21st Century. Obviously, Gillespie has not grown up in the Republic, so its ways - our ways - are new and strange to him. But if he was thought capable by Duncan then that should be all the endorsement you need."

A polite smattering of applause went around the crowd led enthusiastically by Nin, Charlie and Brighid, who also planted a kiss on Gillespie's cheek. Blushing, he stood and held up his hands in acknowledgement.

"Last, but by no means least, we have Kirstie MacNachtan, our local girl who I cannot believe needs much introduction. As the Clan's Eòlaiche Didseatach, she is one of our most important Duine Uasal. And it's in her leadership of our digital gaming business where Kirstie has excelled. Since being appointed, she has rolled out more new gaming variants more quickly than ever before. She has doubled revenue and quadrupled profits. A skilled programmer, she has masterminded our position on the dark web and has contributed more to Clan funds than anyone else in our history. But she doesn't just live by the pixel, she is a firm friend and commanding leader in the real world too."

He paused, letting his words sink in. The crowd cheered and shouted their support and approval. Gillespie could just see Kirstie through the crowd standing by the door to the inner courtyard. She was looking uncharacteristically bashful; her face a bright crimson with embarrassment at all the vocal support.

Having allowed the crowd to express its views in cheers and shouts, Aodhan again raised his hands for quiet.

"Before the vote, in my role as Seanchaidh, I am going to play a pìobaireachd in memory of Duncan, who led us for so many years. When the last notes die away, you must make your choice within 30 seconds. The result will then be immediately displayed on the screen and through the intranet."

Arranging the drones over his shoulder and filling the bag with breath, Aodhan started to play. The notes came slowly and long, held with power and ornamented with a filigree of grace notes. Brighid whispered in Gillespie's ear: "It's the Piper's Lament for his Master - very appropriate, but very long."

The austere and challenging music held the crowd in silence, its power washing over them, the notes reverberating around the stone walls. Gillespie had never really listened to pìobaireachd, the classical music of the bagpipe. It was not easy listening, invariably long and requiring a focus that he struggled to find in an ordinary day. But today it transfixed him; the notes passing over and through him and the crowd, the tempo and complexity building and deepening: spinning, tumbling, gusting, flighting, skewering, pinning, cutting and biting. Time stopped, and the world melted away. There was nothing left but the hypnotic progression of the music, its variations inexorably gaining complexity and momentum. It reached a crescendo of intensity that gripped his heart so tightly, but just as he thought he could bear no more, the music stopped. The crowd slowly awoke from the collective trance and glassy eyed they fished out their phones to vote.

All eyes turned to the big screen. After a brief pause, during which an animation of the black tower fluttered and rippled on the screen like a flag in the wind, the result was announced:

Alexander of Albany first with 42% of votes cast, Kirstie second with 36%, and Gillespie last with 16%. The remaining 6% were undecided.

The crowd burst into shouts, cheers and ululations at the result. Gillespie let out a sigh of relief; never had he felt so happy to have failed so badly. Nin, Charlie and Brighid all grabbed him in a group hug, laughing and congratulating him for getting 16% of the vote, far more than they had expected. He just felt relieved that it was now over, duty had been done and honour more or less preserved. He could return to the crumbling eaves of his home and put some of the cash that Duncan had promised him to work.

He looked across to where Kirstie had been standing. She was no longer there. He assumed she must have retreated to spare herself the embarrassment of being endlessly commiserated over. Alexander on the other hand, was pushing through the crowd arms raised above his head punching the air with joy. He had lost his bonnet and his wild deadlocks bounced and swayed with his exuberant celebrations and that of the Clan around him. He finally made it to the passageway and disappeared from view into the court of the fountain. A few minutes later he materialised at Aodhan's side at the window. Aodhan greeted him warmly with much back clapping and laughing. He must have been Aodhan's choice too.

The crowd spontaneously burst into a football style chant of "Al-ba-nay we love you, Al-ba-ny we do!" that echoed and reverberated off the stonework. Gillespie smiled, everybody seemed happy enough. He imagined some were sorry not to have Kirstie as their leader but after the events of the previous day and the ominous threat that seemed to be moving towards them up the loch from Inveraray, the Clan had decided that a strong military leader was what they needed. And they were probably right, much though he liked Kirstie.

Alexander finally split from Aodhan's embrace and turning to the crowd raised a hand for quiet.

"My dear Clan, what an honour you have done me. An honour which I will hold in my heart and for which I will be ever grateful. We all know that leadership comes with responsibility and that can be a heavy burden. But as I put my shoulder to this wheel, I promise you…." and at that moment he reached into his shirt and pulled a short but wicked looking knife from his oxter, the blade flashing in the weak sunlight, "with every drop of my blood," at which he drew the blade across his palm, a thick red line immediately welling in its wake. "That I will serve and protect this great family, our Clan, our lands, our ideas and our ideals. That I will help us forge a great future together, for our children and our children's children – the children of Nechtan, the children of the Black Tower – I hope in God!" he shouted exultantly and the crowd below erupted, shouting "I hope in God" at the top of their voices; they cheered him to the echo.

25 - THE EAGLE'S FEATHERS

Once the crowd had calmed, Aodhan again raised his hand for quiet.

"Alexander MacNachtan, formerly of Albany, Jamaica, do you now accept the burden and responsibility of leading this Clan, the children of Nechtan the Great. Will you lead us from this day forward, stinting nothing and giving your life's blood to nurture and protect us, defending us, our land and homes from our enemies whosoever they may be?

"I hope in God" said Alexander.

"So be it, you have been chosen by us, to fight for us, to die for us if necessary. I hereby declare under the ancient and honourable law of tanistry that you Alexander MacNachtan formerly of Albany, has been chosen by the Clan and henceforth will be known as Alexander MacNachtan of Dunderave, 36th Chief and Keeper of the Black Tower."

He handed Alexander a large bunch of keys on a steel hoop and two eagle feathers, which Alexander added to the one he already carried in his bonnet. The ceremony over, Aodhan closed the window cutting him and Alexander off from view.

Down in the courtyard, the Clan pipe band started up a set of joyful jigs to get the party started. Gillespie wondered what was going to happen next when he saw Archie Beaton pushing his way towards him through the throng. After exchanging pleasantries, including being congratulated for a fine showing in the vote, Archie told him that he was required inside and that he should make his way to the Red Banner Hall. Nin volunteered to accompany him, and they wended their way through the boisterous crowd that was already starting to make inroads into the hospitality on offer.

Having climbed the steep stairs and arrived at the double doors to the Hall, Gillespie and Nin waited until their knock was answered and they were permitted to enter. As the doors swung open, Alexander strode towards them and embraced Gillespie warmly. His engaging smile and friendly manner quite at odds with his previously rather dour and stern demeanour. Ushering them towards a pair of chairs near the fire, he motioned them to sit. Gillespie noticed that Kirstie was there too, her face red and blotchy, particularly around her eyes. She composed herself and smiled at him in slightly half-hearted manner.

Gillespie immediately started congratulating Alexander on his victory, his enthusiasm was such that Alexander was quite taken aback but gratefully acknowledged his thanks.

"Gillespie, I've brought you here to apologise for the distress and trouble that you have been put to. Aodhan has told me the whole story. But so be it, that is in the past now. I wanted to take this opportunity to speak with you as we do not have much time. I think Aodhan has already told you that as a loser under Clan law you are banished from Clan territory for a year on pain of death. In your case this seems excessive. However, rules are rules, and Kirstie is a different matter. We need to be fair, so both of you will have to leave."

"Kirstie, you know how much I regret doing this. But you also know that I did not make and cannot change the rules. I am truly sorry that you have to leave."

Kirstie nodded dumbly.

Nin asked "So, what is the deadline for them to be across the Clan line?"

"Midnight. After that, there will be a bounty on both your heads for 365 days, inclusive. But once that day has passed, I will welcome you both back here with open arms." Alexander winked. He looked down at the unexpectedly refined gold watch on his wrist: "By my reckoning you have about nine hours to get out of Dodge, so I wouldn't hang around. Oh, and

Kirstie, make sure you share the administrator passwords to the gaming sites before you leave. Can you give them to Aodhan? I'm sure you understand."

Kirstie nodded, and they turned to go, descending the steep stairs and out of the dark doorway into the courtyard of the fountain. Nin left to find Charlie, and Gillespie walked with Kirstie. They had to squeeze their way through the roiling crowd that was getting louder and more boisterous with every pint that was poured. The Clan pipe band had now been replaced by a barrage of fiddlers who were showering the crowd with clouds of rosin as they ripped through reel after reel, propelled by thundering dance beats and a bass heavy backing track. Finally, they escaped onto the strand and Kirstie wandered over to the gaming facility and punched in the entry code.

"Come on in. Take a look at my little empire before I have to leave it all behind." Gillespie followed her inside, marvelling at the high-tech suite. The walls were covered in white boards with algorithms and complicated looking fractions scrawled on them in different coloured pens. The ranks of computers whirred away to themselves processing who knew what. "The server rooms are downstairs. We use heat exchangers out in the loch to keep it all cool. It not only cuts our fuel bill but improves performance. Another one of my ideas, I might add."

A sudden banging on the door interrupted her. Charlie and Nin were both standing on the step, "C'mon let's get a move on," said Nin impatiently "we need to get you out of here". Allowing the others to walk on, Kirstie paused for a moment; her hand pressed to the door, as if the strain of saying goodbye was too much. Finally, reluctantly, she drew her hand away and left to walk up the path to the track.

26 - FIRE AND SWORD

After all the commotion of the celebrations it was surprisingly quiet as they started up the path towards the Kat. Out here the silence hung like a dampening cloud, muting man and nature alike, and while they could still hear the fiddlers, they seemed like a world away.

They had just climbed into the Kat when Gillespie saw the first black clad figure; a masked head that quickly emerged and then retreated behind a tree. In the split second between his eye seeing it and his brain processing it, he felt a hard shove in his back. Something flew past his ear. Then all hell broke loose. The one black head became fifteen, as figures poured out of the undergrowth. Several of them had crossbows, quarrels thudding menacingly into the Kat's bodywork. Charlie threw him onto the floor of the Kat and pinned him there, while Kirstie grabbed the roll cage for dear life as Nin roared straight up the slope ahead of them.

Nin did not slow or turn, except to avoid the occasional tree, as he climbed the steep slope; the wheels of the Kat churning a path through the undergrowth and the suspension delivering a hefty whack to Gillespie's head with every bump of the rough terrain. On and on they went, climbing the hill behind Dunderave for what felt like hours. Gillespie struggled to make out what was going on: was that a vehicle in pursuit? If only he could lift his head from the floor to see. Bloody Charlie!

The vehicle suddenly lurched to a halt and Nin yelled at them to get out. Charlie rolled off, freeing Gillespie who fell out of the back in time to see a Kat crash through the undergrowth below. It was manned by four black dressed figures bristling with weapons: it tore up the slope towards them.

Nin dived across the cab, yanking open a compartment on the passenger side. He pulled out a wicked red oblong disc and without pausing threw it down the slope just ahead of their pursuer. The dull crump of the explosion did not do justice to the impact on the vehicle, which was lifted bodily into the air and swatted to the side, scattering the occupants across the hillside.

While Gillespie stood gawping, wondering whether to run, hide or just piss himself, Nin, Charlie and Kirstie leapt on their assailants. The explosion had put two of them out of action already, lying still and spread-eagled on the slope. One of the others was struggling to get up with what looked like a badly broken leg which Charlie scissor kicked from under him for good measure, before sitting on his chest, dagger drawn. The final protagonist was flattened by Kirstie and Nin, both of whom had blades at his throat. Ripping off his hood, Kirstie hissed with surprise: "Graham Campbell! What the fuck are you doing! You motherfucker! I should cut your throat right now, you piece of shit." Her voice quivering with anger, fear and adrenalin.

Nin smashed his fist into the man's face, splashing blood across his cheek. He gripped him by the throat: "Tell us what the fuck is going on or am I really going to lose my temper." He pressed the tip of his knife into the flesh of Graham's cheek just below his right eye.

Graham pleaded through his bleeding lips, eyes questing from Nin to Kirstie. "Please stop, I didn't know it was you. I was just following orders. We saw you take off; how could I know it was you?"

"What were you doing by the castle? Why did you attack us? And be quick about it." Nin lifted his head to listen for other pursuit.

"We were ordered to surround the Castle; to stop anyone from leaving and await further orders. Something big is going on. I don't know the details. But MacCailean Mòr is moving on the Black Tower and he means to take you down."

"Shit! Look…" Kirstie pointed down the hill towards the castle far below them. It was swarming with heavily armed black-clad men. More vehicles were arriving every moment. She then pointed at the loch; there were three boats heading towards the Castle at full speed, each contained at least 10 men.

"Fuuuuuuck!" Nin was transfixed.

It was then that they heard the first gunshots; short bursts of automatic fire that echoed across the hill.

"What! Why are they shooting?" Gillespie shouted. "I thought you said Canun was sacrosanct!"

Dropping Graham's head, Nin ran to the Kat. He rummaged in the dashboard compartment and fished out a small pair of binoculars.

Gillespie didn't need binoculars to see what had happened; the MacNachtans had been caught totally by surprise. With so many people focused on celebrating, the entrance had not been properly guarded. The attackers had got in easily and had penned the MacNachtans into the far corner of the outer ward under the screen.

The crack of gunfire subsided; some kind of standoff seemed to have been reached. With all the black clad figures milling around the Outer Ward and the Courtyard of the Fountain it was clear that they had control of these, if not the tower itself.

Nin rubbed his eyes. "This has to be an official operation. No other possibility makes any sense. MacCailean Mòr would never dare to move against us like this. Fuck, fuck, fuck!"

Kirstie grabbed the binoculars. The three boats had now beached, disgorging black clad figures onto the shore. She tracked them towards the outer ward, but half suddenly peeled away to the outbuildings: to her office, to the gaming operation!

"What are they doing? Why are they are trying to get in there?"

The figures were huddled around the door, they suddenly they all stood back and there was a puff of smoke: they had blown the door open. The figures disappeared.

"Oh, my fucking God, they've got inside!" Throwing the binoculars at Nin, she pulled out her phone and started to rapidly type, her eyes burning into the screen. "Just a few more moments, just a few more mome…. oh no.."

"What!" shouted Charlie.

She showed them her phone: a blank screen. "They've killed the phone network. We've no service. Which means I can't change the administrator codes to stop those bastards getting their hands on everything."

They froze: faces white, mouths agape.

"Wait a moment." Gillespie fished his phone from a pocket. "They've shut down your service, but what if I still have access. I am roaming after all. Look, I still have signal on Cruachan.net."

"You do?" Kirstie said, disbelievingly. "Give it to me, now!" Grabbing his phone, she bent over the screen tapping furiously. Each second felt like an hour as they stared at her fingers flying over the screen.

"Come on, you bastard, come on…" Kirstie was pale, pouring with sweat from the stress. She held the phone close to her, breathing deeply. "Yes! Done it!" She checked the screen one more time before chucking it back at him. "Thank God for that. Listen, I've managed to change the codes so that even if they get access to the servers they won't be able to do anything. I've also saved the administrator codes and some instructions in your notes pages; if we ever get separated they'll tell you everything you need to know. Don't fucking lose it - OK!"

Gillespie nodded, slipping the phone into his pocket and buttoning it carefully.

In the meantime, Charlie scooped up the weapons and threw them into the back of Nin's Kat. He then stood over the unconscious and injured Campbells to make sure they didn't radio for help and as he did so, something caught his eye. He pointed at a small drone the size of a flying tea tray with rotors at each corner that was slowly working its way up the hillside. "Uh oh, I think we have company."

27 - THE BLACK TOWER BURNS

Allan Stewart held on to the grab rope with one hand while shielding his eyes from the glare off the surface of the loch. The boat was moving fast now, cutting through the water at maximum speed, shadowed on either side by the two other boats. The harbour of Inveraray flashed past on the left, a blur of white. Ahead he could see their destination nestled under the lee of Beinn Bhuidhe. His face was set in a grim half smile, as if he was only half-looking forward to the blood and chaos that he knew was being unleashed ahead. He loved these moments, the thrill of not knowing how those carefully laid plans were going to unfold: this is what it is to be truly alive. Nothing existed but this moment. He exulted in that feeling. He had sucked on the teat of John Lamont long enough to know to enjoy these moments, when the leash was slipped.

The shingle crunched under their bow, and the company spilled onto the beach. Running up the shore, they pulled down their masks and moved towards their preassigned targets. He took fifteen handpicked members to the gate into the castle's outer ward, pushing past some of the Campbell force that were milling around the doorway. They glanced at him and his team, all dressed identically in black with a dark green and blue panel of Campbell tartan on the inside of their forearms: they waved them through. Inside the outer ward, the Campbell force stood with guns drawn keeping the crowd of MacNachtans pressed against the far wall where they skulked in a sullen and dishevelled state. He noted with satisfaction that most of them didn't even have their traditional weapons with them. After all, they had been coming to a celebration. A few bodies lay on the open ground, some of which were still groaning. Ignoring them, Allan led his team down the corridor into the Courtyard of the Fountain. There he found Niall and Archie Campbell, the leaders of the Inveraray force, standing outside the door into the tower. Allan eyed Archie Campbell warily, he was one of MacCailean Mòr's most trusted men, his Curaidh Mòr, a legendary fighter: he had to watch him closely.

Niall was fingering his long blond hair unfazed as Allan approached, pistol in one hand and sword in the other, the Campbell panel continuing to work its magic. Allan then took off his mask: that did take Niall aback, stupid twat.

"What the fuck are you doing here?" He asked, staring wide eyed at Allan and his men.

"Special orders from John Lamont," Allan said, "He and MacCailean Mòr have cooked this up, so we are here to see it goes according to plan. Anyway, isn't it wonderful to see the Wardens working so closely together." Allan smiled his impenetrable smile, his black eyes, hard and unyielding.

"Hhmm, OK. Well MacCailean Mòr didn't mention anything to me, but so be it. Anyway, the bastards got in there before we could seize the door. Can't be many of them inside though. Shall we blow it down?"

Allan pushed him to one side and pulled out a sidearm. He shot out one of the first-floor windows and shouting up to it said "Alexander MacNachtan. I've been sent by order of the Comhairle of Chiefs of the Riaghaltas of the Gaelic Republic to bring to justice you and such of your clansmen that were responsible for an act of piracy and terrorism against our neighbour the Kingdom of Great Britain and Northern Ireland. I demand that you give us entry and that you submit, otherwise we will start killing your dearly beloved clansmen out here until you change your mind."

A figure appeared at the window above. It was Aodhan. Holding his arms above his head in plain view of those below, he said: "We know nothing of your charge. As you can see, we have been celebrating the appointment of our new Chief. I am shocked that you could denigrate such a moment with this violence."

"Never mind about that," said Allan. "You have a choice; either open this door under the Bratach Gheal - the white flag - so that Archie, Niall and I can enter and speak with you face to face like civilised human beings. Or I won't be held responsible for my actions. I will give you the count of ten to decide which it will be: 10, 9, 8, 7, 6, 5, 4, 3…"

At that moment, a key could be heard turning and seconds later the door swung open. Leaving the other clansmen outside, Allan, Niall and Archie went inside, pushing roughly past the woman that had opened the door. They ascended the steep stairs and found themselves opposite the double doors to the Red Banner Hall. The two clansmen standing there were shouldered aside by Niall and Archie, who opened the doors and entered the room beyond.

Alexander MacNachtan of Dunderave sat impassively in the high-backed chair accorded to the Chief of the Clan, his bearing calm and authoritative. It was as if the chaos of the outer ward, the shouts and screams and shots that could still be heard were happening somewhere else. Allan admired his sangfroid.

"How can I help you gentlemen?" Alexander asked, turning his gaze from one to the next, his eyes betraying no fear, his voice steady.

"We have been sent by command of the Council of Chiefs to arrest the MacNachtan clansmen responsible for destroying a Kingdom patrol vessel in the Irish Sea earlier this week. We know they came from here and the Council is determined to make an example of your poxy little Clan, to send a message that such banditry will not be tolerated. I must ask you to surrender those responsible immediately or face the consequences."

Alexander listened carefully and rubbed his white beard while he thought. After a few moments he answered in a considered tone: "Sirs, as you know, I've only just been elected Chief. I do not know what, if anything, my predecessor may have ordered or done. Under Canun law I reserve the right to address my peers in the Comhairle, rather than have to explain the actions of this Clan to you here. I am willing to come freely with you now to Oban to address the Chamber. However, I must ask that you stop harassing and attacking my clansmen, who have done nothing more than be present at my investiture. I demand that you release them to go home immediately."

Niall Campbell then lent forward pointing at Aodhan; "This old goat will know what's been going on. Duncan didn't do anything without his knowledge. I say we take him outside and ask him a few questions."

Allan nodded. "Good idea. But no need to go outside, let's just stay here where it's nice and private."

Alexander did not seem too concerned; he clearly had nerves of steel. Aodhan on the other hand was beginning to sweat, his eyes turning from one to the other, looking for where the threat was going to come from first. Allan was busy making calculations, thinking about his next move.

Niall leant across the table, palms flat, fingers spread, leaning into Aodhan's face. "So Seanchaidh are you going to tell us a little story? Why don't you sing us a song?" Niall's irritating, arrogant whine cut the air.

Allan saw his chance. As all eyes were distracted by Niall's aggressive posture, Allan reached down, and in one smooth movement drew the sgian dubh from his stocking and slashed at Archie's neck. He caught him just below his Adam's apple, the blade biting deep and leaving a thick red streak in its wake. As Archie collapsed, jetting a gout of blood across the table, Allan brought the blade down through Niall's hand, pinning it to the table. Niall screamed.

Without pausing, Allan pulled out his pistol and shot Aodhan between the eyes, blowing the brains out of the back of his head. Alexander erupted, throwing the table into the air and trying to escape. He didn't get far; Allan's first shot winged his shoulder, knocking him to the ground. Alexander groped for something to defend himself, but just as his hand found the handle of his dirk, Allan put a double tap of rounds into his chest.

"That should take the wind out of your sails." Allan said, laughing, as Alexander writhed on the floor drowning in his own blood. "Jesus, what a mess you are all making."

Niall had now regained his senses and was tugging at the handle of the knife, trying to release his hand from the table.

"Not so fast you Campbell cunt." Allan picked up Alexander's dirk and plunged it deep in Niall's chest. Niall's eyes widened in horror at the hilt left sticking from his sternum by Allan's swift hand, before he collapsed forward onto the table and lay still.

Allan stood back to survey his handiwork. While it was true that only one was actually dead so far, the others were all well on the way. Alexander's breathing was already getting shallower and he seemed to have lost consciousness. Archie, that legendary swordsman, was trying to hold the remains of his windpipe in, his movements more like a dying fish flapping on the slab at every passing moment. Niall was silent and still, his hand still stapled to the oak by Allan's knife.

"So, let's see now. What do we need to do next?" Allan mused out loud. Taking his pistol, he grabbed one of Archie's still flailing hands and thrusting the index finger through the trigger guard he shot Alexander again for good measure. Making sure Archie's prints and blood were comprehensively registered on the handle he dropped it to the floor and kicked it away from the twitching figure.

"Can't be too careful now can we," he whispered in the dying man's ear.

Next, he pulled hard on his sgian dubh to release it from the back of Niall's hand and the table. Niall's body, no longer pinned in place, slipped to the floor. Allan wiped the blade casually on Niall's shirt sleeve before sheathing it. Surveying the room, and satisfied with his handiwork, he tore one of the tapestries off the wall. The ancient threads were rotten and weak: so much the better. Tossing one end into the huge fireplace, he trailed the rest across the room, making sure it lay over the table and anything that looked flammable.

The fire roared and crackled, tearing into the tapestry and burning with bright blue and green flames as it consumed it. Soon the room was well alight, and Allan had to beat his retreat. Closing the double doors behind him, he swept down the stairs and out of the castle.

28 - THE PURSUIT

While conscious that they had to get moving if they were not to be spotted by the approaching drone they were all suddenly transfixed by the sign of smoke coming from Dunderave. As the first black tendrils rose upwards, untroubled by the slightest breeze, they split and wove the air above the castle, before gradually diffusing into the pale sky. These first wisps were soon followed by billowing black veils of smoke and tongues of flame as the fire advanced into the roof of the building.

Gillespie watched, struggling to imagine how Nin and Kirstie must have felt, to watch 500 years of history literally going up in smoke. Numb, Nin shook his head, for once speechless. Gillespie could see that there were tears running freely down his cheeks, cleaning a pink path through the mud and grime. Kirstie had the palm of her hand clamped to her forehead, her mouth agape, frozen by the horror of the moment.

It was Charlie that reacted first: "C'mon. We need to shift if we are not to end up like that lot down there. Look at that fucking drone, it'll be here any second."

Snapping out of the spell that the smoke had woven over them, they sprinted to the Kat. Kirstie climbed in next to Nin, while Charlie and Gillespie jumped into the back, holding onto the roll cage as Nin raced off up the hill. They crashed through bushes and round trees, thumping into holes and splashing across bogs. The tree cover was beginning to thin and soon they would be clearly visible to anyone looking from the loch-side below. Nin was making for the ridge line, once on the other side it would be much easier to shake off any pursuit, but to get to that relative safety he had to cross half a mile of open hill along the longest of Beinn Bhuidhe's three ridges.

In between glances over his shoulder, Charlie gave a running commentary to Gillespie on the progress of the drone. It had still not seen them but was advancing methodically up the hillside and was now about where their encounter with the Campbells had been. Sure enough, it stopped, dropping down close to the ground, then regaining altitude it started to circle faster and more widely. Trying to speak to Nin above the roar of the engine and the flying mud was difficult, but Charlie managed to signal that the drone had found the wreckage of their pursuers and was now on their trail. It would surely see them within moments. "It's an observation drone not a raptor," he shouted at Gillespie with a half-hearted smile, "so, no rockets at least."

Far below to their right, Gillespie could see the little hamlet of Clachan where he had met Fiona. He hoped that she hadn't been at the investiture. Judging by her mood she wouldn't have gone, but he dreaded to think what might have happened to her and Mara if she had.

Ahead of them was the crest of the ridge, behind which they would soon be hidden, at least from watchers on the ground but obviously not from the drone in the sky. They broke through the last of the tree cover and were totally exposed as they slugged up the steep hillside. The drone spotted them almost immediately and, banking hard, flew straight at them. As if realising that escape was futile, Nin pulled the Kat over, leaning back to shout something at Charlie who immediately started rummaging through the assortment of weapons they had captured off their Campbell pursuers. The drone hovered overhead, transmitting footage to its controllers down on the shore.

Charlie's first shot missed the main body of the drone, passing through one of its four rotors, sending blade shards flying. This was not enough to bring it down, but it did upset its balance, leaving it seesawing wildly. Charlie didn't need a third shot, as his second bullet exploded the plastic casing of its body, destroying its operating system and leaving it to drop to the ground like a rock.

Nin restarted the Kat and continued up the slope, clawing his way to the crest and the relative safety beyond. Grunting his satisfaction, Charlie dropped the gun back to the floor of the Kat: "That was a bit of luck, just a spy drone. But obviously they know where we are now, so we will need to be quick to escape them." Pointing down towards the loch, Charlie's finger tracked a line of Kats streaming towards Clachan. "See there, they are going to try and cut us off by circling round the other side of Beinn Bhuidhe. If they get past Inverchorchan to the River Fyne before us, we will be trapped like rats."

Gillespie nodded dumbly as if he knew what Charlie was talking about. "Are we going back to Elrig?" He asked, hoping against hope that they could just retreat to that friendly sanctuary away from all this madness.

Charlie looked at him as if he was an idiot, his eyes flashing green to match his mood. "No, I don't think that would be a good idea. Can't you see what is going on? They are burning Dunderave down, God knows what must have happened to Alexander and the others. Do you think they would have just allowed all that to happen? No way. Which can only mean that we need to put as many miles between us and those Campbells as we can."

Finally, they crested the ridge and plunged down the other side. Having left the chaos of the loch behind, the calm of the view down the hill into Glen Shira was seductive. Why couldn't they just go back to Elrig? Surely, they would be safe there?

Having made it to a patch of forestry that shielded them from view, Nin pulled the Kat under the cover of the trees and killed the engine. Gillespie's arms were shaking, the effort of holding on to the steel frame while the Kat had pounded up the hill had wrung every bit of strength from them. His knees too felt like they had been battered and bludgeoned; they trembled even as he tried to straighten them. He was in no shape to do anything but doing nothing was not an option.

Kirstie, Nin and Charlie were all huddled round the bonnet speaking so rapidly that Gillespie's Gaelic struggled to keep up. In any case, they didn't seem much interested in his opinion and he didn't feel qualified to contribute, so he kept his mouth shut. There was a hot debate as to what to do next. Nin was wide eyed and ranting about wanting to drive straight to Inveraray and put a bullet in MacCailean Mòr, while Kirstie was for going to Oban, to the Riaghaltas, to plead for intervention. Charlie was the calmest and having disabused both Nin and Kirstie of the wisdom of their ideas, came up with what seemed the most sensible plan.

"We don't know what has happened down there to Alexander, Aodhan and the rest, but the castle is burning, and it doesn't look good. No one, not even MacCailean Mòr, would move on us in such a way, flying in the face of all Canun law, unless it had been authorised at the highest level. Those were gunshots we heard remember. When was the last time guns were used by one Clan to attack another? 1965 or something? When the Shaws attacked the Roses at Kilravock, and look what happened to them as punishment, wiped off the face of the earth. No, this can only be a Government action. MacCailean Mòr is much too smart to expose himself like this. If that is the case, then we need to get as far away from here as we can until it has all calmed down. Somewhere to lie low and find out what is going on before making any rash decisions."

Kirstie and Nin seemed to accept this logic and certainly did not offer any alternative.

"But where shall we go? Where's safe?" Kirstie asked. "This whole glen will be crawling with Campbells in the next few hours and it's going to be dark soon."

"Unless someone has a better idea, I vote that we seek sanctuary with my people at Kindrochit over in the Cairngorms. We won't be looked for there and we will be a long way from the arm of MacCailean Mòr. We can then figure out what to do next."

"Not a bad idea," muttered Nin. "And we need to get away from here." He nervously eyed the southern end of the Glen. "What's the best route, do you think?"

"They'll be watching the main Tyndrum to Crieff Wade for sure, so we'd do much better to keep up Glen Shira to Dalmally and then head over by Glen Orchy….."

"But doesn't that take us too close to Rannoch Moor? What about the Griogaraich?" Kirstie said nervously.

"Aye, well, maybe we have more in common with the MacGregors now than we did before. In any case, I don't see how we can make it across otherwise. The main road is too busy and will be watched too closely. We've probably got time to get to Dalmally before they can shut it down. Then we strike out off road down Glen Orchy, skirting Beinn Lawers and then through Glen Lyon, turning north east to follow the Tummel until we get to Glen Tilt, which is as good as home and dry." Charlie said confidently.

Nin looked sceptical "That is ridiculous and totally disregards the brutal terrain, including such hardly insignificant obstacles like Schiehallion and the River Tay. Not to mention having to cross two Wades…" at which point Nin cleared his throat and spat on the ground, "…. at Aberfeldy and at Pitlochry. Total madness if you ask me."

"Oh, for fuck's sake, stop spraffing and let's get moving," Kirstie said. "You are like a pair of fishwives. We need to get a fucking move on, now!"

Almost as soon as the words had left her lips, they saw the column of vehicles turn into the southern end of the Glen and start a methodical sweep of either side of the valley.

Firing up the Kat, Nin started along the north-western side of the ridge, jagging his way north. Gillespie could see that they already had a difficult choice to face – did they go over the top of the mountain or follow it round? The former would obviously expose them to the risk of being seen, but also to the rapidly falling temperature which they were already beginning to feel as the weak sun set. However, to descend and follow the base of the mountain would take a long time due to Beinn Bhuidhe's two other protruding ridges. He guessed which route Nin was going to take and sure enough Nin pointed the nose of the Kat up the slope and started to climb.

29 - RED MIST

As he left the castle, Allan pulled his mask down over his face again and gathered his men. They pushed through the milling Campbells into the outer ward. The MacNachtan men had now all had their hands bound with cable ties and sat dejected at the far end, while the women and children had been released. Leaving the Campbells to gaze bewildered at the smoke that was now starting to pour out of the castle roof, he joined the rest of his crew at the outbuildings where they had been at work.

The building's door hung shattered on its hinges, reflecting the significant charge required to blow it open. Inside, papers were scattered, and the room was still full of acrid smoke. His men were busy taking as many hard drives as they could find, scattering paper and screens in their wake. He found the staircase which led down to the server room and descended the stairs to the air-conditioned chamber below. There were neat rows of boxes all tidily connected with cables, green and red lights winking and blinking; it was an impressive sight. It must have cost a lot to buy and to maintain. His men had smashed open a few cases and were extracting motherboards, the floor scattered with broken plastic and shredded wiring.

He finally found Donna Lamont hunched over a laptop in the far corner. Her face illuminated by her screen, her pockmarked cheeks looked even more sallow in this light, and her lanky hair was oozing its way out of the hairband on top of her head. But while personal hygiene may not have been high up her list of priorities, he knew that Donna was a hell of a hacker She was responsible for all the IT and systems technology that enabled the Clan to function and fight in the digital age.

Donna peered at him over the screen. "I need ten more minutes. That bitch must have changed the access codes. But although she thinks she's smart, I am smarter."

Allan nodded, replying, "That you are. Just get me the codes and let's get out of here."

She wordlessly returned her eyes to the screen.

Allan started to pour accelerant around the room, making a big pool in the middle away from the heat exchangers. After five minutes and with a shout of victory, Donna sneered triumphantly: "Yes, done it. Now all I need to do is change the administrator passwords. If only I could see her face, the self-satisfied cow." The smirk on her face was dripping with schadenfreude. She continued to work the keyboard, reaching a frenzy of tapping, only to stop suddenly swearing loudly: "Shit! That fucking bitch has put in an extra security layer. Fuck. I can't hack it and certainly not here. We really need to find her and get the administrator codes. Without those we can't get full control. Have you located her?"

"No. I've been somewhat preoccupied with other matters." Allan felt his blood starting to rise. "No matter, we'll find her. In the meantime, let's get out of here before those Campbells wake up and smell the coffee."

Pushing Donna up the stairs ahead of him, he pulled a flare from his pocket. Having ignited it he dropped it in the accelerant, sprinting up the final few steps and out of the door as the basement burst into flame.

Gathering the rest of his team, he led the way back to the boats where the rest of his crew were now in the boats waiting for him. He stepped into the water pushing the boat away from the shingle with the satisfaction of a job well done.

As they pulled away from the shore, the helmsman shouted: "I've been scanning the Campbell comms channel. A party of four seem to have escaped the castle. They have caused a bit of mayhem and are currently in a Kat fleeing over Beinn Bhuidhe. They seem to think that one of them is Ninian MacNachtan and another is a woman, Kirstie MacNachtan. Isn't she one of the ones you were looking for?"

"Bingo." Allan said. "Take us to the head of the loch. We have some more hunting to do."

Sending the other two boats back to Castle Ascog, Allan directed his boat up the loch towards Clachan, overtaking the line of Campbell Kats that were taking the track along the loch shore. Arriving in Clachan ahead of the Campbell force, Allan jumped ashore and with his three best men hid behind the corner of one of the houses, right where the track bent round the water.

Minutes later, the Campbell column arrived and started to turn the corner. Allan waited until four Kats had passed, before coolly stepping out and waving down the fifth and final vehicle. He held his arm out so the driver could see the Campbell tartan on the inside of his forearm. The driver duly came to a halt and wound down his window. Leaning towards him as if to speak, Allan shot the driver in the face before shooting his companion twice in the chest for good measure.

His team dragged the bodies from the vehicle and dumped them out of sight behind one of the houses, before taking off in pursuit of the other four Kats.

30 - THE BEATON

Archie Beaton was sat in his office reading a few emails when he first smelt the smoke. Initially he thought it might have been part of the celebrations, a hog roast or bonfire perhaps, both were popular at Clan events. The thick walls of the castle normally absorbed all external sound unless it was directly in front of his window, so he was usually unperturbed by any distractions. He pushed back from his desk and walked to the window; immediately he knew something terrible was happening. From his tiny office he could just see into a corner of the outer ward, where clansmen were grouped and bound. He then noticed that the music had ceased and that he could hear the shout of orders.

On reflection, he thought that the smoke did not smell of roasting pig but burning timbers; he rushed to the door, opening it a fraction to see what lay beyond. Smoke was already thick in the stairwell; he knew that he did not have long before he would be trapped. Closing the door, he looked round his office to see what might aid his escape: not much. Taking his sgian dubh he cut the left sleeve off his shirt and, for lack of any other liquid, pissed on it to create a membrane to catch as much of the smoke as possible. He was glad the castle cleaners couldn't see the mess he had made of the carpet. Gagging slightly, he nonetheless thanked the stars that the few pints of beer he had consumed meant that the smell was not overpowering. Binding the sodden sleeve round his face, he dropped to his knees and opened the door.

The draught on the stairs was sweeping the smoke upwards in a spiral and it was already impenetrably thick above him. At floor level he could still see the stairs and he rapidly crawled down them as fast as his hands and knees could bear, cursing each of the sharp-edged stone steps all the way down the two flights to the main floor of the castle. He could feel the temperature rise as he descended and when he pushed open the door at the bottom he could hear the crackle of burning wood too. So far, he had not seen any bodies, but as he came onto the main landing opposite the Red Banner Hall he saw someone lying in the doorway. Although it felt suicidal to be going towards the fire, his sense of Hippocratic duty pushed him forward.

The body by the door was a Campbell judging by his tartan, his eyes were open, but his pulse was gone. One hand was clutched at his throat and was soaked in blood. There was nothing that Archie could do for him. He looked in the Hall for any others. The blaze was roaring; the table and much of the furniture was alight and the roof beams had caught too. It wasn't going to be long before the whole lot would come crashing down. There were two dark and still figures on the far side who he could not reach, but there was one arm lying outstretched on his side of the table. He grabbed it and pulled the body towards him, feeling for a pulse. There was a flutter, no more than that, but he was still alive, just.

Archie yanked on the arm with all his might, pulling the body out of the room and towards the stairs. Once at the top of the flight he cradled the man's head to protect it as he dragged the rest of the body down the steep flight of steps and out into the Courtyard of the Fountain. He could feel his world blackening as he reached the bottom, the doorway seemed to be disappearing away from him down a long black tunnel. With the last of his energy he fell rather than walked through the doorway and into the air beyond.

Unseen but strong hands grabbed him and pulled him through into the outer ward. As he drifted in and out of consciousness all he could hear was a confusion of shouts and people running. Finally, he could resist the black void no longer and he surrendered himself to it happily as it opened up and swallowed him whole.

31- TO THE RIVER

Darkness was almost total by the time that they cleared the summit of Beinn Bhuidhe and started down the other side. For obvious reasons, they could not use the headlights on the Kat, and the battering that the sturdy vehicle was taking as it thumped into holes and through the underbrush meant that a breakage was only a matter of time. Sure enough, it died as they were about halfway down the slope; the front offside wheel being smashed at such an angle that it would move no further. Nin swore and kicked the offending tyre, but there was nothing to be done.

Charlie riffled through the weapons in the back and distributed them around the group. He handed Gillespie a chunky semi-automatic rifle wordlessly showing him where the safety catch was.

The temperature was falling fast, and they were hardly dressed for a night on the hill. Adrenalin was driving them on for now and as long as they kept moving they were OK, but whether they could last a night outside was another matter. A pale moon started to rise, helping to illuminate their way. In any case, Kirstie and Nin knew this area like the back of their hands and the dark was little impediment. There was no cover here of any description, Beinn Bhuidhe slid down into a tight glen with the River Fyne at the bottom flowing east, sandwiched on the other side by Meall nan Gabhar, a steep sided hill. To their left, was Beinn Bhòideach, and the Shira flowed south west from there down the Glen which took its name. In the middle of these three peaks, the two rivers met, creating a natural barrier. This was what they were aiming for and was what they had to cross to have any chance of escape.

As they came off onto the level the ground got softer and soon they were sinking up to their knees in freezing boggy water. Gillespie didn't know how much more he could take; his legs already weak after the Kat ride were now jelly. As they finally reached the river, Gillespie looked despondently at the water swirling below. Although it was not very wide, probably no more than 60 feet, it was cold, deep and fast flowing. There was no way they could wade across and there was no bridge or other means to traverse it. Nin and Charlie split up looking for tree trunks or anything that would float, but there was nothing.

They could now see the headlights of the five pursuing Kats which had split up; two were searching the lower reaches of Beinn Bhuidhe while the other three were exploring the riverbank. One of these had started following the river in their direction. They would soon be caught; they needed to act.

While Gillespie stayed out of sight under the lee of the riverbank, Nin and Charlie crept forward into the undergrowth, their black clothing making them all but invisible. When the Kat was 20 yards away, Kirstie coolly stood up with her hands raised above her head. The occupants of the Kat shouted at her in fast and fierce Gaelic covering her with their rifles as the vehicle drove towards her. As they got closer, they ordered her to kneel on the ground while keeping her hands in the air. At the very moment that the Kat pulled to a stop, when the men were slightly distracted and off balance, the trap was sprung. Nin and Charlie surged out of the undergrowth on either side of the vehicle, swords drawn, grabbing the two men from the back and pulling them to the ground, while Gillespie stuck his semi-automatic rifle through the driver's window. One of them squeezed off a round; but it went high, missing Kirstie. He didn't get another chance as he was battered unconscious by Charlie using the basket hilt of his sword. Nin had meanwhile taken care of the other one before he pushed Gillespie aside and dragged the confused driver from his seat, raining punches down on his head.

However, that unfortunate shot had alerted the other vehicles, and they were now racing towards them across the bog. Kirstie shouted at them to strip the Campbells of their coats; although it took precious seconds, it was imperative that they had some warmer clothing. This was no time for politeness, as they wrestled the coats off the stricken bodies. The other vehicles were almost upon them as Charlie started the engine. Gillespie climbed in the cab, with Nin and Kirstie in the back and they streaked off along the riverbank with their enemies in hot pursuit.

They were just about keeping ahead of them, but there was no way they could outrun them forever. Gillespie saw that one Kat had split off and was going to try and cut them off as the river curved. Charlie seemed unconcerned, focused completely on the rough terrain. Suddenly, he threw the wheel over, driving straight through a dip in the bank and into the river. The water was deep here, and it immediately swept the Kat off its tyres and out into the current. Their pursuers arrived seconds later but did not dare follow into the dark water.

The Kat was tossed like a cork, and Charlie fought the wheel trying to use its tyres to steer it across the water to freedom on the other side. Gillespie sat wide eyed gripping the dashboard as water sloshed over the sides. They only had a limited amount of time before the Kat became waterlogged and sank.

Without warning they hit a submerged rock; the vehicle shook violently. Kirstie, who'd been hanging on the back, slipped with the force of the impact and was thrown into the water. Nin tried to grab her, but there was nothing he could do. She was cast upon the muddy bank and they were immediately swept downstream out of reach. Seconds later, the enemy were upon her, pulling her out of the river and standing over her. Gillespie could hear Nin thumping the roof of the cab in frustration as the vicious current swept them round a bend, out of sight and into the darkness.

32 - CROSSING THE WADE

The rush of water was deafening: Gillespie tried not to think how much longer they could last in this freezing torrent. The water was now nearly at the lip of the door and was seeping fast into the footwell. They were going to sink very soon, at which point they would either drown or once again become fair game for their pursuers. He was briefly relieved when the Campbells had disappeared behind the last bend in the river, but no longer: this was suicidal. Charlie was trying to steer them out of the current and onto the bank of the opposite shore and every now and then the wheels would bite on a rock and the vehicle would be thrown forward, scrabbling for grip. But the river was too deep and once traction was lost they were swept onwards again. So close and yet so far.

Just as Gillespie was contemplating how to extricate himself from the vehicle once it was beyond the point of no return, it was over. As they approached the next bend, Charlie managed to steer them onto a sand bank cast up by the river's course and as soon as their tyres sank into its soft yielding grains they were off, out of the water and racing across the far shore, water pouring from their undercarriage.

They crashed through the bushes and boggy grass that covered the glen floor as Charlie tried to put as much distance between them and the riverbank as he could. Because it was so dark, and Charlie was driving without the benefit of headlights, it was a rough and bumpy ride. After smashing his knees on the dashboard for the umpteenth time, Gillespie was beginning to wonder if he preferred to take his chances with the enemy, rather than sustain any more of this punishment. Finally, as they started to crawl up the hill out of the bog, the going improved and Charlie located a drove path that wound along the side of Meall nan Gabhar to the north. As they followed the glen round, they were soon completely hidden from the view of those in the valley behind, freeing them to use their headlights and allowing them to make faster progress.

The drove road was wet and rutted but nothing the Kat couldn't take in its stride, even in the dark. Soon they could see mighty Beinn Laoigh rising to their right, its top snow-capped, its steep ridges sweeping down to the valley below, forcing the drove road to the north east. After another hour of hard pounding, they were at the bottom of a cleft between the mountains and surrounded by oppressive peaks. Darkness encompassed them and the crunch of ice under their tyres was a reminder of how far the temperature had fallen. They were certainly thankful for the stolen coats now.

Charlie pulled the Kat over and, having turned off the lights, killed the engine: silence and blackness descended. It was the first time they had really had a chance to speak since the river and Kirstie's capture. Nin got down from the back of the Kat, grim faced. He ransacked the various compartments until he found some tobacco and then rolled himself a cigarette which he shared with Charlie. They offered Gillespie a puff, but he politely refused. The glowing orange tip was the only light in the whole glen except for the stars and the waning moon.

Gillespie suddenly felt exhausted, as if a stopper had been pulled and the wind let out of him; he was collapsing in on himself. The long day, combined with numerous stressful encounters, the vibrations of the Kat, the cold, the lack of food: it was all too much. Maybe he should just lie down by the track and go to sleep until the morning. Yes, that seemed like the best idea. If he just lay down, everything would be OK.

It was the icy water that brought him back. He found himself lying by the side of the Kat, Charlie and Nin standing over him with concerned looks on their faces.

"Are you OK?" Charlie asked, "you just fainted away."

"Yes, I think so. I'm just so tired." Said Gillespie, "and hungry for that matter. What time is it anyway?"

"It's just past ten," Nin said. "We've got to try and make it to Glen Orchy before it gets light. My cousin Don lives just over the Wade. If we can make it to him before light we'll probably escape detection. We'll need to stick to the side of Beinn Laoigh and then cut across the Wade. Assuming we don't bump into any Campbells, we'll be up Glen Orchy and settling into a nice cooked breakfast before you know it."

The sound of that cooked breakfast just made Gillespie feel even hungrier, and with his stomach rumbling he asked what the food situation was.

"Pretty piss poor, if I'm honest," said Charlie. "I've found a few chocolate wafers in the Kat, but apart from that, nothing. Obviously, there is plenty of water around so grab yourself a drink." At this, he gestured to the burns and pools of the glen with a sweep of his hand.

They divided up the wafers, greedily devouring them in a matter of seconds. Gillespie bent down and cupped his hands in the freezing burn, scooping some icy but delicious water into his mouth. Feeling a little better, he climbed back into the front seat of the Kat, and Nin got in to drive. Charlie was consigned to standing in the back and making rude comments about Nin's driving. At least in the cab Gillespie had access to the rather meagre heat coming from the engine. He wondered what had happened to Kirstie; her shout as she fell in the river haunted him. It was a subject that they had conspicuously not discussed when they'd stopped. She was gone and there was nothing they could do.

The grinding of the drive train was relentless, as was the jolting of the suspension as they smashed into potholes and bounced out the other side. Every now and then they would come to a burn and consultations would be taken between Charlie and Nin as to which was the best route across. They got stuck a few times, and Gillespie's legs were now caked in freezing mud from helping to push the Kat. Despite the thick down jacket that he had stolen, he was now seriously cold: as cold as he had ever been in his life. He was beginning to lose the feeling in his fingertips and with it his ability to grip anything. He turned to look at Nin hunched over the wheel, those cornflower blue eyes muted in the lamp light from the speedometer, focused on the ruts and bumps in the track ahead.

The cab of the Kat was starting to ice up now and every now and then Gillespie gave the windscreen a wipe, but generally just ended up smearing the screen rather than clearing it. He wondered how much longer it would be as he watched the hours grind by. They would stop occasionally to jump around to try and warm up. Charlie and Nin swapping places while insisting that Gillespie stayed where he was. They didn't trust him to drive, and they didn't want him dying of hypothermia either.

The drove path gave out just as Beinn Laoigh met Glen Lochy. The ridge that had shadowed them to their right melted away into the glen's wide floodplain. They had to be careful here, as there were more houses, and they didn't want the noise of the Kat to waken any trigger-happy residents. There were spinneys of silver birch, rustling their branches in the chill wind, and a few rowans that still carried last autumn's fruits on laden branches. They could now see the Wade road ahead, its tarmac snaking around the bottom of the glen, following the path of the Orchy river from the high mountains down to Loch Awe. It was well lit and even at this hour there was a fair amount of traffic racing up it in both directions.

Nin turned to Gillespie and said: "That is the main route coming up from the border at Arrochar. It goes all the way to Oban and carries most of the business and trade coming into the West of the Republic. It will be difficult to cross unseen. We should sit here for a little while and see if it's being watched." He turned off the ignition and rolled himself another cigarette.

"I'm curious, why do you call them Wades?" Gillespie asked. At which Nin spat a gobbet of phlegm out of the Kat onto the heather. "And why do you always spit at the mention of the name Wade?" Nin looked at him and then very deliberately swivelled his head to spit out of the door again, before returning to look at Gillespie with an added wink.

"General Wade was the motherfucker that was sent to pacify us poor Gaels before Cumberland came to murder us. General Wade," at which he resisted expectorating for once, "came and carved six roads into the flesh of our land so that he could march his troops and not have to contend with the hills, the bogs and rivers. He understood that roads could subdue and enslave us in a way that armies since the Romans have failed to. Of course, we have been beaten in battles and bowed our heads and knees to Kings and Queens in Edinburgh and London from time to time, but we'd never been occupied until Wade came. He built the roads, and bridges and forts and barracks that would have shackled and imprisoned us if King Charlie hadn't slain Cumberland at Culloden."

"They're still here, but there are as many Gaels that wish they weren't, as are happy that they are. Of course, we use them, just don't expect us to be grateful for them. As you'll see, there haven't been many roads built in the Republic since Wade, and like as not there won't be, especially here near the border. We don't want to make it too easy for the British to roll their tanks and troops in. The lack of roads has always put them off in the past, no reason why it won't in the future. Wade deserved a long swim in a deep loch with a rock tied to his ankles if you ask me. Roads are the devil's work and no mistake."

After twenty minutes spent watching the Wade they had a pretty good feel for the flow of traffic. It was erratic but there did not seem to be any patrols operating along it and following a quick consultation they decided to move before they froze. Charlie took over the driving, grateful to be out of the draught of the wind. He nosed the Kat up onto a grass bank that ran across a boggy piece of open ground. There were scrubby willows and a few ash lining the bank on either side to shield them from prying eyes, if there were any. However, there was nothing to mute the sound of their engine which seemed deafening to Gillespie.

Charlie motored along the bank until it was just shy of the road where there was a ditch to negotiate thick with shrubs and bushes. Waiting for a moment when no headlights could be seen in either direction, Charlie accelerated the Kat down the bank into the ditch. Gillespie's window exploded with branches and leaves: the bog myrtle he could smell, the gorse he could feel. The Kat shook from side to side as its wheels churned and gouged a path up the steep embankment and onto the road. Slewing in a wide arc as Charlie wrestled the wheel round, the Kat was soon purring east along the Wade, making for the turning that they hoped was only half a mile or so away.

The black tarmac was smooth as silk and after the hours on the hillsides of Argyll - it felt like a magic carpet ride. Couldn't they stay in its rip and be swept along all the way to Arrochar and beyond? Back to civilisation, with its boredom and mundanity; Gillespie had had enough of this moment by moment, minute by minute existence; his body was drained of adrenalin and his brain was bursting with too many thoughts, fears, memories and hopes. All he wanted was to rest.

A few trucks sped past them in the opposite direction, heading from the border towards Oban, their sides adorned with tarpaulins advertising hauliers from far flung locations such as Krakow or Valencia. They could now see the turning in the distance, just on a corner as the road bent round to follow the glen east. Gillespie could hear Nin chambering a round in his rifle, while Charlie pulled a sidearm out of its holster and laid it on the seat between them. Charlie swung the wheel and made the turn. The blackness of the road ahead was blinding after the lights of the Wade. As the sodium orange started to fade out behind them, Gillespie felt as if he was also relinquishing his last opportunity to turn back, to return to the real world and leave this madness behind.

33 - FIDDLER'S REST

It was only after the second dram of whisky that Gillespie actually felt like he was beginning to warm up. While ordinarily having whisky with breakfast might seem the fastest route to an appointment with the devil, right now it made perfect sense.

The table was a picture of silent concentration: three grown men wolfing down plates laden with browned and split sausages, crispy bacon, crunchy edged hash browns, pale diced mushrooms with caramelised onions, tomato halves blackened and seared, the crumbly slice of black pudding speckled with glistening jewels of fat, fried eggs with yellow domes marooned in puddles of frilled albumen, all swimming in a gloop of baked beans.

Gillespie pushed the crust of toast around the plate chasing down and mopping up the last of the yolk that clung viscously to the willow tree pattern. His eyes drawn into the alluring Chinese water garden with its doves and pagodas, each revealed one by one from under the carpet of cadmium yellow.

At last, Charlie spoke for all of them: "Fuck me, that was good. I haven't enjoyed anything so much since I went down on those four fishermen in Lerwick, and that must have been a good 10 years ago." He belched contentedly at the memory: Nin rolled his eyes and turned his attention to his coffee.

The smoky tendrils of the whisky were probing the muscles and tendons in every nook and corner of Gillespie's body, seeking out his tension and pain points and gently massaging them, kneading them into submission. He felt like a jelly fish washed upon the shore, unable to stand, to move, hopeless and helpless, cast up and accepting of whatever was going to happen next.

The room was starting to spin slightly; he needed to rest, more than anything he needed to rest.

Don MacArthur sat watching the motley crew at their breakfast with an amused eye. Bound in a tattered tartan dressing gown, his shambolic appearance was accentuated by a wild mop of hair. It looked as though it had been backcombed many years previously and left untroubled since. He took a deep pull on his vape, expelling a cloud of apple cinnamon from his lungs: he idly watched as the prodigious cloud thinned and disappeared into the air above them. In the background the radio played, his foot unconsciously tapping away to the rhythm. The first smear of dawn could be seen beginning to silhouette the hills that surrounded the house to the east. Gulping down a tarry slug of coffee from the bottom of his cup, he stood and offered to show them where they could sleep.

When they'd tumbled through his door, they'd looked more dead than alive - the pallid grey of the truly cold. Unable to speak or walk they staggered and clutched their way from the front door to the warmth of the kitchen where his range pumped out life affirming heat all day and night. It was amazing what a cup of tea and dram of whisky could achieve, rousing them to near consciousness. The second dram and a plate of breakfast, washed down with a pot of Guatemala's finest, completed the transformation, its precious alchemy restoring them to speech and humanity.

Nin tried to start thanking Don for his hospitality, but Don waved away his words.

"Nae bother, nae bother. Now listen, youse all need some kip and while you're catching up on some well-earned rest, I'm going into Tyndrum and see what the lie of the land is. There is nothing much on the radio apart from some spraff about MacCailean Mòr being summoned to the Comhairle to explain himself next week. I'll be able to get a better idea from the lads down at the Griogaraich's Lament. That bar is always hotching with loud mouths and strong opinions. I should be able to get a pretty good idea of what's happening."

He led them through the hallway and up the stairs, directing Nin and Charlie into the larger double room and Gillespie into what must have been a child's room, filled as it was with posters and toys. Barely pausing long enough to strip off his road worn clothes, Gillespie was asleep before his head hit the pillow.

34 - STIRRING

John Lamont crossed his office and shoogled round his desk. He ran his finger up the screen to activate the monitor, briefly peering into the retina scanner to access his server and opening up his contacts to find the details he needed.

Flicking through a few names; Macpherson, MacGillivray, MacIntosh, he came to the one he was looking for: Jimmy Singh Davidson of Clan Dhai, over in Dingwall, on the east coast. He dialled the number and turned his chair to look out of the window as the sun began to set at the end of another short late winter day.

"Yes, hallo?" a terse voice came down the receiver.

"Ah, hallo Jimmy, its John, John Lamont. How are you?"

The tone down the phone immediately became much more welcoming.

"Ah, how are you John? Great to hear from you." Oozed Jimmy down the phone. "How can I help you?"

Lamont recoiled with distaste at Jimmy's ingratiating tones. "I was just calling to see if you had heard what has been going on over at Dunderave?"

"No, I haven't. What's been happening – have they chosen a new Chief yet?"

"Well, funny you should mention that, but they have, or should I say had."

"What do you mean?" Jimmy Singh said, uncertainly.

"I mean what I said. They chose a new Chief but that he's already dead. Seemingly, it was all too much for MacCailean Mòr. He has totally over-reached himself. It was supposed to be a simple law and order enforcement action, to try and find the perpetrators of that Irish Sea attack. But what has he done? ... Shot the place up, burned it to the ground, killed Alexander MacNachtan and goodness knows how many others. Its chaos. ...."

"That is what happens when you have over mighty magnates like MacCailean Mòr, eventually it goes to their head and they think they are above the law......... Well us small clans need to stick together, or we'll all be swallowed up. Are you going to be in Oban next week? I think there is going to be a special session to discuss this, and I think it's very important that we small clans make a point. What'll be left of the Republic if we allow him to get away with this! Oh good, so you agree, fantastic, well this is what I've in mind....."

After another twenty minutes, John put the phone down well pleased with his call. Next, he called Euan MacNeil of Barra, then Dugald MacDugal of Dun Ollie, Tam Matheson of Attadale, and Dervoguila Farquharson of Kindrochit. All of them shared the same reaction. Warming to his theme, he picked up the phone to a much more challenging target and slightly hesitantly dialled Catriona MacLean of Duart's number.

"What an unexpected and, may I say, unlooked for pleasure," came a voice as smooth as velvet down the phone. "What could be happening that the Great John Lamont, the Warden of the Clyde, should feel the need to call me at this hour, I wonder?" She continued, letting the words fall from her lips like honey from a knife.

He ran out his spiel, which by and large had worked pretty well with the lesser Chiefs. She listened silently, waiting until the end before saying: "My, my, what a little pot of trouble you are cooking up. Quite surpassing yourself this time. You do seem to have it in for poor old MacCailean Mòr," and with a harder edge to her voice, "not that he doesn't deserve it, mind you. And what, can I ask, are you looking to gain out of this? And what crumbs might there be falling from your table to those of us who choose to support your nefarious little plan, distasteful though it may be?"

"Catriona, why don't you just tell me what you want, that would be much quicker, don't you think?" He knew that he was about to be forced to give away something precious, and he sure as hell wasn't just going to offer it up.

"No, no, no, John, you misunderstand me. As I see it, you called me asking for my help to stitch up the most powerful warlord on the west coast of the Republic so that you might profit from his demise. I really think it's beholden on you to think a little harder on what you are offering first. As for all this bullshit about 'we small clans must stick together', can I remind you that I've over 1,000 men in arms, and probably five times that number of reserves. So, I am not sure if I would categorise myself in that way."

"You know as well as I do that trying to take down MacCailean Mòr will upset the balance of power in the Republic, and who knows how that will end? All I do know is that hooded crows like John Lamont are the only ones that benefit from the likely carnage. If I'm to get involved, I want to do it with my eyes open. Can I suggest that before the Comhairle meeting next week you let me know what you are offering, and I promise to give it my closest consideration."

Before he could respond, she cut the line. He hung up, resisting the urge to smash the receiver in pieces. He could feel the flush of blood rising up his neck and into his face. The tic above his right eye started to twitch uncontrollably, the vein pulsing as his anger was stoked into rage.

Pushing himself back from his desk, he shouted for Allan Stewart. As he entered, John Lamont thrust his finger into Allan's chest, eyes bulging, lips pulled back in a snarl. Saying nothing, he swept past him out of the room and down the stairs to his cellar to vent his anger on a poor unfortunate. Allan sighed and followed; it was likely to be a long night.

35 - THE RUIN

Brighid walked slowly along the lochside, staring at its waves and listening to their lapping on the rocks. She felt weary and sad. She had made the walk from her house at Stronshira to Dunderave so many times, almost beyond count; for Clan gatherings, celebrations, commiserations, weddings, funerals, baptisms, blessings, for the annual games and for dancing, to meet and catch the news, to gossip and love. The castle had always stood at the centre of her life, but now it offered shelter no longer.

No one knew how the fires had started but both the castle and the gaming operation had been badly damaged. Kirstie had disappeared too, so no one knew how to rebuild – even if they felt up to starting. She could see groups of Campbell clansmen standing around idly watching the MacNachtans who'd turned out in force to try and clear the area and see what could be salvaged. She saw Fiona and Mara helping to lift burnt timbers and charred furniture from the outbuildings.

It didn't make any sense to her. Why had the Campbells done this? Why had MacCailean Mòr plunged so precipitously into such dangerous waters. He had no need of the little that Clan Nechtan had. He might admire Glen Shira and be keen to secure a powerful income stream like their gaming business, but in the great scheme of things, to a magnate of his power and influence, it was all small potatoes. After all, hadn't they lived side by side with the Campbells for many, many hundreds of years? In days when relations were far worse than they'd been today. Yes, Duncan Tapaidh had baited MacCailean Mòr from time to time, needling him over some pointless matter, just for pleasure. But that was one of the few joys that any small Clan could expect; like a flea troubling an elephant, it was beneath the dignity of the elephant to react. Even if MacCailean Mòr had wanted to get rid of his pestilential neighbours, why did he burn down the castle and the gaming operation, they were worth far more to him intact, surely?

Brighid turned all these thoughts over in her mind, searching for answers which didn't come. She went down the corridor to the Courtyard of the Fountain. The Black Tower was still there in its pool, although the water had ceased flowing from its crenulations. It was quiet and forlorn, but still standing: that gave her some heart. The entrance way into the castle was a forbidding gaping abscess blackened with smoke. There were a pair of Campbells on the door to deter any looters.

Wandering to the back of the courtyard, she looked up to see the extent of the damage. Fortunately, the fire boat had got there in time to prevent the castle's total destruction. The damage was extensive but seemed to have been limited to the wing where the Red Banner Hall had stood. Here the upper stories had gone, and the roof had collapsed, leaving a jagged line of roof tiles to indicate where the timbers still stood true. The water from the fireboat would also have done its worst and she imagined the cellars must be knee deep in seawater. All that wine Duncan had collected over the years, almost certainly ruined: he had loved his wine.

She walked back down the passage to the outer ward where she bumped into Iain the Rat. He was nursing a black eye and a succession of bruises down the right-hand side of his face. He broke into a grin when he saw her, which he immediately regretted, wincing and flinching, as if to shrug away the pain of his injuries. Brighid put her hand on his shoulder: even that made him shrink from her touch, he had clearly taken a pasting. They wandered over to one of the overturned picnic tables and, having righted it, sat down to chat.

"What in God's name went on here?" Brighid asked. "It just doesn't make any sense. Why would MacCailean Mòr have Alexander and Aodhan killed and burn the castle down? I could understand him wanting to rough things up a bit: to teach Alexander a lesson at the beginning of his Chiefship. But as for all the rest of this destruction, it just isn't logical."

Iain nodded, rubbing his aching jaw. "It seemed to go out of control very quickly. When they first arrived, we all backed right off. It was clear that they meant business; they were carrying rifles and semis - and when was the last time that happened between clans? A few brave lads had a go but were taken out pretty quickly. In any case, most of us were too smashed to put up much resistance. Which is why what happened up there," he nodded towards the black hole of the Hall, "just doesn't make any sense."

"I don't believe this bullshit that Alexander cut Archie Campbell's throat like that; I mean from across the table, while sitting down? Do me a favour. Archie Campbell was the finest swordsman in Argyll in living memory. He was a fucking wizard with that sword. He could turn me into sashimi any day. So, don't tell me he just let Alexander lean over the table and cut him from ear to ear. Anyways, that's not Alexander's style; he was a tough motherfucker, much too tough to panic in the face of that blond cunt Ardbreknish. And another thing, since when did you ever see either Ardbreknish or Archie carry a gun? Taking one to a parlay? It flies in the face of almost every tenet of Canun law."

"What happens now? Said Brighid. "I mean, do we have to elect another Chief or what? Who's going to oversee the process now that Aodhan is dead? Maybe MacCailean Mòr's going to try and subsume us into Clan Campbell - this would be the perfect opportunity."

"Yeah, but when was the last time the Comhairle allowed that to happen? All those little clans that sit on their fat arses would be petrified that they'd be next. The whole Republic could disintegrate. No, the Comhairle won't allow that to happen lightly. But that doesn't mean that MacCailean Mòr will just allow us to go our own sweet way. My guess is he'll let the dust settle, and then put his own appointee in the Red Banner Hall. And I don't see there is much we can do about it."

"What about Kirstie? Where's she? Have you seen her since last night?"

"No," Iain replied, "I haven't, or any of the Elrig lot for that matter. I saw them leaving during the party, just before it all kicked off. God knows where they are now."

"Rather than sitting around on our arses, why don't you go and start asking that lot by the uplink, and I'll see what I can get out of those Campbells on the door. Patrick Campbell is married to my sister's brother-in-law. He'll tell me anything he knows. Let's meet back here in an hour."

Brighid turned and left the castle ward looking for Fiona and Mara; they'd be a good place to start.

An hour later she was back at the table, casually cleaning the tips of her nails with her sgian dubh while she waited for Iain. When he arrived he brought Jamie with him. Jamie was still limping and clearly suffering from his wound, choosing to stand rather than sit. Nonetheless, he was doughty as ever; his peat spade of a beard almost visibly bristling with indignation over the events of the previous day.

"What did you find out?" Brighid asked. "Anything of use?"

"Mmm, well let's just say that this story is getting fishier by the hour. Patrick Campbell told me that several of their men were killed last night in Clachan pursuing some fugitives who sound very much like our Elrig friends. Apparently, they had fled over Beinn Bhuidhe and were making for the other side of the Fyne to escape. It seems like they got away, but not before leaving a trail of dead. The Campbells are hopping mad and looking for revenge."

"Doesn't sound very likely," Jamie interjected. "I mean Nin and Charlie can certainly handle themselves but killing left and right is not their style."

Brighid nodded, adding: "I agree. I can't imagine them doing such a thing. I also heard something interesting from Fiona, you know Malcolm's widow who lives up at Clachan. She said that she saw a boat drop a team of men on the shore and that those same men ambushed one of the Campbell Kats, killing the occupants and driving off in the vehicle. Later she saw that

Kat return and unload the same team plus a woman, possibly Kirstie, she couldn't be sure, into the boat which then disappeared down the Loch."

"There is something very strange going on, right enough," muttered Jamie. "The question is what and what can we do about it?"

Brighid thought for a moment, "I think we need to talk to the Beaton. He was the last man out of the castle alive and was the one that saved Ardbreknish. If anyone knows anything it'll be him."

"Aye, that's as maybe, but he's in the Infirmary in Inveraray being treated. One of us will have to sneak down there and try and get to him. I don't imagine it's going to be easy."

"I'll go," Brighid said immediately. "I've got a much better chance of being allowed through than you two vagabonds. Also, I've an old school friend who's a nurse in the Infirmary, she can probably help me."

They both nodded their agreement. Jamie was not going to be much use due to his wound, and Iain did not have the kind of face that lent itself easily to hospital visits. There was not a moment to lose and having kissed them both on each cheek, Brighid left the castle ward for Inveraray.

36 - THE INFIRMARY

MacCailean Mòr stood over the bed lost in thought. He had one arm wrapped around himself and the other clutched to his chin. His eyes were staring down at the pale youthful face of his cousin Niall Campbell of Ardbreknish. The usual bloom and vigour of his countenance had been replaced with a grey and deathly pallor. His eyes were closed, and his long blond hair was gathered beneath a hospital cap. There was a large dressing in the centre of his chest, pinned by strip upon strip of medical tape. His right hand lay on the sheet, again copiously bound in bandages and dressings, with the added drama of drips and tubes linked to various machines which pinged and squeaked their opinion of his condition.

MacCailean Mòr was no stranger to death or injury, how could he be? But there was something about that moment which upset and disturbed him. He could feel that there was something awry, but he could not put his finger on it.

He knew his cousin well enough; he had watched him grow from a gurgling babe in arms, to a cheeky lad, and now to an occasionally pompous but generally diligent duine uasal. If there was one thing his cousin knew better than most, it was sword play. He had been raised in the dojos and sword yards of Inveraray, not to mention his travels to learn from further flung clans and countries. In all the time that he'd known him, he had barely known Ardbreknish to suffer more than a cut or a few bruises. He did not understand how he and Archie could've lost control of that room and ended up in a room full of dead people.

It had never been his intention to do more than give Alexander MacNachtan a bit of a scare, teach him who was boss. After all, he had been away from the Republic so long he may have forgotten who was the Duke of Argyll and the Warden of the West.

Yes, that old fox Lamont had poured some poison in his ear about Duncan Tapaidh's cheek and encouraged him to assert his authority. But it'd seemed a good moment with the power vacuum left by the dead Chief and that incident in the Irish Sea. Better that he did it than allow Lamont, or one of the other vultures that had been circling Duncan's prone body for months.

He had no interest in trying to destroy the MacNachtans – what did they have that he wanted? Of course, the money from the online gaming would be useful, but he knew that he needed them to run it. Far better to let them have it and just extract a tithe from Alexander. He could then have taken a few scalps to parade before the Comhairle, so that the Kingdom could be shown that justice had been served: everyone would have been happy. Alexander was a sensible man; he would have seen the value in complying.

The slaying of Archie, his friend, his Curaidh Mòr and personal bodyguard, was distressing: slaughtered like a sheep in the fold. If he actually believed that Aodhan or Alexander had done it then it might make sense. But he had fought with Archie countless times, both in the sword yard and in the field. This was a man that had shrugged off a thousand such attempts in the past. However good Alexander had been, MacCailean Mòr did not believe that he was a match for Archie in that kind of situation. It was a puzzle indeed.

Leaving aside the human cost for a moment, he also considered the political price he was paying. Suddenly, he had all the small clans in the Comhairle baying for his blood, saying that he had exceeded his authority, calling for sanctions. While individually they were not much to worry about, collectively, like a school of piranhas, they could tear him apart. He was already wary of his visit to Oban next week, answering a summons from Speaker Urquhart, the little twerp. If it wasn't for Lamont's little plan, he would be worried.

Sighing deeply, he turned to leave. As he reached for the door handle, a nurse entered with a clip board and a harried expression. He tried to ask about Niall's condition, but she cut him off stating firmly that she did not care who he was, but that he needed to leave her patient in peace to recover. She would only tell him that Ardbreknish had not regained consciousness since being brought to the Infirmary. He was still in a critical condition and was in a coma principally due to smoke inhalation, but the loss of blood had not helped either. Given his weak and feeble condition there was no guarantee when, or even if, he would ever regain consciousness. The nurse encouraged him to be patient.

Despite being frustrated at not being able to get Ardbreknish to answer his questions, MacCailean Mòr nodded his thanks, promising to return the next day.

37 - LOOSE ENDS

The grating buzz of his mobile dragged John Lamont's attention away from the double screen on his desk, where he had been reading news of the Dunderave incident in The Raven. It was the usual mix of half-truth and speculations, sprinkled with a few facts to leaven it and give credibility to the rest. He noted with pleasure some of the vitriolic comments from Tam Matheson and Dugald MacDugall, excoriating MacCailean Mòr for over-reaching his commission. The trim smile on his lips broadened further when he picked up the phone to hear MacCailean Mòr's gruff tones coming down the line.

"Lamont," he always knew that MacCailean Mòr was angry when he addressed him by his surname like some naughty schoolboy. "I want to talk to you about Dunderave and the MacNachtans as there is something very fishy going on."

The smile vanished instantly from Lamont's face and he focused his concentration on the voice coming down the line.

"I've just come back from the Inveraray Infirmary where one of my top duine uasal is lying in intensive care, having nearly been murdered during the Dunderave operation. Not only that, but my Curaidh Mòr, Archie Campbell, has been killed, along with Alexander MacNachtan and his Seanchaidh, and half the castle burned down. The Republic is in uproar and I have been summoned to the Comhairle to explain myself. And yet, the strange thing is, I had nothing to do with any of that. I sent my men to shake Alexander up a bit and extract a bit of retribution for the patrol boat as we discussed. But how did everyone end up dead? And who set the castle on fire? None of my men did that, I have been assured."

John Lamont had to stop himself giggling out loud at that. "Yes, I know, terrible isn't it." He commiserated down the phone. "And did you read the bile from old Tam Matheson in The Raven? Honestly, some people have no gratitude, do they? Think of everything you have done for those Mathesons over the years, and for those MacDugalls too. I mean, the temerity of it, don't they know their place?"

He had to stop himself laying it on too thick, but he was enjoying stirring the pot: this was what he loved more than anything.

MacCailean Mòr fulminated for several minutes, swearing and raging at the impudence and ingratitude of the lesser clans, before John cut across him, judging that the moment was right to ask insouciantly:

"So, do tell me how your man is? Is he conscious, has he been able to tell you what happened?"

"What? Oh, you mean Ardbreknish? No, he's in a coma, but could come out of it at any time, and when he does, I am going to find out what happened in that room."

"Look, it would also be great if we could meet the night before the Comhairle meeting, so I can talk through my answers to the enquiry. You know how much I value your support. Why don't I take you for dinner at the Soused Herring? Shall we say 8pm?"

Lamont agreed readily and MacCailean Mòr rang off, leaving him dizzy with the opportunities that were opening up. He was also relishing the thrill of this close relationship; MacCailean Mòr's needy reliance on him was a new and welcome development.

The only grit in his oyster was that damned Ardbreknish. How could Allan Stewart have been so casual as to leave him alive? Most unlike him. Nothing that couldn't be rectified though. Although he had better be swift, the last thing he needed was for that little bird to spring back to life and start singing. Pressing the intercom, he asked his assistant to fetch him Allan Stewart and to be quick about it.

38 - VISITING HOURS

It wasn't until the evening that Brighid slid in through the goods entrance round the back of the Infirmary. She had texted her old friend Claire Campbell, who worked there as a nurse, and she'd promised to help get her to the Beaton. She hovered by the back door until Claire came with a spare white coat over her arm. So as not to attract unnecessary attention, Brighid took off her sword and tucked it behind a parlour palm in the corridor, before pulling on the coat and pinning her hair up in an officious manner – plunging a pencil through it for good measure. With a battered folder in her arms and a hassled expression pinned to her face, she looked every inch the plausible nurse. She followed Claire through the building to take a lift to the life support units on the fifth floor. As they left the lift, they walked down a long corridor, coolly passing the two guards outside Ardbreknish's door, before they got to Archie's room. They knocked quietly on the door before entering to find the Beaton sitting up in bed.

Claire didn't stay as she had to get back to her rounds but promised to look in later. It took Archie a few moments to recognise Brighid, but when he finally realised, his broad smile said it all. "Ah what a welcome sight after all these Campbells. How are you? How's everything at Dunderave? Last thing I remember was that the poor old place was on fire."

"Yes, it's not looking its best at the moment," Brighid sighed, "and there is fair chaos elsewhere too. Not only is the Castle half destroyed, but Alexander and Aodhan are dead, the gaming operation was burned down, and Kirstie has disappeared. As you were the last inside the castle, we were hoping you might be able to tell us what happened."

Archie frowned. "It was hard to tell what had happened in the castle, if I'm honest. I was barely in the Red Banner Hall for more than a few seconds, what with the heat and smoke. I do remember seeing two bodies on the far side of the room, presumably Aodhan and Alexander. They must have both been dead already and that big Campbell was lying by the door with his throat cut. I grabbed the only living thing that I could reach, which was Ardbreknish. What has happened to him by the way? He was still just about alive when I got him."

"I think he's still alive, but in a coma. They have him in the room next door. Claire doesn't seem to know whether he will ever recover. I guess he's the one we need to speak to, the one that will have the answers if there are any. Is there anything I can get you to help speed your recovery?"

"No, they are looking after me pretty well. I don't imagine they will keep me here for too long, just a few days while they clear the smoke from my lungs. To be honest, they are being pretty appreciative, I did save one of their own after all."

Brighid and Archie chatted for a while until he seemed to tire. It was getting late; she should really be heading back home. She also didn't want to be caught in Archie's room, there was no saying what the Campbells would do in the current febrile environment.

She leant over and kissed Archie farewell on both cheeks. Then she straightened her white coat and checked her appearance in the mirror. Satisfied, she picked up the folders and left the room, closing the door behind her.

The long corridor was now empty; its lino flooring stretched away, littered with the occasional trolley or chair, but there were no people and certainly no guards. It was a little odd, given the two burly guards that had previously been stood outside Niall's room. Brighid set off towards the stairwell, stopping to have a quick peek through the window of Niall's room, to check he was doing OK. She had no axe to grind with him, even if he could be a pompous prick from time to time.

She peered through the glass in the door and saw a black masked figure standing over Niall's body holding a syringe up to the light. She instantly knew that was no doctor and, before she could stop herself, burst into the room shouting.

The black clad figure turned dropping the syringe on the bed and reaching for the sword strapped to his back. Brighid frantically clutched at the thin air behind her own head, realising too late that her blade was still carefully tucked behind the parlour palm downstairs. She retreated into the far corner of the room, shouting and swearing as the figure rounded the bed and advanced on her. She grabbed a chair, holding it out to try and keep her attacker at bay. The first swipe of his sword chopped off two of its legs, and the second splintered the seat in half, reducing her shield to useless matchwood. She was paralysed with fear, unable to move, watching helplessly as the sword was raised for a third and final time.

At that instant, the door burst inwards, knocking her attacker off his feet. The two Campbells that had been previously been guarding the room tumbled through the door, dirks drawn. The black clad assailant swiftly regained his balance and turned his attention from Brighid to this new threat. The blade of his sword moved in a shadowy blur, whistling through the air as he brought it down across the body of the first of the Campbells. The room rang to the clash of metal, as his edge was caught on the blade of the Campbell's dirk. A skilled parry in the circumstances. But, without a pause, the attacker compassed his sword around the smaller blade and with a backhanded sweep hacked deeply into the Campbell's lower leg, nearly hewing it through above the ankle.

As the first Campbell fell backwards with a scream, his companion pressed home his own attack. The man in black had no time to raise his sword, and instead caught the slash of the Campbell's dirk on the elbow of his sword arm, grunting with pain as he forcefully pushed the blade backwards pinning it across the Campbell's chest. Simultaneously, and with the speed and accuracy of a striking viper, he used his left hand to punch his sgian dubh into the Campbell's right eye socket, killing him instantly.

A dirk clattered across the floor towards Brighid; she grabbed it. The handle was slippery with blood and she briefly struggled to get a firm grip. Just as the attacker finished his demolition of the second guard, she was able to grip it well enough to slash at the back of his left ankle, severing his Achilles tendon. Yelling in pain and surprise, he turned on her and smashed her with the basket hilt of his sword, knocking her across the room and spinning the dirk from her hand.

She lay semiconscious on the floor, the looming black figure zoomed in and out of focus as her eyes struggled to adjust after the blow. The attacker raised his sword to despatch her, when a ghostly pale apparition trailing cables and tubes, rose from the bed behind him. Niall Campbell of Ardbreknish stabbed the syringe into her assailant's neck and depressing the plunger before collapsing backwards out of sight. The man in black scrabbled desperately at the needle, pulling it free before falling to the ground, writhing like a decapitated snake. Without pausing for thought, Brighid kicked the sword out of his hand and plunged her sgian aslaich repeatedly into his chest.

At last he was still; she lay prone across his body, exhausted. After a few moments she raised her eyes to survey the room: the Campbell with the injured leg needed help badly. Staggering to her feet, she pulled the emergency cord, before sinking down on the bed and looking across at Niall. His eyes were open now and despite the tubes up his nose he managed a weak smile while he brought his two hands together in silent applause.

39 - THE MEETING

The warm water of the shower felt good as it massaged and cleansed her body, washing away the blood of both her attacker and her defenders. She wished that she could stay in the shower's warm jets, luxuriating in their wet pummelling. Reluctantly, she turned the chrome lever to stop the flow and return to the real world.

The Infirmary had found her a spare room to wash and change in. Ali from Khan's Highland Supplies had been round to drop off some fresh clothes, all charged to MacCailean Mòr's account. She gratefully pulled them on, glad to be free of the cold congealed blood that was soaked through her own. She pulled a hospital comb through her long blond hair, wincing as its tightly packed teeth yanked and tugged at the many knots. Finally satisfied, she tied it back in a ponytail and dared to look in a mirror.

There was a knock at the door and an orderly came in with a tray of tea and biscuits. Brighid noted that there were two cups. As if to answer the question that was slowly forming in her mind, the door swung open again and MacCailean Mòr entered. He was wrapped in a great kilt of fine Campbell tartan, so dark it was almost black, with a claymore on one hip and a dirk on the other. He looked imposing: handsome but intimidating.

She didn't know what to do. Should she run? Get away from this man who had just ordered the killing of her Chief and assaulted her friends? Could she reach her sgian aslaich? Wouldn't that be sweet revenge. But she was no Kirstie. She was also exhausted from the earlier fight: he would be too strong for her. Instead she resolved to be patient, to see if another, better, opportunity might arise.

He motioned for her to sit, and she perched on the edge of the bed thinking about what she could or should say. He shook her hand, smiling warmly and thanking her for her bravery. His eyes were grey, crinkle cut with laughter lines round the corners, belying his supposedly dour image. He sat a respectful distance and gently asked about the attack: How was she feeling? Was she injured? What could he do to help? He was warm and compassionate, genuine concern in his voice and eyes. He listened attentively as she recounted the struggle with the black clad foe.

The stress of the day suddenly got to her and she found herself monologing, a torrent of words pouring out: how scared she had been; the single-minded aggression of the attacker; his strength and skill; her rescuers, her poor rescuers; how sorry she was; could she have done more? Her anger at who could have sent such an assassin; how wrong it was to murder a man in cold blood; unconscious and defenceless. She was shaking, her voice breaking. Her chest felt so tight; she couldn't breathe, the room swam.

He put his arms around her and gave her a hug. He said nothing, just held her. Minutes passed; the room silent except for her gasping sobs. Bit by bit she regained control; the outpouring of her emotions slowed; she filled her lungs: calm returned. He poured her another cup of tea.

She asked after the fate of the two Campbells that had saved her life with their timely, if unfortunate, intervention. The one who had been struck in the eye had died instantaneously, the thrust going deep into his brain. His colleague had been saved, despite the loss of blood, but was unlikely to ever dance the Ghillie Callum again.

After sharing their mutual amazement at the fortuitous timing of Niall's return to consciousness and speculating over the nature of what had been in the syringe, MacCailean Mòr asked if she felt strong enough to accompany him to the morgue to try and identify the assassin. Nodding, she took a final mouthful of her tea, before rising shakily to her feet. MacCailean Mòr held out his arm to support her, and she graciously accepted his help. Despite herself, she was warming to him. She didn't know whether it was the stress of the situation or the empathy he had shown. But was it just that? Or was it because the reality of the man was so different from the myth?

40 - PARTING

Gillespie woke slowly, drifting in and out of sleep. The warmth and comfort of the bed was all enveloping and seductive, his conscious mind was reluctant to surface. Finally, he opened his eyes and spent several minutes staring at the artex ceiling, exploring the galaxies contained in its whorls, before he summoned the energy to rise. The room was small and tucked under the eaves of Don MacArthur's cottage. He had to crouch until he got into the middle of the room to avoid banging his head. Popping the blind on the window he rubbed the stubble on his face and looked for a while at the rain lashing the glen outside. Opening the bedroom door, he went in search of a bathroom; he was dying for a shit, a shower and a shave, in that order. He walked past a semi-open door: that must be where Charlie and Nin were staying, judging by the full-bore snoring.

Later, as he dressed, he went over his clothes carefully to check for damage. They had held up remarkably well, considering their escapades. He felt somewhat revived as he belted the kilt around his midriff and pulled on his black combat jacket; the clothes, which had seemed alien only a few days ago, were already becoming well-worn friends: part of him and his story.

Feeling ready to face the world, he picked up his two-handed sword and turned it over in his hands. He pulled it half out of its scabbard, mostly to admire the running wolf on the blade and to run his thumb over its edge to reassure himself of its razor-sharp threat, but also to ensure it wasn't wet. The last thing he wanted was to ruin it with rust marks when he had only had it a few days; he dreaded to think what Fiona or Mara would do to him if he allowed that to happen. Satisfied all was well, he pushed it back into the carbon fibre scabbard with a reassuring snick and headed downstairs in search of something to eat.

He was sat at the kitchen table looking out of the plate glass window when Don's clapped out Kat puffed into sight and ground to a halt outside the front door. Don's cheeks were flushed, it had clearly been a long lunch. Swaying slightly as he leaned round to scoop up his fiddle, Don meandered his way across the yard and into the house. Having joined Gillespie in the kitchen, Don eyed the big brown teapot that was still steaming with a fresh brew and poured himself a cup, heaping three teaspoons of sugar into it for good measure and a hefty slug of milk. With his body anchored to a chair he visibly relaxed and in between humming some indeterminate tunes asked Gillespie about his perspective on everything that had been happening.

After ten minutes of chatting, Don looked at his watch and asked: "Whae's that lazy bastard cousin a mine? Its near three o'clock in the afternoon and he's still lying a bed. I had better roust him out."

"Rather you than me," said Gillespie. "He can sleep through pretty much anything as far as I've seen."

"Ok, well, let see how yon bastard likes the sound of my pipes."

"I didn't know you played the pipes too?"

"Ach well, strictly speaking I don't. But I do have a set hereabouts that I won in a game of cards, and I find they work wonders in this kind of situation."

Don disappeared upstairs. His arrival at Nin and Charlie's bedroom was heralded by the most god-awful ear-splitting wail, two heavy thumps, various shouts and curses and finally silence.

Don returned to the kitchen with a smile on his face. He put the mothy looking pipes on the table and poured himself another cup of tea. "Aye, that's done it; they'll be along in a moment."

Sure enough, Charlie and Nin arrived shortly thereafter, in various states of undress, pulling on garments and looking grumpy. Charlie's pale as milk body had been coloured in with a palette of livid bruises. They looked pretty uncomfortable: not that he showed it. Nin was, as usual, busy spiking his hair, in between reaching for the tea and checking what food was on offer.

Once relative peace had been achieved around the table, with loaded plates and steaming mugs, Don began to tell them about what he had found out at the Griogaraich's Lament.

"So, I walked in there and gets talking to a bunch a Campbell reprobates, nice lads for the most part. They had just come off a night tour sweeping the Coire Laoigh between Beinn Lui and Beinn Oss all the way up along the Cononish to Tyndrum, thinking that youse bastards had gone that way round. I can tell you that they were not best pleased that they didn't find nothing after all their yomping. I expect yon would have a fair few more bruises to add to that fine collection," he nodded at Charlie, "if they had laid their hands on ye."

Charlie rubbed his side, as if vicariously experiencing their blows and kicks.

"They were heading back to Inveraray with empty hands, and I don't think they are going to come along my glen for now. But whose to ken what will happen when MacCailean Mòr learns that his trap has been slipped. Mind you, maybe they don't give too much of a rat's arse about ye, after all they have everything else they wanted."

"So, do we stick with the plan?" Asked Charlie, through a mouthful of hot buttered toast.

"Well I don't have a better idea, and it sounds like staying anywhere near here for the time being is going to be difficult. I still don't have any signal on my phone. They can't have reactivated the Clan network. How about you?" Nin asked, turning to Gillespie.

"I have signal as I am roaming here on Cruachan.net. But I don't have any messages, not that I imagine anyone would really be trying to reach me.

Should I try calling Brighid or Iain?" Gillespie asked, balancing the phone in his hand, finger poised over the screen.

"No!" came the simultaneous cry from both Nin and Charlie: "They'll be monitoring all calls to the Clan network, attempted or connected. If they pick up your number they might track you through the chip in your phone. No, it's better that we stay dark for as long as possible. When we get to Kindrochit we can try through the Farquharson network, they are bound to have someone who can help."

Gillespie swiped open his phone anyway and saw that he had one unopened message - from Kirstie! Competing thoughts raced through his mind, each tumbling over the other in their haste – How could Kirstie be messaging him? What did it say? Where was she? Was she OK? He flicked it open. All it said was:

username: Kirstie.macnachtan@blacktower.net

password: c@mpbellsareCunt5.

Presumably those were the administrator access codes that she had sent him from the hillside last night, although what he was expected to do with them he knew not. There was also a picture file attached with the title: *Follow the rat to the backdoor.* He clicked on the file, it was a picture showed an old photograph of a shinty team standing on a crowded pitch, all knobbly knees and bad haircuts surrounded by a crowd of people. Slightly mystified, he closed the file and returned the phone to his pocket.

Don put down his cup and addressed Nin in his apologetic voice: "Aye, well, you had better move on from here, right enough. With the greatest respect to our honourable shared lineage, I can't be caught helping fugitives from MacCailean Mòr, not seeing as how I'm living here in his backyard."

"Fair enough," said Nin. "Thank you for your open door. We were in a pretty dire condition when we arrived, and the warmth of your hospitality has been much appreciated. We'll pack our things and get on the move. If we leave soon we should be able to get as far as the edge of Rannoch Moor before dark. We can see how far we can get skirting round it, but at some point we need to get north of the Tummel."

"Aye, well, you would be wise to give the Black Wood a wide berth, it sounds almost more dangerous than the Moor itself these days." Added Don. "As for where all the Griogaraich are hiding, it's hard to say, they are elusive buggers and tend to shift about."

They gathered their gear, thanking Don for the thermos flask of tea that he pushed on them as they left the door. As they stowed the supplies in the various cubbyholes and compartments around the Kat's interior, Nin peered through the steering wheel at the fuel gauge.

"Well it's not going to get us to Kindrochit, that's for sure, but it may get us to Pitlochry or somewhere we can fill up away from all these Campbells. Anyway, there is no helping it."

Don stood on the front step watching as they made their preparations. After a few minutes, Gillespie realised that his eyes were following him around and seemed to be drawn to the sword on his back. Seeing that his interest had been registered, Don asked: "Was that Malc MacNachtan's sword you have there? How did you come by it – d'ye kill him for it?"

"My God, no!" Gillespie was horrified at the thought. "I was given it by his widow."

"Well, that was quite the gift. That's a Passau blade, you know. We've been using their steel for near on a thousand years. Germans know steel and the wolf of Passau knows it best. D'ye know how to use it? Or are ye hoping that your opponents are just going to run away as soon as ye pull it out of the scabbard?"

"To be honest, I haven't a clue. I stopped fencing with a claymore once I had done my GCSE, and I never did any studying with a weapon like this. I am only really carrying it to try and blend in."

"Aye, well that's the first as I've heard of any cunt blending in wi'a two-hander, right enough. Here, give it us and I will show ye."

As Nin and Charlie were finishing sorting out the vehicle, Gillespie pulled the sword from its scabbard and handed it to Don. As Don took it in his hands he seemed to grow six inches taller and ten years younger. He flourished the blade, feeling its weight and balance, nodding approvingly. He cut a devastating figure of eight in the air, the huge blade a mesmeric blur; it seemed to encompass all points of attack simultaneously.

"Since ye don't know what the fuck ye doing, I suggest you start with a low guard." At this Don held the sword with the pommel just in front of his crotch and with the blade pointing up and across his body towards Gillespie's right eye. "That way you can parry, poke or compass either way into a cut. If you want to show them you know ye moves, then bring the pommel up to your right shoulder with the blade behind ye, that gives ye tremendous cut potential in riposte, and it hides your reach, makes them bastards wary. As they should be." He smoothly moved the blade from the first to the second guard, dramatically changing the potential approach for an attacker. And with that, he handed the blade to Gillespie who clumsily tried to recreate Don's elegant moves.

"Remember, that's a slashing weapon. Ye just hack the fuck out of ye opponent, don't try and be too clever, just hack. Right? And be a ferocious cunt, 'cos ye enemy may well just drop of a heart attack. Most folks these days never get to fight one, so they may just piss themselves and run away. Ha, ha, think that was always big Malc's strategy. I'll miss that bastard too, right enough."

Nin came over to watch the impromptu lesson. Grinning, he said to Gillespie, "You should come back when things have calmed down and have some proper lessons from Don, he was once the Gaelic and World Champion at two handed."

"Aye, but that was long ago," Don laughed. "And there weren't too many cunts as could wield one, not like an epee or sabre."

Gillespie thanked him, feeling more inadequate than ever. He sheathed the sword and climbed in the front seat, ready for departure. Charlie was starting in the back, and Nin was at the wheel. With a belch and a clatter, the Kat pulled out of the drive and turned down the track heading east.

41 - RANNOCH MOOR

As the Kat made its way down the trough of the glen, sandwiched between the high hills on either side and the meandering Orchy in the middle, Gillespie turned his thoughts to the next leg of their journey. Of course, he had heard of Rannoch Moor, it was infamous in Gaelic circles as the debatable land that lay in the centre of the highlands between the spheres of influence of the eastern and western magnates. This was where the writ of MacCailean Mòr petered out and before that of Atholl or Gordon started.

It was legendary as an inhospitable bog, open and weather lashed, with no farmland and few houses. It had little of value if you didn't count freedom, the freedom to do whatever you pleased as long as you had the strength to do it. Since time immemorial, and certainly since long before the Republic, so called broken men, those that had been expelled from their clans, would come to hide out among like-minded rogues. This too was where most of the Griogaraich had settled.

The MacGregor Clan, or the Griogaraich as they were known, had long been feared by their neighbours. The media was always full of tales of luxury cars being stolen to order and shipped to their clients in the Balkans or South America, or the doings of their mercenary units in far flung parts of Africa. Any unclaimed act of wickedness was generally laid at their door, whether they had anything to do with it or not.

While Gillespie was sure that the stories contained more than a grain of truth, he was also sure that they were amplified to sell newspapers and supermarket novels and scare children into good behaviour. But that hadn't stopped the MacGregors from being excluded and shunned by much of Gaelic society. Over many centuries they had been expelled from most of their ancestral lands or forced to join other clans, but Rannoch Moor was their last redoubt and few risked entering there lightly. This den of iniquity was what they had to cross to have a chance of reaching Kindrochit and the relative safety of Charlie's family.

Shadowing the course of the Orchy River, they bounced and wound their way down the glen to its natural conclusion. Here it was dissected by the other major Wade that ran north east from the Arrochar border crossing, and plugged by the mighty pyramid of Beinn Dorain, whose bulky lower slopes lay ahead of them.

Nin shouted details of their route to Gillespie over the roar of the engine: "We are going to go left at the Wade," at which he spat out of the window, "and follow the bottom of the hill round. We don't want to get drawn across the middle of the moor if we can avoid it. Instead, we are going to skirt the southern corner. We need to hug the side of Beinn Dorain as it pushes the road north to Loch Tulla. Then we will come off the road and follow the Water of Tulla all the way to Bridge of Gaur, where we'll cross the Tummel. It's too dangerous to cross any further east until you are pretty much over the border. Gaur is where the danger really lies, as any self-respecting Griogaraich will have keen eyes on that crossing point. Not that I imagine they get many passing strangers, all things considered. There's an Inn there where we can probably get something to eat and somewhere to rest, but it won't be luxurious, and we'll need to get there without arousing too much attention. On the other side of the Tummel there is a minor Wade that will take us to Pitlochry. From there, we should be safe to travel the rest of the way by Wade to Kindrochit."

Gillespie nodded, it made no odds to him; he was just being swept along, wherever the grinding wheels took him.

Having negotiated the Wade without incident, Nin stopped at a suitably discrete spot to open the thermos, have a smoke and swap places with Charlie, who was already feeling the effect of the cold. The next stage of the journey was risky, they all knew that, but there was no alternative. Charlie puffed at the roll-up while carefully studying the bleak open bog ahead of them, as if half expecting a ragged bunch of MacGregors to appear at any moment.

Darkness was falling and although there was a rough track that followed the Tulla it was slow going, full of muddy hollows filled with freezing water. Gillespie lost count of the times that he and Nin had to get out and help push the Kat out of a deep piece of bog or up a steep bank. Each time he got out of the relative warmth of the Kat to help push, his heart sank. The surface of the moor was soon crisp with frost and the pools and puddles that made up most of its surface had a thin covering of cat ice that made the inevitable plunge into the freezing water below even more chilling. His legs were frozen and although the kilt kept his core surprisingly warm, it was still wet and deeply unpleasant. He had lost the feeling in his fingers which he stuffed under his armpits, while he attempted to keep blood moving in his toes by wriggling them relentlessly.

Eventually, the track improved somewhat, and they made their way through mile after mile of conifer plantation, following forestry tracks that wound their way through the dark impenetrable pines. Within the forestry they were able to use their headlights more freely, without the worry that they might attract unwelcome eyes. Charlie had discovered that Gillespie's phone still had sufficient signal to use the GPS system, and although there was the occasional wrong turn mostly they were making reasonable progress. Finally, the plantation started to thin, and Charlie pulled over so that they could survey what lay ahead.

From the edge of the forestry they had a good perspective out across the moor to the north and east. Charlie explained that the flattest and boggiest parts of the moor were to their north west, and they had escaped the most impenetrable part. He pointed out the track as it wove its way down through dull brown open ground between the two hills that were the gateway to the head of Loch Rannoch and the Bridge of Gaur. They could see the village lying beyond, if you could call it a village: just a few houses scattered around the loch head.

Dawn was starting to lighten the sky and Nin and Charlie shared the binoculars, sweeping the glen to check for any movement. Finally convinced that the coast was clear, they got back in the Kat and set off, Nin at the wheel. Gillespie's kidneys took another hard pounding as they came down into the village, the ruts and bumps of the track were frozen solid, and the Kat's tyres transferred the impact of every ridge and hole through his entire body.

It started to sleet; the prospect of a warm room and a bed became almost unimaginably desirable to Gillespie. He wasn't sure if he had ever been so cold for so long before. As he drove, Nin was concentrating hard to avoid the worst of the holes in the track, His nose and cheekbones were raw with cold; tiny purple tendrils spreading across the skin of his pale face, as his body struggled to deliver heat and oxygen to its extremities. In the back, Charlie was stamping his feet to keep the blood flowing and swearing freely to himself. After 16 hours of these relentless cold and wet conditions they needed shelter, whatever the potential risks.

They slowly made their way between dark and shuttered houses coming at last to a rather surprising Scandinavian-style wood clad building. It had a rough, hand-painted sign swinging in the wind announcing it as the Inn At Gaur. For all the clean modern lines of the building, the silver grey of the wood panels, streaked darker by the rain and sleet, only accentuated the gloomy feel of the hamlet. The antithesis of vibrant it felt abandoned, as if all the energy had been sucked down into the bog.

Nin was uncharacteristically reticent about ringing the bell. It was still early, barely 8am, and they had little way of knowing if the inn keep was awake yet. But the biting cold brooked no hesitation and having discretely parked the Kat, Nin pressed the entry buzzer robustly. A small camera above their heads suddenly turned and stared in their direction. Then there was a clumping of feet and a rather tuneless whistle, before the door opened, and they fell inwards into the warm and dry.

42 - THE INN AT GAUR

As they settled in the bar, gratefully sipping tea and whisky, Gillespie looked around the room. It was a rather unfortunate collision of low-key Scandinavian minimalist architecture and pure English pub vernacular, horse brasses, swirly red carpet, flouncy light shades, well used dart board and large flat screen TV. In this extremely remote and dangerous location this seemed beyond incongruous. He began to wonder if it was real or just a hallucination.

Having introduced himself as John Smith, the inn keep said to them in a broad Lancashire accent: "Right, now that you're all settled, would you mind telling me who you are and what you're doing here? It is not every day that I get woken by a bunch of half frozen Gaels at 8 of the morning. Actually, it happens more often than you might think, but it's still not an everyday occurrence."

Nin and Charlie exchanged a quick glance before Charlie replied "I stay over by Kindrochit, and we're on our way home. There was a spot of bother on the way and we were keen to avoid the main road, if you get my meaning."

"Yes, I am sure I do. You don't need to tell me more; in these parts we understand the value of discretion." John Smith stifled a yawn with the back of one of his ham-like hands.

"If you don't mind me asking," interrupted Nin, clearly unable to restrain himself any longer. "How on earth did an Englishman end up running the Inn At Gaur. You don't look like the type to be a natural bedfellow of the Griogaraich and their friends. For a start you are a Sassenach and there can't be too many of them here in Rannoch."

"Oh, I don't know," John Smith replied. "You'd be surprised." Then leaning in, as if to let them in on a secret, he said in his most conspiratorial whisper: "Maybe it's because I'm a Sassenach that they are happy for me to be here. After all, we weren't the bastards that put a price on their heads and chased them down with hunting dogs, were we now? And I am sure that it was a Scottish King that proscribed the MacGregor name for 150 years on pain of death or banishment. And I am pretty sure that we weren't the ones that took all their land away and sold them into indentured slavery in the colonies. Nope, that wasn't us. So, us Sassenachs actually get along just fine with the Griogaraich, it's you bastards that need to watch yourselves." At which he roared with laughter and clapped Nin and Charlie on the back, spilling their tea and eliciting an exchange of sheepish grins between them.

John Smith was a short but portly man, his belly stretched before him like a prow, reflecting its owner's love of food and beer. His wispy hair was starting to thin and go grey on top, and as if to compensate it was being allowed to hang in a sweep at the back. His red cheeked face was jovial and framed two dark brown eyes that peered out behind a pair of glasses as if through grubby net curtains. His bulbous nose was a livid purple, swollen and pitted, a living record of a licentious life. His glorious laugh, which filled the room, revealed teeth that had not troubled any dentist for some years.

"Anyway, I almost forgot to ask what Clan you are," said John eying them carefully. "These things matter round here, as you might imagine. So, let me see now." He adjusted the glasses that hung round his neck on a lanyard to inspect their tartan more closely. "Campbells, hhhmmm, that may be problematic. Not the most popular Clan here on the moor, I must say."

Nin and Charlie looked at each other aghast, before realising that they were still wearing the jackets that they had captured from the Campbells by the Fyne and they immediately stripped off that layer to reveal the tartan that lay beneath, self-consciously holding up the panels to ease John Smith's identification.

"Ah so it's two MacNachtans and a Farquharson is it now. That should be OK, don't think there is too much bad blood there that I am aware of - at least not in the last few centuries." At which he laughed his belly laugh again, clumping them each on the shoulder for good measure.

"Well, I can see why you don't want to go around by the main road: impersonating another Clan is a serious matter. As a Sassenach I don't think I know what your Canun says about that, but I am sure it wouldn't be comfortable or pleasant. Now, I don't really mind what it is that you have done, as long as you keep your blades sheathed and your bill paid, but there are those round here that might get a little over-excited if they saw some Campbell tartan. So, I would be cautious about flaunting that too widely. Now, can I get you something to eat to go with that fine cup of tea?"

The ravenous response that his question elicited produced another deep rolling laugh and having taken their prodigious order, he disappeared off to the kitchen.

Soon they had demolished everything that John had to offer them, and they asked about renting some rooms for a bit of rest. Charlie was for getting back on the road by midday to have some hope of reaching Kindrochit by nightfall and Nin and Gillespie were in no mood to disagree. After two nights on the hill, sleeping in a bed for a full eight hours that night was suddenly a very attractive proposition. John showed them up the stairs to the rooms, raising an eyebrow at Nin and Charlie as they settled in together, but saying nothing. The rooms were spartan but warm, and Gillespie's eyes barely had time to take it all in before he fell asleep, fully dressed.

Gillespie felt as though his eyes had barely closed when a rough hand started shaking him to get up. He bitterly resented it and tried to snuggle back under the duvet. He imagined himself back home in his draughty bedroom in Antrim, where the act of rising was always carefully premeditated to require the shortest possible time between bed and clothes. But the shaking was persistent and eventually could be ignored no longer. With a final "what the fuck, you bastard!" He lifted his head off the bed and found himself staring down the deep fullered blade of a claymore. At the other end of the sword, his face somewhat obscured by its basket, was a skinny shaven-headed man with a long single topknot that was braided in a plait and which hung down around his face.

"Easy now, tiger. No sudden moves." The stranger said, keeping the blade very still and pointed at Gillespie's left eye. With his free hand he pulled the duvet slowly off Gillespie to check that he had no weapons hidden under the covers. "Okay, now I want you to put your hands on your head and stand up very slowly. If I see the merest flinch I will cut you a new smile from ear to ear. Raise your right index finger if you understand."

Gillespie raised his finger and slowly swung his legs over the edge of the bed and stood up. In the limited space it was hard for him to pass the man without getting very close. His hard, pale eyes bored into Gillespie, as if daring him to try and make a move. But Gillespie was not about to do anything foolish and meekly passed him, going out into the corridor. The man scooped up Gillespie's two hander, giving it an admiring glance as he did so, and prodded Gillespie ahead of him down the stairs and back through the door to the bar. Charlie and Nin were already there, both had been bound with cable ties and sat glumly looking at Gillespie. At least it did not look as though they had been harmed, yet.

The bar was now filled with a rag tag bunch of cut throats and desperados of all shapes and sizes: tall, short, fat and thin, both men and women. The only characteristic that they shared was a haggard confidence. They were joking and laughing while they drank their coffee and beer, casting the occasional glance over at the captives but not really paying them much mind. Assorted weapons, both traditional and modern, were scattered on tables and propped against chairs. Over by the dart board a group were throwing knives at appointed numbers and betting on the outcome of each throw with much ribald laugher.

The skinny man with the shaved head put his sword point down and told Gillespie to hold his wrists forward. He then bound them together with a cable tie, firmly but not too tightly, and sat him down next to Nin and Charlie. They carefully looked him over, as if to check that he still had all his arms and legs.

John Smith was leaning on the bar talking to one of the caterans, a wild looking Indian man with thick matted hair tied up in a ragged bun, a bristling moustache and red rimmed black eyes which burned like coals. John Smith and he were sharing a rather intense joke, and John's easy laugh reverberated around the room at the punchline. Gillespie noted that the Indian man carried no tartan and as he looked round the room many of the others didn't either. Those that did mostly carried the nine green squares on a red ground with a white stripe that was immediately identifiable as MacGregor. Gillespie's mouth went dry. These were the Griogaraich, the most feared and loathed collection of thieves and murderers in all of the Republic, or the Kingdom for that matter.

Once his shock had subsided, he nudged Nin, "What's going to happen? What'll they do with us?"

Nin shrugged, "Depends on their mood. If we're lucky, they might just let us go. If we are unlucky, they might hold us hostage for ransom or rape us each in turn before cutting our throats. Whatever you do, don't say more than you need to."

At that moment, a slight man of medium height came towards them. Gillespie had never seen anyone so striking, he was handsome with an almost beatific cast to his cleanshaven face. His short and neat hair was carefully brushed and very dark, as were his thick, neatly trimmed eyebrows and long eyelashes, and these contrasted with his pale skin and limpid blue eyes. His face had an extraordinary, indistinct and vaporous quality, as if his features moved in smoke and shadow. His face was one that you struggled to remember clearly unless you held it in your gaze; if Gillespie looked away, even for a moment, then it immediately dissolved in his mind's eye, despite his best efforts.

The Griogaraich's manner was surprisingly poised and his delicate hands were well manicured. He had no bulging biceps to flaunt, but his spare physique had the latent energy of a coiled spring: Gillespie found it far more intimidating. Unlike the ragged and dirty clothes that most of his companions wore, his were largely clean and well pressed, each pleat of his kilt hanging sharp. In a rough and god forsaken place like Rannoch this evoked its own power. Gillespie was not surprised to see that his right arm carried the nine green squares on red that identified him as a MacGregor and not just a random broken man.

The Griogaraich was joined by the man with the braided plait and a thick set black woman, who was older than the others and had a battle-hardened calmness about her. They pulled up some chairs and sat looking at their captives. The dark-haired man, who had the bearing of their leader, drew his sgian dubh which he waggled at them as he leant forward:

"What do we have here, I wonder? John over there," at which he gestured with his sgian dubh at John Smith by the bar, "tells me that you arrived first thing this morning dressed in Campbell tartan, but that you shed that skin soon enough and now profess to be MacNachtans and a Farquharson of all things. MacNachtans are usually as rare as unicorns in Rannoch aren't they Sal?" He asked of the woman, who nodded. "And now we have two all at the same time. Very unusual I would say. And as for the Farquharson, well – I don't suppose you are related to Garaidh Farquharson are you by any chance?" At which he put the blade in Charlie's face, checking for any reaction. "No? Oh, that's a shame. Because if you were, I would have to cut your cock off and shove it so far down your throat you'd piss blood out of your arse."

At this vicious change of tone he studied their faces closely, before returning his attention to shaving the cuticles of his nails with the dagger's point. "So, tell me Sal, how do we know that these here gentlemen are telling us the truth and that they aren't Campbells in disguise? Or Murrays for that matter sent to hunt us down?"

The skinny man with the plait said: "maybe we should carve us off a slice – if it tastes of bacon then we will know we have caught us some Campbells." Now it was his turn to hold a dagger to Charlie's face, which went an even whiter shade of pale than usual.

"Honestly, listen to the pair of you," said Sal. "You'll have them believing all the Rannoch stories soon. Here, give me that." And she grabbed the man with the plait's knife and approached Ninian who tried to back away from the advancing blade. She traced the point slowly down his Adam's apple leaving the finest red line in its wake, before laughing at his widened eyes and slicing off one and then another button off his tunic. Reaching down, she then pulled the fabric off his right shoulder revealing the indigo silhouette of the black tower tattoo. A similar operation was performed on Charlie, revealing his sword bearing lion and finally on Gillespie, who aroused some consternation due to his bare milky white shoulder.

"How can you be a MacNachtan if you don't carry the mark of the black tower?" Sal asked, incredulously.

"Believe me, it's complicated." Gillespie said, and before he could add anything further, Nin jumped in. "Although he's Clan, he's really from across the water in Northern Ireland. We kidnapped him from his home in Antrim and brought him to Dunderave under the orders of our last Chief. It was a Clan thing; you know how it is sometimes."

"Aye, as a matter of fact I do," replied the dark-haired man. "All those Chiefs sending you on their silly errands hither and yon, and you clannish sheep meekly doing their bidding without a braincell or bollock between you. That rubbish won't wash here; we are the Griogaraich, and we don't hold with Chiefs. We choose the freedom to do as we please. Anyway, we have had a long day and a longer night, and I don't have the time, energy or inclination to deal with you. But you would do well to mind your own business and keep out of our way. Where are you headed next? I think it only fair to warn you that we're just back from a little altercation over the border at Dunkeld, so it might be a little hot if you are going east."

Without waiting for a reply, the man checked his watch and seeing it was coming up to midday shouted to John Smith: "Turn on the TV, I want to check the news." As John switched on the large TV, the attention of the room focused on the screen in the corner. Having eventually found the BBC news channel, John turned up the sound, so they could hear the concerned looking newsreader's voice:

"Another dark day for relations between the Kingdom of Great Britain and Northern Ireland and the Gaelic Republic as a group of unidentified clansmen terrified the sleepy border town of Dunkeld early this morning. Just as residents were waking up to start their day, a Gaelic warband, which is believed to be led by none other than the infamous Alasdair MacGregor, swept through the town making for the border. This followed a daring raid carried out the previous night on King's Brand Pharmaceuticals in Dundee, where security staff and production managers were bound and gagged while the Gaels ransacked the facility. It is believed they were searching for specific high value medications including Hydromorphone Hydrochloride, a painkiller that is literally worth its weight in gold. It is understood an undisclosed volume of the drug was stolen by the band, which then made for the border crossing."

The camera now swept a heavily fortified border post with guards and police milling about looking earnest. This elicited a few jeers from the occupants of the room, many of whom made a ring with their index fingers and thumbs and waved their wrists at the screen, before being hushed by their leader.

The newsreader continued; "Several prominent local residents were taken from their homes and used as human shields as the warband forced their way through the border crossing. We are relieved to be able to report that all were subsequently released unharmed and that no fatalities have been reported. This is the second major incident in recent weeks between out of control Republic Clan factions and Kingdom forces. A formal complaint has been issued by First Minister Balfour in the strongest terms to the Parliament of the Gaelic Republic in Oban."

"In response, just a few minutes ago, the following statement was released: The Riaghaltas of the Gaelic Republic is shocked by the news of this appalling act and deplore in the strongest possible terms the actions of this renegade band. We would like to convey our deepest sympathies to those that have been affected and are committed to bringing these criminals to justice at the earliest opportunity. The Riaghaltas can confirm that the Black Watch have now been deployed from their Ruthven Barracks and are on the trail of the perpetrators."

"Aye, aye, whatever," said Alasdair MacGregor, while running his fingers through his neat dark hair, smoothing and shaping it. "The bastards will need to find us first."

43 - THE CASTLE

Brighid had never been inside Inveraray Castle before. Of course, she was familiar with its four towers with their witch's hat roofs and brooding black stone walls, but she had never gone inside. Not many MacNachtans had, at least not willingly. The seat of the Campbells for many, many hundreds of years, it had always stood as a challenge to MacNachtan tenure; a challenge which over centuries had turned into a threat and then into the reality of expropriation. She looked out of the vehicle at the dour stone walls and shuddered, what would her ancestors make of her walking through that door with none other than MacCailean Mòr?

MacCailean Mòr swung the 4x4 in a large arc, crunching over the sweep of gravel so that Brighid's door was opposite the port cochere. A much betartaned flunkey rushed out with an umbrella to shelter her from the pouring rain as she took the few steps to the front door. MacCailean Mòr then ushered her into the main atrium, effusively welcoming her to his home.

While Brighid was no stranger to castles, having spent much of her life in and around Dunderave, even she had to admit that this was on a different and more opulent scale. The atrium was double height, festooned with old Clan weapons from King Charlie's time and before, and these had been artfully arranged in geometric patterns on the walls. Most noticeable to her was the relative warmth inside. Dunderave was many things, but warm it wasn't, even in the height of summer. Here the warmth reflected the obvious wealth that surrounded her but spoke more clearly than any Gobelin tapestry.

MacCailean Mòr wove a path through several rooms and up a flight of stairs to a cosy booklined sitting room, complete with an overstuffed chesterfield sofa and range of well-worn armchairs. Turfing out an indignant spaniel that was sitting in the most comfortable looking chair, MacCailean Mòr invited her to sit while he summoned tea and his steward.

Duncan Campbell arrived shortly after the tea and had to clear his throat several times, with ever increasing volume, to catch the attention of MacCailean Mòr who was busy pointing out interesting features of the view to Brighid.

"Will you be my guest here tonight? I would feel terrible if you had to go back down the glen to an empty house after everything you have been through. Why not spend the night and have supper with me? I am sure I can get the cook to rustle us up something edible. And in terms of bedrooms, as you might imagine, there's no shortage."

Brighid thought about this carefully, many of her fellow Clan members would be aghast at the idea of her staying the night in Inveraray Castle, let alone having dinner with their inveterate enemy. But over many years she had developed a sixth sense to know when men were attracted to her, and MacCailean Mòr, with his twinkly eyed chat and empathetic concern, was ringing all her alarm bells. Normally, she would have run a mile or at least fired a shot across his bows, but against her natural instincts, and certainly against the collective prejudices of her ancestors and fellow Clan, she paused. Having spoken with MacCailean Mòr at some length it was now clear to her that he had not intended for the assault to end the way it had, and he certainly had nothing to do with Alexander's death. He nonetheless held the Clan and their future in his grip. Fortune had cast him in her path, and the incident in the Infirmary had created a connection between them. She could feel his attraction and that could prove a very useful lever of influence, something that the Clan needed now more than ever. But beyond altruism, she also had to admit that she was attracted to him, and that wasn't a feeling she had had for a long time. She had grown up with her fellow clansmen all her life, they had no secrets to hide, the good and the bad, all was known. That dull security and predictability was what she had always run away from. She suddenly felt like being a little reckless and not overthinking this moment and resolved to at least stay for supper, relinquishing herself to the flow of events.

Dark had now fallen and MacCailean Mòr drew the curtains and started to fuss over the fire. It was recalcitrant, refusing to light, and with every wasted match his frustration rose. Brighid tutted and calmly pushed him aside. Crouching at the grate, she quickly reassembled the kindling into a little tepee with a twist of paper at its heart and, having relieved him of the box of matches, struck one to light it. The flames caught first on the paper, and then slowly licked up the split sections of kindling, growing in intensity, the yellow tongues soon chasing round the boar's head on the cast iron fireback. Before long, the fire was roaring away and they both stood watching it, silently transfixed: transported. The spell wrought by the infinite patterns of the flames, which have ever hypnotised and captivated humans since those first sparks millennia ago, still held true and wove its magic around them.

She could not remember if it was she who kissed him or he that kissed her first, but after that touch of his lips on hers everything else fell away. The world shrank to that moment, that hot wet kiss, the press of his tongue, the caress of his hands that traced up her back. He tasted sweet, like a distant memory of strawberries, but as she kissed his neck she also smelt animalic: dark, dangerous and alluring. Her pulse raced as he cupped her left breast, squeezing her nipple through the fabric of her top, massaging her with his palm. She pushed him back on the sofa, sliding his kilt up and fondling his heavy balls between thumb and forefinger, causing his cock to jump and stiffen for her kiss. He slid a hand up between her legs, teasing an entry, his fingers questing and probing, her body pulsated. They consummated that moment with an urgent coupling, both caught in the bonds of the other's desire, succumbing to and embracing it as if it was the only thing left in the world that mattered.

44 - ARDBREKNISH

Brighid could not remember when she had slept better. Whether it had been the quality of the bed and the down duvet, the near-death experience of the previous day, or the several hours of vigorous love making, she could not say. As she opened her eyes, she gazed on MacCailean Mòr's profile across the pillows. He was at least ten years older than her, not quite middle aged, but on the way. His rather dull brown hair was beginning to grey at the temples, and it was roughly parted, leaving a floppy fringe across his forehead, giving him a more boyish look than he deserved. His roman nose was distinguished, and he had so far managed to hold on to the cheekbones that nature had given him. His trim physique was not that of a hard, musclebound fighter, but that did not bother her, in fact she was rather attracted to its hint of softness.

MacCailean Mòr seemed different though. She had felt that urgency in him as he had held her, that need for someone: someone to hold, to caress, to kiss, and to fuck and be fucked by. As if he had been too alone since his wife had died. For her own reasons, she had felt that emptiness, exacerbated by the clumsy advances and fumblings of her many suitors. So, she felt good as she swung her legs out of bed and with a smile on her face she pottered around the unfeasibly large bedroom, opening doors trying to find the bathroom.

MacCailean Mòr woke as she was drying her hair and he spent the first few minutes of wakefulness admiring her from afar as she towelled and tousled. She caught him looking at her and realised that he had been watching for some time. To get her revenge she threw the sodden towel over his head while she pulled on her clothes. When he finally got out of bed it was her turn to cast an admiring glance while he crossed the room to the bathroom, and he pulled his silliest face at her before closing the door behind him.

Brighid got the feeling that the staff were unusually quiet over breakfast. Not that she had much of a benchmark to compare it with of course, having never been waited on at breakfast before. She imagined that despite their stony, ramrod-straight postures they were all sniggering on the inside at the look of their master's latest conquest, but she didn't mind, it had been a beautiful moment and if that is all it remained so be it.

MacCailean Mòr peered at her over the morning's copy of The Raven. She could see a dramatic picture on the front cover of a border crossing with the banner headline **Rannoch Rats Strike Kingdom Pharma Gold**. She could see from the smile on his face that as far as he was concerned it wasn't wholly bad news.

"What's happening?" She asked.

"Ha! It's those Griogaraich bastards. They have only gone and raided across the border in Dundee, ripping off some highly valuable pharmaceuticals in the process."

"Doesn't sound too good to me," she said. "Surely that will just get the Kingdom all riled."

"Aye it will, but it also means that there is some other bastard for the Comhairle to get worked up about rather than just me alone. Old Atholl is responsible for maintaining the integrity of that border. He's going to have to answer a lot of questions as to why the Griogaraich could pass with such impunity. And to be honest, from a personal perspective, anything that puts ants in Athol's pants is fine by me."

"Honestly, you Chiefs are like bairns sometimes, most of the time coming to think about it…" Brighid said.

"All the time, I think you will find," he replied with a smile. "And please, for goodness sake, call me Colin. Anyone who survives a night in my bed and lives to tell the tale gets that privilege."

"Ooh I feel so honoured, so special – Colin, is that what you say to all the girls?" Laughing, she went to brush her teeth and get ready for their return to the Infirmary.

Niall was sitting up in bed when they arrived and although he was still deathly pale he at least managed a smile as they walked through the door. He had been moved to a new room, presumably to allow a deep clean of the gore left by the previous day's struggle. This room had a large picture window over the loch and Brighid craned her head to try and catch sight of Dunderave.

"How are you feeling? She asked, getting a wan smile from Niall in return.

"Oh, you know, not too bad now that I don't have assassins trying to murder me in my sleep." He croaked. The subdued laugh that followed caused him to wince with pain.

MacCailean Mòr leant forward. "Aye, well, it's great to see you still breathing! Now we wanted to ask you a few quick questions so that we can try and get to the bottom of what is going on."

Niall nodded, concentrating hard; speaking was clearly an effort and painful due to the chest wound he had sustained.

"It was Allan Stewart…." He winced at both the words and the memory. "The Lamontation's man. It was him that did it all. First, he cut poor Archie's throat, and then pinned my hand to the table, before shooting Aodhan and Alexander. Finally, he stabbed me. I can still see those black eyes of his staring into me as he pushed his blade in." He shuddered and rubbed the bandage in the middle of his chest. "I also remember seeing him set the place on fire, I guess to cover his tracks. The last thing I saw was poor Archie open the doors to get out, he was trying to hold his neck together: there was blood everywhere. Did he make it?"

"No, I am afraid he didn't," said MacCailean Mòr. "He died in there, as did Alexander and Aodhan, and so too should you, if the MacNachtan Beaton hadn't come to your rescue."

"What? The Beaton? Really?"

"Aye, well you were one lucky bastard, and as Napoleon once said, "God give me lucky generals!" MacCailean Mòr stood up and gave him a hug, being careful not to catch any of the many tubes and wires while he did so.

Brighid smiled indulgently from the edge of the bed and put her fingers on Niall's left hand, giving it a little squeeze for good measure, before saying: "None of which helps explain why he did it though, does it?"

MacCailean Mòr stood up. "No, you are right it doesn't. But the one thing I do know about Allan Stewart is that he doesn't do anything without John Lamont having ordered it."

"There is something else." Brighid paused, as both MacCailean Mòr and Niall Campbell looked at her.

"It was something that I heard at Dunderave yesterday. You know those clansmen of yours that were killed at Clachan during the chase of those fugitives over Beinn Bhuidhe?"

MacCailean Mòr nodded.

"Well, one of our Clan saw the murder of your two men on the edge of the village and those same killers later got back into a boat and disappeared south down the Loch. Apparently, they were carrying a prisoner which we believe was Kirstie MacNachtan, a good friend of mine and a senior Clan leader. I'm guessing by the surprised look on your face that she wasn't brought back by your men?"

MacCailean Mòr shook his head, "No, my men didn't come back with anyone. They told me that there had been a scuffle, resulting in one of their Kats being stolen and a few sore heads, but that the enemy," at which he checked himself, "excuse me, the suspects, then escaped into the dark across the river. We sent patrols through the northern glens during the night, but we didn't catch them."

"Just to confirm, you didn't have any men in boats?" Brighid asked.

"No."

"OK, so it seems pretty clear that an interloper is involved, and that if the interloper was Allan Stewart, then the person pulling the strings behind the scenes must be John Lamont."

"Aye," said MacCailean Mòr. "It must be, the scheming bastard. What would I give to have him here so we could ask him a few questions?"

Brighid reached out an arm to his shoulder. "Will you help us get Kirstie back if she is in Castle Ascog? I am worried about what may be happening to her there. Could you help us?"

Standing to his feet and gazing out of the window, MacCailean Mòr said, "Aye, if I can, I will. And if that slimy bastard thinks he can fuck me over he has another thing coming. But he's slipperier than one of his greased eels. If we are to catch him, we need to be careful, very careful."

Brighid nodded and said: "Well the first thing you should do is announce Niall's unfortunate demise."

"What?!" Niall said, wincing in indignation.

"In this game of smoke and mirrors surely we want the clever bastard to think that his plan has been successful, so you can catch him off guard? Forewarned is forearmed, and we have had the warning now. He won't know that we know and that will give us some advantage."

"Aye, you're right." MacCailean Mòr nodded. "I am sure he's laid a trap for me, but I need to catch him in the act. While he thinks he has the upper hand, we can spring our own little surprise." And he pulled her closer to him, kissing her tenderly: "You're smart, as well as beautiful."

Niall looked on in a mixture of surprise, horror and jealousy.

45 - FOR THE WATERS ARE COME IN UNTO MY SOUL

John Lamont took off his glasses and put them down on his desk. He resented having to wear them and hated the dark red marks they left on his nose. Pushing back his chair he stood up and strode purposefully out of the room, crossing the landing that led from the rudimentary and robust 15th century part of the castle to the opulent and elegant 18th century wing. His soles squeaked across the highly polished parquet floor. He stopped in front of a nondescript door his hand falling to its brass ribbed handle. As he opened it, a blast of cold air and the damp mustiness it bore was enervating. Breathing deeply, he paused, before descending the steps which spiralled downwards into the living rock. After a few flights, he came to a studded oak door that which he opened with a clunk.

The room beyond was neat, well swept and smelled of bleach. The stone walls had been whitewashed and the floor was covered in poured rubber with a centralised drain hole set under a sturdy looking chair, each leg of which was screwed to the floor with its own substantial bolt. The legs and arms of the chair also had metal cuffs attached, to utterly restrain any occupant's limbs. He ran his finger chasing the grain, dark brown and worn.

At that moment, a door in the far wall opened and Allan Stewart entered, his black eyes twinkling. Donna Lamont was right behind him, burdened with her laptop and chewing remorselessly on a mouthful of gum. He waved Donna over to a table in the corner to set up her laptop, while Allan helped him with the thick iron ring set in a trap door in the floor. They yanked it open, wedging it in place; he peered into the darkness below.

"Now my dear, I hope you didn't think we'd forgotten about you down there, even if you are in an oubliette. Not just any oubliette, I might add, but my oubliette, which I'm sure you'll agree is a little special. My good man, Allan Stewart, says that so far you are refusing to play ball. I hope you understand that we cannot allow that to continue."

"Why don't I winch you up and we can have a little guessing game? We can see how many turns it takes for you to give me the right answers. I love games. Do you? But I always feel that they are so much more thrilling if there's a forfeit involved, as that really concentrates the player's mind. Rather like gambling: I always say that if it doesn't hurt when you lose, you aren't playing for high enough stakes. Would you like to play, Kirstie? Or shall I leave you down there for a few days to think about it? Most of my guests seem to be very keen to leave my oubliette, I can't think why?"

He nodded to Allan who winched her up out of the hole in the floor. Kirstie was covered in filth and was shaking violently, whether from the cold or fear was hard to say. Allan quickly bound her in the chair.

"I think we can all agree that it's so much more civilised if we can all just get along, don't you?" Said the Lamontation. "After all, this is just a simple transaction; you have something we want – the access codes, and we have something we can give you in return – respite from my good friend Allan. There is no need to make it complicated and unpleasant is there?"

Kirstie was slumped head down: she said nothing. The Lamontation nodded to Allan, who began laying out the tools of his trade on the table in front of her, starting with a lump hammer.

It the brave fool thinks she can tough it out, well she would learn soon enough. He left Allan to it while he went for a coffee, returning half an hour later to find Donna focused on the white lines of code unravelling from her curser. Her pouchy, yellow cheeks were creased in concentration as she sucked and chewed on her gum. Her snub nose was wrinkled in thought, pushing her glasses up her face and making her eyes look even more distended than usual, while the lank tendrils of her hair hung about her head like kelp on the shore, flat and lifeless. Lamont stood behind her left shoulder, watching and gently encouraging her. He knew nothing of computer code or what the endless series of command prompts and flurries of pixels meant. That was why he had Donna after all, and she was the best.

The snivelling from the other side of the room was a little trying though. He idly watched the swelling puddle of piss that was pooling under the seat, following its progress as it started to meander its way across the poured rubber floor towards him. What a mess. Lifting his eyes from the piss to the occupant of the chair, her legs and arms secured firmly in heavy metal bands which allowed no prospect of escape. Her face hung down, hiding the worst of her bruises, her short hair wilted, as if matching her mood. Her nose blew small bubbles in the blood that trickled from her nostrils each time she exhaled, a crimson balloon swelling and bursting in rhythm with her ragged breathing.

"Good, good, we do seem to be making progress, don't we? I am so delighted that you learned that part of the game so quickly. Many of our guests take much longer to learn how to play, and I fear that they later regret their slowness. We can all agree that Allan is a little genius with that hammer. Don't you think?"

From under her fringe, Kirstie moaned.

"Oh, don't be like that, he's barely begun to show you what he can do and where he can take you. To be honest, we were kind of expecting you to hold out a little longer. We thought you MacNachtans were tougher. After all you've survived having those bastard Campbells for neighbours for so long. But no matter, if you want him to give you a full demonstration I am sure that can be arranged." Allan Stewart's beetle black eyes stared back at him like bottomless pits.

Donna suddenly exhaled deeply combined with a little fist pump: "Yay, that's it." Then turning to Kirstie, she taunted her: "Who's the daddy now, bitch. You think you are so goddam clever, but I've got the measure of you. That double stacked encryption was sneaky, but not so very special in the end. And seeing as how you've now given us the admin codes I think we can all agree that Clan MacNachtan's day in the online gaming sun is over. We are officially in control! And if I just change the passwords, like so, we've now officially locked out any of your colleagues that might try and take it back."

"Is that done then?" Lamont felt slightly foolish for having to ask.

"Yes, it is. I've now switched all the passwords and admin codes so that their programmers will not be able to gain access. But the best part is that I've switched all the revenue accumulation into our accounts, so you can see the money coming in – look there at that counter." Following her finger, Lamont was mesmerised by the counter that was clocking up numbers at a rapid rate.

"Is that in Cùinn?" He asked, somewhat incredulous.

"No - dollars! Brilliant isn't it? Just goes to show you how those bastards have been raking it in for years. Well their goose is now well and truly cooked."

"Why thank you Donna, that's reassuring to hear. The question is, what do we do with our guest. It seems that we have everything we need, but to be honest I'm not sure that we can allow her to leave. Castle Ascog is a bit like the Hotel California in that respect. As you can imagine, I can't allow my former guests to run around besmirching my good name now can I."

"But you promised," mumbled Kirstie.

"Yes, I know I did. Shame about that. Still, the question is, shall I give you to Allan to enjoy? Or maybe Donna? Would you like to have a crack of the whip, so to speak?"

"Nah," said Donna, "I'll just stick to computing thanks."

Donna was packing up her computer when she said: "Actually, it might make sense to keep her around for a few more days, I want to make sure I've got all of the code sorted first and I don't want to run in to any more hidden surprises. If we can just keep her on ice until I am sure that we are in the clear that would be good."

"Oh dear, Allan will be disappointed." Lamont looked at Allan Stewart, whose face reflected no emotion whatsoever. Then, beginning to tire of his own charade, Lamont brought the session to a close, ordering Allan to take her to the castle's cells, as there was a fresh guest due in the oubliette.

46 - THE BLACK WATCH

The words had barely flown Alasdair MacGregor's lips when the first detonation went off, showering them with broken glass and throwing them to the floor. An instant later, a further explosion convulsed the room and the wall where the dart board had been disappeared in a thick cloud of smoke. Gillespie's ears were ringing so loudly that although Nin and Charlie were shouting at him he couldn't hear what they were saying. Nin started scrabbling around the floor and finding a jagged piece of broken glass cut the cable tie that bound Charlie's hands. Seconds later, they were all free from their bonds and Charlie made a long arm for their gear which was still lying on the table behind them.

Their captors had all scattered and were seeking cover behind turned over tables and chairs or behind the bar, getting as low to the ground as they could. The room erupted in a violent melee as black clad figures poured through the hole in the wall, spraying the room with automatic gunfire and cutting down any of the Griogaraich that were still on their feet. Gillespie saw the wild looking Indian hurl a war quoit at the first attacker; it buried itself deeply in the man's forehead, nearly severing the top of his head. Three of the Griogaraich to their left scrambled as a grenade was tossed over the table they were sheltering behind, one caught the full impact of the resulting blast and lay still with his guts torn open, while the other two were immediately shot as they tried to flee.

Then Sal was on her feet with an assault rifle pinned to her hip, firing controlled bursts into the oncoming figures, several of which fell immediately while the others retreated back through the smoke-filled hole. As the Griogaraich gradually recovered from the initial shock of the assault, they grabbed whatever weapons were to hand and Alasdair MacGregor started to show his mettle, shouting orders and directing the defence. He sent the man with the plait upstairs to see what was going on outside, while directing small groups to various points around the building to provide a defensive field of fire.

The confusion in the room was now solidifying into something more comprehensible, but Gillespie did not find that reassuring. The building was clearly surrounded, and heavy bursts of gunfire were raking the structure. His eye was distracted for a moment by the bizarre sight of all the horse brasses twinkling, as they shook in the wake of the bullets rending the air.

The man with the plait reappeared and shouted at Alasdair, whose hitherto calm face became grave. He started shouting orders, disposing his forces. Rather than go out of the hole left by their attackers, he pointed at a large plate glass window on the neighbouring wall. Sal shattered the glass with a burst of gunfire and the bulk of the Griogaraich poured through it, while heavy covering fire was maintained by several defenders from inside.

"Come on," said Charlie, "we can't stay here. That's the fucking Black Watch. If we want to live, we're going to have to run, now." Grabbing their gear, he made for the front door, on the opposite side of the building to where the Griogaraich were escaping. Seconds after they left the bar, the room behind erupted in a sheet of flame and cloud of smoke, as their assailants sought to silence the defence. Time was moving in jumpcuts and Gillespie struggled to focus, his brain rattling with one word only: "fuckfuckfuckfuckfuckfuckfuckfuckfuckfuckfuck….".

He stuck like glue behind Nin and Charlie. As they opened the front door, they saw a line of Kats pulled up in front of the Inn, but their attackers had been drawn away to the other side of the building where the Griogaraich breakout was in full effect. Sheltering behind the vehicles, they watched as the battle unfolded.

Despite their rag tag appearance, the Griogaraich were highly organised. Alasdair had split them into a series of smaller strike teams and had pushed out from the building in a fan formation, taking the battle to the enemy and not giving them a grouped target. Each strike team moved as a unit, taking it in turns to provide covering fire as they advanced towards their attackers, rolling smoke canisters to obscure their progress. But their assailants were not amateurs either and the Griogaraich's numbers were being thinned dramatically as they crossed the open ground. Finally, they'd closed the gap and the ensuing melee disappeared behind the thickening smoke.

"Come on, get in the Kat for fuck's sake." Charlie said, throwing their gear in the back as he climbed into the driving seat. Their departure stalled for a few painful seconds as each pocket was patted down looking for the key, before it was found and jammed in the ignition. Racing the engine, Charlie swung the Kat out and tore down the track away from the Inn. As he rounded a corner, he suddenly threw the wheel over, almost spilling Nin out of the back; there was a further line of vehicles beyond, guarding the route that led down the loch to the east.

Fortunately, they'd taken this second line of defence somewhat by surprise, and it wasn't until they were almost back behind the cover of the neighbouring house that bullets started to pucker the mud around their retreating rear. They were now heading back towards the action, where the smoke was starting to disperse, and the gunfire subside. That did not mean that the fighting was any less intense, in fact quite the opposite, as small groups were locked in hand to hand fighting. With all the figures similarly dressed in black it was difficult to see who was getting the upper hand.

Nearest to them, they saw Alasdair, Sal and the man with the plait fighting a group of black clad figures. Sal had clearly exhausted her ammunition and was swinging her assault rifle like a club; while Alasdair had a claymore drawn in his right hand and a pistol in his left; the man with the top knot had been reduced to his sgian dubh. Alasdair was faced by two assailants with swords drawn. Without hesitation he double tapped one with his pistol, spinning him backwards, while simultaneously catching the other's blow on the edge of his claymore, before bringing his pistol round to despatch him. Gillespie would long remember the look of horror on Alasdair's face as his frantic pulling of his trigger finger elicited no response from the now-empty weapon. His opponent sensing his opportunity, shouldered him to the ground, smashing his basket hilted sword into the side of his face. Alasdair was dazed; spread-eagled on the ground, defenceless, waiting for the killing blow.

In a flash, Nin leaped from the Kat onto the attacker, grabbing his sword arm with one hand and choking off his airway with the other. They wrestled for a few moments, but Nin was too strong for him and the would-be killer's body soon went limp. Alasdair looked up from the ground in stunned amazement, before being grabbed by Charlie and pushed into the back of the Kat. Meanwhile, Sal had bludgeoned her opponent to the ground, delivering a mighty roundhouse kick to his head to settle her account, before jumping into the Kat next to Charlie.

All eyes now turned to the man with the top knot who leapt at his opponent, slashing his dagger at the soldier's outstretched hand. As he made contact, his opponent managed to squeeze off a volley of shots into him, but that did not stop his blade which he frenziedly stabbed at the soldier's face, neck and chest. They both went down: neither got up again.

Charlie streaked off up the glen, leaving the fighting behind. Alasdair tried to protest from the floor of Kat, but even if they could've heard him above the roar of the engine, it would've made no difference. Charlie was making for the forestry that covered the hill above the houses; if they could just get amongst the trees then they might be able to escape. For a few minutes as they slogged up the hill, Gillespie hoped that they might have escaped the notice of their attackers, but as the sounds of gunfire petered out behind them, a line of vehicles started out from the village on their tail.

47 - SMOKE AND MIRRORS

As soon as MacCailean Mòr got back to the Castle, he summoned his press team and briefed them on what to tell The Oban Raven. He even allowed them to get creative on some of the detail, complete with the timing and location for Niall's funeral, designated charities and a request for no flowers. He then summoned Fearchar Campbell of Knap, who he packed off to lock down the Infirmary so no news could get out.

Satisfied that a convincing false trail had been laid, he sat at his desk and stared out of the window. There were many things that he should have been thinking about, such as his summons before the Comhairle the following day; or the pressing question of increased day rates for his Independent Company in the deserts of the Tibesti; or how he was going to get timber felling equipment up to his plantation on Beinn Cruachan — all of which were questions that Duncan his steward was remorselessly pressing him for answers over.

Instead, the only thing that came to his mind was Brighid's pale and curvaceous body, the sweep of her breasts and her glorious pear-shaped rear. How he wanted to have her near and to run his hands over her silky contours; the smell of her too, if he closed his eyes he could just pluck it from the air in front of him. And another ten minutes were lost in glassy-eyed reverie as he luxuriated in the memory of their night together.

Finally, resigned to working, he started to leaf through reports on the assault on Dunderave. He wanted to make sure that he had his story absolutely straight before putting his head in the lion's jaws the next day. He sketched out all the questions they might ask and lined up his answers. It was a pity that Ardbreknish was still so ill or else it would have been ideal to reveal him in a coup de theatre in front of Lamont and the whole Comhairle, but it wasn't to be. However, he did have a short video testimony that they had recorded at Ardbreknish's bedside and that would have to be sufficient.

He could barely wait to see the look on that bastard Lamont's face when his double dealing was revealed. There was no way that he was going to be able to come back from this act of treachery; MacCailean Mòr knew the Chiefs too well. They feared Lamont and his ever-increasing power, and this was the perfect example of why they should nip his ambition in the bud. If he dared to move against MacCailean Mòr, the Duke of Argyll and Warden of the West, who was safe?

MacCailean Mòr thought with pleasure about the various fates that might be meted out to Lamont. On reflection, incarceration on the dread island prison of St Kilda was probably the right answer; the idea of Lamont having to dine on guga and herring for the rest of his days while slowly going out of his mind on that wind and rain lashed rock gave him twisted pleasure. His sweet talking would not avail him there, among all the paedophiles, rapists and murderers that were too dangerous to be kept elsewhere.

Having made all the necessary preparations, he went to his apartment to pack. He had not forgotten about his dinner date with Lamont that evening, an arrangement that he was slightly regretting suggesting. Still, he had no choice now, he certainly did not want to give Lamont any hint that his treachery had been rumbled. He would just need to be cool headed and play it straight; in any case, he had the advantage, he knew Lamont's little secret.

48 - THE SOUSED HERRING

The Soused Herring was Oban's best restaurant. It was located right on the sea front, just a short stroll down from the Riaghaltas up on the hill. The dining room was on the first floor and Parliamentarians and Clan Chiefs could frequently be seen locked in discussion over dishes of oysters or lobster, all washed down with the finest claret. The décor could best be described as traditional; dark tongue in groove panelling and ubiquitous stags' heads, supplemented by humorous cartoon caricatures of well-known regulars and some rather poor paintings of former proprietors.

MacCailean Mòr had booked the private dining room in the corner tower. Its major advantage, apart from spectacular views of the setting sun, was that it had its own entrance, so you could arrive and depart unseen. Discretion was frequently critical when dealing with the many factions in the Riaghaltas, riven as it was by internecine rivalries, many of which went back several centuries.

John Lamont was already at the table when he arrived. The bastard smiled up at him with an unctuous grin that was just inviting a good slap. Restraining himself, he allowed the waiter to take his chair and push it in as he sat down. After swiftly filleting the menu and reverting to his usual selection of hand dived Isle of Skye scallops and samphire to start, followed by loin of Assynt venison en croute with a red wine and truffle reduction, he turned his attention to his guest.

John Lamont was at his most companionable, quaffing claret and making small talk, asking after the wellbeing of the Campbell Companies in North Africa and the progress of his drain laying in Tarbert, among other scintillating topics. When they turned to the subject of the next day's hearing,

MacCailean Mòr played his part well, ruminating over the mystery of how two of his best men could've been killed and bemoaning the burning of the castle. He was rather enjoying himself acting up his ignorance and was particularly enjoying the thought that the next day he could despatch Lamont to a life of gull shit strewn misery in the Atlantic.

After they had finished their main course and demolished a fine bottle of Lynch-Bages, he felt in need of a piss. Excusing himself, he returned a few minutes later to find that Lamont had ordered them each a glass of Jurancon instead of pudding. Lamont had been clever to pick his favourite dessert wine, doubtless he had read about his love of the French sweet wine in his entry in Gaels of Today – the who's who of the Republic. He joined the Lamontation in raising a glass to the success of the morrow, rolling the rich, thick wine around his mouth, relishing its acidity and zing.

It was then that MacCailean Mòr began to feel slightly tipsy: the room starting to swirl at the edges of his field of vision. He hadn't had that much to drink, just over half a bottle of wine: normally that wasn't enough to even whet his appetite. He vaguely contemplated his wine glass: it began to swell and shrink before his eyes as if it was breathing. There was a quiet knock on the door which Lamont rose to open. MacCailean Mòr looked up from his pulsating glass to see Catriona MacLean of Duart enter the room, all sweeping red hair and smirking pout.

Slowly coalescing thoughts pooled at the front of his mind: What did that scheming cow want anyway? What was she doing here? Did I invite her? Is that her natural hair colour? These thoughts then became ring girls, slowly high stepping from one side of his mind to the other as he tried to grasp at their meaning. A small faraway voice tucked in a shadowy corner of his head was saying something; he felt it must be important, but he had to struggle to hear it. He fluttered a hand at Lamont and Duart, waving them to be quiet so he could focus on the words. He peered down at them behind his closed eyelids as they bubbled up towards him: "it's in the wine, you fool, it's in the wine." But now that he was staring down into the blackness he could not pull back and he fell, tumbling head over heels, over head over heels, downwards into the dark, with Catriona MacLean of Duart and the Lamontation's laughter ringing in his ears.

49 - BLOODBOND

As the Black Watch started to roll up the hill after them Gillespie was immediately grateful for two things; firstly, that they had a decent head start and secondly, that Alasdair MacGregor was in the Kat with them. He clearly knew this area better than anyone and he swiftly took control, shouting directions to Charlie and guiding them deep into the forest. The dark pines closed in, cutting them off from view and shrouding them in the oppressive silence of forestry monoculture.

Sal was in the cab with Charlie, while Gillespie, Nin and Alasdair stood in the back, holding on to the roll cage. A heated discussion was building, as Alasdair discussed the merits of various routes with Nin, who seemed reluctant to agree to his suggestion. Eventually Alasdair thumped on the roof to get Charlie to stop and they all got out as he tried to explain his plan. With the point of his sword, he quickly sketched the outline of Loch Rannoch in the mud. Jabbing at it, he implored them to listen to his advice.

"Look, we passed along the north side of Loch Rannoch when we came from the border, and that is the same way that the Watch came from their barracks at Ruthven, so they are bound to be all over it. We would either need to sneak past them or somehow get across the loch to the Black Wood on the south side, neither of which will be easy. I know you want to get to Pitlochry to pick up the Wade, but you would be mad to follow the Tummel to do it."

He now outlined a long loch that ran at near right angles to Loch Rannoch. "This is Loch Ericht; it runs north from here all the way to Dalwhinnie. This forestry runs up to its southern shore, meaning we can shelter in it to hide from the Watch, even if they are using drones. Once we get to the Loch there is a rough but passable cattle track that can take us along the East side all the way to the Wade. Then if you are going to Kindrochit you can carry on all the way around Kinveachy, Tomintoul and Crathie to get you to Braemar. I know it looks like a long way around, and it is a long way around. But it's either that or dealing with the Black Watch. I know which I'd rather."

"Apart from anything else, the Watch will not expect you to go that way. They think that you are Griogaraich and that you would naturally be heading deeper into Rannoch where they might fear to follow. The chances of them seeing us if we go via Ericht are slim and non-existent if we follow the east side of the loch."

"How can we trust you," said Nin in an uncharitable voice. "How do we know you are not just going to lead us into some bog, where you can rob and murder us. Isn't that what you Griogaraich do best after all? Let's not forget that it was only a few minutes ago that you had us hogtied and were threatening us with all kinds of violence. I must need my head examined to be trusting any Griogaraich, let alone you, Alasdair MacGregor!"

Alasdair could not hide his anger at this insult; the gauze and vapour that always seemed to shade and blur his features parted, fully revealing two hard pale eyes that burned out at Nin beneath his thick brows. Without speaking, he bent down and picked the sgian dubh out of his stocking and cut a line across his right hand. He wordlessly stretched it out towards Nin, allowing the blood to slowly pool in the cup of his palm. Nin contemplated it for a few moments, before he too slowly bent down and taking his own blade cut his palm likewise. He then clasped Alasdair's in a vice-like grip, their co-mingled blood oozing out red and thick to drip on to the grass below.

Sal stepped forward and grasping their clenched hands between hers, said, "Under Canun, I hereby declare that by blood you have now been joined, and only by blood can you be parted." They both nodded, holding each other's gaze all the while.

They then started to go over the detail of the plan again, as if the argument had never happened.

Gillespie turned to Charlie: "What the hell was all that about?"

"Jesus." Charlie stood frowning, as if struggling to process what had just happened. "They've made a bloodbond, an unbreakable commitment that binds them together."

"What? Is Nin mad?" Gillespie was astonished.

"You saw how Alasdair reacted to Nin's accusation. This was clearly the only way he felt he could show his good faith and preserve Cliù. After all, Nin saved his life back at the Inn. By binding himself to Nin in this way, Alasdair is making a pledge to repay that debt. It is not a gift that is offered or received lightly. They are brothers now in the eyes of the law, with all that that entails."

"You mean Nin now has a Griogaraich brother? Why would he do that?"

Charlie looked at Gillespie beneath knitted eyebrows: "This will bring complicated consequences, but it's too late to worry about that now."

Gillespie looked over at Alasdair who was now locked in an intense but calm discussion with Nin and using his sword to point out the route on his mud sketched map, his features once again blurred behind that enigmatic haze. He wondered how such a young man – and he guessed that Alasdair could not have been more than 30 - could've acquired such a fearsome reputation. He looked more suited to a seminary. But his leadership qualities were not in question and having concluded the discussion, they all jumped back in the Kat and ploughed on into the dour forest.

After 45 minutes traversing the dark green desert of the plantation, Charlie poked the nose of the Kat out of the trees. They looked down the fine vista of a narrow loch hemmed in on either side by high hills. Alasdair pointed out Beinn Alder to the west, its mighty plateau rising sharply out of the water. A dramatic sight, it was snowbound and imperious. There was a clearly visible path that traced the western shore, but instead Alasdair directed Charlie to turn east.

After fording a river, they picked up a droving track that followed a fast-flowing stream which had carved a path between two peaks. This track wound up into the hills behind the eastern shore of the loch, hiding them from the view of any pursuers. As the Kat climbed higher into the corries of the encompassing hills it got increasingly cold and icy, but it nonetheless remained passable. After the previous few nights of exposure, which he wasn't keen to repeat, Gillespie felt a palpable sense of relief as they finally started descending again to re-join the loch-side about halfway to Dalwhinnie. From here the track was much easier, and as dark was falling they could see the lights of the township ahead.

Nin was driving, and as they approached the junction with the Wade he started tapping at the fuel gauge on the dashboard. Unsurprisingly, his tapping made no difference to the position of the needle, which was resolutely stuck on empty. They were going to have to stop for fuel and after a quick discussion all agreed that this was probably the moment to part company.

Although they had only known Alasdair and Sal for a few hours the parting was much harder than it deserved to be. The skirmish at the Inn and the subsequent flight through the hills had created a bond far more profound than the mere passage of hours. Gillespie embraced Sal, hugging her close, feeling her strong arms crush him in return, while Alasdair very formally held out his hand and shook his warmly, fixing him with those pale eyes, wordlessly communicating his thanks and friendship.

Nin on the other hand, qualified for a hug and a smile from Alasdair MacGregor, who also shared the details of the encrypted messaging service the Griogaraich used. They promised to meet, once the dust had settled, with Alasdair promising a tour of the darkest reaches of Rannoch, while Nin offered the convivial charms of Elrig in return. Waving them off into the darkness, Nin started the Kat and turned onto the Wade heading north.

After all the drama of the past few days, the next few hours were dull and mundane. Having stopped to fill the Kat up with fuel near the famous distillery, they left Dalwhinnie and motored north, following the Wade as it circumscribed the high mountains of the Cairngorms. Gillespie spent most of the journey asleep, only stirring when Charlie elbowed him awake as they approached Braemar, the centre of Farquharson territory and the location of Kindrochit, Charlie's family home.

The road was squeezed between heavy forestry on one side and the winding turns of the River Dee on the other. The blackness of the night, with the moon well hidden behind thick cloud, meant that little could be seen beyond that illuminated in the streetlights. Having passed a hotel and a few bars, they crossed the Clunie Water and arrived at a rather battered pair of gates which Charlie opened with his phone. The drive to the house was short and with a flourish Charlie swung the Kat in front of a set of steep stone stairs that led up to the main door.

After the grandeur of Inveraray or the looming presence of Dunderave, Kindrochit was a modest and approachable kind of castle. The narrow stone steps led to a centrally located door tightly sandwiched between two towers, set with arched ashlar-dressed windows and topped by witch's hat roofs. On either side of these towers was a single bay across three stories, with the smaller ground floor windows sensibly elevated 10 feet off the ground to deter unwanted visitors. Like Charlie, it was rough-hewn, but handsome, charming and inviting with no airs or pretences. It had been home to the Farquharsons for many centuries and Gillespie was unimaginably grateful to step across its threshold into the warmth and welcome that awaited therein.

50 - THE WARDEN OF THE WEST

John Lamont could barely contain himself as he strode up the hill to the Riaghaltas. It was a wet and dull morning, but nothing could darken his mood as he walked around the dour granite arcade to get to the main entrance. Although he hadn't had much sleep, he still felt refreshed and with a spring in his step he pushed through the imposing doors.

Having deposited his bag and passed through security, he checked his appearance in a mirror. He had made a special effort with his Great Plaid and had even pinned it with his most impressive hunk of family silver. He wasn't going to have any of those bastards looking down on him today.

Entering the Comhairle chamber he saw that it was already almost full. Of course, his place on the front bench was free, and next to him MacCailean Mòr's was empty too, and so it would remain. Across the aisle was Duart, a discrete hint of a smile her only acknowledgement. Apart from MacCailean Mòr, all the Wardens were there: MacDonald and MacLeod, the Wardens of the Isles; Seaforth, Warden of the North; Gordon, Warden of the East; Atholl, the Warden of the March; and himself the Warden of the Clyde – the smallest and least important of them all.

Bowing to Speaker Urquhart he took his seat and waited for the session to begin. The investigation into the Dunderave incident was the first piece of business, and the full chamber reflected the high level of interest in it. Like sharks, this lot could smell blood in the water, and they all want to get their piece.

The room was shuffling and fidgeting, growing more irritated with every passing minute as they waited for MacCailean Mòr to arrive. Speaker Urquhart kept looking at his watch and muttering to himself, growing more red-faced and irritable. Eventually, judging that the moment was right, and that the mood of the chamber had come to the boil, Lamont stood and addressed the Speaker.

"My Lord Speaker, I am not sure how much longer you propose to keep us here waiting for the arrival of MacCailean Mòr, but can I suggest that we start with today's business? I am sure that I speak for the Chamber when I say that we're all busy and have many other matters to attend to besides considering Argyll's failings."

The room erupted with a cacophony of agreement and cries of "Get on with it!". Speaker Urquhart looked a little nervous but nodded his agreement and called the first speaker, Tam Matheson of Attadale.

"My Lord Speaker, my Lords, my Ladies." Tam started. "We are gathered here today to consider the actions of our colleague Colin Campbell, Duke of Argyll in his recent action at Dunderave, the ancient seat of the Clan MacNachtan. As you know, this House gave Argyll a commission in his capacity as Warden of the West and Colonel of the Black Watch, to catch and bring for trial the miscreants that attacked a naval patrol vessel belonging to our neighbour the Kingdom Of Great Britain and Northern Ireland in the Irish Sea last week. Intelligence pointed to a party of MacNachtans being responsible and he was directed to deploy his militia to take action and detain the guilty party. A simple enough task you might have thought."

"Now I do not need to tell you of the long running antipathy between these two clans, and you are doubtless aware of the desire that Argyll has held for many years to subsume them and take their land and valuable online interests for himself."

"What we have seen in the past week is that he has outrageously and wilfully exceeded the commission this House entrusted him with. Instead of apprehending the suspects - surely a simple task with those 5,000 men of his - he chose to assault the castle when the Clan were celebrating the election of a new Chief – the worthy Alexander MacNachtan, formally of Albany, whom many of you will know. It was not enough that Argyll illegally used firearms to suppress those that opposed him, despite his overwhelming numbers, but that he should also execute Alexander and his Seanchaidh in cold blood under the Bratach Gheal - the white flag of truce!"

"But even that was not enough to satisfy him. He vindictively set fire to the ancient seat of Dunderave and destroyed the Clan's online gaming operation – their only source of reliable income and an important source of tax revenue for the Republic."

"Can I ask my fellow Chiefs if they feel safe in a Republic where a power crazed individual can unilaterally take such action? Do my fellow Clan Chiefs feel that they and their Clans are safe, knowing that they could be next? Do my fellow Clan Chiefs not feel that it's odd, nay an insult, that the Duke could not even be bothered to come here today to answer these charges? Do they not feel it, like a slap to their own face, the disrespect that he has shown to this house and all of us who are in it?"

The Chamber erupted in shouts and jeers and the waving of sgian dubhs as the mood of the room darkened. Dwarfed by his eagle backed chair, the Speaker called for calm, waving his arms dementedly, until at last relative quiet had been restored.

Tam Matheson sat down, but Jimmy Singh Davidson now stood up, smoothing his tightly wrapped dark blue turban as he did so.

"My Lords, surely we have had enough of over powerful magnates usurping the good intentions of this House for their own benefit? Hasn't Argyll held power for too long and done too little for the good people of the Republic, unless their name was Campbell?"

"Wasn't this unapproved appropriation of another Clan's property and the murder of its Chief under the Bratach Gheal complete anathema under Canun?"

"Where would we be if we allowed this kind of activity to go unpunished I ask you? Would any Clan here be safe? Would the Republic be safe? Where would it end? If the House does not take action today, will the Republic still stand tomorrow I ask you?"

And so it went on.

Lamont sat in his place listening to all the impassioned words delivered by his puppets, the very words and phrases they used identical to those he had given them. He wanted to laugh as the rage and fury of the Chamber mounted. Finally, he decided that there had been enough warm up, now was the time to strike. Standing he said:

"My Lord Speaker, my Lords and Ladies. Given everything we have heard today there can be no doubt that we need to act and act quickly. The breath-taking arrogance of Argyll can be seen in his failure to attend today and I fear that if we delay further, who knows what plan he may be cooking up. Can I therefore propose to this House that at the least we require him to surrender his ill-gotten gains? To that end, I am prepared to take the MacNachtans under my wing, to help them to get back on their feet under my protection."

"Furthermore, I propose that the Chamber strips him of his position of Warden of the West and appoints a new Warden, a more worthy Warden, to take his place. Surely, there can be no better candidate than Catriona MacLean of Duart, given her wise council and service over many years to this House and the Republic?"

The roar of the room gave clear affirmation to these requests and as the Speaker was calling for a vote, Catriona MacLean raised her hand to speak.

"My Lord is too kind in his words, and it goes without saying that I would be honoured to accept. Furthermore, can I suggest that at this uncertain time the Duke of Argyll is also relieved of his role as Colonel of the Black Watch. It is critical that the Black Watch can be considered an impartial and trusted service by all. I think it is clear from today's session that few, if any, of us feel that this is a role that Argyll can continue to fulfil. I therefore propose that John Lamont, Warden of the Clyde is appointed Colonel of the Black Watch, reflecting his many years of service to the Riaghaltas and the Comhairle, his steady hand and unquestionable resolve."

More cheers greeted this speech, although Lamont was sensitive enough to note that the noise levels were by no means as conclusive as those as for Duart's appointment. He didn't care, this was not a popularity contest after all.

To a cacophony of shouts and cheers, Speaker Urquhart called the votes.

A little under an hour later, Lamont left Oban with a new commission in his pocket giving him oversight and control of the Republic's powerful internal security force, the Black Watch. With Argyll now removed from his post, the other magnates were rightly nervous, sensing a defining shift in the tectonic plates of the Republic's politics. He had seen Gordon scurry from the building to get back to the security of his lands in the East and the fawning of Seaforth and Atholl as he had left the Chamber had been most amusing.

Yes, things were going to change now in the Republic and anyone that got in his way was going to regret it, probably frequently and at his leisure.

51 - LIGHT OR DARK

He didn't know if he preferred the light or the dark, they both had their positive and negative qualities. He'd had plenty of time to think about them, lying there hour after hour. The dark was the all-consuming utter black of the pit, showing not a chink or crack. He could find a strange comfort in that profound darkness: his brain projecting hallucinations and sparks to fill the void. It did not matter if his eyes were open or closed; they saw the same. The darkness had a mass though, and that weighed on him. Initially it felt bearable, but as the minutes - or was it hours? - passed, the gravity of the blackness bore down on him, crushing him to the floor and smearing his spirit across the stones like a paste.

Then, without warning, LIGHT. It burned and blazed like a southern summer sun. It was relentless and unyielding; there was no hiding from its perpetual zenith. They had taken all his clothes, so he could not even shield his eyes from it with a rag. Occasionally, he would lie with his head pressed against the wall, or even against the side of his latrine bucket to shelter from the piercing glare in its cooling shadow.

The stone cell was about ten-foot square and fifteen-foot-high, the only entrance through a trap door in the ceiling. He had already paced the paving slabs hundreds if not thousands of times. Sometimes he tried to walk on the cracks, tracing a heron toed passage across the room. Sometimes, he hopped from stone to stone, testing his balance and accuracy, forcing himself to begin the crossing again if any toe touched a mortared joint. He had traced mazes and labyrinths in the joins, chasing minotaurs and trailing thread to pass the hours.

He had ascribed each wall a point of the compass, so that he could turn and imagine the world beyond in each direction. Of course, he had no way of knowing which way he was actually facing, but as he stood full square to each wall in turn, he spread his arms and pressed his body against the stones to project himself outwards; as if he could pass through the silent rock into the world beyond, flying across continents and oceans, and wandering the cities and byways of his past.

He had counted the stones on each wall and even the number of stones in each course as they wound their irregular way around the cell. He had tried to concoct mathematical calculations as to the volume and quantities of air and stone that contained his world. But he was rubbish at maths and never felt confident in his calculations. He had nothing to write with or even to mark the stone to assist in his calculations, he had tried to gouge the mortar and use its flakes and crumbled grains as a miniature abacus to stack and measure, but somehow he always lost which grain was what and had to start again.

He tried to count, counting the minutes and then the hours to give the passage of time a form and meaning. But he had stopped once he realised that there was no rhythm to the light and the dark. He knew that this was deliberate, to disorient and discombobulate, and he wasn't going to play that game. Food came from time to time, lowered on a tray by an unseen hand. At each mealtime he tasted it carefully and sipped the accompanying water drop by drop. He knew enough of the hospitality of some highland magnates to beware MacLeod's Meal; the salted ham and seawater repast that would drive its diner insane with thirst. He would rather starve.

He spent time thinking of how it had come to this, this cell, his world. He thought of Lamont and Duart, their laughter ringing in his ears, but he chose to push those thoughts into a deep dark corner of his mind and turn the key on them for the moment. Raging would achieve nothing.

Instead he thought of the pleasures of the world. Tracing memories, of his parents, their home, their garden, of holidays and presents, laughter and smiles. He frequently turned his thoughts to the women he had known and loved; he caressed their imaginary limbs and traced their contours with his tongue, nuzzling and spooning, clasping and fucking. He tried to remember all their names, not that the list was so long, but some were fleeting and others enduring. Of course, some stood out – Mairead, the first, the sweetness of youth. Her passionate kiss and chocolate skin transported him back to a teenage time of urgent moments and tender hours. She dissolved, to be replaced by Jane, the glorious Jane, how he missed her laugh. When they'd married he had known that he would die with her at his side years hence, old and worn. But he'd been wrong. Life's cruel joke was to twist that vision until he was stood by her bed for days and weeks and months watching her fade: to shrink and dry like a raisin in the sun, until there was nothing left. The bloom of youth burned away to a withered husk filled only with the grit of wasted seeds and tannic bitterness.

To expunge that unwelcome thought he turned to Brighid, her memory so fresh it could still be smelt and tasted. Her sharp chin framed by that long blond hair, her grey eyes flecked with fire like rare agate; how long he could stare into their galaxies and vortices, spinning and whirling free from this stone cell.

And so MacCailean Mòr waited.

52 - KINDROCHIT

The dining room was like a battleground, but one from which Gillespie couldn't flee. The long mahogany dining table stretched away on either side of him; to his far right at the end sat Torquhil Farquharson, Charlie's father; to the far left was Dervoguilla Farquharson, whose generous and welcoming personality wanted to smother you in its all-encompassing bosom. If looks were weapons, then the pair of them were at dirks drawn, fencing and fighting the length and breadth of the table's polished leaves.

Torquhil sat there bulge eyed, flushed and shaking, his sticking out ears waggling in indignation while his wispy grey hair frizzed itself into a demented halo. He was clearly building up a head of steam for his next sally when Daracha, Charlie's sister, abruptly stood up, propelling her chair backwards across the floorboards, and flinging her napkin onto the half-eaten lunch in front of her.

"For God's sake give it a rest, Papa. We are not living in the 19th Century. Anyone would think that you have been living under a stone. It is not as if Charlie's relationship with Ninian has been a secret, they've been living together for five years! How could you be so rude to your own son and embarrass him in front of his friends? You should be ashamed."

Dervoguilla butted in to add, "I think it's simply wonderful that Charlie has brought Ninian to see us at long last. I'm so looking forward to getting properly acquainted."

With that she pressed her hand on top of Ninian's and smiled warmly at him. Nin's whitened knuckles and clenched fists betrayed the feelings that his calm face was hiding. He turned and flashed her his most charming grin, and while patting her hand said "It has been such a pleasure to meet you all at last. Charlie has told me so much about you. I've never been to the Cairngorms before, so it's great to have a reason to come and visit."

"Sharing a room, nay even a bed, under my roof? Never! I mean the shame of it. I have my honour and reputation to think of." Torquhil retorted, his whole body bristling to his eyebrows and beyond.

"Well, strictly speaking darling, it's my roof," said Dervoguilla. "And, if we're talking about Farquharson honour, I think I am best placed to be the judge of that, don't you? Seeing as how I am the Chief. It's been so long since you were a MacTavish. When you took my name, you took the lion and forsook the boar's head, you really can't have split allegiances. Anyway, surely that feud has been laid and the blood debt paid?"

For once stumped, Torquhil muttered and shook his head, outnumbered and outgunned he knew this was not a battle that he could win. Gillespie had sat watching the exchange with the dispassionate interest of the anthropologist, observing and learning, happy not to have a dog in the fight. Just as the table returned to relative calm and Daracha had regained her seat, Gillespie mischievously asked: "I had no idea there was an outstanding blood feud between the MacTavishes and the MacNachtans, how did it happen?"

It was an innocent enough sounding question, but Gillespie knowingly lobbed it like a grenade onto the table and stood well back to observe what happened next. Charlie caught his eye and raised his eyebrows, as if to say – did you really have to do that? Nin sighed, Dervoguilla slumped and Daracha stood up again and left the table. But Torquhil seemed to swell as if attached to an airline, rolling his shoulders and cracking his knuckles as he turned his full attention away from his son's dubious partner to observe his other guest, a stranger in a strange land.

"Well Gillespie, that is an interesting question and one that you as an outsider is certainly free to ask, although I should caution you that even such a simple question can lead to unexpected and complicated answers. Can I suggest that you charge your glass while I tell you the story and you can then tell me whether you think my disquiet is unwarranted."

"It all began in 1936 when Diarmid MacTavish, the 20th Chief of the Clan, had two daughters. The fair Rosa, as lissom and bewitching as any dew dropped rosebud, the flower of the county, desired and loved by all, and the doughty Ealaseachd, who was as plain as her sister was beautiful. To cement the relationship between the MacTavishes and the MacNachtans it was decided that a wedding should be made, to bolster their friendship and strengthen the ties that us small clans need if they are to hold out against our powerful neighbours. Anyway, Tormod, the middle son of the MacNachtan Chief, was the lucky recipient of this honour and the fragrant Rosa was proposed as the perfect match. They were engaged and spent many a happy hour in each other's company getting to know each other and preparing for their life together."

"The wedding day was set, the guests invited, the feast prepared, and the two clans met for the ceremony in the Parish Kirk in Inveraray. This Kirk conveniently has two identical halves, perfect for just such an occasion, so that each Clan may arrive without meeting through their own entrances. This wise arrangement was created to reduce the risk of feuding and fighting during a service. The bride duly arrived, robed and veiled in virginal white and was piped up the aisle to Dunardry's Delight. The Minister duly conducted and concluded the ceremony at which point he invited Tormod to kiss the bride. But imagine Tormod's horror when he withdrew the veil and found himself staring at none other than the moustachioed face of Ealaseachd!"

"This bait and switch approach to marriage was a common feature of highland weddings of old, so quite why the MacNachtans were so surprised is a mystery to us MacTavishes. I think they were just sore that we'd outsmarted them. However, it's fair to say that Tormod took umbrage at this arrangement. After the party had retired for a tense wedding breakfast at Dunderave, he persuaded the fair Rosa, who he had successfully wooed during their engagement, to flee with him through the lavatory window into a waiting boat and away. In the ensuing altercation several clansmen were killed on both sides, triggering a long-running and sanguineous blood feud."

"The official feud was suspended in 1973 by the Court of Canun, all sides judging that the passage of time and the number of bodies had more than exceeded the acceptable level for Cliù to be satisfied. And no one knows what became of Tormod and fair Rosa; they disappeared without trace. But to this day there are few MacTavishes that you will find to sit down with a MacNachtan, let alone take one into his bed."

Gillespie looked from Torquhil to Nin and Charlie and then to Dervoguilla, for once stunned into silence. Nin was flushed, whether from the wine or his rising ire at the story. Charlie twitched nervously, while his father was like the cock of the heap, all puffed up with pride at the clever double cross that his MacTavish ancestors had performed.

Dervoguilla turned to Gillespie and said in a carrying whisper that all could hear: "You see, that is the problem with the Gaelic Republic – all bawbags and no brains. You'd think that if all the killing and ill temper was enough for the Court of Canun to end it over forty years ago that the Clan of today could just forgive, forget and move on. But no, there is more pride than sense in some, that's for sure."

To mollify the tension in the room Gillespie stood and proposed a toast, raising his glass to each in turn: "To Diarmid MacTavish, the smart and slippery, to Rosa, young and fair, to Ealaseachd, the sour and jilted and Tormod, who ran like a hare."

It was as he said the words that he felt a horrible realisation creeping up his throat from his stomach to fill his airway. He gasped and instinctively drained his glass: it was wine. Spluttering, he put the glass down on the table. No one else seemed to have noticed. They had all raised their glasses and were drinking down the contents. Torquhil even starting to chuckle with Nin over the outrageous and unjust exploits of ancestors past.

But Gillespie's mind was blazing, computing dates and ages, transliterating names, his doubts dissolving as he did so. It couldn't be true: but it suddenly seemed inarguable. It was the names that did it, more than the dates. His grandfather's name was Norman. Gillespie had always thought it an odd and strangely English name for a man of Gaelic heritage. A man who did not suffer fools and had little time for small boys. He could see him now in his battered tweeds, socks rolled over his gumboots, his hat slouched low. His grandmother had been called Ros: he had barely known her. She had died in a car accident when he was five, leaving Norman bereft. The key piece of the puzzle was only obvious to him now having heard Torquhil's tale. Because the Gaelic translation of Norman was Tormod. Could this have been his grandparents? Is this why they left the Republic? Why his grandfather would never return or even speak of the Clan or the Republic? Was it guilt over all those unnecessary deaths? Or was it wounded pride at being duped? His head span with the revelation: but he said nothing. This was not the time or place. Gillespie now desperately wanted to move the conversation on away from Tormod and Rosa.

Fortunately, Charlie did it for him: "Enough of all that, we need to get down to some serious business and find out what is going on back at Dunderave. Mum, what have you heard?"

Dervoguilla wiped her mouth with her napkin: "I am afraid nothing good. In the Comhairle it feels like the wheel is turning and that we're in for a period of upheaval. Now that Catriona MacLean has been made Warden of the West, the Chiefs are waiting to see how she's going to change things. Given that this is the first time in two centuries that there is no Campbell as Warden of the West, we can expect change a plenty in time. For us in the east it may not matter that much, we have our own breed of overlords in Gordon and Atholl, but for you folks in the west it surely will."

"There is also more to this than meets the eye. I had that slime ball John Lamont on the phone the other day trying to drum up support for his scheme to censure MacCailean Mòr. Although I've no love for MacCailean Mòr, I went along with it to find out what was going on: it's always useful to know what is going on in John Lamont's head, when one has the opportunity. At that stage he was just sounding out support for a censure motion, I had no idea it would lead to this power play. What is particularly fishy is that there is still no sign of MacCailean Mòr, he has vanished off the face of the earth. One has to wonder if he's languishing in one of Castle Ascog's dungeons or worse.

"This move propels Lamont to the top of the heap. With the Black Watch at his back he now not only has more men than anyone else, but he can also swathe it under a veil of legitimacy. It was quite disgusting to see how fast Atholl and Seaforth went around to offer him their congratulations. They clearly know which way the wind is blowing!"

"The final fly in this ointment for you, I'm afraid, is that he also had himself appointed as "guardian" of Clan Nechtan, to protect you from the ravages of your over-powerful neighbour, at least until you have a new Chief. And we can all imagine that the appointment of a new Chief may now be some way in the future, if he has anything to do with it. Which he will!"

"What?!" Exploded Nin and Charlie simultaneously, eyes and mouths agape at this shocking news.

Nin continued: "How can that be allowed? We've never had to submit to any other Chief before! We are one of the oldest clans and have always been independent. There is no way the Clan can submit to this."

Dervoguilla sighed, "I know, it's a mess, and not something that would ever normally be countenanced. It just happened. He played the Comhairle like a cheap violin, and while some of us bridled at the tug of his bow, none of us could resist the tune. I'm sorry."

Gillespie had never seen Nin look dumbstruck before, but he now sat there silent holding his head in his hands staring down at the table. Charlie lent over and put his arm around him, squeezing his shoulder. Nin shrugged off his attempt at empathy.

Torquhil started wittering about how maybe this meant it was a good idea for them to stay at Kindrochit for the foreseeable future, at least until things had calmed down. Dervoguilla nodded her agreement and started proposing different long-term accommodation arrangements for them to consider. Daracha just stood in the doorway, listening.

Gillespie's head swam, no longer really sure which way was up. The idea that the infamous John Lamont of the Sorrows, the Lamontation himself, was going to become the overlord of the Clan was impossible to bear. He thought of Brighid and Kirstie, Jamie and Iain the Rat, not to mention Fiona and Mara and Archie Beaton and all the others he had met during his few short days at Dunderave – what would happen to them now? Were they just to become meat in the Lamontation's grinder, indentured to the Republic's most notorious and cruel despot?

The unexpected thump of both of Nin's fists hitting the table caused the plates and glasses to jump and eliciting a gasp from the assembled company. Lifting his face, he stared around the table at each in turn, his irises transformed from their normal soft and gentle cornflower blue to glittering sapphire.

"No! This cannot be allowed to stand while I or any MacNachtan has blood in our veins and breath in our lungs. If Lamont thinks that he can take us so easily, we must learn him another lesson. We haven't endured 500 years of Campbell depredations to roll over and be plucked by that bastard." At which he looked at Charlie and Gillespie, searching from one to the other for support.

"Aye," was all Charlie said. And Gillespie heard that brief but resolute affirmation echoed by another's lips: his own.

Dervoguilla frowned and rubbed her forehead, as if to dispel the creases and wrinkles that were now crowded there. "You're awful brave or awful foolish. I know the Lamontation better than any round this table and I can assure you he's every bit as cruel and relentless as his reputation. Courage will not be enough; you will need to be patient and devious too. You can't just walk up and ask him to leave. You'll not only need to take back what is yours, but to hold it you'll need to prise it out of his cold dead hand. His vanity will not allow him to relinquish what once he's held."

"Well I'm sure that can be arranged," said Nin, pushing back from the table and getting to his feet.

53 - FELICITATIONS

John Lamont picked up the phone, his thin lips stretched into a broad smile. For years he had had to listen to that self-important prick moaning at or threatening him over some perceived slight or failure. So, it was a welcome change to have Andrew Balfour, First Minister for Scotland, offering congratulations on his appointment as the Colonel of the Black Watch.

Balfour had been the very model of diplomatic politesse, pouring platitudes down the line over how he wanted to establish a closer working partnership; or how grateful he was to at last have a partner in the Republic that could get things done. John Lamont was not so old or forgetful that he couldn't remember the vicious call of only a week or so earlier, but he had already filed that memory away so it could be drawn upon at an appropriate future opportunity. For the time being, he was gracious in his acceptance of the plaudits and promises offered by the First Minister.

Having completed his metaphorical backrub, Balfour clearly felt that the moment had arrived when he could turn to more serious business and extract some action on the pressing matter of border security.

"I can't tell you how relieved both the Prime Minister and I are that at last there is someone in post that can show some leadership and bring about the changes that are needed in the Gaelic Republic. We need to know that our neighbours respect and enforce the law. I'm interested to hear what progress has been made in both the Irish Sea incident and the hostage taking at Dunkeld."

Lamont knew that the Kingdom's Prime Minister was under pressure. The tabloid media had predictably foamed at the mouth over the Irish Sea incident, and with the Dunkeld hostage taking following so soon on its heels, the spasms of outrage had reached an incendiary level. Lamont was wise enough to know that this couldn't be ignored, and he had already helpfully constructed a narrative to pour oil on these febrile waters. It was all part of his game plan, he needed to play the First Minister like a grilse if he was to land the bigger fish of the Prime Minister. But first he had to hook his grilse.

"Andrew, I want you to know that we've already taken firm steps to punish the perpetrators of both incidents. Thanks to my own investigations I identified a renegade group from a small Clan as being responsible for the Irish Sea incident. Consequently, I've seized control of their base, sequestrated their assets and burned their castle. I can also confirm that their Chief was killed resisting arrest and that I've a number of suspects in custody. I've prepared some video footage that can be shared with Kingdom media and across your social channels which I hope will go some way to assuaging their concerns. I also hope that you'll find it shows the Prime Minister and yourself in a good light."

"Secondly, in respect of the Dunkeld hostage crisis, I can confirm that we now know the identity of the perpetrators: an infamous band of outlaws. Unfortunately, these individuals are very hard to control as they do not answer to any Chief and live outside of our society. However, the Black Watch rapidly located and intercepted the warband, which was vigorously suppressed. I can confirm that there were 22 fatalities, 16 of which were Griogaraich and the remainder from the Black Watch. We have also secured a few prisoners who are currently being questioned. Finally, we have located the stolen pharmaceuticals, which we will return. Again, I've prepared some content that you might want to share across your broadcast and social channels."

"Goodness me, John, you have been busy. You've only been in post a few hours and you're already achieving great results! What a relief to be able to report some progress for a change. I know that the Prime Minister will be grateful. I think it's only fair to ask if there might be anything that we can offer in return?"

"Since you mention it, there's one thing that I would be grateful if you could look into." Lamont said, judging that this was as good a moment to ask as any. "I was hoping that we could reach an agreement in respect of online gaming. It is a very small part of our overall economy, but it's a growth area and one which we are keen to expand. If you could see your way to lifting the prohibition you have on earnings from gaming, it would be a small but valued gesture. Although Republic companies have small operations in the Kingdom, we do have substantial interests in the Far East."

Balfour's silence signified to Lamont that the cogs in his tiny brain were whirring, trying to work out what the catch was. Eventually, the computation finished, presumably inconclusively, and Balfour replied that he would see what he could do and rang off.

The idea that he might be able to onshore the money that was pouring in from the MacNachtan's gaming operation was almost erotic. As with politics everywhere, follow the money: money attracts power, power attracts money - a virtuous and vicious circle. Even in the Gaelic Republic, the one with the most cash was almost certainly going to win, and the Lamontation wanted to make sure that was him.

54 - THE BURNING EMBER

Kirstie paced her cell working her leg muscles and counting the number of lengths. She was up to 1,657, which she then tried to convert into miles as she walked. She had always been quite good at maths, and she quickly worked it out that at roughly three paces to each length and two and a half feet per pace she had done 12,427 feet, that was roughly two miles she had paced that morning. Satisfied, she paused to do a few squats, sinking low on her haunches to stretch out her muscles. Her hands were still too sore to put any weight on them, so press-ups were out of the question. She looked at the baby fingers on both her hands and winced at their mangled state; they were black and swollen, more like morcilla sausages. She still couldn't bend them even the slightest amount without intense pain and she doubted that they would ever heal fully. Using her teeth, she had torn off some strips of her shirt which she had used to bind each to their neighbour to try and keep them supported and straight.

She thought back to the hours in that chair, how she had wanted to gouge and claw at Alan Stewart, to feel his flesh tear beneath her nails and teeth, not just to make him stop but to exact her revenge, her toll for the pain and misery he had visited on her. She'd briefly felt ashamed of how quickly she had given up her secrets. But she knew that she had little option. Pride and cliù dictated that she should have held out and allowed them to crush and mangle each joint and bone in her body before revealing such secrets. But she knew, as did anyone else who had actually been faced with the choice, that few if any can take that route. She was not one of them.

In any case, she had made a contingency and it was important for her to live to be able to put it into action. She did not know how long she had left, but anything that postponed the inevitable moment was to be grasped.

The cell was rough cut stone and largely featureless. She didn't care, it was a huge improvement from the nightmare of the oubliette. That had been true terror. It had not been a hole in the ground – more of a slot. One that was so narrow that she could not turn around, or lie down, or raise her arms or barely move. It had been pitch black, cold and she could feel the gnawing bite of the damp needling its way into her bones. She had felt like she was suffocating, the blackness pouring into her lungs and smothering her. The tears running down her face had left an icy trail down her skin. She wanted to rub them away but could not lift her arms to reach them. Piss and shit had flowed and fallen where gravity took them, but at least these had diminished over time as her body emptied itself.

The shame, like the hunger, lit a fire deep in her soul, an ember of pure red-hot hate. She blew on that ember in the darkness, nurturing its glow, stoking its first lick of flame into a blue burning coal of white-hot power that melted and consumed her from within, expunging all other thought. She still carried it with her like an isotope in her heart, its heat and mass an ever-present weight. She prayed that she would have the chance to unburden herself, to free herself from its negative charge, and to be ready for that moment she paced.

55 - THE SIGN OF THE TWO STAGS

It was getting dark when Brighid left her house at No 6 Stronshira and walked along the loch. It was damp – that in between highland weather that is so prevalent in Argyll, where it's not exactly raining but not exactly not raining either. Mist was draped thickly over the trees and spilled wetly down the sides of Beinn Bhuidhe, pooling on the loch edge. Across the loch at Ardkinglas she could see curtains of rain being blown along the shore, fortunately for her the prevailing wind was keeping it away from the path she had to tread. As she walked under the trees she breathed in the green scent of the wet pines, the evocative smell of her childhood, the sharp tang of the fresh needles from the low hanging branches overlying the warm musty brown of the old ones that had fallen on the path, their deadening carpet yielding softly to each footstep.

As she walked past the castle the trees parted and the comforting aroma of times past was subsumed into a more complex blend of dank stone and burnt wood. The blackened ribcage of the charred roof timbers was silhouetted eviscerated against the grey sky. She'd not been down on the shore since the Lamontation's men had arrived to take control. It had been bad enough having the Campbells standing sentry and acting like they owned the place, but at least they were all lads that she had been to school with; boys who she had played shinty against or kissed at a ceilidh and fooled around with on the hill away from prying eyes. The Lamontation's men were different. As with any organisation, if you want to understand its culture look no further than its leader; the tone they set and their demeanour seeps and permeates through the rest of the body. Now that she knew MacCailean Mòr better, she could see that the officious and arrogant aspects of his character could be found easily across the Clan, but also the more tender and open natured elements too. The Lamontation's men, on the other hand, were overbearing, brusque and harsh, with no obvious redeeming features.

The black beetle eyed Allan Stewart had been given Dunderave by Lamont, and had spared no time in asserting his authority, facing down the few Campbells that had tried to hold on to what they'd taken. With MacCailean Mòr having vanished, the Campbells were like decapitated chicken; the legs and wings were flapping, but there was no purpose or direction to their movements. They were swiftly outmanoeuvred and retired to Inveraray to lick their wounds.

Brighid didn't spend any time looking down at the castle, a quick glance showed her that the flag of the black tower that had always flown from its flagpole had gone. It had been replaced by the Lamontation's hand turned palm outward. Many of the Clan crests were apposite to their nature and none were more so than Lamont's – a palm raised in warning, a warning to stop and go no further; aggressive and dismissive.

She was soon threading her way through the houses at the edge of Clachan. She passed that of Iain the Rat and Fiona, the grass in their gardens still winter brown, looking as tired and worn as she felt. Nothing a little sunlight wouldn't cheer; this winter had lasted for ever. Raising her eyes to the snow that still lay on Beinn Bhuidhe, she cursed its ever-present reminder that spring had yet to come.

The path now opened out onto a wide grass space tucked under the hill and fronting onto the rocky shore. Standing foursquare in the centre was the Two Stags Inn, her destination. The Two Stags was the favoured drinking hole of the Clan, it was where you knew you would always find a friendly face, cheerful chatter and a roaring fire. Its long low frontage hunkered down under the lowering mass of Beinn Bhuidhe behind. It was a single storey of white harled blocks, with a steep pitched slate roof above. It seemed to seamlessly blend into the rocky massif behind. Two gabled ends sandwiched the main body of the Inn and in the pitch under the roof of each side was painted a red deer stag festooned with antlers bellowing a challenge at its painted rival in the other gable. Underneath these in now traditional highland fashion, were two large picture windows which gazed blankly out over the loch towards Ardkinglas on the other shore.

Brighid was grateful to step over the threshold, out of the penetrating damp and into the warm and cheerful atmosphere of the bar. Shedding her coat and hat, she shook out her long blond hair. She paused by the fire, holding her hands out to warm them against the smouldering peat and once she felt life returning to the tips, turned and approached the bar.

As usual there were two of the Clan soaks propped by the counter: Tam and Davy. A comical pairing, they were always found sat together on the high stools at the bar and were an excellent source of information on the ebb and flow of visitors. They drank slowly and steadily from the opening hour to the closing bell, never havering but steadily racking up the pints and gills. Davy was as thin as a rake and was always smartly dressed in a crusty old tweed jacket over a rather mothy kilt, always the same kilt. His face was lined from years working for the Clan Company in far flung tropical climes and it was as if his skin had absorbed so much sunshine that it could never completely relinquish its tan, despite the mounting number of in-door hours. Tam on the other hand was always a little dishevelled, his straggly hair pulled into ever more wild peaks and promontories as the day wore on. His mind and chat were rapier sharp though, despite the years of booze, and Brighid always loved to spend time discussing the rights and wrongs of the world with him.

Having embraced each of them, she turned to Dolina, the Two Stags' barkeep and owner, and ordered a glass of claret. Not wanting to be waylaid by Davy and Tam, she took her glass and went to the far gable end of the bar. There gathered around a table were Iain the Rat, Jamie and Archie Beaton and having kissed them each hello, she took her place at the table.

After several minutes of gloomy reflection on the Lamontation's outrageous move and how Allan Stewart was no neighbour for those who wanted a long and peaceful life, the conversation turned to what they could or should do to alleviate their situation. Jamie, who was still wincing occasionally due to his wound, spoke for all: "I just can't believe that it's all fallen apart so suddenly. Only a few weeks ago Duncan was still alive, and the money was rolling in. Now what are we left with? Nothing? A smoking ruin, two dead Chiefs, our land and livelihoods sequestered by that unscrupulous bastard. Everything that has held us together for nearly a millennium is under threat or destroyed. If we don't do something soon, the Clan is just going to fall apart."

For once Iain the Rat was in agreement: "Aye and we need to be quick about it. The sharks can smell blood right enough and are starting to rip chunks out of us. I heard that Donald Hendry over by Inverchorachan had a bunch of MacArthurs sniffing round his farm. He saw them off, but they have their eye on him, no question. And I am sure that is being repeated all across our land."

"Has anyone heard from the Company?" Brighid asked. "I think that before he was killed Alexander had said they were still in Jamaica on leave. Do we know if they have even heard about what has happened?"

The gathered heads all shook in unison.

"Well it seems to me, that we need to get a message to them. They will be furious when they hear what has happened to Alexander and will surely want to avenge him. We need their muscle if we are to have a hope in taking and holding the Castle. The problem is that our network has been down ever since the Campbells took the castle. Without it we can't communicate with anyone – it's like we have been gagged. Do any of you know how we can turn it back on?"

They all shook their heads and sat there glumly, silently contemplating their glasses. Eventually it was Jamie who spoke:

"Didn't Fiona, Malcolm's widow, work with Kirstie? Maybe she will have some idea of how to do it?"

Looking at the knitted brows of her companions, Brighid decided that this was the best idea they could hope for. Taking a large slug of claret from her glass, she stood up: "OK, I am going round to her house and see if I can get her to come and join us. We'll find out soon enough if she can help."

Twenty minutes later she was back with Fiona at her side. Fiona's haggard face was not improved by the streaky mascara trails left by the rain that was now lashing down outside, but there was a steeliness to her that Brighid thought was much needed. After greetings had been exchanged and a glass of claret poured, all eyes turned to Fiona, more in hope than expectation.

Fiona pulled her vape out of a pocket and taking in a deep lungful, slowly breathed out a cherry flavoured cloud while she contemplated the faces round the table. Having marshalled her thoughts, she said:

"Aye, I worked with Kirstie on the network systems. I won't say that I am exactly up to her standard, but I know my way around it. But to be honest, I am not sure that is much use, as there are some other big issues that we need to address first."

"You are all familiar with the fact that they burned down our server room, right and along with it our access to the internet through our satellite uplink? We do have a backup of our data stored across a variety of mirror sites around the world and if I can access that I can get the network back online. But we need to have an internet connection and a mobile data signal. Currently, they have shut down our mobile transmission towers and destroyed the satellite uplink. So not only does the Clan not have a signal, but even if we did, there is no entry point for it onto the net. We need to find a way to turn the towers back on and somehow to connect them to an internet gateway. If we can do that, then I can activate the remote back up and get the Clan systems back online, no problem."

They all sat there despondently, nursing their glasses. Brighid was beginning to think that it looked hopeless. She had never thought that access to communications was so important. In the old days the Clan would just send out the fiery cross to raise the men, but in the 21st century there wasn't the time for such old-fashioned methods.

Iain now spoke up, rubbing his scraggy stubble as he did so: "The switch for the mobile towers' power supply is in the Castle's main sub-station. That's under the Courtyard of the Fountain. It will be tricky to get to it without being spotted and even if we switch them on, what's to stop them just switching them off again? Also, that still doesn't solve the problem of the gateway."

Archie Beaton hadn't said anything yet, and he rubbed his fingers through the white woolly ring of hair that sat down on his ears, his bald pate shining under the lights.

"OK, so let's talk this through logically. We need to turn on the mobile network and to do that we need to gain access to the Courtyard of the Fountain and flick the right switch. Then we need to connect it to an internet gateway, but our own is destroyed. The question is, who else has one that we could connect to? Presumably, the Campbells have one in Inveraray?"

"Don't be absurd," interjected Jamie. "There is no way the Campbells will allow us to piggyback through their gateway!"

"Slow down, no need to get so feisty." Archie said calmly, and turning to look at Brighid, he said "I believe that some of us have rather better relations with the Campbells than others at the moment."

Brighid blushed fiercely, hoping that none would see in the rather dim light of the bar.

Archie continued, "Brighid here performed a valuable service to the Campbells, saving the life of one of their top duine uasal in the Inveraray Infirmary the other day. I believe she has established a rapport with MacCailean Mòr. If you ask for support, will he help us?"

"Aye, I could ask," Brighid replied. "But MacCailean Mòr has disappeared, no one knows where he is. The Lamontation has probably had him killed or kidnapped as part of his grand plan."

"Even more reason for them to help," said Archie. "They want to get their Chief back and we want to get our castle back. The Lamontation seems to be the key to both, it must be better that we join forces. Surely, you can go and speak to his steward and see what they could do? If you do that, then we can think about how to turn on the mobile towers and I've an idea of how we might do it......"

The group all leant in and listened to what the Beaton had to say, until even Jamie was nodding his agreement to the plan. It was a bold plan, maybe too bold, but no one had a better one.

56 - PARTNERS

The first part of the plan was relatively easy. Brighid rose early and waited for Fiona to join her at Stronshira before heading into Inveraray. Fiona had turned up on a single cylinder trail bike: the engine thumping a deep staccato rhythm while she waited for Brighid to climb on the back. Perching on the tiny seat, Brighid had to grab on tight to Fiona as she twisted the throttle, propelling the bike over the bridge and down the few short miles to Inveraray.

As they pulled into the gravel sweep in front of the castle, Fiona pulled a neat slide, scattering chips far and wide. Both of them were grinning as Fiona popped the bike on its side stand. "Ach, I haven't done that in ages, feels so good to be out and in the open air!" Her face was alive and positively glowing with energy after the short and frankly rather hair-raising ride. Brighid slid off the back and walked towards the porte cochere, where the two Campbell clansmen on duty eyed them suspiciously. Brighid was a relatively familiar face given her recent stay at the castle, and they were certainly less assertive than they would normally have been had two MacNachtans arrived in a cloud of dust and gravel. One kept them at the door, while the other went inside to find Duncan Campbell, the steward, who was responsible for the castle and Clan in MacCailean Mòr's absence.

When Duncan arrived five minutes later he was effusive in his welcome for Brighid, ushering the pair of them through the door and into the splendour of the atrium. There was a modest fire burning in the grate and he invited them to warm themselves on the fender while he pulled up a chair.

After the welcome and introductions were out of the way, Brighid asked after MacCailean Mòr. Duncan looked crestfallen as he admitted: "No one has seen him since he went to Oban for the Comhairle meeting. He was supposed to be having dinner the previous night with Lamont at the Soused Herring, but after that he just disappeared. We've been making enquiries in Oban, but no one saw him leave. We can only imagine that he's in the hands of Lamont. We pray that he has not been murdered already. I would like to think that he's worth more alive than dead, but with Lamont you never know."

The burly clansman looked like he was about to burst into tears, his eyes reddening. Pausing to allow him to regain his composure, Brighid put her hand out and squeezed his shoulder. "Don't you fret, Duncan. We'll find him and bring him back. I don't know how, but if we work together then I am sure we can do it."

"And that is why we are here," said Fiona. "We need your help too. They have disabled our mobile network and our satellite uplink. We need to route our signal through your connection so that we can start organising the Clan – without communications we are helpless."

Duncan looked from Fiona to Brighid. "I am not sure what to say, obviously we have never countenanced such an action before. Giving another Clan access through our network – it's unprecedented. But then these are not normal times."

He stood up and gestured for them to follow. He led them outside and around the castle to a range of buildings built out of the same dark grey black stone. It must have been the old stable yard. He punched an entry code on the door, and he ushered them into a gleaming white space with row upon row of desks and computers. The banks of programmers briefly raised their eyes to see who had entered, before returning their gaze to their screens.

"This is where we co-ordinate our Clan companies around the world, as well as manage our various other business interests. We have a pretty big backbone network that is plugged straight into the Vac-90 transatlantic cable, so we have plenty of bandwidth. Here let me introduce you to Fergus MacIver who runs the operation and see what he can do to help."

Fergus was a small and neat man with a fastidious manner. Clean shaven and with carefully parted hair, he wore thick horn-rimmed spectacles that gave him an owlish countenance. He started engaging Fiona in an impenetrable patois of contention ratios and terabytes that made Brighid's head spin. Fiona on the other hand seemed to positively bloom, throwing her shoulders back, pointing and asking questions. Soon she was laughing and spraffing with the otherwise dry-looking Fergus. Brighid was grateful to be able to leave them to it, and she and Duncan returned to the castle.

Brighid now had the opportunity to tell Duncan the rest of the plan, and after twenty minutes discussing various details and variants, she left him and wandered back along the loch shore towards Stronshira.

57 - UNTIL THE BLOOD FLOWS

Allan Stewart was enjoying being the laird for once and not the servant. Although Dunderave was no Castle Ascog, not least because it had the sky pouring through one half where the roof had been burned away, it still gave him a thrill to walk its empty halls and rooms. He had ensconced himself in what had been Duncan MacNachtan's bedroom in the unburned half of the building. He had no time to clear out all the clothes or get rid of the possessions that littered every surface. But he did get a vicarious thrill from lying in that bed; that bed where Duncan had famously bedded stars of the stage and screen and a few politicians to boot.

It was starting to get dark when he heard the first shouts. He was unable to see anything from the window, so he went down the stairs and out through the Courtyard of the Fountain into the outer ward. From there he could see that a crowd of Lamonts had gathered around two figures who were shouting at each other, fingers jabbing, swearing and making threats. From the look of their tartan one was a Campbell and the other was a MacNachtan, both were red faced and furious.

As he approached, one of his junior officers, Ned Burdon, started briefing him on the situation. "Sir, these two just appeared and it wasn't long before an argument started. This one," he gestured at the Iain the Rat, "accused him," at which he gestured at Duncan Campbell, "Of being a motherfucking Campbell cunt bastard. While this one," he pointed at Duncan "threatened to cut off his pointy yellow nose and feed it to his dog."

Allan immediately saw the potential for a bit of entertaining mischief, one where someone else's blood was at risk. Entering the ring of Lamonts that had encircled the pair, he said, "Well, well, what do we have here. Seems like there is a little bad blood between the pair of you. Having heard some of the terrible language you have been using, I can't imagine that anything will assuage it but blood and steel?"

Both Iain the Rat and Duncan nodded, their eyes locked, their posture menacing.

"OK, I hereby declare Canun has been invoked. You must fight until the blood flows. May the first blood not be your last."

"May the first blood not be your last," echoed the surrounding Lamonts, stepping back to create a wider arena for Iain the Rat and Duncan to fight.

Swearing, they both drew their blades and circled each other. Duncan adopting the unusual inside half hanging guard, with his sword point down, the basket at shoulder height, thereby protecting his lower body. Iain had adopted the more assertive St George's Guard, with his sword arm raised up at head height and with the blade held horizontal. His leg was in shift, so that Duncan would have to lunge at full stretch to make contact. They circled each other warily, lobbing occasional insults as each in turn laid a desultory cut or feint at the other.

Allan laughed to himself, these clansmen were so puffed up on pride they would fight at the drop of a hat, the fools. Anyway, it provided good entertainment for others, especially his men who had gathered round to watch and who had had a busy few days. If there was a better way to pass the time that see two men fight and spill their blood Allan Stewart did not know it, and he happily settled back to enjoy the contest.

58 - THE SWITCH

Archie, Jamie and Brighid had been watching the castle from the tree line for nearly an hour and with the gloaming upon them, the light was now failing fast. They were on the far side of the castle, away from where Duncan and Iain were hopefully conducting their pantomime and were dressed head to toe in black. As if on cue, they saw the sentry on the parapet of the wall become distracted by something happening on the other side of the ward and he disappeared from view. They swiftly crossed the open ground from the trees to the bottom of the castle wall.

Archie was carrying a carbon fibre pole that was about ten-foot-long and as thick as his forearm. He swiftly unscrewed one end and untelescoped and locked two further sections together; he now had a thirty-foot flexible pole that was stronger than steel. Barely pausing for a second, Brighid gripped the end of the pole at right angles to the wall while Jamie and Archie held the far end. As they pushed, she walked it up the wall with her feet, until she was up and over the twenty-foot-high parapet. As she disappeared over the top, Archie and Jamie retracted the pole and disappeared back into the cover of the pines to watch and wait. The whole operation had taken less than a minute.

Brighid dropped down into the Courtyard of the Fountain, rolling softly as she landed. Springing to her feet, she hugged the shadows as she made for a doorway in the far corner. When she got to the smooth steel door, she prayed that the skeleton code would still open it. She punched the numbers into the keypad and breathed a sigh of relief at the soft click and green light. She opened the door as little as possible and squeezed through the gap into the darkness beyond.

Once the door was closed behind her, she felt safe to switch on the lights that illuminated the rough cast concrete steps leading down into the sub-basement. Following Iain's directions, she ran down a long corridor to the third room on the left, here she was confronted by a wall of olive-green electrical cabinets, covered in jewel like lights of different colours and sizes. They all looked remarkably similar and for a moment she wished that the Rat was with her; she could not afford to make a mistake.

She pulled a piece of paper from her breast pocket and held it up as she studied the bank of cabinets. Counting in from the right wall she found the third cabinet and ran her finger down the winking lights to a large black button labelled on/off next to a brightly burning red light. She depressed it and the tell-tale red light went out and the green one next to it lit up. Thrusting the paper back in her pocket, she pulled out a small pair of pliers which she used to grip and unscrew the red plastic cover of the light from the panel. Next, she unscrewed the neighbouring green plastic cover and swapped them over, so that the green was where the red had been and vice versa.

To any but the most informed observer nothing appeared to have changed, just that the red light had moved an inch to the right. In reality, power had now been restored to the Clan's mobile tower network which was once again beaming signal up the glens and along the shore. Now all they had to do was to open the gateway, but that was Fiona's job.

Her heart was pounding as she pulled the door to the cellar closed and walked back up the corridor and climbed the stairs. She extinguished the lights and opened the door into the Courtyard a crack. She could hear just hear the muffled chattering of guards as they watched the duellists, shouting their encouragement at the pair. She closed the door again and shrugged the small draw string bag off her back. From it she took out an apron and a cap, identical to the ones worn by the kitchen staff in the Castle. Having put them on, she calmly walked out of the door with her head held high, walking down the passageway into the outer ward. She fussed over a few of the picnic tables, collecting glasses, stacking plates and rearranging dirty cups, until she was certain no one was interested in her. Then she slipped through the entrance gate, skirting round the back of the crowd of onlookers to the duel and walked away up the hill to the track, shedding the apron and cap as soon as she reached the sanctuary of the trees. There she was joined by Archie and Jamie, and they looked down to the shore and the duel that still seemed to be in full flow.

Brighid did worry that Iain and Duncan were over doing it. As any seasoned blade fighter knows, duels were almost always short, sharp and definitive. The florid sweeps and elegant ripostes that the pair were performing were almost comical. Their audience didn't seem to mind too much though, and the bellowed insults that the Rat and Duncan were exchanging seemed to compensate for the lack of venom in the strokes. Then, as if to a predetermined signal, they both clashed their swords together and closed into a tight melee. After several seconds of wrestling to and fro they sprang apart, each nursing a small cut to their upper arm.

The tension of the crowd evaporated, as their hopes for blood were dashed by these meagre trickles. Even Allan Stewart, who had been goading the pair to stoke their anger, lost interest. As the crowd scattered back to their posts, Duncan and Iain gathered their possessions and studiously ignoring each other, walked the path back into the trees away from the Castle.

59 - CONNECTED

Ping, ping, ping, ping, bzzzz, bzzzz, bzzzz, wiwoo, wiwoo, wiwoo.

The table in front of them suddenly erupted in a cacophony of buzzing chirrups and ringing bells, as long queued messages poured out of the ether into their handsets. Charlie and Nin dived for their respective phones, gazing mesmerised at the screen full of messages as if for the first time. There it was, as bright as day in the top corner - An Tùraidh Dubh, with the little emoji of a black tower. They were back online!

Although in the great scheme of things this was a very modest triumph, there was no denying the effect it had on their morale. The simple act of reconnection seemed to transform their prospects, now they could at least communicate, access money, connect with friends and family and figure out a way to fight back.

Nin and Charlie were alternately laughing and agonising over the information that was flooding their screens as they caught up on news. For half an hour no one spoke as the updates were digested. Gillespie, who was in any case unaffected by the data embargo, exchanged a few emails with Eammon and Kate on the farm, not because they really needed his input, but as much to make him feel he was doing something useful. Finally, the screens were lowered, and an assessment could be made of their situation.

Rubbing his eyes, Gillespie said: "So, what's the plan?"

Charlie looked at him as if he was an idiot. "We don't have one, that is the point, you great bell-end! That is why we are sat here like a bunch of numpties." And those greeny brown eyes flashed fire at him.

Feeling somewhat ashamed at Charlie's overwrought reaction, Gillespie concentrated as best he could. He felt beholden to propose something, anything, and without having thought too deeply he said:

"It's obvious, isn't it? We need to find and rescue Kirstie. I mean, I don't know enough about the Republic and your ways to even get started with all the politics and the law and how you can reclaim Dunderave and kick Lamont out. We can't take on all that other stuff in one go, there are too few of us. But we can try and do something about our friend. And besides, if not us then who? We now know that Kirstie wasn't captured by the Campbells, and Brighid has it on good authority that she was taken by Lamont to Castle Ascog. That makes a lot of sense, since they have also taken control of the gaming operation and to do that they must have got the admin codes from her. The idea of her being stuck in that dreadful place is too awful."

Nin started to nod, "Aye, maybe our Irish MacNachtan is right. Fuck the castle and the Chief and all that bullshit. We need to try and save Kirstie - I don't imagine they are they are going to keep her alive for very long now they have what they want from her."

"OK, so that is where we start," said Charlie. "But how are we going to get in there to find her? You can't exactly stroll up to Castle Ascog and asked to be let in. Besides, that place has an evil reputation, I don't think I've ever heard of anyone attempting such a thing. It's a place people run from, not to."

"Which is exactly why they won't be expecting anyone to try," interjected Nin, his new-found focus burgeoning his innate confidence. "And now that I'm thinking about it, I've just the person to help us."

"Who?" Said Charlie and Gillespie simultaneously.

"Why Alasdair MacGregor, of course!" Nin beamed, delighted at his stroke of inspiration.

Gillespie looked at Charlie and then at Nin, slack jawed.

60 - THE SUMMONS

Alasdair MacGregor paused, straining his ears for the slightest sound. Nothing. He was not so foolish to believe that meant he'd shaken his tail, just that they were being cautious; as well they might. He was annoyed that he had sent Sal ahead, leaving him exposed in this way, but he was not unduly concerned. He had already led them a merry dance through the hills and given he was approaching Rannoch Moor proper they had better be on their guard. This was Griogaraich country and none knew it better than he.

He was now skirting the upper slopes of Sgòrr Gaibhre, with Rannoch Forest stretched out below him. If he could cut round behind the bouldered slopes of Garbh Mheall Mòr ahead he could catch his pursuers in the rear as they made their way across the tight sided valley which led down to the forest and ultimately out onto the Moor. He duly increased his gait to his favourite loping run.

After years in the hills he could keep this pace up for many hours, long after most pursuers had given up exhausted. Surefootedly, he sprang from rock to rock, deliberately avoiding any mud that might leave a revealing footprint. The air was cold, and he pulled it deep into his lungs, enjoying its burn. He was in his element and relished these moments and here on the edge of Rannoch, the home of the Griogaraich, it would take the devil himself to cow him.

He picked his way through the boulders, leaping the gaps and scrabbling over their tops, and had soon completed the circuit of Garbh Mheall Mòr. Pulling out a small pair of binoculars, he hunkered down to watch as his pursuit made their way down the shoulder of the ridge into the Coire below.

There were five of them, Black Watch judging by the dark green and blue government tartan that he could just make out on their uniforms. Not that he was surprised. He thought that they might have given up by now, but clearly not.

They had stopped just past where his tracks had ended, where he had doubled back. They were clearly discussing what to do next and he was keen to see if they would stick together or separate. After some debate they elected to follow the Coire down towards the Forest, assuming that he would have to go that way to get to the safety of the Moor. They were also sticking together and that made his task that much harder.

He pressed his cheek to the cold damp rock; this boulder had lessons to share. Alasdair MacGregor's pale eyes suddenly snapped into focus.

He now shadowed his pursuers; the hunters had become the hunted. For his plan to work he had to get to them before they left the Coire, it was also important that they didn't see him. He flitted from boulder to boulder as he climbed the Coire's slopes high above them, as they continued to meander, looking for his tracks. He knew that he was running out of time. They were almost at the end of the Coire now; he had to slow them down.

Bending down he found a palm sized rock and, having picked a spot on the far side of the narrow valley, he threw the stone as hard as he could. The stone soared and then clattered down into a mound of smaller stones and gravel, scattering them and sending the impact echoing around. The five froze, turning to face the sound, hands on their weapons as they scanned the rocky mountainside.

While he had them staring in the wrong direction, Alasdair found what he was looking for; a collection of boulders at the top of the scree run that lined the slopes of the Coire. He rapidly appraised the boulders and having found the best candidate he placed a thick black disc under its edge before retreating a safe distance. This movement attracted the attention of one of the Black Watch, who shouted at the others and pointed towards Alasdair on the hill far above them. At that same instant, the landmine detonated, shattering the boulder and dissolving the hillside above which started to move, slowly at first but swiftly gaining a terrible momentum as it rumbled down the slope. The figures scattered, trying to escape as the tide of rock engulfed the Coire floor.

Alasdair saw two of the Black Watch disappear under a cloud of dust and stone, while a third was struck by a rock the size of watermelon that tumbled and bounced in a lazy but inexorable arc towards its target, downing him with a sickening thud. Two remained, but they were dazed by the dust and shock of the impact. Having tracked the avalanche down the hill, Alasdair did not hesitate and leapt on the first with sword drawn. It was not much of a contest and having parried his opponent's rather feeble attempt at a cut, Alasdair ducked under his upstretched sword arm and houghed the man's hamstrings, leaving him to collapse with a scream while he turned to face the fifth and final pursuer.

The man's face was covered in dust and sweat; he was blinking furiously trying to clear his gummy and clogged eyes. He thrust his pistol at Alasdair and the crack of gunfire filled the Coire, reverberating from stone to stone, as he chased Alasdair's shadowy blur. But his aim was unsurprisingly poor, and Alasdair was moving fast, dodging from left to right as he zigged towards him. From ten feet, Alasdair unleashed a whip crack of a left hand, the smooth stone flying straight and true to bounce off his opponent's forehead, dropping him to his knees like a stunned ox. After a second's pause, the figure fell forward flat on his face, out cold.

Alasdair picked up the pistol, tucking it into his webbing and turned to survey the scene. He could do nothing for the two of the Watch that had disappeared completely under the rocks, while the man with the crushed chest was still breathing and would live but was clearly in a lot of pain. The man he had houghed was lying on his back yelling. Alasdair went up to him and traced a thin red line across the bottom of his neck with his sword point to attract his attention.

"Now five against one is not very friendly odds is it?"

The man stared back, saying nothing.

Alasdair continued, "Maybe I should cut your throat and let you bleed out on these cold wet stones? No? Well, it's lucky for you I am feeling like one merciful motherfucker today."

Turning away from the groaning figure, Alasdair gathered some useful bits of kit and ammunition before setting off at a jog down the mouth of the Coire and into the trees beyond. It was as he was about to enter the trees that he got the message, his phone vibrating in his sporran. He frowned as he read it and paused for a few minutes while he decided how to reply. His mind made up, he tapped out a response and then tucked the phone away. Turning south, he headed away from the safety of the Moor.

He knew he had a hard step ahead of him if he was to make the rendezvous in time. But these hills were his backyard and having checked his watch again, he disappeared into the landscape at his loping run.

61 - FOLLOW THE RAT

Fiona pushed herself back from the desk with a smile. It was possibly the first smile that had crossed her lips since she had heard the news of her husband's death only a few short weeks ago. It was as if, at least for a few moments, she had shrugged off the deadweight of grief that she had felt smothering her. She did not expect the feeling to last, but it did show her that there was hope. The world was a little more colourful, as if the spectrum of her vision had widened from the drab greys and duns, to at least include blues and yellows. She heard a laugh, and it took almost a minute for her to realise it had been her own.

She exchanged a high five with Al, the next-door terminal operator who had been helping her navigate the Campbell systems, sharing the moment of triumph when An Tùraidh Dubh had come back online. She imagined all the pings and alerts around the glens as the Clan was reconnected to their digital life, all the social posts and photos, the gossip and memes, as well as the serious stuff. Al had been a great help and she had been impressed with the power and subtlety of the Campbell operation. But despite its scale and reach, ultimately it was no more effective than the unit that Kirstie had developed at Dunderave of which Fiona had formed a part.

Once the Clan mobile network had been restored, it had been relatively straightforward to hack a patch to route access to their network through the Campbell's internet gateway. Now the Clan could communicate and access the outside world. She had never imagined that being isolated could have been so debilitating, it was as if the bonds of time and history were being dissolved. If it had gone on indefinitely who could say what would have happened to the Clan. As it was, it was only a step on the road, by no means their final destination. For a start, this was just their portal and communications hub, it did not include any of their gaming operations which had always been kept completely separate and which were still beyond their reach.

The brief celebration over, she went and got herself another cup of coffee to join the mounting tower of cups on the desk. Light was falling, but she had no intention of stopping while she could still keep her eyes open. She turned to Al to pick his brains on what to do next.

"I want to try and hack Castle Ascog, I need to see if they are holding my friend Kirstie, at the same time we can see if they are holding MacCailean Mòr. Have you guys ever managed to gain access?"

"No, unfortunately not. We've tried occasionally, but their system is pretty secure, and we have never found a chink to wriggle through."

"OK, but do we think they may have left any code or links that might give us a clue or way in from when they shut down An Tùraidh Dubh?"

Al scratched his scraggy beard while he thought, "I doubt it, they didn't seem to really touch your intranet, just destroyed your ability to access it. On the other hand, they have now integrated the gaming site into their systems, so if we can get into that then then maybe we can hack backwards up into their network. I can't imagine that we'll find a connection from here, but I'll run a scan just in case we've missed something."

Fiona glanced at her watch; it was just after five. She needed to jump on a conference call at six with Brighid, Iain and the rest of the crew and she had hoped to be able to have some more good news to share. She went back to her terminal and called up the Clan Lamont site. She tried playing around with their HTTP and FTP entry ports but got flamed each time. She was getting nowhere and hoped that Al was having more luck with his diagnostic test. The sigh from across the desk told her the answer before he could even speak the words.

Checking her watch again, she picked up the computer's headset and dialled into the call, which was already populated by Nin, Charlie and Gillespie at Kindrochit and Iain the Rat, Archie, Jamie and Brighid.

After graciously accepting their thanks for her work on activating the gateway and hearing all about Brighid's daring break-in at Dunderave, the mood became darker when the fate of Kirstie was discussed. Nin outlined the plan that he'd made to rendezvous with Alasdair MacGregor and to get his help with the search of Castle Ascog. Iain and Jamie were highly sceptical; getting the help of a Griogaraich with anything seemed absurd, let alone teaming up with the most feared Griogaraich of them all to break into one of the Republic's most terrifying locations. Certain of a double-cross, or just a no show, they poured cold water on his plans. This left the atmosphere on the call even blacker than before, if that was possible.

To try and maintain a bit of positive momentum, Fiona then went through the various steps that she had gone through to try and hack the Lamont systems to no avail. She bemoaned the fact that they were unable to connect to their gaming programmes, as that might have offered a route in.

It was then that Gillespie spoke up: "Well there is one thing, which probably doesn't mean anything and almost certainly won't help, but I thought I should mention it."

All ears swung in Gillespie's direction. "Yes, what is it?" said Fiona. "For God's sake, out with it!"

"Nin, remember when we were on top of Beinn Bhuidhe and Kirstie sent me a message with the admin passwords?"

"Aye, I do," said Nin, "and I also know that they don't work now."

"Aye, right enough," said Gillespie. "But she also left another strange message which I didn't understand at the time: in fact, I still don't. But there must be a reason why she sent it to me. Maybe one of you knows the answer. I'm just going to forward it to you now. It's an old black and white photo of a shinty team and the accompanying message says, "follow the rat to the back door". It must mean something, otherwise she wouldn't have sent it to me, but what it is I do not know."

There was a general murmur down the line as each opened the message and looked at the attachment.

It was Iain the Rat that spoke first: "That is a picture of the Glen Shira shinty team when they won the Argyll cup in 1979. Look there is old Cal MacNutt and Fraser Henderson in the front row. Christ, look at Fraser's teeth!."

For a moment the older members of the group, essentially Archie and Iain, were lost in a ball by ball re-enactment of the last game of the '79 season, when Lachie MacNachtan had scored the unlikely winning goal with 5 seconds to spare when his wild strike rebounded off the head of a MacArthur defender into the goal, winning the game and hospitalising his opponent at the same time.

"Yes, yes, OK all very interesting, but how does that help us solve the riddle? What did Kirstie mean? Is there a message hidden in here that we aren't seeing? And who does she mean by the Rat? Iain is the only Rat we know, and he's not even in the photo." Said Fiona, exasperated.

"Yes, I am."

"What? Where?" came the reply from several lips simultaneously.

"There, in the far-left corner. I remember being there, but I've never seen this photo before."

All eyes turned to the far-left corner where a young boy of 10 or so with a pointed face and bad haircut was stood, arms raised in triumph, toothy grin splashed across his face. It was a tiny figure in the background, so it was not surprising that they hadn't seen it before.

"OK, so there you are, but what is the significance of it?" Fiona asked.

"God knows, I was just celebrating that we were the champions, I don't think it has any significance." Said the Rat.

There was silence while everyone stared at the picture on their various devices.

"Wait a minute," said Gillespie. "I am looking at this on a phone and the picture is really small even if I blow it up, I can't see anything. Who's on a proper screen – Fiona? Can you zoom right in?"

"Aye, give me a moment, if I just stretch it out…. there. Fuck me…. clever cow, how did she do that?"

"What!" came an exasperated chorus down the line.

"Well if you can blow up the image of our friend Iain, you'll see that he has his arms raised and index fingers pointing up, presumably to show that the wonderful Glen Shira shinty team is Number 1. But if you look above where his fingers are pointing you can also see the old Double Diamond advertising hoarding that used to be in Castle Place in Inveraray where this photo was taken…."

"Aye," said Nin. "I can see it now you mention it."

"OK, shit for brains, what are his fingers pointing at…"

"It's just a web address on the bottom of the poster, what's so special about that?"

"Either Charlie has sucked your brain out of your cock, or you really are as thick as two short planks – the internet hadn't even been invented in 1979, you great twat!" Fiona said, exasperated.

All the other call participants murmured their acknowledgment of this, as if it was obvious and how plain it was now they saw it. Nin, who was feeling slightly foolish, said nothing; he was quietly trying to imagine a time before the internet had existed and failing.

"So that address and the numbers that follow, they are a code to access the site?" Gillespie asked what everyone else was thinking.

"That is what we are going to find out in about 20 seconds." Fiona's fingers tapped away in the background. "OK, so yes, this appears to be a back door into the gaming site. Kirstie must have created it to make sure she could always get in. This was a clever way of storing the codes in plain sight, where she could always access it but anyone stumbling across that image would never have seen them buried in the background."

"Now, I want to be careful so that I don't trip any alarms and alert Lamont. Let me look around and see if we can find a way out of this back up the control chain into their systems. I can't do it while I am on the phone, so we'll have to reconvene. Give me a couple of hours."

For the next two hours Fiona worked furiously, trying to feel her way through the Clan Lamont network. Once she had left the familiar territory of the old MacNachtan gaming system, she was into unknown territory and had to be careful. She imagined that it was a bit like being blind, you had to feel your way down unfamiliar network paths and junctions, keeping an eye out for security code, tiptoeing round protocol traps and being careful to leave no trace.

The backdoor that Kirstie had left only gave her administrator rights on the old MacNachtan code, as soon as she hacked up into the Lamont network she was exposed. To gain access to their full system, she needed to escalate her access privileges without ringing the alarm bells. After poking around for a few minutes, she was surprised to find that the Lamont site had been written in C++, which meant that there were no inbuilt system blocks to a buffer overflow hack. She was not naïve enough to believe that it meant the site wasn't protected, just that she could at least try and initiate a discrete stack-based exploitation to see if that could secure additional system privileges. She had already spotted the "canary" that had been left by the most obvious data stack, and she carefully tiptoed round it to find a less obvious and unprotected target.

Her eyes burned into the screen, line after line of white code scrolling up and away into the surrounding black ether. After 45 minutes of mounting tension, she suddenly got the result she wanted: **ACCESS GRANTED**. She breathed a sigh of relief. She had had to upgrade an old profile from the MacNachtan system and had been worried that the cloaking she used wouldn't fool the Lamont security, but it had worked, at least for the time being.

Now she had to look for where the information on prisoners was kept. She imagined that any system area explicitly dealing with prisoners was likely to have high security and be closely monitored too. Instead she decided to look for a softer target. Scratching her head to think of alternatives, she tried the castle kitchen – everyone has to eat after all. There she was able to pull up a schedule of catering requirements for the week, including in what was described as the secure area.

Although there were no names next to the various cells, just numbers, she could toggle back through previous days to see when the cells were occupied, and by cross referencing with a calendar she could match the first entries against two of the numbers to the disappearance dates of both Kirstie and MacCailean Mòr. One of the numbers, which she identified as most probably Kirstie, had been moved from one location to another a few days after her appearance on the register, but the other, which she presumed was MacCailean Mòr had been in the same unit since his arrival. Although she could not be 100% sure without a much deeper penetration, Fiona was as confident as she could be that these were their missing targets. "Kirstie" was currently being held on sub-basement 4/3 and "MacCailean Mòr" on sub-basement 6/2.

Wracking her brain for anything else she could usefully do while she was inside, she suddenly had a brain wave and without further ado pulled back from the catering rota and headed off to another area of the network to see if she could dig out the information she needed.

62 - DOUNE

Gillespie couldn't believe that they were really going to leave the peace and comfort of Kindrochit for the danger and uncertainty of the plan that had just been outlined. Having been nearly drowned and frozen, not to mention shot at and blown up, during his journey over the Grampians, he was in no hurry to leave. When he'd protested, Charlie and Nin had looked at him with condescending understanding. They suggested that this was not his fight, and that he'd be very welcome to stay safe at Kindrochit until the situation had become clearer, or even to try and make his way home. Charlie pointed out that the border was close, and with a bit of luck he would be able to cross and make his way to Aberdeen or Glasgow and then fly back to Belfast. They waved off his concerns over his lack of passport or ID, saying that once he was over the border he wouldn't need them.

He felt irritated at how quickly they wanted to let him off the hook, almost as if they expected him to run away back to his real life at the earliest opportunity. Maybe he had been hanging round Gaels for too long already, but his cliù felt affronted. He also had a sense of loyalty to Kirstie. He knew that if he left now that would be it, he could never come back and so he had made up his mind to throw in his lot with the rescue team, to do what little he could.

He busied himself shadowing Charlie and Nin as they got ready. This time they would be better prepared and at least have proper winter clothing. Charlie had the added distraction of his Mother fussing him and his Father making suggestions that were neither needed nor wanted. By necessity, Charlie had been very cagey about where they were off to and had certainly not told his parents the truth. The idea that their son might be disappearing to fraternise with the Republic's most wanted man and then attempt to free a hostage from the lair of the Lamontation, a feat that no one in their right mind would even contemplate, was not one that any parent could countenance.

Finally, they were ready and having piled all their gear in the Kat, they waved off Torquhil and Dervoguilla before heading south out of Braemar. Soon the bright lights of Perth were illuminating the sky through the darkening gloaming. The border road turned west at Dunblane, skirting the city at a distance and leaving it to sit secure behind prodigious barriers of razor wire and ditches. They headed west and Nin took the next exit ramp while gritting his teeth and wringing the steering wheel in his hands.

Doune, even the sound of it rang like a bell, like a forger's hammer on an anvil, like your ears after a clap of thunder, it struck a note of warning. For more than half a millennia Doune had been a centre of the Gaels' weapons industry, founded on their insatiable desire for ever more sophisticated armaments, as well as meeting the needs of militaries from around the world. Nin explained that Doune was run by the Ateliers, the arms producers, each of which was specialised in certain areas. The best-known was the Atelier of Thomas Caddell and Sons, which had been founded in 1646. They had never been at the commodity end of the market; they were artists, who made the best for the best, and at a price.

The Kat swept into town, passing low houses of stone: some white, some red, some unharled and bare schist, Nin pulled in by the Mercat Cross and parked. Across the road was the steep corbie-stepped gable of the town's leading hotel, its stone walls towering over them. Above its studded oak double doors swung a sign made of a crossed pair of old-fashioned steel pistols. This was the infamous Sign of the Silver Pistol, the location of their proposed rendezvous with the outlaw Alasdair MacGregor.

63 - THE RENDEZVOUS

The Wild Geese had been a popular restaurant with the more nefarious clientele of Doune for centuries and over the next few hours Gillespie, Nin and Charlie gradually sagged on their bar stools as the row of empty glasses in front of them proliferated. Plates of food came and went as the hour hand of the clock relentlessly marched around the dial. Gillespie was beginning to feel nervous that Alasdair MacGregor might not show after all – bloodbond or no. Even Nin was beginning to wonder if such things were still accorded due respect in the modern age, in any event a MacGregor was hardly the most reliable counterparty.

It was as Charlie ordered their third bottle of Claret, that the door opened, and a dark figure entered. The Maitre d' bustled over and with a slightly fawning manner relieved him of his coat and bag, ushering him down the few stairs into the bar area. The shadows seemed to lengthen as the man descended the steps, as if the illumination cast by the dim bulbs could never quite keep up with him. It was only when he was practically by their side that they could be sure that Alasdair MacGregor had kept his word.

MacGregor's pale eyes parted the vaporous brume that hazed and shrouded his features, their evident delight at seeing Gillespie, Nin and Charlie was almost matched by their surprise at his arrival. He grabbed them in a two-armed bear hug, while calling for whisky from the barman. Now that he was close, Gillespie could see that he was in quite a state, his kilt and stockings were sodden and covered in mud, and his whole body was drenched in a mixture of sweat, blood and bogwater. He had clearly come straight off the hill and his journey had not been an easy one. Nin got him a chair, so that he could sit down before he fell down.

Nin poured him a glass of claret, "Here's to you MacGregor, I had my doubts but you're a true man of your word."

"Aye, well it wasn't the easiest journey, that I can say. You didn't leave me much time to get here, so I've had to run those Balquhidder hills through night and day, and they don't get any smaller with time I can assure you."

Having ordered some more food, they waited for Alasdair to regain his composure and for the whisky, wine and mound of carbohydrates to work their magic so that they could start to plan their assault on Castle Ascog.

64 - THE ATELIER OF THOMAS CADDELL

The next morning, after a hearty breakfast of kippers and kedgeree, sausages, crispy bacon, Stornoway black pudding, toast and coffee, lots of coffee, they felt ready to face the world. After a mile or so outside of town, Nin took a discreet turning on the left, sandwiched between two neatly clipped hedges and came to a brief stop at a simple black five bar gate. This swung silently open to admit them and they drove onwards through a sweep of parkland dotted with mature trees.

The Atelier was an extraordinary building, famous in the Republic and beyond for its bold architecture. Built in reinforced concrete, the central section rose 100 feet into the air and was fretted with a looming De Chirico-style arcade, whose neat round topped arches teetered on very tall narrow piers, a motif that was repeated throughout the building. This was flanked on either side by paired drum towers, also pierced with tall thin windows. From his previous visits, Nin explained that as you rose through the building there were many different levels and layers, including the famous roof garden.

Nin parked the Kat in the Visitors' carpark and they crunched across the gravel to the main entrance. This was sunk in huge round pipe on its side and led like a vein straight into the Atelier's heart. Waiting at the mouth of the pipe was an imposing woman in a white lab coat, her dark hair bound in a bun, wearing a pair of thick black framed glasses. She proffered her hand to Nin, who shook it politely as she introduced herself:

"Natasha Caddell, at your service. We are delighted to be able to welcome you to The Atelier of Thomas Caddell."

She stared closely at Gillespie and Charlie in particular, before leading them into the building. After mounting a few steps, they came to a wall of glass, at least a foot thick, with no obvious joins. She placed her palm flat on it and, as if by magic, a pair of huge doors were suddenly revealed in the glass as they swung inwards on hinges hidden in the floor and ceiling. Natasha ushered them through and led them to a screen mounted in the wall, while the doors swung closed behind them. As they approached, Charlie's face appeared on it with his name and address, and various biographical details. Natasha gestured at the screen and said:

"Can you confirm your details please Mr Farquharson. As we have not had the pleasure of receiving you before, we need to ensure we have an accurate record. If you could also just place your right hand and thumb on the screen to acknowledge the details are correct." Charlie did so and stood back while the screen added his fingerprints to his file.

Next Natasha turned to Gillespie and invited him forward to the screen.

"Mr MacNachtan, we have not had the honour of serving you before, and you must register to enter the Atelier. We have created a profile, but could you please check that it's accurate." At which the screen was populated with Gillespie's name, address, height and weight, eye colour, the schools he had gone to, his University degree, and a variety of photographs, including several taken since their arrival.

Gillespie looked startled and a little shocked: "How did you get so much information about me? He asked. "In fact, how did you even know my name?"

Natasha looked at him as if speaking to a young child: "As you drove in through our gate, your face was captured and matched against a variety of social platforms. We then were able to scrape all the other information we need. We find it saves a lot of time and arguing with reluctant visitors. As I am sure you can understand, security and discretion are our priority."

"For example, let's take Mr MacGregor here." She pointed at Alasdair. "He's wanted by the security forces in the Republic and the Kingdom, not to mention 14 other jurisdictions. However, as a longstanding client we would never divulge his presence here, or his account details, to any external party."

"Now, if you could just put your right hand on the screen, including your thumb…perfect, thank you. That concludes the check in process. Now, please follow me to the sales suite."

Natasha led the way deeper into the building until they came to a huge room filled with presses and machines. There were not many people, but the odd white coated figure could be spotted between the rows of automated production units. Along one side of the wall was a massive cantilevered staircase that rose the full height of the building in one long inexorable flight. The rough concrete treads were set into the wall with their far end suspended in space, there was no handrail to catch if you fell, just a long drop to the factory floor below. Gillespie's jaw sagged, not only at the size of the room but also the height of the staircase. Health and safety worked to different parameters in the Republic.

Finally, they reached the second floor, and entered a large triple height room. On the far side there was a wall of glass that looked out towards the highland line, where the green grassy slopes of the lowlands broke against the rough-hewn hills to the north. The room was divided into three sections with one half occupied by a very long table and the other half divided again into a seating area with display cases and finally a firing range. Natasha invited them to sit at the table, where tea and coffee were served.

"Now," said Natasha fixing them each in turn with a studied look over her glasses. "How may the Atelier of Thomas Caddell be of service?"

65 - WIRING

The first alert popped up in the right-hand corner of her screen and she closed it without really giving it a glance. The system frequently sent her reminders, alerts and warnings and over the years she had learned to ignore most of these. She was so deeply embedded in her network that, like a spider sat in the middle of her web, she already knew when there was something to be really worried about. It was only when the second one popped up a few minutes later that her mind focused on the little black box that winked from the corner of her screen:

UNUSUAL INFORMATION REQUEST, FILE DOWNLOAD QUARANTINED

She started exploring the network to see what was going on. Firstly, she wanted to take a look at what this file request was and who had requested it. Of course, the network was large with hundreds if not thousands of users, it could be really hard to stay on top of who was doing what. Which was why there were strict permissions protocols and a few of her own little security checks to ensure no one could run around unhindered without her knowing. This was probably nothing, but she wanted to check it out, nonetheless.

****

Fiona was worried she had pushed it too far. In her desire to make the most of her access to the Lamont systems she had chanced her arm trying to get a floorplan of the castle as this would be invaluable to the rescue team. The idea had come to her when she was looking at the catering schedule trying to find the location of Kirstie and MacCailean Mòr. Of course, these files were not stored in a folder helpfully named Castle Ascog blueprints on it in big red letters, but it had been while she was in the catering department's folder that she had got thinking a bit more laterally. She toggled back up a few layers and went in search of the castle maintenance files. She was hoping that the maintenance team were not very computer savvy and didn't spend much time in front of a screen.

Having found the right network tree, she dug down until she got stopped by a password point. She reckoned she had three goes before setting off any alarms and promised herself two attempts before heading for the exit. She needn't have worried, she got it in one: password.

She now had to think where the best place to look was; she tried plumbing, but all she found were orders for a new soil pipe, caustic soda for drain cleaning and a few old and rather inappropriate photos from a past Christmas party involving a pair of plungers. She tabbed back and tried Housekeeping, but that was even duller, with invoices for floor cleaner and hoover bags. She was beginning to run out of ideas when she tried the folder marked Power and Light. In there, under the System subfolder, she found what she was looking for: a wiring plan of the Castle showing the routing of all the powerlines and cables. More importantly, it showed, entry and exit points, stairwells and floorplans for all levels, including the sub-basements.

She right clicked and tried to download the file. Nothing happened for a long time and then a box came up saying "your request has been submitted to an administrator for authorisation, please wait". Fuck, fuck, fuck, someone was bound to spot and query the request. But she needed those plans. Instead of waiting for the download that would probably never come, she reopened the files and carefully took screen shots of every level before closing them and fleeing the network. She realised she was sweating with the stress and the tension, but she had what they needed, even if they were just screen shots, that was going to have to be good enough. At least she had not been caught: their backdoor was still undiscovered.

****

Donna sat at her computer and activated a trace to see what users and devices were active on the network at that moment. Scrolling through the operating system, open ports and IP addresses she did not spot anything unusual, but she needed to go deeper to be sure. Next, she launched a packet sniffing programme to see what data was being sent and where it was going to. Nothing untoward came up. She then went into the quarantined request, pulling up the file and opened it. Why would anyone want electrical wiring plans? She picked up the phone and rang the maintenance department. It was answered by Dougie MacLucas. She sighed; Dougie was always flirting with her but couldn't hammer a straight nail if his life depended on it; she didn't imagine she was going to have much joy with him.

"Hey Dougie, how you doin' this evening?" She said in an attempt to be friendly.

"Aye, all the better for having you in my ear." He replied, in way that made her feel slightly ill and violated at the same time.

"Ah thanks Dougie. Look, just a quick question for you. Is anyone from your team doing anything that would need the wiring diagram for the castle?"

"Ah, I can't rightly say." She could almost hear him scratching his head as he did so, as if the rubbing of his greasy hair might ignite some braincells into action. "I know that Jess had some trouble with the fuses in the west tower during the week, maybe she was looking at the wiring for that?"

"Aye, that's probably it. Sorry to bother you, have a nice evening."

"Och the night is yet young. Why don't you come around, we could go for a bevy in the bar?" Dougie asked, rather too boldly for Donna.

"Thanks Dougie. That's a kind offer, another night maybe. I need to clean my computer keyboard tonight. Thanks all the same." Donna hung up the phone and, feeling satisfied, shut her computer for the night.

66 - SHOPPING

Gillespie sat fascinated at the exchange that was taking place between Alasdair, Nin, Charlie and Natasha. Every time they specified a need, she recommended a product which would meet or exceed their specifications. They discussed the basic parameters of what they were looking for, in this case a close quarters indoor assault. Natasha then made various suggestions which were in turn discussed and considered by the group. It became rapidly clear to Gillespie that not only was Natasha an expert in her own right, but that Caddell's was operating at the near science fiction end of the munitions spectrum and although they'd had nearly 400 years of continuous innovation and development it was still impressive.

The conversation started with assault rifles but swiftly graduated from such run of the mill considerations of accuracy and rates of fire. Natasha invited them over to a particular display case from which she produced a boxy black machine gun not much more than a foot long. The trigger was about halfway down its body and it had the curved scimitar of an extended magazine protruding from the base of its pistol grip. Flicking a few clips, she extended a stock from the rear and dropped down a forward grip, transforming what had been a pistol into more of an assault rifle.

She handed it to Alasdair, who immediately said: "Heckler and Koch MP7a1, 4.6mm calibre and 40 rounds in that extended magazine. Popular with the US SEALs and other counter terrorism units."

"Very good," she said. "Except this is our own variant with some special features. You see there," at which she pointed at a thin black tube that was mounted on the body of the gun. They all nodded. "Well that is a special extra which we think transforms this weapon, particularly in close quarters combat situations. It may not look like much but it's what we've called a Boma-solais, or light grenade. When you push this button here," she carefully pointed the gun away from them down the range before indicating a small stud on the side of the tube, that she then pressed, releasing a flash of coruscating light down the range. "That is a unidirectional bolt of ultra-bright light, in this model about 32,000 lumens, equivalent to over 160,000 candles, which will temporarily blind and disorient those you point it at, particularly in an indoor scenario where opponents will be rendered unable to see for at least 30 minutes. The battery allows you up to five discharges before it needs to be plugged in."

The assembled group cooed over the weapon, which Natasha carefully placed back on its stand.

Alasdair then stepped forward and asked: "Could you show us some of your latest drone units? I've heard they are pretty special from some of my colleagues."

Natasha looked at him and paused for a moment, as if deciding whether it was a reasonable request, before leading them over to a robust sealed door on the other side of the walkway.

Natasha closed the door behind them: "These are our tactical drone units; they are normally only available to our Government clients due to their highly specialised nature. But because Mr MacGregor is such a long-standing and valued client and given the special relationship between Atelier Caddell and the Griogaraich over many centuries, I am prepared to make an exception in this case."

"In respect of your scenario I can recommend two units in particular. The first is this." She pointed to a tiny grey painted drone about the size of a flying matchbox. "This is our C4-X108 unit, otherwise known as the Hornet. It can be controlled by the gyroscopes in your phone, like so." At which she held her phone in her hand and lifted it up to make the drone rise and pushed it forward to make it move away around the room. As she moved her hand the drone would track it. "Here, you have a go." She passed the phone to Gillespie, who immediately navigated the drone around the room. It was supremely intuitive and delicate, with an incredible level of control. There was an obstacle course of wooden posts hanging from the ceiling and Gillespie was soon slaloming the drone through these as if he had been flying it for years.

"Very good. Easy isn't it?" Natasha held out her hand to take back her phone, before parking the drone back on the table. "The Hornet is packed with a charge of C4 explosive that is sufficient to knockdown all human targets within a radius of four metres. It is therefore very useful to be able to fly up to an entrenched position or around corners to clear away opposition. It is most effective in an indoor environment."

"Finally, there is this unit which we call the Woofer." She pointed to a larger unit, the size of a thick book, with rotors on each corner. "This uses an acoustic-dynamic energy charge to stun and incapacitate targets over a small area. It would probably still be effective in a room of this size for example. The beauty of it is that it's silent to human ears, so it can be drifted into an enemy position and detonated, unleashing a sonic pulse that will literally have your opponents on their knees, probably vomiting. It works by disrupting the inner ear with a massive blast of ultra-low frequency sound waves. Because it's such low frequency, it cannot actively be heard. It is a little less portable than the Hornet, but it can obviously be used more than once. You fly it in the same way, using your phone."

"That now concludes our demonstration for this morning. I think that's all that we have that is relevant to your needs. I will now leave you for a few minutes while you consider your order." Natasha turned and left the room, leaving them to chatter over what they had seen and discuss what they were going to buy and how they were going to pay.

Half an hour later, having agreed on a shopping list and said farewell to Natasha, they found themselves walking back down the entrance tunnel into the fresh morning air, carrying a variety of packages.

Gillespie suddenly felt that time was running very quickly now, they could not afford to waste a moment if they were going to be in time to save Kirstie. The glamour of their visit to Caddell's soon began to wear off, as the reality of what they were about to try and do came front of mind once again.

As they drove down the snaking driveway back towards the entrance gates, he could feel a sense of foreboding rise, gripping his guts in its suffocating clench. He closed his eyes and focused on pushing it down, thinking about his friends, not just Nin and Charlie and now Alasdair, but also Brighid and Iain and Kirstie. This helped him to push away the crushing coils of self-doubt, freeing him again to breathe and think, and while the gnawing demon of fear wasn't banished, it was subdued for the time being.

67 - THE RAT'S NEST

For the sake of discretion, Fiona, Brighid, Jamie and Archie had decided to convene at Iain the Rat's house on the outskirts of Clachan. This was a simple highland cottage, white harled and with two dormer windows peeking out from the roof. They trooped into the spotless kitchen and having kissed Liz, the Rat's bounteous wife, on each cheek, they each pulled up a chair and surrounded the table to talk. The warmth of Liz's welcome was renowned throughout the county and soon the table was groaning under drop scones and shortbread, teacakes and squashed flies, whose oozy, treacled raisins tumbled from the grip of the flaky short pastry. In between hot buttered mouthfuls they tried to focus on the grim task ahead.

Once the contents of the table had been cleared away, mugs of tea were filled, and Fiona propped a tablet at one end of the table so that they could conference in Nin, Charlie and Gillespie. The first thing they saw was the immediately recognisable top of Nin's head, the spiky prongs waving in the camera lens as he tried to prop his tablet up. Once he had pulled back from the camera, they could see four figures looking back at them.

Charlie leant towards the screen and said: "Before we get started, let me just introduce you to our good friend and ally on this operation Alasdair MacGregor." At which he held up his hands as if to frame Alasdair's face. Fiona couldn't work out if it was the screen or the lens of their camera, but Alasdair's face seemed to shimmer and weave, as if behind a heat haze or greasy fingerprint, it made it very hard to make out his fine features under those dark brows.

There was a stunned silence around the table as they contemplated the reality of what was being discussed. To team up with this most notorious cateran, famous for kidnaps and murders, robberies and assaults, seemed reckless, although no one could deny that those skills might be very helpful in their current situation.

Having got over their initial surprise at their new ally, Fiona started by updating them on what she had discovered from her excursions on the Lamont network. She circulated print outs of the screen shots she had taken of the electrical wiring floor plans, with yellow highlighter around the cells that she thought held Kirstie and MacCailean Mòr. They all felt nervous over how deep they were, particularly sub-level 6; that was an awful lot of floors to fight your way out of.

They rapidly agreed that a frontal assault would never work and that they would need to use stealth to have any chance of success. But how were they going to get in, and more importantly yet, how were they going to get out? For every route that was proposed more questions and issues were raised. The mood round the table began to get gloomy; no one had the answers: they were out of their depth. The glimmer of self-confidence that had been sparked by Fiona's success was now guttering and in danger of being extinguished.

Then an unexpected voice piped up; Liz, the Rat's wife, who'd been plying them with pots of tea and her astounding range of home baking, had been standing at the kitchen counter listening to the bold and ambitious plans. She had said nothing as ever more extravagant stratagems and tactics were passed back and forth both by the team. As the black cloud of hopelessness started to settle on the gathering, she plucked up the courage to speak.

"Excuse me for asking, but am I right in thinking we're looking for a way to get into the castle that won't attract too much attention?" The group nodded and invited her to pull up a chair. "Aye, well if that is the case, I may have a crazy idea. I'm sure many of you are familiar with MacFarlane's bakery in Tarbert, across the water from Ascog? Aye? Well that's run by my cousin Morag and I don't think I am exaggerating when I say that it's famous for the best baking on the west coast." The nodding of heads and involuntary licking of lips was all the confirmation she needed to continue. "I happen to know that she is always making stuff for Ascog, it seems that the Lamontation has a sweet tooth to go with all his other vices. How about we hold up the next delivery they have to the Castle and take the order there ourselves? That should get at least two of you inside the castle walls."

There was general wonderment around the table at this brilliant idea, but the hope that sprang in their breasts was almost immediately doused by Archie. "That's all very well Liz, but how do we know when the next order will be? It is quite possible there may not be one for weeks, and we can't afford to wait."

The seesaw of hopes raised and then dashed was almost more than Fiona could bear, it always seemed as though someone was trying to pick holes and look for problems when they weren't coming up with their own ideas. She wracked her brain trying to think of a solution but answer there came none. She stood up to walk around the kitchen to better aid her thought processes. She looked at the cupboards with their neatly stacked plates and upside-down glasses, the tea towels hung from hooks and stacks of baking trays, the calendar on the wall with each day neatly struck out after it had passed with a single line, the pin board with jobs to do and useful numbers, deliveries expected and appointments that had been made.

It was then that she saw it, and she gave a squeak of excitement as the idea popped into her mind, fully formed. The others all turned to see what she was so excited about. She reached down and picked up a folded copy of the latest Oban Raven, where on the front cover in big black type it announced:

Lamont Invested as Colonel of The Black Watch

She held the paper up in front of her as she turned, eyes gleaming: "Don't you see? We don't need to wait for a delivery, we can order our own! We can commission and send him a cake to celebrate his investiture as

Colonel of the Black Watch. There's no way they are going to turn that back at the Castle gate."

There was a stunned silence as the room contemplated the brilliance of this idea, before Archie said dryly: "So, this is a bit like the Trojan horse but in a cake…."

After the laughter had died down, the mood soared as they discussed the plan. Finally, it was decided that Alasdair could place the order, and pay for it from an offshore MacGregor account, leaving no trace back to the MacNachtans. As they'd placed the order, they could specify when they wanted it to be delivered, making it very straight forward for them to intercept the delivery boys, substituting their own team, who could thereby gain access to the castle.

The buoyant mood round the table did not take away from the fact that this plan, clever though it was, would only get them into the castle, not necessarily out again. But the positive momentum pulled them onwards and they had soon agreed the remaining details. It was almost insane in its ambition, but this was no time for timidity, they had to be bold.

68 - THE GREAT IMPENETRABLE FOREST

After the call finished, Charlie and Nin disappeared to pack, while Gillespie sat in the Bar with Alasdair. Gillespie had worked hard to persuade him, Nin and Charlie that he should accompany them. They had pointed out his lack of military experience and the dangers that they were going to face, but Gillespie had been adamant. He hadn't come this far to turn away now. On one thing they did agree, he would not be part of the team that actually entered the castle, that would have been foolish beyond words. Instead, he would be their eyes and ears on the outside.

The wheels of the plan were now turning and gaining momentum. Alasdair had spoken with Liz's cousin at MacFarlane's Bakery in Tarbert and placed the order, paying with one of his many offshore accounts. Charlie and Nin's giggles had almost given the game away as they sat listening to him place the order. Alasdair had to ensure that the cake was sufficiently large that it would require two people to carry it and he went into great detail of the flavour and shape of the cake, the type of icing he wanted, and the dedication written on it. The incongruity of listening to a wanted man like Alasdair MacGregor going into such detail on cake icing was almost more than Nin and Charlie could bear; Gillespie eventually had to usher them from the room.

Finally, the order was placed, for delivery the following afternoon, which gave them precisely 24 hours to get in position. They split into four different teams: Alpha was the penetration team of Nin and Alasdair, their two most experienced fighters; Beta was Charlie and Gillespie, the on the ground back up outside the Castle; Gamma was Brighid, Iain and Archie who were going to intercept the cake and provide the getaway; and finally there was Omega which was Fiona, who would be based at the Campbell digital unit and provide online infiltration of the Lamont network. Brighid also had the task of briefing Duncan Campbell, MacCailean Mòr's steward on details of the plan.

When all was agreed, they stood back to admire the plan, rather like an inventor admires a prototype, all held together with baler twine and tape. They knew it could work, they felt it should work, but would it actually take to the sky, or fall apart on the ground?

The clock was ticking: they had to get a move on. They piled their gear into the Kat and headed out of Doune to the west. The first part of the journey was straightforward and took them along the Wade that marked the border to reach the east shore of Loch Lomond, where they crossed at Rowardennan ferry before making their way to Arrochar. There they had to leave the Kat, and Alasdair had arranged for a trusted Griogaraich boatman to take them down Loch Long and out through the Clyde estuary before heading up the eastern coast of Bute to reach their drop off at Loch Riddon on the southern coast of Cowal. This was as near as they could get to Castle Ascog without attracting unwelcome attention, although it still required a sharp walk through the Great Impenetrable Forest and over the hills of Cowal to get to their target.

It was around midnight when the boat pulled away from the quay. The journey had so far been uneventful, but it was now that the real pressure started. As the whine of the boat's engine faded into the night, all Gillespie could hear was the lap of the tide on the shore and the whistle of the wind through the inky blackness of the trees ahead. Alasdair had chosen this spot as it was as close as they could realistically hope to get without being spotted. The reason that he could be so confident of this was that Cowal was almost entirely subsumed by the Republic's infamous Great Impenetrable Forest, which true to its name was near impassable to man or beast.

BLOODBOND

Gillespie had studied the Great Impenetrable Forest in both geography and biology at school, where it had been used as an example of how the reckless introduction of non-native, invasive species can wreck an ecosystem. In the late 18th and 19th centuries many rare plants were brought to the Republic to be cultivated and sold to collectors from around the world. However, the success of one of the introductions had surpassed all others, with a particular variant of Rhododendron Ponticum coming from Spain finding the climate of Cowal very much to its liking. In the intervening centuries it had spread to cover the entire peninsula in its writhing choking branches. It crept over and smothered the hillsides, was seemingly immune to destruction and had incredible powers of self-resurrection. Its only positive feature was that it made a very effective barrier to Kingdom aggression, its interlocking branches creating a continuous and impregnable bio-fence which rendered the movement of troops near impossible.

Gillespie was now contemplating the deep black reality of this forest with its rustling leaves and spiky branches. Although Ascog was only a few miles away, it might as well have been on the moon. Alasdair claimed to have some knowledge of the Forest and took the lead, using the GPS on his phone to try and find a forestry path in the interior. As they pushed through interminable clumps of bushes the cold wet bog and pitch black of the night made progress impossibly slow. Gillespie was beginning to regret coming; how were they ever going to find their way out of this maze? He was constantly ducking under or climbing over branches, being slapped in the face by the wet leathery leaves or poked by their sharp twigs. Hour after hour they trailed Alasdair in a silent conga as inch by inch he led them deeper into the forest. Every now and then Gillespie would look behind to see if he could see where they had come from, but the branches seemed to close ranks behind them, sealing their path with an oppressive black wet wall.

As if contending with the obstructive vegetation wasn't bad enough, they also needed to clamber their way over a spine of hills before finally coming out onto flatter terrain on their western slopes. This was forested with plantation pines, and within their dull and serried ranks they finally stumbled on the access track that Alasdair had been looking for.

Once on the track they made good time and were soon only a short distance from Ascog. Gillespie was cold and exhausted after the gruelling slog through the forest: by contrast, Nin and Alasdair looked like they'd barely got started. They had a few hours to kill until the appointed hour, so they at least had time to get some rest. Here the forestry had reverted to ponticum and having left the trail they pushed a few yards into the blackness until they found a small clearing where they could safely have a bite to eat and sleep away from prying eyes.

69 - INTERCEPTION

The bow window of the Boar's Head Inn made the perfect viewing point, and Archie had arrived mid-morning to ensure that he could get the table tucked into the curved curtain of glass that looked out over the harbour. While he sat and waited, he drank endless cups of coffee and tea; he tried to alternate them, as if that would fool his body over the amount of caffeine it had consumed.

Despite the flow of plates and cups to his table, his eye never wandered from the large plate glass window of MacFarlane's Bakery. He could even see the zinc counter top groaning under sweet confections of all colours and flavours: millionaire's shortbread, fly cemeteries, apple turnovers, flapjacks, cat's tongues, krispie cakes, fairy cakes, cupcakes, doughnuts, almond slices, coconut macaroons, scones, and pancakes: not to mention the savoury section with stovies, black pudding wraps, bacon slices and sausage rolls, the list went on and on. If it hadn't been for the size of the lunch he had just eaten he could've easily demolished a few platters of their products too.

His job may have been the most comfortable, but it was a critical one; he had to alert Brighid and the Rat at the precise moment that the cake was about to start its journey and, given the very public environment, they couldn't afford for anyone to be suspicious. Down the quay, Iain The Rat was leaning against a bollard looking out across the water. Brighid had a black cap pulled low over her fair hair and was slowly feeding chips to the seagulls that crowded the quayside, hustling to get their share. She had attracted quite a flock of those noisy and vicious avian thieves.

Archie tested his microphone, making sure that they could all hear him in their discrete earpieces. Now all they had to do was wait.

The weak sun shone: a welcome change from the drizzle and rain that had wrapped the west coast for much of the previous week. Of course, weather here rarely stayed the same for long, but it appeared to be calm and fine for the time being. Archie looked at his watch: just gone 2pm. If they did not get a move on they were going to be late. Just as he was wondering what ingenious and uncomfortable punishments the Lamontation doubtless had for tardy delivery boys, Archie saw a boat slip across the harbour and pull up, stern-to the harbour steps.

It was a classic west coast taxi boat, about 20-foot-long and with a generous enclosed cabin and powerful engine. These boats could be seen puttering up and down the coast all day making deliveries and dropping off customers, they were the lifeblood of coastal commerce. With the tide quite low, the roof of the wheelhouse cabin was below the quayside wall, shielding the interior from view: a point in their favour. The two boatmen sauntered across the road to MacFarlane's. Simultaneously, the Rat set off from his bollard towards the quay steps, so that as they were distracted going through MacFarlane's door, he was calmly walking down the steps onto their boat and out of sight.

Brighid was now surrounded by a cloud of gulls; they flapped, screaming and cawing as she tossed the occasional chip among them. She expressed no interest in anything that was happening behind her in the bakery, but she didn't need to, as Archie was giving her and the Rat a running commentary from his vantage point. Finally, the bakery door was hooked open to allow the two boatmen to squeeze through carrying a huge Tupperware cake box, at least two-foot square and a foot high. They carefully walked it over the street, successfully negotiating the kerb and avoiding the storm drain. They got to the quay steps and gently started to descend, struggling to keep the box flat. They were now out of Archie's sight, so it was over to the Rat and Brighid to work their magic.

Brighid waited until they had got to the bottom of the steps, had negotiated the transom and were trying to get the cake past the wheel into the cabin. This was her moment. She dropped the steaming bag of chips to the ground causing a white winged explosion of gulls as they fought to get to this generous bounty, screaming and flapping in their fury at the competition. The cacophony was deafening and distracting, something Brighid was relying on to hide any noise they were about to make and to focus all eyes on the gulls, and not the boat. As the gulls fought and tore at each other, Brighid slipped silently as a shadow down the steps and over the transom. The two men were completely focused on the delicate task of placing the cake on the table in the cabin, one had his back to her, while the other had his back to the chain locker in the bow.

As the cake hit the table, the chain locker door exploded outwards. The Rat grabbed the man from behind, passing a thick garrotting band around his throat and cutting off his air supply as he wrestled him backwards. Before his companion could even react, Brighid tapped him on the shoulder. As he turned, conveniently wide eyed and mouth agape, she sprayed him liberally with mace, incapacitating him instantly as he clawed at his eyes and throat. Brighid looked over to the Rat to see if he needed any help, but the boatman's struggling was getting fainter, and it wasn't long before he was still, unconscious but breathing.

They swiftly bound and gagged the two men, covering them with a pile of blankets. She tried to wipe as much of the mace off the man's face as she could, to limit his discomfort, but his rage at the unexpected assault was obvious. She just hoped that the bonds would hold until their mission was over.

With their prisoners secure, she went back up the steps to cast off. The only sound on the quayside being the screams of the gulls as they finished the last of the chips. She nodded at Archie and cast off the ropes, before getting behind the wheel and slowly guiding them out of the harbour, threading her way through the maze of buoys and boats towards their destination across the loch.

It was a lovely day for a cruise, even if their destination was not one many would have chosen. The water of Loch Fyne was looking its most seductive, its silvery sheen reflecting the green craggy hills. It was not a long crossing and within twenty minutes they had moored up at the small harbour of Portavaddie which sat a mile or so below Castle Ascog. There, waiting for them on the quay, was the familiar grin of Nin, and the new face of Alasdair MacGregor.

Brighid embraced Nin, she had not realised how much she had been missing him, but now that she had his sparkling blue eyes staring back at her, she felt her day had improved. She then turned to Alasdair MacGregor: he was not what she had expected at all. She had imagined a big beefy cutthroat, probably covered in scars and tattoos. Instead, with his lithe frame and average height, he was almost nondescript, except for those pale eyes, neat dark hair, thick eyebrows and fine features. His face was extraordinary and indescribable at the same time: like the itch which you cannot scratch, the word on the tip of your tongue, the thought at the back of your mind; you know it's there, you can feel it, you reach for it, but you can't pin it down. He shook her hand politely and that of the Rat, before Nin and he took the cake and set off up the hill towards the castle.

70 - THE EXTRACTION

While it hadn't looked far on the map, by the time they had got to the top of the short hill that led from Portavaddie to the castle driveway, both Nin and Alasdair were pouring with sweat. The cool air did not offset the sunshine and steep gradient, not to mention the weight of the cake. Nin was cursing Alasdair under his breath all the way up the hill for the size and extravagance of the offering.

As they got to the Castle, they were stopped by the sentry at the gatehouse who patted them down for weapons and then inspected the cake. Satisfied that there was nothing suspicious, he radioed ahead to the kitchen and sent them on their way. While the main drive curved to the south and ran along a small loch to the Castle, the back driveway went straight up the hill and was sandwiched on either side by forestry. After a few hundred yards it started to bend around the back of the stumpy hill - Cnoc a' Chaisteal, the Castle Rock - against whose southern flank the Castle sheltered, before swinging round to arrive at the rear of the Castle itself. They needed to time their rendezvous with Charlie and Gillespie very carefully, to the exact moment that they were out of sight of the gatehouse but before they were in view from the Castle. It was as the drive made this final climb around the rock, and with forestry close on either side, that they had planned to meet and collect all their gear. This was a key part of the plan, since there was no way they would've been allowed to walk through Castle Ascog's gates carrying weapons, but without them the rescue was doomed.

As soon as they turned the bend out of view of the gatehouse, Nin could see Charlie's camouflaged face peering out through the branches of a massive ponticum bush. Nin's eyes followed the line of Charlie's pointing finger to the two slim black backpacks lying under a bush right by the tarmac. If you didn't know they were there, you could've walked past them a hundred times without seeing them. Nin steered Alasdair and the cake over to the bush and having placed the cake box on the ground he lifted his kilt to take an extravagant piss. He reckoned that any watchers would likely avert their gaze, and, once he'd finished, he discretely swept the bags up from under the bush. Moments later, they each had a pack on their backs and had picked up the cake again to walk the last few hundred yards to the back door.

Castle Ascog was an unusual combination of 18th Century refinement and medieval brutality; it was as if two houses had been smashed uncomfortably together. Most of the Castle was 15th century, with a huge round tower on the south eastern corner surmounted by a spiked roof. But there was also a more refined 18th century wing. This was where Lamont spent most of his time, preferring its gracious proportions and high ceilings to the dark and rather mean rooms in the old building. As at Dunderave, there were windows scattered across its façade with no seeming logic to their placement and two bartizan turrets hung above the man entrance set under a corbie-stepped gable. The front of the Castle looked out over Loch Ascog to the south, which was really more of a large pond, while the later wing looked across Loch Fyne towards Tarbert.

A vertiginous wall of rough masonry towered above Nin and Alasdair as they arrived at the back door. As befitted an ancient stronghold there were no windows on the ground floor, instead there were gunloops and arrow slits that scrutinised their approach. The door itself was pale studded oak, with a massive wrought iron ring for a handle.

They rang the bell and waited. A voice came over a small speaker asking who they were and what the delivery was. Nin tried to keep his voice calm as he explained that they had come from MacFarlane's Bakery in Tarbert and had a special delivery for Lord Lamont. There was a brief pause before a buzzer sounded and the door swung open.

A shotgun toting Lamont met them at the door and ushered them into a spotless white hallway. There was a counter at the far end behind which sat a hatchet-faced woman who was eying them suspiciously beneath a mountain of coiffed and coiled hair. As they approached the counter, she put down the nail file that she had been buffing her already perfect nails: "Who are you? You've come from MacFarlane's, right? Where are the usual delivery boys? This is highly irregular. We've not placed an order, so I don't understand why you are here."

As Nin tried to answer her, she put her palm in his face and shushed him. "No, don't talk, you're here to carry things, not speak. Let me do the speaking. I'll have to call MacFarlane's and find out what is going on. This is all highly irregular."

As she picked up the phone, Nin felt a chill go down his spine; if the alarm was raised now they would have no chance of making it down into the sub-levels: he couldn't allow her to make that call. He tried to speak but again found himself staring at her palm, and for emphasis she brought her index finger across her lips and pointed at him. He was speechless, and not just because she wanted him to be.

The Lamont with the shotgun was standing in the corner, not exactly poised like a coiled spring, but certainly alert. Just as he was about to do something reckless, Nin heard Alasdair's honeyed tones pour like a soothing balm across the counter.

"Madam, I am really sorry that we are putting you to so much trouble. My colleague and I would only be too delighted for you to call MacFarlane's. But as you can see, the cake is a special delivery for Lord Lamont on his investiture as Colonel of the Black Watch. Look here, take a close look at the design…" and he made a strange pass with his hand in front of her eyes while directing her gaze at the surface of the cake. Her eyes immediately became slightly glazed and seemed to follow his hand over the ornate writing iced onto the cake's white surface.

"Yes...." She said, suddenly dreamy. "Lovely, isn't it. What pretty colours, and I do love the battle honours: a charming touch. His Lordship will be pleased...."

"Should we take it to the kitchen?" Alasdair asked slowly, the syllables rolling and dripping off his tongue like nectar. The whole room seemed to shrink in, to listen to every word as they emerged and fluttered free from his lips.

"Kitchen? Yes.... the kitchen..... what are you waiting for?..... You should take it to the kitchen. Here, Davey," She clicked her fingers at the man with the shotgun. "Take these gentlemen to the kitchen, they have an important delivery."

As they were about to leave, Alasdair suddenly returned to the counter. "Could you also please tell me the Wi-Fi code?"

"Wi-Fi code? Yes, of course, it's 123456. Thank you and have a nice day." The receptionist returned her gaze into space.

Davey slung the shotgun on his back and led the way down the corridor, swiping them through a steel blast door and on into the castle.

Nin was seriously impressed by Alasdair's hypnosis technique, he had even found himself hooked on the drip of those delicious syllables, unable to think beyond their perfect golden drops. It had gotten them into the Castle, now they just needed to dump this goddam cake.

Davey took them down a flight of tight wound, rough wooden stairs onto a long dim corridor lined with linen presses and cupboards. They passed exotically labelled doors that echoed the house's long history - dairy, scullery, still room and pantry. Eventually they came to a large stainless-steel door with a glass observation panel set in the centre: this was the kitchen proper.

Dressed in white and with his hair tied up in a net, the Chef was hard at work glazing some pastries with dribbles of caramelised sugar. Without deigning to speak to them, he gestured that they should leave the cake on the counter. Nin turned to Davey and asked him to hold the cake for a moment.

As the Davey unquestioningly took Nin's end of the cake, Nin reached across the steel counter and picked up a heavy wooden rolling pin. Before Davey even knew what was going to happen, let alone react, Nin smashed him around the head with it knocking him out cold. Davey collapsed headfirst into the cake, soaking its white Royal icing in a carmine flood of blood.

At the sound of the blow, the Chef raised his eyes, but before he could do more than squirt caramel over Nin's kilt, he too had been battered with a sharp blow to the temple: he dropped like a stone.

Alasdair and Nin knew that the clock was now ticking. They roughly tied the bodies up, stuffing rags in their mouths, before manhandling them into a huge plate warmer that ran down the middle of the kitchen. They kicked the remains of the cake under the counter: from a distance nothing appeared untoward.

They extracted the assault rifles from the backpacks, screwed the silencers on and primed the various features. Then, having distributed grenades and side arms, they pulled on their back mounted scabbards and Alasdair produced a pistol crossbow and loaded a bolt. Finally, they put in their earpieces and logged onto the Lamont Wi-Fi so that they could connect with the team while they were below ground.

"Fiona, are you there?" Whispered Nin.

There was a brief silent pause, which felt like it lasted for an hour before Fiona's calm voice came on the line. "Yes, I am here. Sorry, I was on mute, so stupid, sorry."

"No problem, OK, let's do this. We are in the castle kitchen, probably on level minus one…can you see it?"

"Aye," said Fiona. "Got you. Now you need to come out of the kitchen and turn left down that long corridor; when you get to the end you should see a stairwell, that should take you down to sub-level 3, after which I will need to give you more directions."

They moved off, leaving the relative sanctuary of the kitchen. Alasdair was in the lead, the pistol crossbow in his hand, the assault rifle slung across his chest. Nin followed. The corridor was empty, and they moved quickly and quietly down to the stairwell at the far end. Alasdair paused at the junction, pressed flat to the wall, straining to hear any sounds from the lower levels. Someone was whistling tunelessly somewhere, but whether it was coming from above or below was impossible to tell. The stairwell was a gloomy, dimly lit, concrete shaft with treads of black painted steel, puckered with heavy non-slip cleats. Nin knew that this would reverberate to the sound of their footsteps unless they were very careful.

Alasdair slipped around the corner and crouching low hugged the wall; he seemed to float down the first flight of stairs as silently as a breath of wind. Nin followed, doing his best to emulate the grace and silky smoothness of his partner, but feeling like a bull in a china shop by comparison: even the rustle of his webbing seemed deafening to his heightened senses. At the bottom of the flight, Alasdair put his hand up to hold Nin on the half landing. There were footsteps, but it was impossible to tell where they were coming from: the echo of the stairwell cheating them of any clues. After a few seconds, the footsteps died away and silence descended again. Alasdair moved into the corridor holding his crossbow at the ready. Nothing, just a long dreary dark corridor, flanked by closed doors.

Nin was already pouring with sweat; the more he rubbed his brow, the more it seemed to run down his face, its salty sting blurring his vision. He tried to blink it away and focus. He had not done any active service for a few years, not since he had been going out with Charlie, and the tension of a field deployment was something that he hadn't missed. Despite the situation, he found his mind wandering to Charlie and that night in Doune: would that be their last night together? He tried to push that thought out of his mind. Meanwhile, Alasdair walked around the turn of the bannister and down the next flight of stairs as if he had every right to be there. Nothing, no shouts or questions. Nin followed his lead, and they then quickly worked their way down the next flights to sub-level 3.

"OK, Fiona, are you there?" Nin asked, heart in his throat. With each level they were getting deeper and, like a diver without a clear route to the surface above, the mental and physical pressure were mounting.

"Aye, are you in position?" She replied.

"Yes, we are just about to enter sub-level 3, where do we go?"

"Turn left, I mean right, sorry right, definitely right."

"Fucksakedoyenoknowyerleftfromyerfuckingrightnow?" muttered Nin under his breath, as he and Alasdair turned the corner. He could swear that the whistling was getting louder, and was that a scream he just heard? Yes, that was definitely a scream, a long high-pitched, soul wrenching scream: it just trailed away. It wasn't close, but it was there.

The corridors also now had an oppressive musty foetid funk, the smell of recycled air mixed with sweat and fear, air that has never blown across the open hill, just been breathed and breathed again: belched and farted, coughed and sneezed, screamed and cried. This smell encapsulated claustrophobia and oppression better than any locked door. What was this place? What the fuck were they doing? How were they ever going to get out?

Fiona broke into his mind, stopping the negative thoughts in their tracks: "From the look of the plan, there should be a turning on your left in about 15 feet, follow that and you should find the stairwell to the remaining sub-levels. When you get to sub-level 5 there is an open landing, just up from the stairwell to your right, that might be a meeting area, so be careful."

Nin felt that they needed to pick up the pace: there was no saying when the mess in the kitchen would be discovered, or when the receptionist would figure out that Davey hadn't returned. He tapped Alasdair on the back and whispered in his ear. Alasdair nodded, and moved out into the corridor.

As he turned the corner, he ran straight into a middle-aged man carrying a laptop and an armful of folders. The man did not even have a chance to react before Alasdair put the crossbow to his forehead and pulled the trigger. The bolt thudded into his skull, disappearing entirely, leaving a black hole as the only evidence of its passage. The man's body started to shake with shock, the only sound a dreadful wheezing like a deflating balloon. Alasdair hugged him, trapping his arms and stopping him from dropping the laptop and folders. They need to find somewhere to leave his body. Nin opened the first door across from the stairwell: it was empty apart from a few filing cabinets and a desk. They sat him on the chair allowing his body to slump forward. To the casual eye it looked like he was asleep; as long as you ignored the steady seep of blood that was pooling on the desk in front of him. Nin frisked him, pocketing his security pass.

They moved to the next stairwell: this led to the deep sub-levels. Alasdair clipped his crossbow to his webbing, instead favouring his assault rifle. The time for stealth was over, now they were this deep they needed speed more than anything.

They passed sub-level 4, Nin felt a pang of angst that they were not going to save Kirstie first, but the agreed plan was to start deep and then to work their way back up. If they didn't get MacCailean Mòr now, they'd never reach him. He prayed that nothing was going to prevent them from coming back for her.

On sub-level 5 it became obvious that Fiona was right: there were voices and a radio playing country and western music just up the corridor. Nin hated country and western. There were at least three voices, maybe more. Nin decided to deploy some of the tech they had bought from Caddell's to even the odds. He rummaged in his backpack and pulled out the Woofer drone. He launched it into the air, keeping it in the shadows as close as he could to the ceiling above the pendant lights. He flew it very slowly along the corridor, its camera confirming that there were three guards, all of whom were distracted: drinking coffee, reading The Raven, gossiping and vaping.

The drone was almost invisible above the lights and it was only when it was nearly over them that one of the three guards suddenly pointed up at it, slack jawed. Nin activated the sonic pulse and the three figures were instantaneously convulsed, as if by an invisible and silent explosion that splayed them across the table. He and Alasdair sprinted around the corner and down the corridor kicking away their guns and pulling away any knives. They needn't have worried, the men were incapable of putting up any resistance: they were like jelly, as if all their bones had been sucked out of their bodies. Manhandling them was difficult but they had no time for pleasantries. Finding the nearest cell, he and Alasdair just dumped them in a heap on the floor before locking the door with a big bunch of keys from the table. Nin stashed the drone back in his pack and ran to join Alasdair on the stairs to the sixth and lowest level.

He not only felt the weight of the earth now but also that of John Lamont and his cruelties; it was a physical burden that was exuded by this evil building, as if it was trying to choke them as it had so many others. But they had come too far to turn back, and as he descended that last flight of stairs, Nin replayed Charlie's last words to him before they had parted earlier that morning: Don't think, just do it. That is just about all he could hold on to now: no thought, just action.

71 - THE SIXTH FLOOR

They had already had enough of sneaking about those infernal dimly lit corridors, he wanted to get out, back towards the light; they were too deep, and the pressure was beginning to show, even on the iron-nerved Alasdair MacGregor.

Fiona was in their ear giving them directions as they descended the final flight of stairs onto the sixth and deepest level. This was the most secure area of the castle, where valuable and dangerous prisoners were kept. It was no surprise that when they came to the bottom of the stairwell there was solid steel door with a keypad and swipe but no handle. Nin did not like the look of this one bit. He fished out the security pass that he had taken off the dead clerk and tried it in the swipe. The LED flashed green: the door opened with an audible click.

Nothing could've prepared them for the sight that confronted them. In contrast to the dimly lit corridors, this room was brilliant white, with blazing strip lights, a hard poured-rubber floor, and a long wall of identical cell doors. With a few paintings on the walls it could have been a SoHo art gallery, but the only colour here was red; it was puddled on the floor, splashed up the walls, sprayed on the ceiling. There were flicks and dribbles, splodges and gouts, trickles and streaks; as if Jackson Pollock has been let loose, but with only one colour in his palette: from scarlet and vermillion, through fire brick to maroon and crusty brown. In the centre of the room were two men, standing by an unfortunate recipient of their attention, who was suspended from the ceiling by his arms on a rope that barely allowed his feet to touch the floor.

Alasdair did not even pause, squeezing off a burst from his assault rifle into first one and then the other torturer. The only sound being the soft thud of the bullets finding their target, the *shrink* of the self-cocking mechanism reloading the chamber after each round, and the *tinkle* of the casings falling to the floor. The impact of the bullets threw the men to the ground and Alasdair immediately ran over to deliver a head shot to each. Nin felt like he was going to be sick. He had seen death and injuries up close, but not like this. This was beyond barbaric. He cut down the man hanging from the ceiling, what was left of him. He felt for a pulse: nothing.

Just as he was standing up from the corpse, a door opened on the far side of the room and two men entered. They were taken by surprise and Nin managed to drop one in the doorway with a well-aimed burst, but the other turned and fled through the closing door, a line of bullets pitting the wall behind him. Without a word, Alasdair set off in hot pursuit.

Nin ran down the line of doors until he found Cell 2. As he opened the door he saw a hatch in the floor which he lifted and flung to the side. The hole was black and stank; he could see and hear nothing below. He called down to MacCailean Mòr, praying that they were not too late or that Fiona's reconnaissance had not been wrong. Initially, a hoarse croak answered, which grew into a desperate yell. Nin flicked through the switches until a light came on in the hole. There, on his knees, covered in excrement and filth, was the bloodied and naked figure of MacCailean Mòr, his arms raised in supplication to his potential saviour.

In the corner of the room was a ladder, which Nin lowered for MacCailean Mòr to climb up. He was initially worried that after what he had been through MacCailean Mòr might not have the strength to get out by himself, but the desperation with which he scrabbled up those rungs told their own story. As he clawed his way over the lip of the hatch, Nin was shocked at the state he was in; after all he had only be missing for a week or so: he was a mess. He pulled him by the hand back to the torture chamber and told him to grab whatever clothing he could off the dead bodies on the floor, while he looked for Alasdair.

He stepped over the body of the dead Lamont in the doorway and poked his head into the long dark corridor down which Alasdair had disappeared. He whispered in his microphone, calling for him, and then, throwing caution to the wind, shouted Alasdair's name into the darkness.

Nothing.

Fuckfuckfuckfuck.

Where was he? Should he go after him? What if he'd been wounded and needed help? How long was this corridor? How deep were these goddam tunnels?

As far as he could hear, the alarm had not been raised: yet. He needed to get to Kirstie, and while he hated leaving Alasdair in this hole, he had to fulfil their mission. Alasdair would just have to look after himself. He returned to the torture chamber where MacCailean Mòr was tightening the last buckle on the Lamont kilt he had taken. He had no shirt but grabbed a jacket from the back of a chair and buttoned it up. As long as you didn't look at his legs and feet, which stuck out bare and bloody below the kilt, he looked almost like a normal Lamont clansman. They had no time to search the bodies, but Nin did see MacCailean Mòr filch a sgian dubh from the stocking of one of the dead and Nin passed him one of his sidearms for good measure. They needed to get to Kirstie before the Castle was locked down.

Running to the steel door, he swiped the card and breathed a sigh of relief as the LED went green and the door clicked open. At least they were out of that hell hole, he couldn't bear the thought of dying down there. He quickly explained to MacCailean Mòr what they were about to do and to follow his lead. Although he was in a weakened state, MacCailean Mòr's eyes shone with adrenalin. Nin had seen that look before on the battlefield and knew that although it could carry a man a long way, it didn't last forever.

Stepping smartly up the stairs, they passed the still empty sub-level 5, before coming up onto sub-level 4. This was another of those interminable dim empty corridors lined with closed doors that reminded Nin of the violent computer games he used to play as a child, maybe this was their original source of inspiration?

"Fiona?" He whispered. "We are on Sub-level 4, I've MacCailean Mòr but have lost Alasdair, I need you to guide me to Kirstie's cell, fast!"

Fiona's calm voice came over his earpiece: "She is in Cell 3. From the stairwell turn right and it's the first turning on the left, second door along."

Nin ran down the empty corridor to the corner, where he paused waiting for MacCailean Mòr to catch up. He checked the safety was off on his assault rifle and turned the corner. There were two guards chatting about twenty yards away. Nin's first few shots went wide as he ran towards them, but he had the advantage: he had an automatic weapon and it was in his hands, while their sidearms were holstered. He stitched a burst up the nearest guard who screamed and fell back against the wall. His colleague at least managed to draw his weapon and raise it before Nin caught him too, propelling him backwards into a writhing heap on the floor.

At that second the alarm sounded.

Nin left MacCailean Mòr to deal with the two wounded Lamonts, while he opened Cell 3. As earlier, this had two parts; the upper part giving access to the trap door and the lower part was where the prisoner was kept. As there was no way for the prisoner to reach the trap door far above them, the security to the upper room was light – essentially there was only a handle on the outside but no locks. Nin opened the door, flicked on all the light switches, lifted the hatch and peered down into the cell below.

The cell was empty; Kirstie was gone.

72 - DEEP

The figure ahead jinked from side to side as he ran, pushing off the walls as he turned each corner to try to maintain his momentum. He was fast and knew these corridors well and Alasdair was encumbered with all his gear, but he was still gaining. Just as he was within touching distance, the man ran into a large storeroom filled with stacked boxes. As he passed the first stack, he pulled it down behind him on top of Alasdair. The jumble of boxes tripped him over, sprawling him onto the floor.

In an instant, the Lamont leapt on him, grabbing him around the throat with one hand while scrabbling for his knife with the other. Alasdair could feel the crushing pressure of the man's fingers on his windpipe, the fingernails gouging. The Lamont's shaven head and shining face loomed over him; the face warped in a look of triumph at having turned the tables so effectively. Alasdair's gun had been knocked from his hand and he couldn't reach it with the Lamont on his chest. He punched at the Lamont with his left hand, landing a few ineffectual blows that his assailant shrugged off and maintained his grip. With his right-hand Alasdair groped for the sgian dubh tucked in the top of his stocking, and as he brought his knee up to try and dislodge his assailant he was able to grip its hilt. Pulling it free, he started to frenziedly stab the Lamont's back: anywhere, it didn't matter. As the blows rained down, the Lamont realised with horror what was happening, clutching at his side in shock, blood pouring from the multiple stab wounds. Alasdair was now finally able to catch him with a solid punch to the jaw, dislodging him from his chest and sprawling him to the ground.

Shouting and screaming, the guard started to try and drag himself away, smearing a trail of blood behind him. Alasdair judged that given the volume of the red stuff he must have caught his liver. He picked himself up rubbing his throat, looking for his gun to finish the bastard off. The guard scrabbled for his communications unit and before Alasdair could do anything had pressed the thick red, emergency response button.

A second later the alarm sounded.

Cursing, Alasdair found his pistol under a box and without a second thought put a bullet between the guard's eyes. He quickly patted the corpse down for anything that might be useful. Most of all, he wanted a security pass, as Nin had the one they had taken from the earlier victim. He eventually found one in the man's breast pocket and turned to retrace his steps.

The alarm was sounding continually which made it very hard for him to communicate with Fiona; he just had to work his own way back to the torture chamber and the stairs, hoping that Nin was still going to be there waiting for him. They had no chance of getting out of here alone; the only hope they had was to work as a team.

He ran down the corridors, trying to retrace his steps. They all looked the same, dull brick lined, gloomy corridors lined with doors leading to cells with who knew who inside. He was beginning to think that he had got lost when he saw the blinding white of the torture chamber ahead. Stepping over the body of the dead Lamont wedged in the doorway, he saw the room was empty – Nin had left him.

Trying to remain calm, he ran to the big steel entrance door. Fumbling with the security pass, he swiped it through the reader.

The LED flashed red.

He tried again.

The LED flashed red.

The door would not open.

They must have deactivated the doors, probably standard practice in the event of a prison break-out or infiltration. Fucking fuck trapped like a rat in a trap, six stories below ground in the Lamontation's torture chamber. In terms of scenarios, he was struggling to imagine a worse one. What the hell was he going to do now?

73 - DONNA

Kirstie and Donna Lamont had hated each other ever since they had met at Stornaway University over twenty years before. Rivals since the first day of their degree course in computer science and applied mathematics, they had vied for top spot all the way through. They should have been friends, after all they were both highly talented programmers. To have two such talented female programmers on the course at the same time had given the faculty a frisson of glamour. It had allowed the Principal to bask in their reflected glory, as their growing enmity spurred them on to outdo each other in international competitions, bringing fame and a wealth of new fee-paying applicants for his courses. Eventually they had gone their separate ways, but fate had now brought them together again.

Except this time, Kirstie was bound to a chair in Donna's office, while Donna barked questions at her, delivering a slap for a slow response or a wrong answer. Although her face stung, Kirstie could tell that Donna had not done this before, the slaps were too feeble. Not that she let on though, moaning and groaning as best she could to make Donna feel powerful and in control. But the bitch was enjoying this a little too much for her liking: all those years of hatred bubbling to the surface.

While Donna was letting her sadistic side loose on her, Kirstie was busy working at the webbing that bound her to the chair. When the guard had sat her down, she'd bulked her arms and held her breath to preserve as much wriggle room as she could and now the bonds began to loosen.

Donna was asking her about the deepest layers of the MacNachtan network's architecture, as she'd found an anomaly which she didn't understand. Kirstie knew that she was talking about the back door, and the last thing she wanted was to give away anything that might increase Donna's suspicions. Donna was sat behind her desk; that greasy hair of hers hanging lankly down her face, grey and lifeless. Her eyes glued to the screen of her laptop as she kept interrogating the code, prodding and testing it from a variety of directions. Kirstie was beginning to get nervous that Donna was just going to delete the whole section, thereby sealing them off from the gaming operation for ever. Just when she was giving up hope, the alarm sounded. The guard who was stood behind her immediately left the room to head to a muster point. Donna didn't seem concerned but did toggle away from the network drive to try and find out what was going on.

"Seems like there some kind of altercation in sub-level 6. If I just activate the cameras I should be able to get a good look at what is going on. Ah yes, there we go. Now I wonder who that is. Anyone you know?" She turned the screen towards Kirstie, who stared at it under her blood-soaked fringe; she shook her head.

"Very curious." Donna thought for a moment. "Anyway, he's locked behind that steel door in John Lamont's torture chamber. Two inches of solid steel, hhmmm, I don't think he will be getting past that. Silly fool. I wonder how it will end for him, I imagine that whatever it is, will be slow, very slow. Maybe John will use the eels? Still, that's not our problem and there's no way he's getting out of there, not with that security door sealed. So, I think I can safely turn my attention back to you."

Kirstie knew that it was now or never. Donna had already dropped many hints that this would be their last session together; she had everything she needed; she was really just toying with her – for old time's sake. Kirstie was due to be transferred to the care of Allan Stewart later that day, which might even mean a trip back to Dunderave for him to butcher her there – oh the irony.

She had loosened her bonds as much as she could and hoped that what she was about to do would work. Lifting her foot from the floor she placed it against Donna's desk and pushed hard, tipping her chair backwards onto the floor while simultaneously wriggling with all her might. As the chair hit the floor it splintered and the webbing which bound her came loose enough for her to slip it off the chair's back. She could now stand, and she busily worked to free her hands.

With horror Donna realised what was happening and picked up her laptop to batter Kirstie's head with. Finally, Kirstie managed to shrug off the last of her bonds and launch herself across the desk at Donna. They both went down on the floor, Donna still trying to hit Kirstie with her laptop, Kirstie using her fists to pour punches down on her opponent. Kirstie wrestled herself on top of Donna and, sitting astride her, wrapped a network cable around her neck, pulling with all her strength. The plastic was slippery, with sweat or blood she didn't know, but she double wrapped it around her fists as she pulled, the cable biting into her hands. The wounds on her hands screamed with pain, but the adrenalin was pumping and there was no way she was going to stop now. Donna's eyes started to bulge as she clawed at the cable trying to get her fingers underneath it: anything to relieve the crushing pressure. Kirstie pulled with all her might, until Donna's scrabbling diminished, her face turning blue and tongue protruding from her tightly drawn lips. Finally, she was still.

As she released the tension on the cable, Kirstie realised that she was weeping, with relief rather than over the demise of the dread Donna. The ordeal of the last week threatened to overwhelm her; part of her just wanted to curl up in the kneehole of Donna's desk, to hide away. Surely, if she just tucked herself away no one would find her? But a louder, more strident, voice forced her to her feet, and to look for a way out. If she stayed here, death was the only outcome.

She quickly stripped Donna of most of her clothes and picked up Donna's laptop. She was about to stuff it in her bag when she had an idea. She quickly opened it and pulling Donna's limp head up from the floor by her greasy hair to allow the facial recognition software to scan her face and log on. Once she was on the network it only took Kirstie a matter of moments to change the security scan to a password of her choice. That way she would be able to access all of Donna's password protected areas and administrator codes at her leisure, assuming she got out of there alive.

She was about to shut the screen when she had another idea; she needed a diversion if she was to have a chance of escape and the maniac on the 6th sub-basement was the perfect tactic. She pulled up a command prompt and punched in a few lines of code, questing for the right commands to open the steel security door. Finding what she hoped was the right location she wrote the instruction and pressed return.

She could do no more, now she had to get away. Fortunately, Donna's office was on the first floor, so she did not have far to go, but with the sound of running feet coming from all directions she was going to have to pick her moment carefully.

74 - RELEASED

Alasdair had stood at the door for at least two minutes trying different sides of the security pass or swiping it in different directions: all with the same result. He had even patted down the corpses to see if he could find any other cards that might work: nothing made any difference. He thought about trying to shoot the hinges off, or the lock, but the thickness of the door meant that was hopeless.

Thinking laterally, he went to the cells, opening each of them and dropping the ladders down to release any prisoners still held inside. The wails as he lifted each hatch were terrifying, reflecting the misery these poor wretches had suffered. He didn't have time to tell each in turn, but as soon as the first prisoner had made it out he explained that he was going to try and free them, but they would need to fight their way out. Ultimately, there were about nine or ten prisoners and they ransacked the white room looking for anything that could be used as a weapon: knives, hammers, saws and a few fire extinguishers. As soon as the guards came through the door, Alasdair said he would shoot as many as he could and that they should then all rush the door. Any weapons that came to hand should be grabbed and put to good use.

His fellow Gaels were in a bad way, they had no clothes, some had obviously broken bones or were missing fingernails and they were all covered in cuts and bruises. But he could tell that for the most part they were duine uasal: fighters. By the assortment of tattoos they bore, they were from a range of clans, but they knew their fate if they stayed and would do everything in their power to escape. He was counting on them causing serious confusion and mayhem, hopefully enough to allow him to slip away if possible: he did not owe them anything more. Had he not freed them? Surely that was enough.

The alarm was still blaring in his ear, it was beginning to drive him insane. He had long since given up trying to talk to Fiona and was now reduced to sitting staring at the steel door. It was during this vigil that the LED switched from red to green. With a shout he ran at the door, yanking it open before it could change its mind. As the heavy door swung inwards, the tattered mob that were his foot soldiers surrounded him and they started the long climb towards the surface.

Sub-level 5 was still quiet, and he forced the prisoners he had released to free the other prisoners they could find, dividing them into groups of two, they ran down either side of the corridor, opening hatches and dropping ladders. Weight of numbers was going to be invaluable as they got to the higher levels. But more than that, he wanted to give the prisoners, whatever they may have done, a fighting chance.

Finally, he found a corner where the alarm was not so loud that his brain felt like it was dissolving and tried to raise Fiona on the earpiece.

"Fiona, Fiona are you there?" He shouted.

Nothing.

"Fiona, for fuck's sake, its Alasdair, where are you? I am down on sub-level 5 and am awful keen to get the fuck out of here."

Fiona suddenly responded: "Alasdair, thank God! Where have you been? We were so worried."

"Aye, well let's not spraff about that now. I need you to turn that fucking alarm off. It's not only driving me insane, but it will be attracting every member of Clan Lamont in the whole district to the castle. Can you not kill it? Pull the fuses? Anything?"

"Got it, am on it." She was gone. He had not even had a chance to ask about Nin, but he needn't have worried, Nin's cheerful voice suddenly crackled on the line:

"Fucking hell, Alasdair MacGregor. Where the fuck are you? Do you need my help?"

"No, think I'm OK for the moment. Just on sub-level 5 with a bunch of crazies at my back. Figured we could do with evening the numbers a little. Just working our way up now."

"OK," said Nin. "I am on sub-level 4, I've got MacCailean Mòr, but Kirstie is nowhere to be seen." He paused and then said to Fiona, "Fiona, can you check the castle records, has she been taken anywhere – the Infirmary or for questioning. I'm fucked if we're going to leave her behind."

"I can't do two things at once, can I?" Irritation creeping into Fiona's voice for the first time. "I'm almost on top of the alarm though, it looks like I just need to kill the whole emergency response system and that should do it."

"Whatever it takes, I can't take any more." Alasdair shouted, exasperatedly.

The ringing stopped.

For a few seconds he felt that he could still hear its penetrating insistent rhythm. But the calm that descended was worth at least five extra men as far as Alasdair was concerned; he could think now, and thinking was the only thing that was going to get them out of there.

Judging by the stench behind him, the number of freed prisoners was growing, He could barely bring himself to look at them; the misery they had been through was written in their eyes and carved on their flesh. Retribution was coming for Lamont; of that he was sure. But his priority was to get out of this fucking hole.

Sweeping up his ragbag band, they ran up the stairs to sub-level 4. He kept a close dialogue going with Nin, to make sure they did not shoot each other by accident, and as he came to the top of the stairs, he saw Nin with the dishevelled figure of MacCailean Mòr at his shoulder.

Once more directing his men to release any prisoners, he and Nin huddled on the stairwell to agree a plan; getting to the surface was the only priority and to get there as soon as possible. As the freed prisoners milled around, they put MacCailean Mòr between them and ran up the stairs, each tread taking them closer to the surface and freedom.

It was as they turned out of the stairwell to the deep levels that they ran into serious opposition. As they approached the top of the stairs, Alasdair could see the red pencil beams of tactical gun sights crisscrossing the corridor ahead. With the press of the crowd behind them, their momentum was too great to stop in time. Instead, as they reached the top of the stairs, he put his arm out across MacCailean Mòr and grabbed Nin's webbing, throwing all three of them forward onto the floor and halfway through an open door across the passage. The corridor behind them exploded in a hail of gunfire, as bullets bit and chipped at the walls and ricocheted around the passage. Some of the prisoners behind were not so lucky and were gunned down, leaving the floor strewn with a pile of screaming and thrashing bodies. Their opponents, in no mood for mercy, poured another sustained burst of fire into the writhing mass, silencing them utterly.

Alasdair knew they only had seconds before grenades or gas would be rolled down to finish them off. He crouched by the door, yelling at Nin to cover him, before throwing himself on top of the bodies in the corridor. As he hit the floor, he pressed the Boma-solais stud on the barrel of his assault rifle, praying that Natasha hadn't over-played its effectiveness. The explosion of light that strobed the other end of the corridor illuminated it in a horrifying post-apocalyptic diorama; at least a dozen black clad and heavily armed men staggered, clutching their eyes, shouting and falling over each other in total disarray. Nin sprayed them with automatic gunfire, pouring lead into the confined space: they were trapped like fish in a barrel. While a few tried to return fire blindly, their shots were wild and hit their own men rather than the grim and desperate horde that poured up the corridor towards them. In seconds they were swamped, and the scene descended into a one-sided melee, with the sighted unquestionably having the advantage. The prisoners' revenge was medieval, and it only took seconds for the remaining Lamonts to be torn apart.

Alasdair and Nin caught their breath and allowed their allies to help themselves to clothes and weapons. Although they were still on sub-level 3, Alasdair felt like they were almost on the home straight. Once their motley crew had stripped all they could from the dead Lamonts, they moved to the next stairwell, the one that would take them to the surface.

Frenzied shouts came over his earpiece with Charlie and Gillespie excitedly talking over each other. Charlie won out: "Oh shit, guys, you've got to get a move on. There are trucks of men massing by the front gates; if you don't get out of there now you're never going to. We can lay down some covering fire to try and keep them back, but it's not going to hold them for very long."

Grabbing Nin and MacCailean Mòr, Alasdair sprinted for the stairs: he hadn't come this far to be entombed in the Lamontation's dungeon. The horde behind followed.

The next few minutes passed in series of jump cut scenes, as they fought to get out; the stairs; a burst of fire to take down a crouching figure; fingers fumbling with his webbing; loading a fresh magazine; diving for cover under a hail of fire from behind an upturned desk; throwing a grenade; an explosion followed by silence; on his feet, running; out of the stairwell now; down the corridor towards the kitchen; the door opening; a looming shadow; a pointed gun; a flash of light; a giant's punch throwing him backwards; stars; the ceiling; nothing.

75 - THE GATE

Charlie and Gillespie were looking down from their vantage point towards the gates in the glen below the Castle. Two covered trucks had arrived, and the gatekeeper was speaking to the lead driver. They did not look particularly concerned, and it seemed possible that although they knew the alarm had gone off they thought it was a drill or a false alarm.

Charlie fretted as to what to do. On the one hand if he started shooting, he would confirm that there was a serious incident underway, on the other hand, if he did nothing, then two truckloads of troops would soon arrive, tipping the odds firmly against them.

Gillespie took the binoculars from him, studying the gates and the gatehouse, the next second he was on the earpiece to Fiona.

"Fiona, see if you can find the electrical system for the front gates, the power or fuses, anything you can do to seal them and buy us some time would be amazing."

Fiona tapped furiously in the background, searching for the right system folders. It was taking too long. Fiona came back on the earpiece: "OK, I think I've found the right system prompt and have just put a little block on there. Hopefully, they won't be able to open the gates, at least electrically. There is probably a manual override, but this will buy a little time."

Squinting through the afternoon sun, he could see that the men at the gates were wrapping up their conversation. The gatekeeper returned to his booth to open the gates. Nothing happened. He came out and looked at the big steel gates mounted on their heavily rusticated stone piers. He shrugged, rubbed his head and went back inside to try the button again. Nothing happened. The driver of the lorry now got out and came to look at the problem and for a few minutes there was an almost comical scratching of heads and pressing of the button. Eventually, they gave up and the gatekeeper went to find the equipment needed to open the gates manually.

While the gatekeeper was rummaging in his booth, a flash from the rear elevation of the castle caught Charlie's eye. Someone was trying to open one of the first-floor windows. It was clearly stiff and some of the planes of glass got broken judging by the faint tinkle he could hear. Then a familiar head poked out, looking to left and right – surely that was Kirstie! He grabbed the binoculars off Gillespie – it was Kirstie! She was clearly making her own escape. She pulled herself onto the window ledge before turning and starting to lower herself to get as close to the ground as she could before letting go.

At that moment, two Lamonts burst out of the backdoor, guns raised and shouting at her as she hung from the ledge. There was nothing else for it: Charlie shouldered his rifle in a flash, squeezing off two shots. The first caught one of the Lamonts in the torso, the impact crumpling him forward onto the grass; the other went low, hitting the remaining Lamont in his right thigh, buckling his leg from under him. Once on the ground it was a simple matter for Charlie to put another round into each of them, to ensure they moved no more.

Kirstie dropped to the ground and looked around, trying to locate her saviour. Unable to identify where the shots had come from, she stooped, took the guns from the dead Lamonts, and headed for the cover of the forestry. This was directly below their position and Charlie urged Gillespie to go and catch her before she disappeared into the Great Impenetrable Forest. While Gillespie crashed off into the undergrowth, Charlie turned his attention back to the gate.

Due to his very efficient silencer, the force at the gate couldn't hear his shots and were still standing round chatting while the gatekeeper tried to manually open the gates' mechanism with what looked like a huge Allen Key. With every turn of the key, the gates opened a little more; it was slow progress, but they were getting there. Charlie thought about popping a few shots in the gatekeeper just to slow them down, but that would just broadcast the real state of affairs at the Castle, and he wanted to keep them in the dark about that for as long as possible.

Which wasn't very long, as the unmistakable sound of machinegun fire now rent the calm afternoon air: a long, controlled burst coming from inside the castle. Charlie could hear screams and yells too, as people poured from the front and back doors. Some of these stopped to fire back at the Castle, as they ran across the lawn to the Loch below. There could now be no doubt as to what was happening and the group at the gates redoubled their efforts to get the gates open.

Rather than shooting the gatekeeper, Charlie waited until the first truck was accelerating through the gates before firing a burst at its front tyres, both of which exploded, and then at the engine grill, in an effort to immobilise it. The driver persisted, trying to force the truck through the gates, knowing that he could not leave it blocking the entrance. Reluctantly, Charlie put a bullet in the fuel tank behind the driver's cab; the resulting fireball engulfed the vehicle, propelling a thick black cloud high into the sky. To his relief, most of the men in the back seemed to escape unscathed, but the driver was not so lucky.

Then he saw them fall out of the backdoor. Nin and MacCailean Mòr either side of a slumped Alasdair, soaked in blood and clearly unconscious. Nin was shouting at MacCailean Mòr and they staggered like a trio of drunks across the grass towards the trees. A wild and motley crowd spilled out of the Castle after them, brandishing weapons and adding to the chaos as they scattered in all directions.

Charlie shouldered his rifle and pack, he had to get to Nin.

76 - BREAKOUT

It had been that cunt Davey Lamont that had caught Alasdair with the shotgun. Nin regretted that he had not hit him harder with the rolling pin. An easy thought to have now, but that that sort of violence was not in his nature. As Alasdair was blown backwards by the force of the blast, Nin found himself staring down the barrel of the shotgun. In the nano-second before Davey pulled the trigger, three shots rang out, throwing Davey backwards and spraying blood up the wall behind him. Nin turned to see MacCailean Mòr lowering his hand, the pistol still smoking. Without a word they both turned to Alasdair's blood-soaked body. Nin grabbed one arm and MacCailean Mòr the other, and they dragged him up that last flight of stairs. Fortunately, there did not seem to be any resistance left on the ground floor, but as they staggered out through the backdoor and into the late afternoon sunshine, Nin rued that he had missed the opportunity to put a bullet in that bitch of a receptionist.

Alasdair was a deadweight, and after the stress of the day it was a load that was almost too much for him to bear. MacCailean Mòr was also weak, and Nin felt that he was having to drag them both across the lawn to the shelter of the forest. The bushes to his left suddenly exploded as a black clad figure leapt out in front of them, Nin was too slow and too tired now, he half-heatedly raised his assault rifle before realising with spine chilling relief that it was Charlie – fucking idiot, he could get himself shot doing that - his legs then turned to jelly and he crumpled to the floor.

He and Alasdair were dragged by Charlie and MacCailean Mòr into the cover of the ponticum where Charlie splashed water on his face from his canteen, the cool water snapping him back into focus. He grabbed the canteen from Charlie's hand and drank greedily from it, before handing it to MacCailean Mòr who drained every last drop.

Nin knew that it was critical to use the confusion of the mass breakout to get to the boat; if the Lamonts got themselves organised they would be caught, no question. He wracked his brain to think of what to do next, what would tip the odds in their favour. Remembering Fiona, he realised that because they were now out of range of the Castle's Wi-Fi his connection to the communications channel had been cut, he needed to log back in. He pulled out his phone to dial the number and immediately realised what they had to do. As soon as he was reconnected to the group he splurted: "Cut the fucking network Fiona, cut the bastards' phone network. Shut them down! Can you do that?"

Fiona, somewhat flustered by the dramatic and strident intervention, replied: "Aye, well I probably can do something, maybe by just by shutting down the entire network server. That should cut everything for a good few hours, at least until they can figure out how to restart it."

"Aye, whatever. Just do it, anything to make harder for them to get organised and to give us a fighting chance of getting out of here alive."

"OK, OK, I am on the case."

Nin looked around at the group, Alasdair was lying unconscious at his feet, peppered with shot and still seeping blood; MacCailean Mòr was still with them, but clearly fading fast as his body burned through the last of his adrenalin; and Charlie, good old Charlie, how he wanted to hug him, but now was not the moment. They had to get moving towards the boat.

"Where's Gillespie?" He asked Charlie.

"He's disappeared to look for Kirstie, we saw her escape the Castle and he went after her to bring her to the boat. We've been trying to raise him on the comms channel but are not getting any response. He could be out of signal or battery, who knows, but we can't reach him for the moment."

Nin gasped: "What? Kirstie is alive?! Oh my God! I don't believe it! You've no idea how that makes me feel…. to hear those words…..to think that we could have gone through all that" – at which he gestured with a bloody finger at the Castle – "…for nothing. Jesus." He sank to his knees clutching his hands to his face, his eyes shining with tears, the stress of the last few hours threatened to overwhelm him. He caught himself and sucked in a deep lungful of that damp Cowal air, its leathery mustiness infinitely preferable to the foetid rank of Ascog's sub-levels. He breathed it out slowly and by the time his lungs were empty, he'd regained his composure. Getting to his feet, he gave Alasdair's assault rifle to MacCailean Mòr, and with Charlie on the other side, he picked Alasdair up and started down the hill.

They kept in the shade of the ponticum as much as possible to stay out of view from any onlookers below. For the time being, they were hidden from the main Lamont force at the front gates or any that were left in the Castle. They obviously could not retrace their steps to the harbour but had planned a contingency. This took them down the glen behind the Castle Rock and over the neighbouring promontory to the north, known as the Bàrr nan Damh or the Stag's Pinnacle. If they kept heading west through the forestry they would eventually hit the Glenan Burn, a stream that flowed into Loch Fyne. By following this they would come out on the shore at Glenan Bay, the next bay up the coast from Portavaddie. Iain the Rat and Brighid would pick them up from there as soon as night fell.

While that had seemed like an entirely sensible plan when scouting the terrain on a map, it didn't take into account the thickness of the ponticum and the condition of the walkers. Nin had serious doubts that they were going to be able to make it, given the state of Alasdair and MacCailean Mòr, both of whom were fading fast, not to mention MacCailean Mòr's lack of shoes. He called a halt at the next clearing to blind Alasdair's wounds to staunch the flow of blood, they also needed to get some calories into MacCailean Mòr or else he was just going to topple over.

They didn't have much in the way of field dressings, but Charlie did have a can of spray-on wound sealant and having exposed the mess of Alasdair's chest, he gave it a good going over until the can was empty. At least the blood from the many pellet wounds stopped seeping. They could do no more, but if he was to survive he needed proper treatment as soon as possible. MacCailean Mòr was an easier fix, at least for the time being; Nin found a couple of high energy bars, one quick release and one slow, to give him the best possible boost to his reserves.

The distance was not far, probably less than two miles, but it was through thick cover, and that would slow their pace dramatically. They needed to get to the pickup point as soon as possible, they couldn't afford to tarry to look for Gillespie and Kirstie; the Lamonts would soon be combing the entire peninsula, using dogs, thermal imaging equipment, night vision, anything and everything to try and find the perpetrators. The Lamonts knew better than anyone that to fail would be to risk the wrath of the Lamontation and that was not something anyone would want to bring on themselves.

77 - THE GLENAN BURN

Gillespie ran down the hill trying to get to Kirstie before she disappeared into the undergrowth. He felt like he was under assault from the ponticum as he struggled through it, flailing his arms to try and push it aside; in return it tried to trip him up with its gnarly branches, slap him in the face with its leathery leaves and poke him in the eye with its sharp pointed twigs, anything to impede his progress. It was like it was alive, part of the malevolent force that seeped from Ascog into the landscape. As he got to the bottom of the Castle Rock, he just caught sight of Kirstie's back disappearing into the undergrowth on the other side of the back drive. Sprinting across the tarmac he called out, but she'd already disappeared into the green curtain of forest.

He crashed after her, calling her name, desperately looking for evidence of her passage through the bushes. He could now hear her just up ahead, as she desperately tried to escape from what she must have imagined were Lamont pursuers. He redoubled his efforts, finally catching her as she was sent sprawling face first into the dirt by a low-lying branch. As he put his hand out to her, she turned with ferocious force and tried to throw him to the ground. Fortunately for Gillespie, she recognised him as she turned, eyes widening in astonishment, and she was able to pull her blows. Even in her weakened state she was a formidable opponent.

Her blows turned into a bearhug: she held him close, lying in the muddy bog of the Great Impenetrable Forest. He could hear her crying, sobbing in his ear, and a wet trail of tears coursed down his cheek. He comforted her, telling her that it was OK, that they had come to rescue her, all they needed to do was get to the boat. She couldn't speak yet, but she nodded, releasing him so that they could both get up.

It was Kirstie that spoke first: "We need to get out of here, they'll be coming for us. Don't let them take me back there: promise me." And the look she gave him would have melted stone. He reassured her that he had no intention of allowing them to be caught and they stood up to survey their surroundings. Under the canopy of the ponticum there was a thick greeny gloom that hung in the air. In every direction it looked the same, bare gnarled branches reached up their leaved tips to the light. There were occasional clearings where the sunlight could penetrate, but mostly they were covered by the thick leathery umbrella of the rhododendron forest. He tried to figure out the way they had come, but despite the violence of their passage through the undergrowth, there was now no obvious sign of their route.

He took out his phone to check for signal: there was nothing. He had been roaming on the Clan Lamont network, something that as a foreigner he was able to do. But it seemed like the network had now disappeared completely; he didn't even have one bar; it was very strange. He had to figure out a way to get to the pickup point. He knew he had to go due west, that would take them to the Glenan Burn which bisected this part of the peninsula and would ultimately take them to the beach pickup point. He would normally use the GPS on his phone to guide him, instead they would have to rely on the position of the sun. But the thickness of the cover in the forest was such that the sun could barely be seen, unless you stood in one of the occasional clearings. This made it very hard to follow a direct line, and the terrain was so uneven, due to rocks, undergrowth, bogs and burns, not to mention the dread ponticum, that they frequently had to stop to try and reassess their direction – the last thing they wanted was to go around in a circle and find themselves back at the Castle.

After they had been walking for what felt like hours, Gillespie realised that the sun was beginning to set, and while this meant that they had a reasonable idea of the direction they needed to follow, it also meant that they were running out of time to make it to the shore. Once night had settled there was no way they would be able to navigate their way through this impossible undergrowth.

Another consideration was that Kirstie was in a bad way. Initially she had been surfing a tide of adrenalin, but as that had ebbed, her energy levels had plummeted, and their progress had become leaden. Part of the problem was that her feet were being torn apart by the forest floor, which despite the abundance of mud had its fair share of sharp and lacerating objects too; fallen branches, stones, roots; all of which had taken their toll on the soles of her feet. As the adrenalin had worn off, so too had her ability to ignore the pain, and she was now leaning heavily on Gillespie as they picked and staggered their way through the undergrowth.

Time seemed to stand still in the Great Impenetrable Forest, as if each moment lasted an hour in its turgid, energy-sapping, green gloom. Even though their eyes were accustomed to the half-light under the leaves, Gillespie knew that dusk was now upon them. And with it the trips and stumbles over tree roots and branches became more frequent, the eye threatening pokes became more determined and the sudden appearance of rocks or holes to stub or swallow a foot, meant that progress was glacial. He was exhausted. He began to wonder if they were lost, despite the fading glimmer of light on the unseen horizon ahead of them. Surely, if the sun sets in the west then they could not go wrong? He found himself doubting even this most basic logic. He was now carrying Kirstie, her feet dragging behind. She was still conscious, but unable to walk a step further. This made it impossible for him to push the ponticum out of his face and the steady wet slap of the leaves as he walked through its branches left cuts and lacerations in their wake.

As the last of the light faded, he heard voices; they were muffled through the leaves but close. He sank to the ground, tears welling at the thought that they were going to be caught now, when they had come so far. He had failed, failed Kirstie and failed himself, even the simple task of getting to the extraction point had been too much for him. He shuddered at the thought of the fate that awaited him in John Lamont's basement. And Kirstie, brave Kirstie, who had already endured so much and had escaped, only to now be sucked back to that circle of hell.

He then heard the voice saying crossly "For fuck's sake Charlie get a fucking grip under his arm, we can't drop him now." Gillespie could've burst with joy at the relief of hearing the unmistakable sound of Nin chiding Charlie.

Gillespie tried to call to them, but only a hoarse whisper came out. Instead, he used the last of his energy to push through the ponticum that separated them and in so doing practically fell into the Glenan Burn at their feet.

78 - ONTO THE LOCH

They knew that something must be going on as the men on the quayside all started up the hill towards the Castle jabbering and calling to each other while checking their weapons. Brighid and Iain quickly agreed that they should cast off while the going was good and before anyone could try and lock down the pier. Having unlooped their cable from the mooring bollard, Brighid put the boat in gear and puttered out of the harbour.

It was a beautiful clear evening, with the sun starting to set almost directly behind Tarbert across the Loch. The gentle hills of Knapdale shone a brilliant emerald green in the hazy yellow light. The Loch itself was still very calm, barely a ripple on its surface, but the temperature was falling with the sun: it was going to be cold on the water. She left the harbour wall behind and followed the coast of Cowal north up Loch Fyne. She passed the ferry terminal and the salmon cages and turned out past the tidal island of Eilean na Beithe, which marked the southern end of Glenan Bay. This island was covered in the birch trees that gave it its name, the tips of their branches just whispering in the almost non-existent breeze; she marvelled at how calm and beautiful the world was when left to its own devices.

The bay was pincer shaped, with the northern claw being closed by another small island, Eilean a' Bhuic, the Island of Goats. The shore itself was divided by three small headlands, separated by sweeps of sand that run up to where the canopy of ponticum and forestry ended. She moored off the deepest part, where she could get her stern as close to the shore as possible. Now all they could do was to wait as the gloaming slipped into night.

She had almost given up hope, when she saw the first dark shapes stagger onto the sand. It had gone 8pm and the blackness of the forest lay thick and brooding on the shore, so its disgorging of the ragged group on the far side of the bay was unexpected and very welcome. That relief was tempered when she first heard the sound of the helicopter. It wasn't overhead but it could be heard in the distance circling the castle.

She chucked the binoculars at Iain while she went below to check on their prisoners. For the most part they had been pretty patient, after all it cannot have been much fun lying under a blanket with your arms bound for most of a day. That patience seemed to be coming to an end and the struggling and muffled yelling had been getting on her nerves. With the arrival of their new passengers, the vessel could not afford the extra weight, so it was time for them to get off. She ushered them both at gunpoint out of the cabin and onto the deck. While the Rat held her pistol, she cut their bonds and pushed them backwards overboard into the shallow water of the loch. They spluttered and swore as they hauled themselves onto the beach, cursing Brighid and the Rat with all manner of feuds and bloodletting. After being bound for so long they were stiff and cramped and were unable to do more than sit on the sand and swear.

It took all Brighid and Iain's strength to help lift the shore party aboard. The only one who was actually able to climb the short ladder unaided was Charlie, who came last. They delicately laid Alasdair and Kirstie on the benches in the cabin; he was still breathing but hadn't regained consciousness, which Brighid thought was a bad sign.

After putting the injured below, she could finally turn to MacCailean Mòr. She wrapped her arms around him holding him close to her. How she had feared this moment would never come. He looked at her, too tired to speak, to groan or even to cry; he just held her in his gaze, before pressing his forehead against hers and giving her a kiss, a single solitary gentle kiss that embodied more pent up emotion than Brighid had ever felt in her life before.

There was no time for more extravagant welcomes, they still had to get beyond Lamont's grasp and that meant getting up the Loch to Inveraray. She was concerned about that helicopter too.

The Rat pulled up the anchor and they moved off onto the Loch. Everyone on board felt an undeniable sense of relief to be at last moving away from the shore and putting some distance between them and the Lamontation's lair. They were not out of the woods yet, but there was no question that the further away they were from Castle Ascog, the happier they all felt.

The Rat was running with no lights, to minimise the chance of being spotted and he pulled a large arc around the Isle of Goats to ensure they did not run aground. Once in the main body of the Loch he steered for the silvery water in the middle of the channel and opened up the boat's engines, powering them up the Loch at high speed. Brighid looked back to the harbour of Portavaddie: it was brilliantly lit and ablaze with activity. She could also see the helicopter which was sweeping the Great Impenetrable Forest to the north of the Castle with a search light, presumably hunting down the other escapees. She shuddered as she wondered if the helicopter had thermal imaging equipment on it; if it did, then picking them off would be child's play. She watched the aircraft circle before holding still over a particular spot, pausing for a moment, before moving onto a fresh target.

They were making good progress down the loch, when she realised that the helicopter seemed to be coming in their direction. Despite the speed they were making, the helicopter was unquestionably faster and after a few minutes there could be no doubt that it was chasing them. It moved out over the Loch surface, still a mile behind, but gaining, the white disc of its searchlight racing up the water of the Loch towards them. Through the binoculars she could now see other boats setting out from the harbour in hot pursuit. These were high speed rigid inflatable boats, faster yet than their boat. She had no doubt that despite their head start they would be caught before they got to the safety of Inveraray.

She shouted at the Rat to warn him and he raised his hand in acknowledgement, but all he could do was keep the boat flat out and hope for the best. She spoke to Fiona on the comms channel telling her to make sure that whatever brilliant ideas Duncan Campbell had, they had better be good or else his Chief was going to end up dead, along with the rest of them.

Charlie reloaded his rifle, while she and Nin grabbed the assault rifles. Finally, she sent MacCailean Mòr below, he had nearly passed out and was clearly in no state to do anything. She also told Gillespie to get below, a little more brusquely than she meant to, and to take all the backpacks and other junk that was clogging the deck with him. He meant well, but this was no place for a greenhorn, she needed clear decks.

As the helicopter closed in, Charlie squeezed off a few shots, several of which hit it, sending sparks flying but not bringing it down or seemingly doing any real damage. The helicopter passed over them. It had its port-side door open and a man with a rifle was hanging out of it on a tether, his first few shots went wide, but as his aim improved the bullets started hitting the vessel, tearing great chunks out of the deck and the gunwale. Brighid and Nin both opened up with their assault rifles, trying to track the aircraft as it passed over them. They could see their bullets were hitting its fuselage, but they did not seem to make any impact. Brighid realised with horror that Lamont must have had his helicopter armour plated.

The sniper in the sky kept raining down fire on them and there was a terrible sense of inevitability to what happened next, with the boat suddenly slowing to a crawl as a bullet hit some vital piece of equipment. The crack of shots from above continued relentlessly and without warning the boat turned so dramatically that Brighid was almost thrown overboard. As she picked herself up, she looked across to the helm: Iain the Rat was lying dead on the wheel, blood pouring from his side. The bullet had entered at his shoulder and exited from his waist leaving a gaping hole through every major organ: it must have killed him instantly. The next shot caught Charlie, throwing him into the scuppers with a scream and spinning the rifle out of his hands.

There was then a pause while the sniper reloaded. Brighid, with tears in her eyes, went and stopped the engine. There was nothing more they could do. She raised her hands in the air. Nin was down in the scuppers with

Charlie, cradling his head in his arms crying, his world shrunk to that square foot: nothing else mattered.

The helicopter hovered over them and came lower so that they could hear the voice over its loudspeaker. "Put your hands on your heads. Everyone in the boat must come on deck with your hands on your head or else we will sink your vessel now. Come on deck with your hands on your head. Now!"

Kirstie and MacCailean Mòr came out first, their faces white with horror at how close they had come to escaping, they were downcast and silent. Next, Gillespie came up the companionway, his hands clasped above his head. Brighid could hear the boats approaching, they were that close. They all looked up at the helicopter, its downdraft beating the surface of the loch, the sound deafening.

From the corner of her eye Brighid caught something tiny flash out of the cabin hatch. She then looked over at Gillespie who was doing something strange with his hands, as if trying to cast a spell. He was moving them in barely perceptible, but very deliberate movements above his head. What was he trying to do, the idiot? She then realised he had something small in his right hand, too small for a gun; it was a phone, his phone. Why was he waving his phone like that? She tracked his focused gaze to the open door of the helicopter where it was hovering twenty metres behind and above them, the sniper covering them with his rifle. Suddenly, out of the gloom of the night, a tiny drone, no bigger than a bat, flew in through the open door of the helicopter past the shoulder of the sniper and before he could react or utter a word, the helicopter disintegrated in a fireball.

Brighid dived for the helm, apologising to the Rat's corpse as she roughly cast his body to the floor and started the engines. The debris of the helicopter dropped into the Loch between them and the Lamont pursuit, covering the loch surface with burning jet fuel, the blades still circling their lethal arc. She hoped that would slow their pursuers down, at least for a while, as she could only crawl away up the Loch towards Inveraray and safety.

She needn't have worried; a few boats did warily follow them as far as the Tiger's Mouth, but Duncan Campbell had been on the phone to Lachlan MacLachlan who, while vigorously protesting his neutrality, did at least direct his men to fire a few shots across the bows of their pursuers, forcing them to turn back and allowing Brighid to finish the remainder of the journey in peace.

Never had the white painted town of Inveraray look so sweet to a MacNachtan as it did that night. A crowd lined the quayside to cheer and marvel at the rescue of their Chief, who was pulled from the boat and hoisted on the shoulders of his Duine Uasal in a tail of triumph back to his Castle.

The crowd of Campbells also cheered the crew of the little boat as they disembarked, and Duncan Campbell embraced Brighid with such enthusiasm, that she thought she might be crushed. An ambulance was waiting to take them all to the Infirmary, and with the shouts and cheers of the crowd ringing in their ears, including unprecedented Campbell refrains of Strong Stands the Black Tower, they clambered aboard. As it pulled away from the crowd they were grateful for the silence that fell, a silence which gave them time to think and reflect, not only on their fortuitous escape but also on the heavy price that they had paid.

79 - REFLECTION

Brighid walked down the Infirmary corridor pulling her hospital gown tight around her. She wrapped her folded arms across her chest, not because she was cold in the stifling heat of the hospital, but more in apprehension as to what she might find in the rooms beyond. She yawned, shaking her head to dispel the fatigue that still lingered despite sleeping for nearly 16 hours. Her friend Claire had not been very forthcoming when she had asked about the condition of her companions, citing client confidentiality and other nonsense, so when the suspense had got too much, Brighid had eased herself out of bed and taken to the corridor to get her news first hand.

The first door she came to was Kirstie's, and she couldn't help breaking into a smile when she opened the door and saw Kirstie sitting up in bed talking to Gillespie. Despite the bruises on her face and the bandages that bound her hands and feet, Kirstie beamed as Brighid entered the room. They sat and talked for hours, catching up on the details of the rescue, trying to piece together a coherent story from their multiple different strands. Brighid shuddered when she heard about Donna Lamont's demise and the fate that had awaited Kirstie.

She then asked Gillespie about how he had conjured the fireball which had downed the helicopter. He explained about the tiny explosive drone that they had bought at Caddell's and how he had stumbled across it when he was desperately going through Alasdair's backpack trying to find something, anything, to shoot at the helicopter. It had been pure luck that the helicopter had been hovering so close to them, but even so he'd no idea that it would be quite so effective. Brighid and Kirstie enveloped him in a double sided bearhug, promising him that his place in the Clan annals was guaranteed for all time.

Brighid now asked about the remainder of the extraction team, in particular she wanted to know about Charlie, who she had last seen being stretchered off the boat. Gillespie said they were in the next-door ward and leaving Kirstie for a moment they walked down the corridor together. As they entered the ward, they saw that the two beds had been pushed together as close as the medical equipment would allow. In one, his cornflower blue eyes twinkling beneath his spiky black hair, was Nin, a smirk plastered across his face. In the neighbouring bed, his head swathed in bandages and his right arm encased in plaster was Charlie, his eyes just visible beneath the bands of crepe. Brighid rushed to his bedside and clutched his good hand in hers. "Thank God you are alive, you have no idea how worried I've been!"

"Ach you great pussy, it will take more than a fucking helicopter gunship and fleet of Lamonts to take me away from you lot!" Charlie said weakly, squeezing her hand, before leaning back and closing his eyes, the effort of speaking clearly still too much for him.

Brighid turned to Nin. "What happened to him? Is he going to be OK?"

"Aye, well, the surgeon offered a brain transplant, but the stupid twat turned it down, so I guess we are stuck with him the way he is." Nin said, to gentle laughter. "But seriously, he's OK. The bullet from that cunt in the helicopter smashed through his forearm and hit his rifle, it was that what clobbered him round the head. He's going to be sore for quite a while as his arm heals, they have put a plate in to hold it all together. But in a couple of months he should be right as rain. He's just come back from theatre, which is why he's even more out of it than normal."

Relieved at this prognosis, Brighid then asked about Alasdair MacGregor. It was Gillespie that had the news on Alasdair's condition, as he had already paid him a visit. He was in the intensive care unit up the corridor and had spent many hours in the operating theatre as they had extracted all the shotgun pellets embedded in his torso. He had also lost a lot of blood and his arrival in the Infirmary had been none too soon. But he was at least stable, if unconscious; the doctors expected that he would recover in time.

The room's mood darkened as they exhausted news on the living, since that meant they could no longer put off discussing the fate of Iain the Rat, their stalwart friend who had been gunned down so cruelly. They all wept anew when they thought of his resilience and the outcome that fate had ordained. Brighid did not know how she was going to be able to look Liz in the eye again, except that everyone knew these were not normal times. The Rat had gone on the mission with his eyes wide open, they had all known the risks, but he was a great loss. There would be the wake and the funeral to consider and time to reflect on the contribution that he had made to the Clan. For now, she had to push the grief from her mind.

Their rescue of MacCailean Mòr meant that at least they now had a powerful ally in their fight to restore Clan MacNachtan's fortunes, but in John Lamont they also had a powerful enemy. The unprecedented assault on his home, the killing of so many of his clansmen and the emptying of his dungeons, meant that he could not pause until he found out who was responsible and exacted a very public retribution. As the Colonel of the Black Watch he could bring huge military resources and the fig leaf of legitimacy to his vengeance, so she was in no doubt that they would need all of MacCailean Mòr's strength and guile to help them survive. That evil bastard Allan Stewart also still occupied Dunderave, a running sore on the honour of the Clan, and from there he would be able to wreak Lamont's vengeance on them with relative impunity. While there was no tangible evidence for him to link the assault to the MacNachtans yet, there was no question that he would be merciless in his pursuit of any information.

But those were worries for another day, today was a day to be glad to be alive and to savour life and love. Having said goodbye to Nin, Charlie and Gillespie, Brighid returned to her room and made a quick call. Then, having got dressed, she left the Infirmary and walked along the harbour front, pausing only to smell the briny air and feel the sun on her face, before heading though the gates at the bottom of the Castle drive. She wandered slowly through the cool shade of the trees, their pine scent layering an evocative astringent note on that of the sea-loch; the sweep of the drive gracefully leading her through the park and around the foursquare castle with its pointed witch's hat roofs, until she arrived at the porte-cochere, where MacCailean Mòr was waiting for her, arms outstretched.

GLOSSARY

Below is a glossary of Gaelic words with a phonetic guide to their pronunciation in italics:

Beinn *(Bain/Bine)* - Hill (there are no mountains in the Republic)
Broken man - Someone who has been expelled from their Clan
Labhraiche *(Lau-ree-cheh)* - Speaker of the Council of Chiefs
Canun - The honour code of the Republic
Cateran - Bandit
Claidheamh dà làimh *(Clieyiv da lev)*- Two-handed sword
Cliù *(Klyu)* - Honour
Comhairle *(Cor-lyih)* - Council of Chiefs
Curaidh Mòr *(Cooree More)* - Personal bodyguard of Chief
Duine Uasal *(Doon-you-asil)* - Literally, gentleman - effectively the elite fighting men of the Clan
Eòlaiche Didseatach *(Yo-leecheh Didge-tach)* - Digital Expert
Gallowglass - Mercenaries
Griogaraich *(Grigoreech)* - MacGregors
Pìobaireachd *(Peebaruchk)* - Classical music of the bagpipe
Riaghaltas *(Ree-ultus)* - The Parliament of the Republic
Seanchaidh *(Shen-achee)* - Bard / Senior adviser
Seanadh *(Shen-ugh)* - Senate
Sgian Dubh *(Skee-an dooh)* - Black knife
Sgian Aslaich *(Skee-an asleech)* - Armpit knife
Tapaidh *(Tahpee)* - Brave / Vigorous / Clever

Nick Bastin

CAST OF MAIN CHARACTERS

Prologue

Prince Charles Edward Stuart – Leader of the rebellion
Prince William, Duke of Cumberland – Son of George II, Leader of British Army
Colonel Robert O'Shea – Commander of Fitz-James's Horse and the Life Guards,
Prince Charles's bodyguard

Clan MacNachtan (Clan Nechtan)

Archie Beaton – the clan doctor
Charlie Farquharson
Alexander MacNachtan – Leader of the Albany MacNachtans in the Blue
Mountains of Jamaica
Aodhan *(Eu-ghan – Aidan)* MacNachtan
Brighid *(Breedge)* MacNachtan
Duncan Tapaidh *(Tahpee)* MacNachtan
Gillespie MacNachtan
Iain 'The Rat' MacNachtan
Jamie Ruadh *(Roo-agh)* MacNachtan
Kirstie MacNachtan – Head of the gaming operation
Malcolm, Fiona and Mara MacNachtan
Ninian 'Nin' MacNachtan

Clan Campbell

MacCailean Mòr *(Mac-Calan More)* – Colin Campbell, Duke of Argyll and Chief of
Clan Campbell, Warden of the West and Colonel of the Black Watch
Duncan Campbell – MacCailean Mòr's steward
Niall Campbell of Ardbreknish – Duine Uasal of MacCailean Mòr

BLOODBOND

Clan Lamont

John Lamont of the Sorrows – Warden of the Clyde and Chief of Clan Lamont
Donna Lamont – Clan Lamont's Eòlaiche Didseatach *(Yo-leecheh Didge-tach)* - Digital Expert
Allan Stewart – John Lamont's right-hand man

Clan Farquharson

Daracha Farquharson – Charlie's sister
Dervoguilla Farquharson – Chief of the Clan and Charlie's mother
Torquhil Farquharson – Dervoguilla's husband and Charlie's father

Other Characters

Andrew Balfour – First Minister of Scotland
Natasha Caddell – CEO of the Atelier of Thomas Caddell and Sons
Alasdair MacGregor – Leader of the Griogaraich
Catriona MacLean of Duart – Chief of the Clan MacLean
Ross Urquhart – Speaker of the Comhairle

Nick Bastin

ABOUT THE AUTHOR

Nick Bastin lives in London with his wife and three children and two cats. His mother's family come from Argyll in the West Highlands and the Island of Islay. He met his wife, who is from the Isle of Skye, studying Gaelic at an evening class in London – she was always much better at it than he was.

In 2007 he co-authored a Very Canny Scot – Daniel Campbell of Shawfield and Islay, a biography of one of Scotland's leading figures of the early 18th century.

BloodBond is his first novel and the first book in the Black Tower trilogy.

Printed in Great Britain
by Amazon